JUSTICE DELAYED

THE SEEKING JUSTICE SERIES
BOOK ONE

SARAH HAMAKER

ISBN: 978-1-958375-08-2

Cover design by 100 Covers.

Edited by Liz Tolsma.

✺ Created with Vellum

Also by Sarah Hamaker

Meet me by the moonlight, oh meet me
Meet me by the moonlight alone, Lord, Lord
I have a sad story to tell you
All down by the moonlight alone
If I had the wings of an angel
Over these prison walls I would fly

From "Meet Me by the Moonlight," circa 1880s traditional American folk song

"What time did the alleged robber come into your store, Mr. Patel?" *Northern Virginia Herald* reporter Brogan Gilmore asked. Mid-August in the metropolitan Washington, DC, area meant slow news due to the congressional recess, thus an attempted robbery at a local convenience store took top priority.

"Excuse me." Vihaan Patel, owner of the Kwikie Mart at the corner of Main Street and Chain Bridge Road in Fairfax, Virginia, rang up a customer purchasing a pack of cigarettes and beef jerky, then waited until the customer left before answering. "It was one-thirty in the morning. Very late."

Standing on the other side of the counter, Brogan jotted down the details in his notebook. "And you had two other robberies within the last two weeks?"

"That's right." Mr. Patel clenched his fists. "Those *badamaash* young men—"

"Badamaash?" Brogan interjected.

"Hooligans." Mr. Patel's lip curled, leaving Brogan no doubt that hooligans was probably a more civilized translation. "They come in

1

thinking they can just take my hard-earned money. Last Monday and Friday, different men, come in late at night and take what isn't theirs."

"How much was taken in the two previous robberies?"

"Three hundred on Monday, fifteen hundred on Friday. Friday was very busy night. Special lottery promotion brought in lots of people, who thought they would be lucky. Big jackpot." A shadow crossed the lines of his expressive face. "Both times, robbers came when I opened safe to remove cash for bank deposit. Usually, no one here to open safe."

A familiar gut feeling coursed through Brogan's body. Maybe these robberies weren't so random after all. This was looking more like an inside job. "Do you open the safe to ready the deposit at the same time each night?"

Mr. Patel shook his head. "That would be foolish. I vary times each day. Sometimes right before bank opens. Sometimes mid-afternoon. Sometimes during the evening. When bank not open, I take deposit bag home with me. The Monday robbery was at ten in morning. The Friday one at nine in evening."

Brogan tapped his pen against the notebook. "Who worked on Monday?"

The door's bell announced more customers. A group of teenagers poured in, their raucous laughter filling the small store.

Mr. Patel craned his neck to keep an eye on the teens. "My son, Veer, working both times. He filling in for worker who called in sick."

The tingle increased. "Is that spelled V-E-E-R?"

"Yes." Mr. Patel greeted one of the teens, who set down a large slushie and a giant candy bar.

Brogan waited while the owner rang up the group's remaining purchases. It could be a coincidence that Mr. Patel's son had been working during the two robberies. Still, at the risk of offending the man, Brogan had to follow up. "Was Veer working last night?"

"He was. He usually works overnight shifts on weekend to let me spend time at home with my wife."

Definitely something there, but Brogan let the subject of Veer Patel drop for now. "But you were here last night. Why was that?"

Mr. Patel shrugged. "I was waiting until jackpot numbers were called at midnight. People buy lottery tickets in cash."

"Did you see the robber?"

"Yes, but he wore werewolf mask."

"Like a Halloween mask?"

"Exactly. Other two robbers had similar masks. The werewolf robber much shorter with lighter skin on his arms. His hand holding gun shook."

Brogan, writing furiously, gestured for him to continue.

"Then she threw soda bottle. Knocked him in head." Mr. Patel's grin stretched wider.

Rather than interrupt with questions as to who "she" was, Brogan let Mr. Patel finish his story.

"Miss Mel's such a little thing. I forgot she was here. She grab soda bottle and, *wham!* Clipped masked man in side of head."

Brogan finished jotting down Mr. Patel's quote, then looked up. "Who is Miss Mel? Did she knock the alleged robber out?"

"No, but Miss Mel scared him. Robber ran out without money." Mr. Patel rang up another customer. "I want to give her bonus for quick thinking."

"Do you mean a reward?" Maybe this story wouldn't turn out so bad after all. A regular customer thwarting a robbery in such an unusual manner would play well. He'd also do some digging into Veer Patel before he questioned the son. Something about Veer working during all three incidents was one coincidence too many in Brogan's book.

"Reward?" Mr. Patel laughed. "Yes, I will give her reward even though she's like an employee."

"Employee?" Brogan frowned. "I thought she was a customer."

"No. She cleans. Every Friday overnight."

"She works for you one night a week?"

"Didn't I just say?" Mr. Patel called out a hello as a burly man

3

walked in and headed straight for the fountain drinks. "I hired company, Squeaky Clean, and they send her. First time she cleaned, I call manager and tell him to only send her. So she cleans my store once a week for six months. Very good worker. My store sparkles. Good for customer service."

As Mr. Patel chatted with the burly man and rang up the customer's purchases, Brogan took the opportunity to check his phone for messages. Nothing. He wasn't expecting anything big to break, not with much of the greater DC area on vacation. But all he needed was that one story to catapult him back into the big leagues.

Mr. Patel waved goodbye to the customer. "Any other questions?"

"Just one." Brogan poised his pen over the notebook. "What's her name?"

"Mel Harman." Mr. Patel gestured toward the door. "You can meet her. She just pulled into parking lot."

MELENDER HARMAN PUT HER HONDA ACCORD INTO PARK OUTSIDE THE Kwikie Mart and checked the dashboard clock. Four-thirty. Good, she'd have enough time after her visit with Mr. Patel to stop by the grocery store down the street before starting her overnight shift. She enjoyed the solitary nature of her job, cleaning stores and offices while most of the world slept. Tonight, she had a new client on her list, which meant Squeaky Clean's owner, Janice Butram, would be sending along another cleaner to keep them on schedule.

Melender, who had shortened her unusual first name to Mel at her job to avoid questions about its origin and to camouflage her background, stepped into the convenience store, the overhead bell announcing her entrance. Behind the counter, Mr. Patel chatted with a tall, handsome blond man wearing jeans and a faded t-shirt. The man held a small notebook and fastened his gaze in her direction when she entered.

4

"Miss Mel." Mr. Patel slipped around the end of the counter and approached, a broad smile on his lined face.

Melender lifted her own lips into an answering grin. The joy on the older man's face made it impossible not to return his greeting in kind. "Mr. Patel, Janice said you wanted to see me. Is everything okay?"

Mr. Patel grabbed her hand and pumped it up and down. "Everything fine, thanks to you." Not letting go of her hand, he turned to the man at the counter. "I was telling Mr. Gilmore about what you did last night in—what was word you said?"

Mr. Gilmore smiled. "Foil."

Mr. Patel nodded. "Yes, foil robbery attempt."

Melender gently freed her hand from Mr. Patel's grip and looked from one man to another. "It was nothing."

"It was not nothing!" Mr. Patel slapped his hand on the counter.

Melender automatically stepped back as her heart rate skyrocketed. *There's no danger. You're not inside anymore. Nothing to fear here.* But no matter what she told herself, the scent of danger hovered in the air. If she sniffed, she would smell its familiar tang, a mixture of sweat, fear, and power.

"Mr. Gilmore is writing about your story for *Northern Virginia Herald*."

No, no, no! "I didn't do anything special. And I'd rather not have my name mentioned."

"It is okay," Mr. Patel nodded. "I spoke with Ms. Butram. She said it would be okay to have company name and your name in article."

Melender didn't alter her expression. Of course the owner of Squeaky Clean wouldn't mind free publicity, never mind that Melender wanted to fly under the radar. An article, even in a regional paper like the *Northern Virginia Herald*, could shift the spotlight back on her.

"Mr. Patel told me what you did, chucking a two-liter bottle of soda at the would-be robber." The reporter studied her with knowing blue eyes that weren't buying her false humility act for one second. The scent the reporter smelled wasn't danger but a scoop. She'd seen that lean, hungry look in the courtroom too often to mistake it now.

The name Brogan Gilmore had a familiar ring to it. She rarely read the news these days, so she hadn't recognized his name from seeing it online on the *Herald* site.

"What kind of soda was it?"

"I'm sorry, what?" She'd lost track of the conversation. Not a smart move, given the very real danger the man posed.

"The two-liter. What brand was it?"

"I don't know." She shrugged. Although the brand of soda wasn't important, if giving him that tidbit of information would satisfy his curiosity, then she would happily oblige. She had been wiping down the cooler doors and had made it to the one on the far end, which was why the would-be robber hadn't seen her when he'd come in with his mask and gun. A free-standing display of two-liters had been near the endcap of the salty snack aisle right beside her. Picturing the display, she snapped open her eyes. "Dr Pepper."

"Good." The reporter scribbled it down. "Can you describe the robber?"

Sure, she'd give him the exact description she gave the police. "About five feet, eight- or nine-inches. He wore a black t-shirt with a grinning skull on the front and a pair of baggy jean shorts. He had on a werewolf mask."

Gilmore asked her a few follow-up questions about the incident, but Melender kept her replies short nearly to the point of rudeness. Gilmore raised his eyebrows at her clipped answers but didn't say anything. Finally, he snapped his notebook closed.

Melender snuck a quick look at the wall clock above the door. 4:45. If she hurried, she could make it to the store and home again before reporting for work at seven o'clock. "I need to go. Mr. Patel, I'll see you Friday night."

"No, wait, wait, Miss Mel." Mr. Patel waved at her as he hurried to his office. "I have something for you."

Melender shifted her feet, wanting nothing more than to flee the store and the reporter's scrutiny.

"Have somewhere to go, Ms. Harman?"

Melender whipped around to lock eyes with the reporter studying her. "Yes, as a matter of fact, I do."

He edged closer to her, dropping his voice to nearly a whisper. "Don't you think it's strange that Mr. Patel's son was here during all three robberies?"

Melender frowned. She never liked Mr. Patel's son, who generally worked overnight on Fridays when she cleaned. While Veer had never bothered her, she steered clear of the younger man for reasons she couldn't articulate. "Veer was working the other two times?"

"Yes." Gilmore started to say something else, but Mr. Patel's return interrupted him.

"Miss Mel, here you go." He thrust an envelope into her hand.

Melender opened the unsealed flap and gaped at the bills stuffed inside. "I don't understand." She looked at the money, then into Mr. Patel's beaming face.

"It's ten percent of what robber didn't get. One hundred and seventy dollars." Mr. Patel tucked his hands into his pockets. "You did tremendous good deed. You take, keep, give away—it yours."

Blinking back tears, Melender put the envelope into her purse. "Thank you, Mr. Patel."

The reporter jotted down the exchange in his notebook. "That will make a nice ending to this piece. Thanks again." With another look at Melender, he headed toward the door.

Thanking Mr. Patel again, Melender hurried after Gilmore to plead that her name be kept out of the article before he drove away. But all she saw was the taillights of the reporter's SUV as he drove out of the parking lot, taking with him her quiet life.

CHAPTER

TWO

"Solid piece on the Kwikie Mart robberies." Marcus Fallon stood near Brogan's desk.

Brogan automatically hit the save button on his current work before turning his full attention to his boss. The seasoned editor and owner of the *Northern Virginia Herald* rarely complimented his reporters. "Thank you, sir."

Despite Brogan's fifteen years of experience, Fallon hadn't treated Brogan any differently from his fresh-faced colleagues who populated newsrooms of small newspapers like the *Herald*. Nearly a year into his job as a general assignment reporter for the daily news outlet, Brogan still had the uncomfortable feeling he had to prove his integrity and journalistic chops with each piece he submitted. But if that's what it took to redeem his career, he'd do it.

"It looks like there's more to the story than the heroic efforts of a cleaning woman." Fallon unwrapped a piece of chewing gum and popped it into his mouth.

"I agree. The timing of the robberies seemed too convenient to me." Brogan paused to gauge the older man's reaction to his statement. He wanted to pursue the angle of Mr. Patel's son working each time the robberies happened, but if he pushed too hard, Fallon was just as likely to assign it to another reporter. If Brogan played his cards right, this story had the potential to springboard him back into the investigative work he craved.

Fallon didn't speak for a moment, the clacking of computer keyboards and muted conversations of the three other reporters signaling a busy newsroom. The editor straightened. "Okay, why don't you do a little digging into that and have a follow-up piece on my desk by three p.m. on Saturday."

"Sure." Brogan kept from showing the relief and delight coursing through his body. Three on Saturday meant he had a shot at the Sunday edition, the biggest print run of the week. Like most community newspapers, the *Herald* lived online except for the Wednesday and Sunday print editions.

"Keep me abreast of any developments and fill out a photographic request with Seth." Fallon took a step away from Brogan's desk then tossed over his shoulder, "And be sure he gets a photo of the soda-throwing cleaner."

Brogan agreed. He'd certainly like to see Mel Harman again, and if the reason had more to do with her dark-blue eyes and hair as white blonde as the sands of a Caribbean beach, he wasn't going to say so.

By Friday afternoon, Brogan had the basic outline of Veer Patel's life, and it was much as he had suspected. According to some of his friends, the younger Patel frequently stopped by MGM National Harbor in Oxon Hill, Maryland, an easy distance from Fairfax. A source at the casino told him that Veer owed thousands of dollars to the casino, although Brogan hadn't managed to nail down the exact amount.

Patel's parents had no idea of their son's gambling, telling Brogan about Veer's veterinary medicine studies at the University of Maryland, along with his volunteer work at a local animal shelter. But a check with the registrar at the university revealed Veer had dropped out last semester, and his fellow volunteers at the animal shelter hadn't seen him for months.

"Hey, Brogan." Seth Whitman, the paper's sole photographer, propped himself against the top of Brogan's cubicle wall. "We on for stopping by the Kwikie Mart tonight?"

"Yeah, I'll meet you there about one thirty a.m. Mr. Patel said Mel, the cleaner, arrives at one." Brogan kept the fact that Veer would also be working that night to himself. He would, however, call the Fairfax City detective assigned to the case, just to check the status on catching the robbers—and to give him a gentle nudge in Veer's direction. It usually paid to make detectives look good, and Brogan could use a few friends inside the local police department.

MELENDER OPENED THE HATCHBACK TO ACCESS HER CLEANING SUPPLIES, pausing to wipe the sweat from her forehead. August in Virginia was never pleasant. Even though the sun had long gone to bed, the temperature still hovered in the upper eighties, wrapping everything in a snug, heavy blanket of humidity. She wasn't looking forward to buffing the floors at the Kwikie Mart in addition to her usual sweep and mop. Squeaky Clean's motto was Never Let Dirt Win, and that meant rotating deep cleaning throughout the month for regular clients. With the small square footage of the store, buffing only added an extra half hour to her usual time, but the hot weather would make the task exhausting.

Carrying in her mop, bucket, broom and dustpan, and a carryall of various supplies, she called out a greeting to Veer Patel, who merely grunted before returning his attention to his phone. The twenty-one-year-old had become even more surly over the past month. The thought planted by that reporter of Veer being involved in the robberies hovered at the back of her mind.

She headed straight for the single-stall bathroom at the back. While the clerks cleaned it daily, she did a deep clean on Friday nights. Tonight, the small, windowless room reeked of body odor and something she didn't want to identify. After propping open the door with the mop bucket, she snapped on her ventilated mask and long rubber gloves, then set to work. Once into the rhythm of the chore, her mind drifted to Tuesday's online article about the convenience store robberies. There was her name, Mel Harman, sprinkled throughout the article. In fact, the piece seemed to be more about her thwarting the robber than about the previous two robberies.

Worrying about the publicity was "borrowing trouble without any intention of paying it back," as her grandmother Sudie had always said. But Melender could only disappear for so long.

Thirty minutes later, she'd finished the bathroom and dusted the display shelves. On her way to tackle the front windows and entry door, she glanced at the wall clock above the door. 1:35. Good, she was a little ahead of schedule. Moving a spin rack of summer hats and sunglasses to the left of the door, she sprayed the floor-to-ceiling window then began to wipe down the inside glass using a long-handled squeegee. She'd made it to the far-left corner when the door's bell chimed.

"Miss Harman?"

At the familiar voice, Melender stilled. She bit back a groan at the sight of Brogan Gilmore, the handsome reporter, along with a dark-haired younger man holding a camera. "Just a minute." She squeegeed the dripping liquid off the window with quick fluid motions before turning to the two men who approached her. "Can I help you?"

Sudie would have taken her to task for the borderline rudeness in her tone, but Melender didn't care. The sight of the camera only meant one thing—the pair had come to take her photo, something she couldn't allow under any circumstances.

If Gilmore noticed her tone, nothing in his expression showed it. "I hope so," he said. "This is Seth Whitman, the *Herald's* photographer. We're running a follow-up piece to the robbery story."

It was even worse than she'd feared. Another story with her name *and* picture. Her heart rate kicked up, and she struggled to maintain a calm expression. She'd gotten soft during her eight months on the outside, allowing someone like this reporter to rattle her. But she liked her life, liked the quiet and the solitude. Liked the way she slipped like a ghost through it with no one really noticing her. After years of scrutiny, this little slice of anonymity was pure heaven.

"Thanks, but I only did what anyone else would have done. I don't want my picture taken." She moved around them to start on the right side of the windows.

She wasn't surprised when the two men followed her, but she largely tuned out Brogan's voice as he attempted to persuade her to agree to the photo. Instead, she concentrated on spraying her cleaning solution on the window, then using her squeegee to carefully remove the liquid along with the grime. If she ignored him, surely he'd give up and leave her alone. As she shifted the metal rack holding newspapers away from the second window, another thought hit her with the force of a tree being felled in the forest. They couldn't take and publish her photo without her permission, could they?

The doorbell tinkled the arrival of someone else. Melender nearly sagged with relief at the distraction. Maybe Mr. Patel had come in after all.

"Did you think you could hide from me?"

Melender froze, her squeegee halfway down the glass. Slowly, she turned to see Ruby Harman Thompson. Her aunt glared at her so fiercely that Melender would have taken a step back if the newspaper rack hadn't been digging into her hip.

"You little conniving..." The words Ruby uttered didn't make Melender flinch, but the venom behind them did. "How dare you come back to this area as if nothing happened!"

Melender stopped listening as her father's only sister continued to spew foul language like a broken sewer pipe. Ruby's auburn hair had been expertly colored to maintain its natural color, while her expensive yoga pants and fitted top showed off her still-trim figure at fifty-six. Ruby had indeed done well for herself in the years since she'd shaken the dust of Maple Hollow from her bare feet. But a closer look showed the years Melender had been away hadn't been kind. Faint lines bracketed her eyes and mouth, and Melender could see pain behind her aunt's anger. It was the pain that kept Melender's mouth shut. That her aunt had suffered, Melender had no doubt.

"Excuse me, ma'am? I'm Brogan Gilmore with the *Northern Virginia Herald*. What's going on?"

Melender glanced at the reporter. The hungry look had returned to his eyes, one she'd seen all too often from those eager to feast on the pain of others.

Ruby turned to the reporter, the semblance of a smile crossing her red-painted lips. "You wrote the story about the robberies." Ruby eyed him, tapping a red-tipped nail against her cheek as her smile broadened.

The words flowed like lava from her aunt's lips and would consume Melender if she let them.

"I suppose you want to know why I'm harassing this—how did you put it in your story?—ah, yes, heroine." Ruby cut her eyes to Melender, then back to Gilmore.

"I admit to being curious." Gilmore took out his notebook and pen.

A prayer looped over and over in Melender's head. *Please, God. Help!*

"You see," Ruby's voice sharpened as if she was honing a knife, "this person you called Mel Harman is really my niece, Melender Harman."

"Your niece?" Gilmore's forehead creased, as if he recognized her name but couldn't immediately place it.

Ruby's eyes glittered as she drove the knife home. "Yes, my niece. The one who killed my one-year-old son."

CHAPTER
THREE

"Killed your son?" Brogan stopped writing in his notebook to gape at the older woman. His gaze traveled to Melender, who clutched the squeegee and spray bottle. Clearly, she'd been caught off guard by the woman showing up at her place of employment and accusing her of murder.

"That's right." The cleaner's accuser narrowed her eyes. "For a reporter, you don't know much, do you?"

The woman had mistakenly assumed he knew about the death, but Brogan couldn't recall anyone named Melender Harman connected with the killing of a toddler since he'd been at the *Herald*. He scrambled for a response that would mollify the woman in hopes of eliciting more information.

"I've been out of this area covering other stories for a while and only returned last year. Why don't you fill me in on some of the details?"

Her lips thinned, but she complied. "Then allow me to catch you up." Sarcasm clung to every word like kudzu on a roadside sign. "I'm Ruby Harman Thompson. My husband is Quentin Thompson of Thompson Energy."

That explained the expensive air the woman wore like an invisible mink coat.

Mrs. Thompson continued, "Nineteen years ago, my brother's only child—Melender Harman—killed my son Jesse."

A cold case. Brogan frowned. It seemed unlikely the police would let the murder of a toddler go unsolved for nearly two decades. Before Brogan could question Mrs. Thompson, an older man with silver-streaked hair and wire-rimmed glasses hurried into the store.

"Ruby!" He stopped short at the sight of the four of them standing near the windows.

"Quentin." Mrs. Thompson pointed a finger at Melender. "The person who killed my baby is being called a heroine." Mrs. Thompson started crying, sobs shaking her thin shoulders. "In the name of God, why won't she tell me where my baby is so I can bring him home!"

Mr. Thompson pulled his wife into his arms, his hand rubbing her back. "Now, Ruby. Calm down." The man barely gave Brogan and Seth a second glance and only flicked his gaze to Melender for a split second before refocusing on his wife. "This isn't the time or the place for this."

"I don't care. I had to let her know we haven't forgotten what she did."

"I know, my dear." The older man cradled his wife as if she were a piece of porcelain.

"Mr. Thompson? I'm Brogan Gilmore with the *Northern Virginia Herald*." Brogan spoke quickly, sensing that Thompson was about to bolt with his wife. "May I call you at a more convenient time to speak to you and your wife about this matter?"

"Please, Quentin," Mrs. Thompson said as she pushed away from her husband. "Say you'll speak to him. We have to get the truth out about what she did."

He barely glanced Brogan's way as he answered. "Call my office on Monday."

Brogan jotted the date in his notebook, biting back the flood of questions that threatened to trip off his tongue.

"It's very late." Mr. Thompson spoke softly to his wife. "Let's go home."

At his words, Mrs. Thompson frowned. "I'm not ready to go yet."

"Come along, my dear." Mr. Thompson guided her to the door with a firm hand on her back.

Mrs. Thompson started to argue, but her husband leaned down and whispered something in her ear. Then the older woman turned to spear Brogan with a glance. "Mr. Gilmore, I expect your next story to have the truth about this person. People need to know she's not heroic at all."

As the Thompsons left the store, Brogan nodded to acknowledge her words. Already, his fingers itched to get to his computer to search for what had happened to little Jesse Thompson.

Beside him, Seth blew out a breath. "Wow, that was kind of wild. And here I thought this would be a rather humdrum assignment." He leaned closer to Brogan. "Want me to snap a few pics of her working?"

Brogan had nearly forgotten Melender's presence. He could have sworn he'd seen tears in her eyes when Mrs. Thompson accused her of killing Jesse, but now she ran her squeegee down a window as if nothing had happened. Until he knew more, he would be careful not to antagonize Melender. If there was a bigger story here, he needed to make sure he would have access to the key players.

"She doesn't want her photo taken."

Seth fiddled with his camera lens. "What if we didn't show her face?"

Brogan considered it. "Let me ask." He walked a few steps toward Melender. "Ms. Harman?"

Melender wiped down the squeegee with a rag, keeping her head down. "I'm working."

"Would it be okay if we took some photos of you working? We wouldn't show your face." Her movements didn't slow. Brogan tried again. "My editor can be rather cranky, and he insisted the follow up story include a photo of you. After all, your quick actions did thwart the robbery."

The door's bell chimed as four firefighters came in. Brogan inched closer to her as she moved the racks back into place then picked up her spray bottle, her gaze still directed away from him. "Look, I won't mention what happened here tonight in my follow up piece on the robberies."

Melender threw him a look. The sadness in her eyes surprised him. He'd expected anger or frustration, not sorrow that ran deep below the surface.

"It doesn't matter." She moved past him toward the back of the store.

He followed on her heels, motioning to Seth to stay put for now. "What doesn't matter?"

She put the squeegee and bottle into a supply caddy, then grabbed a push broom. "You're going to go back and write the follow up story before Googling Jesse Thompson."

"And what will I find?"

Melender gripped the broom with both hands, turning the knuckles white. "Please don't bother me at work again. I have no interest in talking to you or any other reporter." With that, she pushed the broom down the aisle.

As he rejoined Seth at the front, Brogan contemplated her words, telling his colleague no photo for now. As Brogan drove them back to the office, he mentally composed his lead to the follow up piece. Melender was right. He would finish the assigned story—and then find out what happened to Jesse Thompson.

Quentin Thompson uttered an expletive as his wife continued to sob against his shoulder in the back of the Lincoln. Ruby had been determined to confront Melender in the hopes the girl—now a grown woman—would finally reveal the whereabouts of Jesse's body. It had taken nearly eight months for his wife to track her niece down. Quentin admired Ruby's tenacity, but living with her grief for nearly two decades had eroded his patience. He felt the loss of their son just as keenly, but he hadn't let it derail him completely. Why couldn't the woman simply move on with her life?

He rubbed Ruby's back again, his mind not on comforting his wife but on how to handle Melender. Even as a teenager, his niece had exhibited a stubbornness indicative of her Appalachian heritage, forged by generations of people eking out a hard living in one of the poorest places in the United States. Ruby had that same stubborn streak, although she loathed to admit to a comparison with Melender on anything.

"Quentin?"

"Yes, dear?" Glancing down at his wife's beautiful yet tear-streaked face, Quentin recalled his first glimpse of Ruby at the reception desk of his company nearly twenty-five years ago. Her graceful movements as she answered the phone and greeted visitors had fascinated him. He smiled even now at the image of how the cream-colored linen sheath she wore accentuated her slender figure and tanned body. On impulse, he'd asked her to lunch, and within three months, he had married her. Only later did he find out about Ruby's hillbilly past.

"She shouldn't be able to go about her life as if nothing had happened." Ruby righted herself, then flicked open a lighted makeup mirror she kept tucked into a seat pocket of the car. She dabbed at her mascara-streaked cheeks with a handkerchief she'd pulled from her purse. Her mercurial moods never ceased to amaze him. She retrieved a compact and began to repair the damage her tears had caused. "We need to bring Jesse home."

As she applied fresh lipstick to her collagen-injected lips, a familiar stab of desire shot through Quentin. Despite her frequent bouts with grief, he still fiercely craved his wife. He brushed his hand over her smooth hair. "Don't worry, my love. She'll come around." *Even if I have to resort to more persuasive methods.*

"There's no reason why she won't tell us other than pure spite." Ruby recapped her lipstick and dropped it back into her purse. "She's always hated me for taking her away from the homestead."

Quentin didn't contradict his wife, but not for the first time, he wondered at Ruby's ability to see only what she wanted to see. It wasn't that Ruby, as the only living relative with the means to take on a teenager, wasn't partially right. Melender had been melancholy about leaving her beloved mountains. However, Quentin suspected Melender's quietness stemmed more from losing her father and grandmother within months of each other than moving from the country to the city.

"That's why she did it, you know," Ruby continued, her voice taking on a peevish edge. "She wanted to punish me for taking her away." Fresh tears sprang to her eyes.

He patted his wife's hand. If only Ruby talked less, their relationship would be much more enjoyable. "My dear, I think you should take one of your pills. I hate to see you so upset."

Ruby nodded. "Of course, you're right. This has been a very trying time for me." She reached into her purse and pulled out the bottle of pills her doctor had prescribed at Quentin's insistence to help moderate his wife's mood swings. After swallowing a pill with a sip from a water bottle, she replaced the medication container in her purse. Resting her head against his shoulder, she closed her eyes.

Within a few minutes, she drifted off to sleep, whether from the pill or exhaustion, he couldn't tell.

Quentin gently leaned her head against the opposite door and pulled out his cell phone. The soundproof privacy glass shielded his conversation from his driver. Connecting the call, he held the phone to his ear.

"Montgomery speaking."

"Quentin Thompson."

A short pause, then Montgomery said, "What can I do for you?"

Quentin smiled. It was always good policy to have leverage over people from whom you wanted favors. In Montgomery's case, he'd scrounged up some interesting tidbits a man with political ambitions would rather keep locked away. "My wife found her."

"What happened?" Montgomery asked.

Quentin succinctly relayed the situation. "She's not going to stop."

"I'm not sure what you want me to do about it." Montgomery's irritation sounded loud and clear over the cell phone.

Quentin bit back the word he wanted to call the other man. "I've already shown you my support. It's time you showed me yours." He let the implication hang in the air.

Montgomery grunted. "Listen, I can have the police pay her a visit based on a citizen complaint, but that's about all I can do. These people have rights too, and I can't have my name linked to anything that smacks of harassment, not with this being an election year."

That would have to do for now. Melender wasn't stupid, and perhaps a friendly reminder that she would always be on the police's radar would be a good thing. He punched off the call without saying goodbye.

As the car pulled into their driveway, Quentin tapped his fingers on his knee. Melender wouldn't be as easy to influence as she had been at eighteen. If she remembered the map and a certain conversation with a senator, things could get even trickier. He would have to be very careful, or everything he'd accomplished could cave in like an old mining shaft.

CHAPTER

FOUR

Brogan returned to the *Herald* office to drop Seth, who shrugged off Brogan's apology for not getting any photographs at the Kwikie Mart. Once they'd parted ways, Brogan made a beeline to his computer and Googled Jesse Thompson. As a result, he'd been sucked into reading about the case for hours. But instead of feeling tired after staying up all night, all his senses were on high alert. Finally, after years in journalism exile, he had the story that would propel him back into the national news arena.

He would have to be extra careful, triple checking his facts and sources, documenting every step with notes and recordings. No way would this story have even a whiff of scandal clinging to it.

Brogan picked up his coffee cup only to find it empty. After rising, he stretched on his way to the break room for a fresh cup.

"Gilmore!" Fallon paused in the break room doorway. "You're here early." The editor peered closely at him. "Did you go home last night?"

"Nope." Brogan grinned.

The older man raised his eyebrows, but Brogan wasn't fooled by his nonchalant appearance. Fallon might run a small newspaper, but he was a first-rate journalist and could catch the scent of a good story quicker than any bloodhound. "Give me five minutes, then come to my office to tell me what's got you all excited."

Brogan hurried to his desk to organize his notes. Exactly five minutes later, he knocked on the editor's door and entered when Fallon barked, "Come in!"

Juggling the printouts and notebook, Brogan shut the door behind him with his foot and took a seat without waiting for Fallon to offer it. "Sir, I don't want anyone else to overhear our conversation."

Fallon straightened in his chair. "This must be some hot tip."

"You won't be disappointed."

Fallon only stared.

Brogan returned the gaze with equal candor, resisting the urge to tap his fingers on the arm of the chair, a nervous habit since childhood. "I've always been honest about what happened in New York, and I appreciate your giving me another chance. I hope over these past months, I've proven to you that I've changed, that I care more about getting the story right than about making a name for myself."

Fallon sipped his coffee. "I'm glad to hear you say so because you're a good writer, and maybe one day, you'll be a great writer—if you can keep that ego of yours at bay. As the Good Book says, 'Pride goes before a fall,' and your fall was spectacular."

Brogan winced at the truth behind the older man's words. He had been prideful, ambitious, and willing to cut corners to make his star rise farther and faster.

"Gilmore, if you had approached me for a job ten years ago, I'd have turned you down flat, because even after you destroyed your career, you still acted proud that you had fooled some of the most respected newspaper men and women in the country with your writing."

Fallon's words fell like hail, hitting him hard. Brogan broke eye contact with the editor, fixing his gaze on the man's paper-covered desk.

"But when you came to me last year asking for a chance—a chance no other newspaper or news organization in the country would have given you—I saw a man who was ready for a fresh start."

Brogan looked up. The compassion in the editor's eyes made him swallow hard before speaking. "I've appreciated your confidence in me and hope I've worked hard to be worthy of that chance."

"That you have." Fallon smiled. "You've written every story I've asked, not once complaining to anyone in the newsroom when I left off your byline, chopped it into bits, asked for a rewrite, or assigned the same story to another reporter just to compare it to yours."

Fallon had done all of that and more in the nearly twelve months Brogan had worked for the *Herald*. But Fallon had also taught Brogan how to write a tighter story, how to play up the personal angle, and how to question reluctant sources. He'd been humbled at how much he'd learned as a journalist under Fallon's direction.

"So what's this big story that had you up all night?"

Brogan opened his notebook. "It turns out that the Mel Harman who thwarted the Kwikie Mart robbery is Melender Harman."

Fallon frowned. "Melender Harman. Unusual name."

"Yes, sir." Brogan waited a beat to see if Fallon made the connection to Jesse Thompson, but the other man waved at him to continue. "Seventeen years ago, Melender Harman was convicted of murdering her fifteen-month-old cousin Jesse Thompson."

MELENDER RUBBED THE SLEEP FROM HER EYES AS SHE MOVED THROUGH HER darkened apartment. As she stumbled to her front door, someone alternated ringing the doorbell with banging on the door. Since no one except her boss at Squeaky Clean knew her home address, whoever assaulted her door wasn't a friend. Which meant trouble had found her at eleven o'clock on a Saturday morning.

When she reached the door, she peered through the peephole. Two uniformed officers stood on the other side. All vestiges of sleep vanished as her senses went on high alert. Drawing in a calming breath, Melender slowly counted to ten to slow her heart rate and to evaluate the situation. One guess as to who had sent them—her uncle. Quentin Thompson had friends in high places. With the chain on, she cracked open the door. "Officers, what can I do for you?"

The shorter of the two men stepped closer. "Ma'am, may we come in?"

"May I ask why you're here?" Melender didn't move. She'd read a lot of law books over the years and knew her rights backwards and forwards. Just because someone from law enforcement asked to enter her home, didn't mean she had to let them past the threshold.

The officer narrowed his eyes. "Are you Melender Harman?"

She had no intention of answering their questions, but she would mentally note their names.

"Ma'am?" The shorter officer whose name plate read Jones sounded irritated.

"What brings you to my door?" she countered.

Before Jones could speak, the other officer interjected. "Ma'am, we received a complaint of excessive noise from this apartment."

"Excessive noise? The only excessive anything associated with my apartment is your aggressive knocking on my door."

Jones hitched his duty belt. "Now calm down."

She again counted to ten in her mind to dose her bubbling anger.

The other officer, whose name plate she couldn't quite read because of the sun's reflection on the shiny surface, added, "We only know what the dispatch officer tells us. And the report is a noise complaint."

Melender knew with ninety-nine percent certainty it had originated with Quentin. "Let me guess. The caller didn't give a name."

"We're not required to tell you who called it in, ma'am." The other officer moved forward enough that Melender could read his name plate. Gutierrez. "We're just here to issue a warning."

"And did this concerned citizen say what type of noise and when it occurred?

Officer Gutierrez consulted his small notebook. "Music loud enough to be heard outside number 347 at four in the morning."

Quentin must be slipping if he hadn't told whoever had made the call that she worked nights. Not that Melender would tell these cops that tidbit of information. She was through sharing anything with law enforcement. "Hmm, and why has it taken seven hours for the fine officers of the Fairfax City Police Department to show up at my door?"

The pair shifted on her stoop before Office Gutierrez replied. "We just got the information. It was a busy night."

"I see." And she did. No sense sending someone to her apartment while she was at work. Better to wake her up and ruin her entire day. Maybe Quentin had planned this better than she initially thought. "Thank you for stopping by, officers. I'll be sure to keep the noise level down from now on."

"You have a good day, ma'am." Officer Gutierrez turned to go.

Officer Jones stepped forward and shoved the toe of his boot in the crack to prevent her from closing the door. "You shouldn't have come back here."

Melender maintained her smooth tone with effort. "Kindly remove your foot."

"Jones? You coming?" Gutierrez called from just beyond Melender's line of sight.

Officer Jones didn't move. "Don't think anyone would care if something were to happen to you." He stepped back and turned to join his partner.

Melender closed the door quietly, then reached up to turn the first of two deadbolts. Her fingers shook so much it took her several tries to secure the knob as well. Sliding down the door, she buried her face in her hands as the sobs overtook her. The cop's veiled threat echoed in her mind. No one would care.

❧

Fallon leaned back in his chair. "Didn't the prosecutor get a conviction even without a body?"

Brogan nodded. He'd been struggling to reconcile the sad-eyed woman who cleaned for a living with an eighteen-year-old murderer. "I've been reading the news accounts of the case, and it was quite the legal feat given that all of the evidence was circumstantial."

Fallon steepled his fingers. "Wasn't there a ransom note?"

"That's what clinched it for the jurors. The toddler went missing overnight while the parents were at a charity fundraiser, and Melender was supposed to be watching Jesse and his older sister, three-year-old Jillian. A frantic search uncovered Jesse's sock in some shrubs along the driveway, but no sign of Jesse."

Brogan didn't glance at his notes. He'd spent so much time reading about the case since he'd left the Kwikie Mart, he had memorized the key details. "The police flagged it as a potential kidnapping given Quentin Thompson's business connections and wealth. Then forty-eight hours later, a ransom note showed up, demanding payment of $1.5 million."

"When did police suspect Melender's involvement?"

"That's not clear from the news reports." Brogan had hunted through hundreds of articles to find when police attention turned to Melender. Not one of the early stories mentioned any hint that law enforcement considered Jesse's disappearance as anything other than a kidnapping by outsiders. "Once the ransom note came in, the FBI got involved."

"Standard procedure, but I bet it slowed the leak of news."

Brogan agreed with Fallon. The Feds ran a tighter ship when it came to releasing information about a case than a local police department. "So the ransom drop was made, the money left in a trash can at a local park at a specific time."

"I recall that the FBI left the money but didn't see who picked it up."

"At the time of the drop off, a huge group of teenagers descended on the park as part of some scavenger hunt, making it pure chaos. In the melee, the trash can wasn't visible, and the kidnappers got away with the money." The audacity of the plan pointed to someone who had brains.

"And no Jesse?" Fallon asked, an emotion in his voice Brogan couldn't identify. Grief, or perhaps anger at a toddler's death.

"No Jesse. The kidnappers never contacted the family again." Brogan consulted his printouts. "That's when the FBI turned its attention to the family members. From there, the investigation quickly focused on Melender, the outsider who had come to live with her rich aunt and uncle two years prior. Ruby Thompson, the sister of Melender's father, took the girl in after the death of her brother and their grandmother—Melender's great-grandmother. By all accounts, Melender wasn't happy living with the Thompsons."

"She kidnapped and killed her cousin because she was unhappy?" Fallon queried.

"That's what the prosecution alleged." Brogan rubbed his hand over his face. "The entire Thompson household testified to Melender's unhappiness, but only the immediate Thompson family ever said anything about Melender being jealous toward Jesse. Apparently, Mr. and Mrs. Thompson left Jesse and Jillian with Melender quite frequently in the evenings when they had plans."

"Doesn't sound like the Thompsons were concerned about their niece harming their kids."

"I agree." Brogan hesitated. "There's a lot that seems strange about the case." The story had the potential to be the one that redeemed his career, but he had to do everything strictly by the book. And that meant getting Fallon on board with his digging deeper into Melender and what might have happened to Jesse. "Melender served every minute of her seventeen-year sentence, then was quietly released eight months ago. Instead of heading back to Maple Hollow,

Virginia, and the mountains everyone said she loved, she chose to return to Fairfax."

Fallon ignored the buzzing of his cell phone. "If I remember correctly, Melender never revealed the whereabouts of Jesse's body. It seems to me that the original investigation left a lot of stones unturned."

As the editor regarded him steadily, Brogan held his breath. But his pulse to accelerated with anticipation, something he hadn't experienced since his fall from grace.

"Gilmore, this has the earmarks of being a good investigative piece." The editor picked up his cell phone. "You'll still need to turn in your regular assignments on time. I'll expect to be kept abreast of any new developments too."

Brogan let out a measured breath, then stood as Fallon began to scroll through his phone messages. "Yes, sir."

He'd opened the door when Fallon added, "And Gilmore?"

Brogan turned to face his boss. "Sir?"

"Don't blow this."

"No, sir. I won't." Brogan hurried back to his desk. It had been a long time coming, but finally, he had his chance to show off his investigative skills. And perhaps spend more time with a certain woman with sad, blue eyes.

CHAPTER

FIVE

J ared Thompson groaned as his half-sister's number flashed on the screen of his cell phone. He wanted to let voice mail pick up, but experience taught him that to ignore Jillian would only make her more persistent. He swiped to the right and put the phone to his ear. "What's up, sis?"

"I'm out front. Open the door. We have to talk." Jillian's voice had an edge to it Jared hadn't heard before, so he quickly rose from the couch and rushed to his front door. After yanking the door open, he lowered the phone as Jillian shouldered her way inside his apartment.

"Well, hello to you too." He shut the door, then followed her into the living room. "Why are you here?"

She shrugged and nibbled on her thumbnail.

Jared blew out a breath. It was just like his sister to pretend she needed something pronto, then dither when it came to asking. He really wasn't up to playing twenty questions. "Jillian." He dragged her name out.

His sister continued to worry the skin around the cuticle with her teeth. "Melender's out of prison."

"What? She's out already?" He sank onto the leather recliner.

"Obviously you haven't called Mom and Dad recently." She flopped down on the sectional but started tapping her fingers on the arm rest.

Jared pressed his palms into his eyes before lowering his hands. Melender was free. With Melender in prison, questions about what happened that night had stayed largely under the surface. Her release changed everything. "When did she get out?"

"Months ago. Dad tried to keep it hush-hush, but Mom found out. It's all Mom talks about, ranting and raving about how justice hasn't been served."

His stepmother, Ruby, had never gotten over her grief when it came to Jesse.

"Apparently, Mom tracked her down and confronted her at a convenience store late last night—or I should say, early this morning."

"What convenience store?"

"The Kwikie Mart near the Auld Sheeben restaurant in Fairfax." Jillian pulled out her phone and scrolled through it. "Mom read a news article that mentioned a Mel Harman and thought it might be our dear cousin Melender. Last night, Dad and Mom went to the Kwikie Mart to confront the woman, who did turn out to be Melender." She thrust the phone toward Jared. "Read this."

Jared took the phone. Jillian had pulled up an article on the *Northern Virginia Herald* website dated four days ago.

Cleaner Foils Robbery

By Brogan Gilmore, Herald reporter

FAIRFAX – A two-liter bottle of Dr Pepper stopped a would-be robber from taking hundreds of dollars from the Kwikie Mart convenience store on Chain Bridge Road early Saturday morning. "She grab soda bottle and, wham! clipped masked man in side of head," said owner Vihaan Patel, who had been transferring the day's cash out of the safe at the time of the incident.

Mel Harman, an employee of Squeaky Clean, was cleaning the store in the early morning hours of Saturday. "I didn't do anything special," she said. "I saw someone in a werewolf mask holding a gun on Mr. Patel, so I chucked the bottle of soda at his head."

"I was very lucky she had such good aim," Mr. Patel said, adding that had the attempt been successful, it would have been the third time in less than two weeks his store had been robbed. "All three times, robbers wore masks."

Police continue to investigate the incidents, cautioning against actions such as those employed by Ms. Harman. "We strongly urge civilians to dial 911 if they see a robbery or other crime in process rather than attempting to stop the crime," said Capt. Bill Donovan with the Fairfax City Police Department. "While Ms. Harman's actions did chase off the would-be robber, it doesn't always happen that way."

Mr. Patel sees Ms. Harman as a heroine. "This time, the robber seemed more nervous, jittery. I was very scared. Her actions probably saved my life," he said. "I reward her for keeping me safe."

Mr. Patel said he would hire a security guard until the thieves are caught. The police urge anyone with information related to these incidents to call 703-555-1212.

He handed the phone back, hoping she wouldn't notice his sweaty palm. "What happened when Ruby showed up?"

"That reporter was there doing a follow-up piece, so Mom told him all about what Melender did and how Jesse hadn't been found."

Jared clenched his fist, wanting to pound something. He'd have to stop by the gym for a few rounds in the ring to work off his rising anger. Once again, Melender was messing up his life.

"Are you okay?" Jillian peered at him. "You look upset."

"I'm fine," he snapped. "What's Dad going to do about this fiasco?"

"He said he was going to make sure Melender didn't cause any

35

trouble." Jillian waved her hand at him. "Whatever that's supposed to mean."

He winced at the raw skin encircling her thumbnail. "How's he going to do that?"

Jillian shrugged. "Who knows? I wouldn't worry about it."

Then why was she here? Jared didn't voice the question that was on the tip of his tongue because he knew why—to warn him that Melender was out of prison and in town. And that Ruby would likely have one of her "spells." Granted, Dad would do his best to convince Melender to leave town. Her presence meant no one in the family was safe. But if Melender decided to try to prove her innocence, there would be no stopping her. Unless... No, he wouldn't entertain that possibility.

"Mom wants you to come to dinner on Thursday."

Jared started to decline, but maybe it would be best to hear first-hand any updates from his father. "Tell Ruby I'll be there."

"Sure." She moved to the door, and Jared followed.

Ruby wouldn't let the issue of Jesse alone, not with Melender free from prison. All of them would be forced to relive those terrible days leading up to Jesse's kidnapping. And he knew for a fact, Jillian didn't want to rehash the time Jesse disappeared any more than he did.

Jillian opened the door and stepped outside. "I imagine Melender will start asking a lot of questions about Jesse's abduction now that she's out of prison. One of her first stops will probably be here. After all, you were supposed to be watching Jesse that night."

～

MELENDER PULLED THE TAB ON A CAN OF CHICKEN AND GRAVY CAT FOOD, dumping half the contents into a bowl. Her Siamese-Maine Coon mix wound around her ankles, mewing his hunger. "Patience, my friend."

She set the bowl on the floor. "Here you go, Goliath." With one more yowl, the cat dove into his food.

She plopped another coffee pod into the Keurig, slid her mug beneath the funnel, and hit the start button. Her third cup of the day, and it was barely past noon. After the cops left, she hadn't been able to go back to sleep. Usually, she slept until three or four in the afternoon after arriving home around seven-thirty from her overnight cleaning shift. The encounter with Ruby had contributed to a restless sleep, and the early wakeup call from the cops meant she was operating on less than her best. At least this was her day off, so she could have an earlier bedtime.

Her cell phone trilled Donna Summer's "I Will Survive." The ringtone never failed to remind her that she would make it through. She had to. Donna belted out the chorus as Melender retrieved the phone from her back pocket. She glanced at the screen. Fairfax, Virginia, along with a 703 area code, which didn't confirm anything, given spoofers had perfected the art of identity camouflage. So few people called her that her curiosity got the better of her, and she answered the call just before it rolled to voicemail.

"Hello?"

"It's Dr. Silloway."

She nearly dropped the phone at the sound of the psychologist's voice. How had she gotten her unlisted number?

"Melender?" The older woman repeated in her calm, measured tone.

"Dr. Silloway. What a surprise." Melender had been forced to spend an hour each week with the prison psychologist, who had been more interested in probing the depths of her mind than actually helping Melender cope with her circumstances. The Keurig signaled her cup of coffee was ready. After hitting the phone's speaker button, she set it on the counter before adding a dash of cream to her cup.

"How are you doing?"

"I'm fine." As if she really cared. Melender suspected the doctor

37

reported the content of her sessions to her aunt and uncle, a viola-
tion of doctor-patient confidentiality, but Dr. Silloway wasn't one
restricted by conventions, not when money was involved. Melender
had no doubt Quentin paid a great deal of money to learn what she
said in those sessions.

"Hmm."

Melender took a sip of her coffee to stem any reaction to the
doctor's infuriating "hmms." Dr. Silloway had usually uttered that
sound while staring at her as if she were a bug under a microscope.
Two of Goliath's paws touched her calf. Melender reached down and
scratched the feline under his chin. *You're right. I don't have to talk to
her anymore, now do I?* "Dr. Silloway, what do you want?"

The woman chuckled, a sound that grated on her nerves. "You
always were direct."

Melender balanced on one foot to steady her thoughts, a technique she'd learned from the prison yoga instructor. As the silence
stretched out, Melender had had enough. "You're no longer my
doctor, so I'm hanging up now."

"Isn't it time you gave the Thompsons closure about Jesse's
disappearance?"

Of course. The question confirmed what Melender suspected all
along, that the psychologist didn't believe she was innocent, despite
her attempt to be sympathetic to Melender's incarceration.

"Do not call me again." Melender punched the end call button
then blocked the other woman's number before slipping the phone
back into her pocket. She picked up her coffee, then moved toward
the sliding glass door, Goliath at her heels. Once she'd opened the
door and screen, she stepped out into the small enclosure, closing
the door behind her to keep the A/C from escaping. The mid-
morning sun hit the balcony full on, turning it into a sauna. But
Melender didn't care. She settled into the lounge chair, coffee on the
end table and Goliath in her lap. With her eyes closed, she let the
sun's slanting rays soothe her body.

She had been biding her time over the past eight months, letting herself adjust to freedom in easy stages. The events of the last twelve hours meant she could no longer coast. The obstacles she faced loomed larger than her beloved Blue Ridge Mountains.

Quentin Thompson had been adept at manipulating public opinion for years and had many powerful friends as head of an international energy company, that much she'd understood at eighteen. His influence would only have grown larger during her years away, which probably fueled the rumors she'd read online about a possible political career in the next Virginia U.S. Senate race.

How to counter that influence occupied her thoughts. But now that the time had come to put her plans into motion, she vacillated. True, she wasn't the same girl who had gone to prison. She was stronger, harder, more determined, and less trusting. But she had yet to test those qualities in the real world.

Unbidden, the reporter's face with its strong jawline popped into her mind. Brogan Gilmore had already picked up the scent of a story. Maybe she could use that to her advantage. She needed an ally, and if her heart beat a little faster at the thought of spending time with him, she was entitled to a little flirtation, wasn't she?

CHAPTER

SIX

Brogan unfolded the *Northern Virginia Herald's* Sunday edition across the table, moving his coffee to one side. There, on the right-hand column below the fold, was his first front-page byline in more than a decade, a more than respectable accomplishment with the Sunday circulation of the *Herald* cresting 150,000. Sipping his coffee, he read the headline.

OWNER'S SON ARRESTED IN CONVENIENCE STORE ROBBERIES

His call yesterday morning to the detective working the robbery case had been more fruitful than anticipated, as the detective already had Veer Patel on his radar. Brogan's information had been enough to turn the case in a new direction, resulting in an early afternoon search of the son's apartment and the recovery of the masks used in the two robberies and one attempted robbery. With the arrest of Veer Patel, his follow-up story had barely mentioned Melender Harman.

Now that the robbery story had been wrapped up, the editor assigned him an investigative story about the disappearance of Jesse Thompson. First thing tomorrow morning, Brogan planned to call Quentin Thompson's office and schedule a meeting. His phone buzzed and interrupted his thoughts, probably another spammer call. He'd received two such calls already this morning, but in his line of work, a camouflaged number could lead to a good news tip.

"Gilmore."

"Mr. Gilmore? It's Melender Harman."

Brogan nearly dropped his coffee. "Ms. Harman. This is a surprise." When he'd given her his card at the Kwikie Mart, he hadn't expected her to call.

"I enjoyed your story on the robbery in the *Herald* this morning. I'm glad the police solved the case, although I suspect they had more than a little help from a certain reporter."

Brogan smiled at her backhanded compliment. "Thank you."

"I never really liked Mr. Patel's son but didn't think he would do that to his father."

"He might have seen it as the only way out of his gambling trouble."

"I guess you're right." She paused. "I'm sure you're wondering why I called, especially after I refused to cooperate Friday night."

The lady certainly didn't mince words. Granted, she had phoned him, but if he appeared too eager, he would likely scare her off. "I admit to being intrigued."

Melender made a noise between a chuckle and a harrumph. "Now that I have your full attention, I would like to ask you something."

He straightened in his chair. "Okay."

"What's more important to you—your byline or the truth?"

The question hit him like a sucker punch to the gut. For a moment, he couldn't find his voice, couldn't respond to the query he had been struggling with ever since his banishment from the news world. When he'd started at the *Herald*, his goal had been to redeem his byline. But his desire for reporting the truth had been re-awakened as he covered small-town politics, personalities, and events over the past year. While he admitted to a thrill in seeing his byline on the front page, he had more pride in his role in uncovering the person behind the robberies.

"Mr. Gilmore?"

"I'm here." He cleared his throat. "In the past, I was solely focused on my byline as an investigative reporter, which led to unethical tactics. I'm not proud to admit that I wanted recognition at any price."

Melender stayed quiet for a moment. "Thank you for your honesty."

"Don't get me wrong," he added. "There's a part of me that still longs for the spotlight, but nowadays, I want to write stories for more unselfish reasons."

"Would you be willing to meet with me in person? I have a proposition I'd like to discuss with you."

Brogan tightened his grip on his phone, his reporter's antenna quivering as he caught the scent of a story. "Sure. I'm free anytime today."

"Good. Let's meet at one o'clock. The Old Town Fairfax Plaza. I'll be near the fountains. Please don't be late."

MELENDER LIFTED HER SINGLE BRAID OFF THE BACK OF HER NECK IN AN attempt to cool down. Even in the shade, the summer heat was sweltering. Children splashed each other in the ground fountain, reminding her of what she'd lost while incarcerated. She might have had a husband and children of her own by now. Drawing a deep breath to both calm her nerves and banish the sadness that accompanied that last thought, she coughed as the humid air choked her.

"Are you okay?" Brogan Gilmore slid into the seat across from her and removed his sunglasses.

Nodding as she drank from her water bottle, Melender used the time to regain her composure. She set the bottle on the table and studied the reporter, who had been looking at her. What did he see besides a thirty-five-year-old woman of average height and weight? Nothing much to recommend to someone of the opposite sex other

43

than perhaps her long, silvery-blonde hair. Not that she was interested in Gilmore that way. She shook her head to dislodge the unwelcome thought that she was here not to get a reporter's help but because she liked the way the man across from her filled out a pair of faded jean shorts and plain blue t-shirt.

"Hot today, isn't it?" Mr. Gilmore eyed her as he unscrewed the cap on his Nationals branded reusable water bottle.

"Yes, it's a scorcher." She fanned her face with her hand, more to chase away the beginnings of a blush than to cool down. "I've lived in Virginia all my life, but I'm still not used to how temperamental the weather can be."

"August is always miserable. That's why Congress goes on summer recess and everyone with any sense leaves town."

"Yet here we both are, sweating in the August heat." She took another swig of water.

"Here we are." He leaned back in his chair. "What can I do for you, Ms. Harman?"

"Call me Melender." Better to put him at ease with less formality between them, given what she wanted to ask.

"Melender." He drew it out slowly, as if savoring the taste of her name on his tongue like a juicy ripe peach. "And please call me Brogan."

"Sure." She straightened in her chair. "I believe you know the basic facts of why I went to prison."

"I know you went to live with your aunt and uncle at sixteen." Without referencing a notebook, Brogan recited that fact from memory. "A year later, just shy of your eighteenth birthday, you were convicted of killing your one-year-old cousin, Jesse Thompson. But although the body was never found, you were sentenced to seventeen years. You served all your time, even though you were eligible for parole after ten years."

Melender blinked back tears. She'd spent nearly half her life behind bars for a crime she hadn't committed.

"So why am I here?" Brogan shifted his sunglasses on the tabletop. "A jury convicted you. You served your time. Justice has been served."

"Not if the wrong person went to prison. Not if whoever took Jesse is still out there. Free."

"I'd read that you never wavered from proclaiming your innocence."

"I am innocent."

He snorted. "That's what they all say, isn't it?"

"They?" His dismissive tone spiked her blood pressure along with her voice. "You mean convicted felons."

"You did the time." He shrugged.

"Yes, I did. Every single minute of it." Her voice shook, and she paused to gather the shreds of her composure like a child trying to repair a sandcastle after a wave crashed over it.

"I don't expect you to believe that I am not guilty of this crime. But there are things that don't make any sense, avenues the police didn't pursue because they thought they had their perpetrator."

His expression unreadable, Brogan leaned in. "What avenues?"

"The ransom money for one thing. It was never recovered. There was never any evidence linking me to the financial aspect of the case at all."

Disbelief flashed across his face, tightening the faint lines on his forehead and around his mouth.

"Read the court transcript, and you'll see that the prosecutor did not even try to pin the ransom on me."

He sat back. "Okay, I will."

"There's the lack of a body."

"That's what your aunt attacked you about, wanting to know where you buried her son."

"I didn't bury anybody!" She lowered her voice, frustration nibbling along her spine. She had to convince Brogan to help her. She couldn't find the killer on her own, especially not with Quentin watching her every move. And she had no doubt he would hire someone to keep a close eye on her. Should she warn Brogan to be careful? Maybe not yet. She couldn't afford to have him thinking she was paranoid. "The prosecutor's case was all circumstantial evidence that could be interpreted differently if you start at another point."

"That point being you're innocent of killing Jesse?"

"That's right." A wave of tiredness enveloped her, and she slumped against the back of her chair. "Look, I'm not asking you to believe in my innocence. All I'm asking is that you read the court transcript. If you think I deserved what I got, then no harm, no foul. However, if you see the trial as a miscarriage of justice, then please help me find out what really happened to Jesse."

The silence built between them as squeals from children splashing in the fountain a few feet away filled the air.

"I Googled you too." She let the statement pull up a chair and sit down. "You were a very good investigative journalist, despite your unethical ways of getting to the truth."

His cavalier expression wavered as he dropped his gaze.

"Sometimes, the path to redemption takes some strange turns," she said softly.

Brogan jerked his head up, meeting her gaze straight on. "You think this investigation could be that path for me."

"Maybe it's redemption for both of us." She firmed her lips. "It depends on you."

"The truth should matter more than one person, one byline, one story. It's been a long time since I've felt that way."

"Now you do?" Melender noted the lines of fatigue around the corners of his eyes. This may well be a man with as many demons as she had.

"I want to seek the truth, no matter the personal or professional consequences." Brogan paused. "But I can't promise what I find will be what you want to hear."

"I'm not asking you to find what will please me. I want you to help me find the truth." She reached down and put a tote bag on the table. "Here's a copy of the court transcript. Call me when you've read it."

Brogan stood and picked up the bag. "Okay."

As he walked away, Melender drained the rest of her water bottle. She might have made a huge mistake trusting a journalist like Brogan Gilmore, but maybe, just maybe, she could use his need to prove his integrity to her advantage.

CHAPTER

SEVEN

Brogan tossed the court transcript on the coffee table, then scrubbed a hand across his chin. Questions spun in his mind, the answers of which should have been contained in the stark pages of a week-long court case. Questions that had him doubting Melender's guilt. Questions that had him not entirely convinced she had no role in Jesse's disappearance. In other words, reading the court transcript had ignited a driving need to uncover the truth of what happened to Jesse, because if one thing kept bubbling to the surface as he read through the testimony, it was that what really happened that long-ago night hadn't been told in court.

He pulled his laptop onto his legs and looked up Melender's attorney, Dan Stabe. The lawyer had left the public defender's office he'd been with at the time of Melender's trial and now was an associate at the law firm of Davis, Ramsey, and Stevens. According to Stabe's posted bio on the firm's website, he had spent just three years with the public defender's, then moved to the larger firm. Brogan doubled checked the dates. Yes, Stabe had made the change less than a year after Melender's trial and sentencing. Davis, Ramsey, and Stevens wasn't a criminal firm. The attorneys practiced corporate law, a far cry from a defense law practice.

On a hunch, Brogan pulled up the website for Thompson Energy. There, buried on the About Us page, was the name of the company's law firm. Davis, Ramsey, and Stevens. He leaned back on his couch, staring at the words on the screen. That kind of coincidence— Melender's attorney ending up working for the law firm representing her uncle's company—ignited his Spidey sense.

Grabbing his phone, Brogan called Melender. As it rang, he glanced at the clock on his computer. 1:00 a.m. He probably should hang up and make the call in the morning.

"Hello?" She sounded cautious but wide awake.

In the background, the faint sound of traffic and the muted tones of an instrumental tune captured his attention.

"Ms. Harman, Melender? It's Brogan Gilmore."

"What can I do for you?"

"Did I catch you at a bad time?" Brogan smacked his forehead. Of course he had, calling her after midnight.

"I'm driving to my next cleaning job, so I have a few minutes."

Some of the tension eased out of his shoulders at the reminder she worked the overnight shift as an office and business cleaner. Why he should be glad he hadn't disturbed her rest, he didn't want to contemplate. Better to focus on the story.

Brogan cleared his throat. "I read the transcript." Her silence encouraged him to plunge on. "I agree there are some major inconsistencies in the evidence and testimony presented."

"Some major inconsistencies."

Brogan winced at her flat tone, but he wouldn't make promises he couldn't keep. "Here's the thing. I don't know if you're innocent or guilty."

"I see. Thank you for reading the transcript."

Sensing she might disconnect the call, he hurried on. "But I do agree there are some rather large holes in the testimony and evidence from court."

"So you said."

"So I did." The old Brogan would have told a source whatever she wanted to hear in pursuit of a story, but the new Brogan, the one who had clawed his way out of a hole of his own making, wanted to do justice, to love kindness, and to walk humbly with God.

Drawing in a deep breath, he shot a prayer heavenward. *God, please grant me the right words to say that will not give false hope to this woman, but would honor You.*

"Are you still there?"

Brogan snapped his attention back to the phone call. "Yes, sorry." He rubbed his forehead, then plunged in. "If we're going to be working together, I need to lay out some ground rules."

"Working together?" A wariness invaded her voice. "Does that mean you're going to look into Jesse's disappearance?"

"It means I'm going to take a closer look at the evidence and testimony presented at your trial to see where it leads." He paused. "It doesn't mean I'm out to prove you were wrongly convicted."

"All I ask is you view it with an open mind."

"That I promise you I will do. What I won't do is pursue any personal vendetta you might have against your aunt and her family."

"I wouldn't ask you to do such a thing."

The conviction in her voice warmed his heart, but he needed to keep her at a distance while he chased down potential leads. After promising to call her later to set up a time for an in-person interview, he disconnected. He needed more background before he started questioning other people. Why not go directly to the source? If the source happened to be an attractive, single woman, well, who said journalism had to be all work and no play?

RUBY THOMPSON TRIED TO PUT THE ENCOUNTER WITH MELENDER OUT OF her mind as Velma kneaded the tight muscles in her neck, but she couldn't shake the image of her niece having a job like a normal person.

"You are very tense today, Miss Ruby," Velma said.

"It's been a dreadful week." Ruby closed her eyes as she lay on her back on the portable massage table in her sitting room. She would call the owner of Squeaky Clean and demand he fire Melender. Her niece shouldn't be able to go about her business as if nothing had happened.

Velma gently turned her head to the side to work the muscles from hairline to shoulder. Ruby kept her eyes closed and attempted to relax. She'd had her husband call the prosecutor's office each of the three times Melender came up for parole to ensure they would be able to attend the hearing to speak for Jesse, but all three times, Melender herself refused parole. Strange her niece would insist on serving her entire sentence. Certainly, it made her ultimate release more galling. What could you threaten someone with if you couldn't send them back to prison?

"Turn over, please." Velma held the sheet up for her to flip over.

A whisper of air tickled across her bare back as the massage therapist folded the sheet back, tucking it snug around Ruby's hips. The scent of lavender permeated the room as Velma rubbed the lotion into her skin with long, sure strokes.

Even if Jesse's body was found, Melender couldn't be prosecuted for the same crime. Anger bubbled up inside her, undoing Velma's calming technique.

It wasn't fair. Melender should tell her where Jesse was. That revelation couldn't send her niece back to prison, but it would, finally, give Ruby some peace. Lately, though, Ruby couldn't shake the feeling her niece had no idea where her little cousin was buried. That Jesse was dead, she had no doubt. A mother just knew. When the ransom money disappeared without another word about Jesse, Ruby had clung to the hope the kidnappers might have given or sold Jesse to some couple desperate to have a baby.

Jesse had been such a sunny boy, always smiling. Even at

fifteen months, he displayed none of the characteristics of a typical toddler. But hope faded when Melender had been arrested for his disappearance and eventually convicted of murdering Jesse. Ruby should have never taken that snake into her home. She should have known nothing good could come from mountain people. Bobby Ray had been an ideal older brother when he and Ruby were kids, protecting Ruby from their volatile father. Their mama worked herself into an early grave, dying in her mid-forties a worn, thin woman who faded into the rough floorboards of their cabin. At eleven, Ruby vowed she would not follow in her mother's footsteps. Five years later, she left the hollow and never looked back.

Until social services called to tell her about a niece Ruby had forgotten existed who needed a place to stay. The small, thin sixteen-year-old who showed up in the dead of winter in a too-big tattered pea coat initially bore little resemblance to Bobby Ray. Then Melender had stared straight into her aunt's eyes, and she had seen centuries of hardy mountain ancestors in that direct gaze.

"Miss Ruby?" Velma's soft query yanked Ruby back to the present. "All done."

Ruby didn't move. Velma covered her shoulders with the sheet. She waited until the door clicked shut behind Velma, then rolled over, clutching the sheet to her naked body.

The unbidden thought came that she had failed Bobby Ray by repaying her brother's many kindnesses and his assistance in her escape to a better life by not helping his only child. Nonsense. What was she supposed to do with a teenage niece she hadn't seen in more than a decade? With a surly teenage stepson, a toddler under foot, and heavily pregnant with Jesse, she had done her duty to Melender, given the girl a place to sleep, food, and an education at the finest private school in the area. And the girl had responded with ingratitude and murder.

Yanking on her clothes, all the tension Velma had valiantly tried to erase came flooding back into her neck and shoulders. Ruby snatched her cell phone. "Siri, what's the number for Squeaky Clean in Virginia?"

"That number is 703-555-2741," the virtual assistant intoned. "Would you like to be connected?"

"Yes."

Ruby thinned her lips as the recorded greeting for the cleaning company came on the line. If things went according to her plan, her darling niece would soon be out of a job.

～

"Mel?"

Melender turned from putting away her supplies to see Janice Butram's assistant standing in the doorway of the supply room.

"Boss wants to see you." The older woman shrugged as if answering Melender's unspoken question. "And no, I don't know what it's all about."

"Okay, thanks. I'll be there once I've finish here."

"I'll tell her." The assistant disappeared, leaving Melender to finish restocking the caddy and slid it into the designated slot.

Melender hadn't spoken face-to-face with the owner since she was hired. Slipping into the bathroom, she washed her hands, splashed cold water on her face, then used her damp hands to smooth back the hairs escaping from her single French braid. About as presentable as she could be after working a ten-hour shift.

Unable to shake the feeling that Ruby's visit on Friday night had something to do with this summons, Melender went into a stall and locked the door. During her incarceration, Melender had wrestled with her faith, gradually coming to realize how much she needed God. Now, praying seemed as natural as drinking water.

Lord, thank you for this job. Thank you for Ms. Butram and her willingness to give me a chance. I pray that my work these past months would speak louder than any calls from Ruby or Quentin. Please help me to show your love to those who persecute me. Amen.

She exited the bathroom, then walked down the hallway to Ms. Butram's office. The assistant, phone to her ear, waved Melender to go in.

With a knock on the door, Melender walked into the office, hoping she wouldn't be thrown to the hungry lions.

"Mel, thanks for coming in." Janice Butram, a tall woman in her late fifties with a curly bob and cat-eyed glasses, rose from behind her desk. "Shut the door please."

Melender complied, her heart rate pounding in her ears. "How can I help?"

"Have a seat." Ms. Butram retook her own seat as Melender sank into one of the club chairs on the other side of the desk. "This morning, I received a phone call from Ruby Thompson."

With more calmness than she felt inside, Melender acknowledged the name. "My aunt."

"Yes." Ms. Butram leaned forward, her gray eyes steady on Melender's face. "She informed me of your imprisonment, then demanded I fire you."

Melender fought back tears. She'd known Ruby would do something like this, but the hurt caught her off guard. Beyond a paycheck, she genuinely liked this job, the mindlessness of the cleaning tasks, the solitude of the work. Dirt didn't care if you were a convicted felon.

"I, of course, told her I would do no such thing."

"Really?" Hope shot through her. Melender didn't care if the older woman saw the tears in her eyes.

Ms. Butram smiled slightly. "I informed Mrs. Thompson that I knew all about your past, including your incarceration, but that I preferred to let the present speak for itself. I also told her I would be a very poor businesswoman if I let one of my top employees go."

Melender brushed the tears away with the back of her hand. "Thank you."

"As I told you during your interview, I'm willing to give second

55

chances as long as my employees are honest and hard-working. I will not tolerate liars or slackers."

Melender discreetly took in a deep breath, letting it out slowly as the prison yoga instructor had trained her to do. Another set of breaths brought her pulse back down within a normal range.

"My answer did not make your aunt happy." Ms. Butram turned her focus back to her laptop but suddenly looked up and peered over the top of her eyeglasses at Melender. "Please be careful. Your aunt sounded very determined to make life difficult for you."

"I will." Melender stood. "And thank you again."

Leaving the owner's office, Melender hurried down the corridor and out to her car. Once inside, she started the vehicle and blasted the A/C to ward off the sweltering heat, then leaned her head against the back of the seat. Tears of relief dripped down her face.

Thank you, God, for this job and for Ms. Butram. I pray for my aunt, that you would help her to find peace. And Lord, please help us find out what happened to Jesse.

CHAPTER

EIGHT

Quentin Thompson sunk a forty-foot putt, then jabbed his fist in the air, Tiger Woods style.

His golf partner, Judge Greg Moloney, grinned. "With that kind of putting, we'll cinch next month's charity golf tournament for sure."

"I knew I shouldn't have taken that bet," grumbled the third member of their quartet, U.S. Senator Edward Johnston, as he lined up his shot at the eighteenth hole.

"Some guys have all the luck." Wilton Brown, a partner at the law firm of Davis, Ramsey, and Stevens who handled Quentin's business interests, selected his club. "Look at you. You have a booming business, a beautiful wife, and a game under par. I say that's the epitome of injustice."

"What can I say?" Quentin chuckled, spreading his arms wide. "I'm just a great guy." His cell phone vibrated, and he pulled it out of the clip at his waist. The bright sunlight made reading the caller ID difficult, so he simply hit the accept button. "Hello?"

"Are you sure it's wise to play golf at a time like this?"

Quentin looked around, then angled his body away from the other golfers. "How did you get this number?"

"I think that's the least of your worries, don't you?"

"Now is not a good time for me to talk." Quentin threw a glance over his shoulder in time to see Edward sink his shot.

"Make it a good time."

Quentin muted the phone, then faced the others. "Excuse me, but I need to take this."

Edward pointed at him. "You're buying the first round."

"I know the rules." The first of the foursome to take a call on the course had to buy the initial round of drinks at the clubhouse. "Tell Henry to put it on my tab. Greg, can you take my clubs in the cart?"

"Sure, no problem," Greg replied. "Everything okay?"

Quentin nodded. "A pressing matter with a current project. I'll catch up to you at the clubhouse."

As the other three loaded golf bags into the two carts, Quentin rushed to the paved pathway that circled the course and unmuted the phone. "This had better be important."

"I don't think you're in any position to make demands. It sounds like you've forgotten who helped you out of that bind you were in eighteen years ago."

Quentin opened his mouth to respond but thought better of it and reigned in his temper with some effort. No sense in riling up someone who could easily destroy all he had. "You were paid for your assistance. Quite handsomely, I should add."

"Which is why you've managed to stay out of harm's way for so long."

Quentin waved as his buddies passed him in their golf carts, waiting until they were well out of earshot before continuing. "According to my calculations, we're even. There's nothing left to discuss."

"Even?" A chuckle that held no mirth crackled over the line. "I think we have a lot to talk about. I see your niece is back in town."

"Melender served her time." Quentin quickened his pace along the path.

"We both know your wife is going to hound Melender into revealing Jesse's whereabouts."

Quentin stayed silent.

"And we both know digging up that particular body is only going to bring more grief upon your family."

Quentin spotted a somewhat secluded bench set behind an overgrown leafy bush and made a beeline for it. Too many friends kept passing him in their carts to make this conversation private. He settled on the bench. "What urgent matter do we need to discuss?"

"Your plan to keep Melender Harman from figuring out what happened to Jesse. There's more than the secret of where your son's body is buried that could spill out."

Quentin sucked in a breath, the pain of losing Jesse striking him hard. "I thought there was nothing to worry about on that score." He had been foolish to think Ruby had let go of her need to find Jesse's body. Just because she had stayed quiet about it for years didn't mean she'd resigned herself to never having a place to visit her son. Now he could see she had merely been waiting for Melender to serve her time and get out before relaunching her quest to bring her son home.

"When it concerns your wife, there's always something to worry about."

"I'll do my best, but Ruby has a mind of her own." Quentin tried not to think about what else might float to the surface if his wife pushed Melender too hard. So far, his niece had done nothing to reveal she even recalled what had happened prior to Jesse's disappearance, but rooting through the past might bring that memory back.

"Your job is to make sure nothing new comes to light. Because this house of cards will come tumbling down if someone starts fiddling with the construction. Are you ready to pay that price?"

∼

Brogan hit send on a story about the retirement of a Fairfax City School Board member. His next assignment—to cover tomorrow morning's ribbon cutting to officially open Potomac Landings, a new mixed-use development with residential townhouses and upscale businesses—meant he had the rest of Monday afternoon free to start digging into Jesse Thompson's disappearance.

But not at the newspaper office. This was best done away from the prying eyes of his editor and colleagues. With a wave to the receptionist, Brogan headed toward his car. Once inside, he pulled up the contacts list on his phone. Didn't his old college roommate still work for the FBI? He'd called Tim a couple of times when he'd worked on other investigative stories, but it had been more than a decade since they'd talked. He hit the call button.

"FBI media relations, Tim Nash speaking."

"Tim, it's Brogan Gilmore."

A beat passed. "Brogan, it's been a long time."

Ignoring the less-than-cordial tone in Tim's voice, Brogan plowed on. "Yes, it has been. Would love to catch up with you now that I'm back in the area."

"That so."

"I'm working at the *Northern Virginia Herald* these days." Brogan continued as if Tim had asked. "I have some questions about an old kidnapping case that I thought you might be able to provide some background on."

"This is about a story?"

Brogan couldn't tell if Tim sounded relieved or disappointed that he hadn't called just to shoot the breeze. He decided the only way to relieve Tim's hurt feelings was to be completely honest. "I'm not sure if there is a story or not. I really just wanted to pick your brain about the case."

"You want my advice about an old kidnapping case."

Brogan turned down the A/C. "Yes."

"Off the record?"

"Most definitely off the record."

Tim sighed. "I'm assuming it was a local case?"

"Yes, happened in McLean, Virginia."

"What's the name and year?"

"Jesse Thompson, eighteen years ago." Brogan resisted the urge to drum his fingers on the steering wheel as Tim clacked on a keyboard.

"This isn't an unsolved kidnapping case."

"I didn't say it was."

"Why are you looking into the kidnapping where the perpetrator was arrested, tried, and convicted?"

The very question Brogan had been asking himself. The answer most certainly did not lie in the fact that he couldn't say a hard no to those beautiful yet haunting blue eyes. "I read the trial transcript, and some things didn't quite add up."

"Have you met Melender Harman?" Tim's matter-of-fact question echoed in Brogan's ear.

Fighting the urge to jack up the A/C again as heat inched up his neck and face, Brogan acknowledged the hit. "Yes, she's the one who asked me to look into it with her."

"I thought she would be out of prison by now."

"She was released eight months ago."

"That's strange. She would have been eligible for parole after eight to ten years. Wonder why she served the entire sentence?"

"You met her too?"

"No, but I remember seeing her during the trial when I was working for the Fairfax County Court House media relations department. She always looked so bewildered and scared."

"Guilty-scared or innocent-scared?" Brogan balanced his notebook on the steering wheel to jot down Tim's comments for background. The more he learned about Melender, the more he'd be able to figure out the real story.

"My gut at the time said she had nothing to do with Jesse's

disappearance." Tim paused. "Back then, I wasn't in law enforcement, so I can't say whether that was because she really wasn't guilty or because I felt sorry for a kid who took off her shoes every chance she got."

"You mean in court?"

"No, she came to court in shoes, but she would kick them off during recesses and anytime she went outside. This was in November, so it wasn't freezing but still, it was rather strange."

Brogan noted the story, then shifted the phone to his other shoulder. "She grew up in Maple Hollow, Virginia, in the foothills of the Blue Ridge Mountains near the Shenandoah Valley. It's so small, it doesn't even show up on most maps."

"Hold on a minute." Tim muffled the receiver on his end, then came back on the line. "I've got to go. Did you need anything else?"

"Is there any chance I could take a look through the FBI files on the case?" Brogan could have filed a Freedom of Information Act form to see the documents, but he'd rather try to get the information quietly. A FOIA would proclaim his interest in the Thompson kidnapping to the world at large.

"Is that all?"

But Brogan heard acquiescence in Tim's voice, not annoyance. "I could file a FOIA, and since the case is closed..." He left the thought unfinished.

"You're right that a closed case means the files aren't classified. However, I will need the official form on file."

Brogan sighed. "I'll email it to you this afternoon."

"But don't worry. I won't log it into the system right away. There's a huge backlog of those requests, so yours could easily get pushed down in the pile for a few weeks."

"Thanks, Tim. I owe you. When do you think I could get a look at the files?"

Tim snickered. "She must have grown up nicely."

Heat fanned Brogan's cheeks despite the cool temperature inside his car. During their collegiate days, Tim always knew when Brogan was interested in a member of the opposite sex. No sense denying his interest in Melender. "I'll admit I find her intriguing, but the fact that she served time for murder puts a damper on things romantically."

"If you say so. I'll give you a call once I've located the files."

Brogan ended the call and snapped on his seatbelt. Putting the car into drive, he headed home. With any luck, he'd have the files in a couple of days and then he could see what, if any, evidence pointed to someone other than Melender for Jesse's disappearance.

CHAPTER

NINE

The overhead bell announced Melender's arrival with a soft jingle as she pushed open the door of Fox's Music Store in Falls Church, Virginia. She loved coming to the shop, crammed with musical instruments, sheet music, and old record albums, especially near the end of the day when the store emptied of customers. It was her rare foray into the world, but she found the musty air of the shop comforting, as if musical notes hovered on the dust motes that danced in the sunlight.

"Hey, Mel. How are you today?" Jimmy Stork, the long-time owner of the independent shop, smiled from behind the counter. With a pencil tucked behind one ear and his reading glasses perched on top of his balding head, Mr. Jimmy, as he was known, appeared more like an absentminded professor than a musician. But the talented man could play nearly every instrument in his store, much to the delight of children who came in with their parents to rent or buy instruments for school bands and orchestras.

"I'm doing okay." Melender wandered over to the counter. "Anything new?"

"Ah, I have something that I think you will enjoy." Mr. Jimmy's eyes sparkled as he moved from behind the counter to one of his worktables. With the flourish of a magician, he whipped off a cloth covering a boxy object.

Melender gasped. On the scarred table lay an Appalachian dulcimer. The three strings of the instrument stirred memories of sing-a-longs with family and friends. The old instrument had a battered black-walnut finish. For a long moment, she simply stared at it. It had been way too long since she'd touched, let alone played, one.

Closing her eyes, Melender could hear her grandmother ripple her fingers over the strings of a dulcimer as they sat on the porch in the cooling evening after a long day of canning in a hot kitchen. Blinking away tears, she pushed down those precious memories and sucked in a deep breath to regain her emotional balance.

"I see someone else admires my latest find as much as I do."

A male voice behind her made Melender jump. Turning, she faced an older man in his late fifties with short salt-and-pepper hair and a closely trimmed goatee, who stood a few feet away from the table.

"She'll be ready to join your fine collection soon enough." The shop owner moved aside to allow the other man to examine the instrument. "Nolan Trent, this is Mel Harman."

She nodded acknowledgement of the introduction, then both men studied her expectantly. Melender cleared her throat to banish the thick emotion that hovered there. "It reminds me of my grandmother's dulcimer."

Mr. Trent pointed toward the curved body with his forefinger. "I found this in a pawn shop and recognized its worth right away. Got it for a song, pardon my pun." Mr. Trent winked at her.

No wonder the instrument had called to her like a mother's call to her children at dusk. "Do you play?"

Mr. Trent shook his head. "I'm only a fan of the music."

"Don't let Nolan fool you." Mr. Jimmy waggled a finger at Mr. Trent. "He's a renowned scholar of American folk songs."

"I wouldn't go that far," the man protested. "It's been a pleasure of mine to have studied the origins, lyrics, and instrumentation of ethnic American music."

"What he's not saying," Mr. Jimmy rejoined, "is that he's written numerous articles and several books on the subject and is considered one of the foremost authorities on this type of music."

"Do you collect folk songs?" Melender's curiosity overcame her normal reticence to talk with a stranger.

"Most of that work was done in the early part of the twentieth century by men like Cecil Sharp and James Madison Carpenter, who went into the mountains of West Virginia, Virginia, and North Carolina to write songs that had only been passed down orally among small communities." Mr. Trent ran a finger down the side of the dulcimer's smooth wood. "Their work, along with later scholars, provided the basis for continued scholarship on the subject."

"Nolan is always on the lookout for unknown folk songs." Mr. Jimmy kept his eyes on Melender.

Melender bit her bottom lip at the silent question behind Mr. Jimmy's words. She rarely shared her music anymore, but the instrument's silent strings beckoned to her as clear as the morning song of a bobwhite to its mate. Almost against her will, she stretched out her fingers to pluck the strings.

"Do you play?" Mr. Trent observed her, but for once, Melender didn't feel like her privacy was being invaded by a stranger's interest. His perusal had a more scholarly feel to it.

"Yes, she does." Mr. Jimmy spoke before she could, a challenge in his eyes.

Melender started to shake her head, but the dulcimer drew her heart, its strings promising sweet memories. "May I?"

Mr. Trent nodded, and Melender gently drew the instrument toward her, leaving it on the table. Deftly, she tuned it, then she paused, closing her eyes briefly to consider which song would best fit this moment in time. The haunting tune of "Forsaken Love" overwhelmed her senses, and she played the simple melody on the dulcimer's strings, using only her fingers as Sudie had taught her, rather than a pick. Without fully realizing it, she broke into sing.

They stood in the moonlight near by the gate.
Goodbye, my darling, I know you'll wait.
She ceased her weeping and smiled through tears
Saying, "I've been true love through these long years."
For on tomorrow at the break of day,
He was to journey far, far away
He held her closer, his promised bride.

Her voice choked as memories of Sudie singing that same song in her quavering voice flooded her mind. Melender's fingers slipped off the dulcimer, and one of the strings snapped with a ping. In the sudden silence, the shop's grandfather clock chimed five o'clock.

"That was magnificent." Mr. Trent spoke softly, as if hesitant to intrude.

"I broke one of the strings." Melender brushed the back of her hand across her wet cheeks, then bowed her head. She hadn't cried this much since her first night in prison, when she vowed never to cry again, a promise she'd kept for seventeen long years.

"Jimmy can fix it," Mr. Trent said.

Melender met Mr. Trent's gaze. "Thank you for letting me play this beautiful instrument."

"Your voice is astounding." Mr. Trent touched the instrument. "I don't suppose you would be willing to sing and play for a little gathering I'm having for some of my academic friends?"

Melender frowned. "I don't sing in public."

"It's not open for the public." Mr. Trent didn't keep the eager note from his voice. "Next month, I'm previewing parts of a new book I'm working on about modern American folk songs to some of my musicology colleagues."

"I don't know any modern folk songs." Melender tried to

discourage the well-meaning Mr. Trent. If he knew her background, he wouldn't be asking her to perform.

"You could sing whatever you'd like. I would be honored to lend you the dulcimer for practice." Mr. Trent smiled. "Once it's fixed."

Drat the man for tempting her with the lure of the instrument, but Melender firmed her resolve. "I'm sorry, Mr. Trent. I can't accommodate your request." She turned to leave. "Mr. Jimmy, see you later."

Melender fled the store as fast as she could without breaking into a run. Behind her, Mr. Trent discussed her decision with Mr. Jimmy, but she ignored them both. If she stayed a second longer, she would cave and accept his offer for the chance to take home that beautiful instrument. But Mr. Trent's reputation would have been in shreds had her identity as a convicted felon been revealed. She might have the voice of an angel, but her background labeled her a devil.

QUENTIN FROWNED AS HE PACED ON THE VERANDA, THE ONLY PLACE HE could be assured of privacy. The private investigator Quentin had hired that morning to keep an eye on Melender's movements was late in calling with an update. The sun might have set an hour ago, but the temperature had barely dipped below ninety degrees. He hated August in Northern Virginia. Usually, they spent the month in their summer home near Bar Harbor, Maine. However, his chief lobbyist had recommended sticking closer to Washington to solidify their strategy for getting the votes to pass a bill that would bring his energy company a lot of business. Even though Congress wasn't in session, there was enough behind-the-scenes strategizing to set the stage for September's return to session.

His phone buzzed, and Quentin answered with a clipped, "Yes."

"She went to Fox's Music Store in Falls Church," said P.I. Dillion Raines.

"What did she do there?" The last thing Quentin needed was more surprises from his niece.

"Talked to the owner, a Mr. Jimmy Stork, and a customer, Mr. Nolan Trent."

"Who's Trent?" Quentin paused near the far end of the porch to gaze out into the landscaped backyard. Lightening bugs blinked in the gloom, the flashes of light more annoying than soothing.

"A musicologist."

"A what?" Quentin didn't care that he sounded irritated. With what he was paying Raines, the man should call on time and not expect common courtesy.

"Trent collects and studies American folk music. He's considered an expert on Appalachian folk songs and has written several popular books on the topics."

"Anything else?" Who cared if Melender visited music stores in her free time? He was hoping for something meatier that he could use against her in case she started causing trouble.

"I checked out that reporter, Brogan Gilmore." Raines didn't offer any more information.

"Am I going to have to pull every last bit of information out of you?" Quentin snapped, his irritation inching closer to volcanic. "What did you find out?"

"He's been with the *Herald* for nearly a year, writing mostly local news stories, such as the one on the Kwikie Mart robberies."

"He seemed older than someone just starting out as a journalist." Gilmore had phoned Quentin's office earlier this morning to schedule a brief meeting for Wednesday. Quentin had instructed his secretary to fit the reporter in right before lunch to give him an excuse to cut their meeting short if necessary. He wanted to find out all he could ahead of time.

Raines cleared his throat. "Gilmore spent his early years as a journalist bouncing around in the Midwest at medium-sized city papers in Nebraska, Indiana, and Kentucky, where he was a finalist for a Pulitzer in investigative reporting for a series on the abuse of mentally ill adults in state-regulated homes. That landed him a job as an investigative journalist for the *New York Dispatch*."

"Why did he leave New York?"

"Ten years ago, he wrote a series of sensational stories that showed prominent board members of a national charity headquartered in New York diverting the organization's funds to their own pockets. That series snagged Gilmore another Pulitzer nomination. But then a reporter at the *Washington Leader* writing her own story on the scandal discovered that Gilmore had based his reporting on a single source, which had fed him altered documents showing the misappropriation of funds. That single source, a disgruntled former employee of the charity, had spun circumstantial evidence into corruption. Gilmore would have found out the same thing had he actually investigated the story instead of relying on that one source."

"I bet the *Dispatch* wasn't too pleased to find out their star investigative reporter had done such shoddy work." Quentin resumed his pacing. A clearer picture of Gilmore began to emerge.

"The paper launched a full investigation and discovered that not only had Gilmore neglected to corroborate the source's accusations in the charity scandal, but he also had fabricated unnamed sources to collaborate his findings in the Kentucky series that netted him the job in New York."

Quentin allowed a small smile to cross his lips. People like Gilmore he understood—always looking to get ahead any way they could. "He sounds like a rather shady character."

"That he was. After the *Dispatch* booted him, he didn't work in journalism until the *Northern Virginia Herald* hired him."

"Good work." Quentin's irritation with the other man's delivery style had vanished with the information on the reporter.

"Do you want me to keep following Harman?"

"Yes."

"What about Gilmore?"

Quentin debated whether or not having someone keep tabs on

the reporter would be worth the expense. "Not yet. But send me daily updates on the woman's activities."

Raines agreed, and Quentin ended the call. Now that he knew what kind of man Gilmore was, he knew just how to ensure the reporter wouldn't be overly eager to help his niece.

CHAPTER
TEN

Melender set her grocery bags onto the kitchen counter, then picked up her ringing cell phone. Caller ID displayed a local number, one she didn't recognize. Probably a telemarketer but maybe it was Brogan calling with an update. "Hello?"

"Digging up the past is never a good idea." The softly spoken words breathed a chill over her like the wind roaring up the mountain ahead of a storm.

Silence.

She pressed the phone to her ear. "Who is this?"

"A friend who's concerned that you might be taking on more than you can handle."

She pushed her fear down enough to respond more calmly. "Friends introduce themselves."

"You wouldn't want to meet me."

Melender recognized the menacing tone, even though she couldn't say whether the caller was male or female. It was the same tone she'd heard from bullies in prison, those who made promises they had every intention of keeping. But seventeen years behind bars had shown her the only way to handle a bully was to call their bluff. "I've met worse."

The caller chuckled, a sound more sinister than light-hearted. "Ah, so the wildcat has grown claws." A short pause. "Keep your eyes on the future before someone gets hurt. I'm sure you wouldn't want to find yourself back in that cell, now would you?"

She snorted. "You think you can scare me with prison? I served my time. Every. Single. Minute."

A low growl emanated from the phone. Melender had heard a similar sound once from a cornered mountain lion right before the big cat clawed a black bear to pieces.

"Ah, but it's not just you, now is it?" The hushed voice continued. "There's Brogan Gilmore, not quite a saint but perhaps useful to your quest? I think you'd really hate to have his handsome face disfigured, now wouldn't you?"

The ominous warning sucked the anger and bravado out of her.

A mental picture of Brogan with his tousled blond hair and blue eyes flashed in her mind. Just when she thought she might move forward, might find the answers she so desperately sought, another person was threatened. Fear coiled around her like a python. She untangled herself from the dread of anything happening to Brogan and opened her mouth to respond. Too late. The caller had hung up.

Sliding down to her knees on the kitchen floor, she did the only thing she could do that would make a lick of difference.

Dear God, please. Please help me to discover the truth about what happened to Jesse. Please keep Brogan safe. Please let my actions be honoring to you.

Her phone trilled again. She checked the caller ID. Again, a local number. Surely the anonymous caller wouldn't contact her again so soon.

Right before it rolled to voice mail, she picked up the call. "Hello?"

"Melender? It's Brogan. Did I catch you at a bad time?"

"No." She cleared her throat, automatically wiping the inflection from her voice to give the appearance of not being ruffled by the threats. In prison, showing any weakness after the confrontation could be as dangerous. "I just got home from work." If ever she needed to hear a friendly voice—even from someone who wasn't sure if she was innocent of a heinous crime or not—it was right now.

"I should let you get some sleep." Brogan let the silence build between them, making no move to end the call.

Melender found she didn't want to break contact with him either. Hearing him breathe on the other end of the line brought a measure of comfort to her frazzled nerves. "It's okay. I have to put away the groceries first."

"Are you all right?"

"I had a threatening phone call." She hadn't intended to say anything, but the concern in his voice had broken through her normal defenses and loosened her tongue.

"What? Who?" Brogan's sharp question instantly reminded her of the caller's words about the reporter.

"Probably a wrong number." The explanation sounded lame as soon as she spoke. "It was nothing."

"What did the caller say?" Brogan softened his voice, but the firmness undergirding the words told her how serious he took the situation.

Putting away the groceries might distract her from making another mistake. She rose, laying the phone on the counter and hitting the speaker button. "The usual menacing ultimatum."

"Melender, what exactly did the caller say?"

She reached into one of the reusable shopping bags and pulled out a carton of cream. "It doesn't matter what was said. It's merely an attempt to intimidate me." She opened the fridge. "Have you found out anything?"

"It does matter. Someone deliberately frightened you."

Melender froze. "How did you know that?"

"It was in your voice and what you didn't say." He paused. "I know it's an easy thing for me to ask, but do you think you can trust

75

me? I promise to be honest with you about what I find out, even if it affirms your guilt."

She closed her eyes, hugging her arms around her waist. Brogan was offering to partner in the search for the truth. She hadn't hurt Jesse, but a trial of her peers convicted her of the act. The person who had done those crimes was still out there, hiding in the shadows. She had originally wanted someone on her side completely believing in her innocence, but working with Brogan would be even sweeter. The chance to investigate the crime with an unbiased colleague.

Drawing in a deep breath, she repeated the conversation with the unknown caller as close to word for word as she could. When she finished, Brogan stayed quiet for several seconds.

"Thank you for trusting me. I'm so sorry you had to deal with that."

His words set her heart fluttering. No one had ever expressed sympathy for her plight. She swallowed a lump in her throat and turned back to putting away the groceries. Better move the conversation back on neutral ground. "I know you didn't call to chat."

"I wanted to let you know that I've submitted a Freedom of Information Act petition to the FBI for the kidnapping case files. Anyone can file it to see unclassified documents from government agencies."

The thought of gaining access to the FBI files had occurred to Melender, but she hadn't considered that would actually happen. "Does that mean I could have filed a petition to see the FBI files?"

"Yes, I suppose you could have." He paused. "I know someone in the media relations office at the bureau's Washington, DC, headquarters, and I'm hoping that will expedite the request."

"I didn't think it would be possible to see the original files." Her mind buzzed with what might be contained in the documents. "Would I be able to see them too?"

"I'm going to ask for copies to be made of the entire file."

"That's a good idea." She finished emptying her grocery sacks.

The oven clock read 9:34. She stifled a yawn. "Was there anything else? I need to get to sleep. I have to be at work by seven tonight."

"That was all. Sweet dreams, Melender." Brogan clicked off, leaving Melender to savor his final words. A handsome man wishing her sweet dreams had never happened. He probably meant nothing by them, but she hugged them close to her heart all the same as she made her way down the hall and into her bedroom.

QUENTIN SMILED AT HIS WIFE AS SHE STEPPED AWAY FROM THE FULL-LENGTH mirror in their bedroom, then smoothed her pencil skirt. Two babies hadn't spread her hips or thickened her waistline, and he was still smitten with her girlish figure.

"Have you talked to that reporter yet?" She uncapped a tube of lipstick from her dressing table.

"He's coming by the office tomorrow morning."

"I'm sure you'll make him an offer he can't refuse." She applied the soft peach color to her mouth, then tossed the tube onto the glass surface of the table.

"Don't worry. I know what to do to get Gilmore on our side." Quentin removed his tie and unbuttoned the top button of his dress shirt.

His wife paused in front of him. She laid a cool hand on his five-o-clock shadow. "Thank you, my darling. I'll see you downstairs for dinner."

Quentin didn't move until Ruby's footsteps grew faint, then he crossed to the adjoining bathroom. After opening the linen closet, he knelt and pushed aside the cleaning supplies on the floor. Pressing a button that had been cleverly designed to blend into the tile, he released the hidden compartment. For a long moment, he stared down at the combination lock. Withdrawing the contents of the safe would mean bringing more pain to his wife, but it could also redirect attention to Melender. Without giving himself any more time to think, Quentin punched in the combination on the electronic keypad. Then he plucked the bag from the safe before closing the fireproof door and concealing it once again. As he shoved the item into his gym bag, a sliver of unease wrapped around his heart. What he was about to do could also rip his family apart.

Downstairs with the others, he didn't have time to contemplate what his actions might cost him. Quentin paused to rake his gaze across his family seated around the dining room table. Jared slouched in a chair, his eyes glued to the phone in his hand, thumbs flying. Jillian mirrored his posture in the seat opposite. Ruby twirled a wine glass, half empty of its red liquid. As always, a pain shot through his chest at the empty space beside Jillian where Jesse would have sat had he lived. Although Ruby still held out hope that Jesse would one day walk through their front door, Quentin knew better.

"Jillian, Jared." Quentin pulled out his chair at the head of the table and sat. "It's so nice to have the family together again."

Quentin nodded at the maid silently hovering near the serving cart. As she placed covered dishes on the table, Quentin made small talk with Ruby, mostly to gauge her level of intoxication. By her coherent responses, she had only started on her first glass of wine since leaving their bedroom. Good. They had a lot to discuss with Jared and Jillian.

Once the dishes were on the table and Quentin's wine glass had been filled, he asked the maid to please close the double doors as she left the room. Tonight's conversation would require privacy.

"Consuela has outdone herself tonight." Quentin surveyed the prime rib, lemon-parmesan green beans, and mashed potatoes with homemade gravy. He heaped a spoonful of potatoes on his plate and handed the bowl to Jared, who didn't bother to look up from his phone.

"Son, would you care to join us for dinner this evening?" Quentin hoped the sarcasm in his tone would capture the young man's attention, but instead Jared kept tapping away on his phone, seemingly oblivious to the question. Opting for a more direct approach, Quentin set the potatoes on the table, then reached over and snatched the phone out of Jared's hands.

"Hey, Dad, I was in the middle of a text!"

Quentin parried, "And we're trying to have a family dinner."

"So? You never complained about phones at the table before. I need that."

"Not until after dinner." Quentin eyed his daughter and held out his hand. "Jillian?"

Jillian glared at him but slapped her phone into his outstretched hand. "Since when do we have family dinners?"

"Yeah, it's not as though we're some picture-postcard family." Jared scooped out a serving of mashed potatoes.

"Maybe not, but that doesn't mean we can't enjoy this meal together." Quentin threw his wife a look, but she merely raised her eyebrows. No help from that quarter. Not that he had expected any. Ruby hadn't parented Jared or Jillian since Jesse's disappearance. As if emotional distance would result in less hurt should either of them go missing. Thank goodness Jared more or less lived on his own, and Jillian at least pretended she was interested in her community college classes.

"Dad, we all know why you called this meeting, ahem, family dinner." Jillian grabbed the service bowl of green beans and slid a few on her plate before passing it to Quentin. "So why don't you get on with your agenda?"

The snippiness to his daughter's tone shouldn't have hurt, given that was how she nearly always spoke to him, but it still produced an ache in his heart. He served himself from the bowl and smiled at her. "Always so impatient, Jillian. Let's wait until we're all served first."

"Of course, we must at least pretend to be a gracious family, is that it?" Jared speared several green beans. "Heaven forbid we simply dive right into business." He shoveled the food into his mouth and chewed, still talking. "We must do everything by the Quentin Thompson rule book."

79

"Jared, that's enough. Your mother deserves..." Quentin attempted to bring some semblance of order to the dinner but instantly recognized his mistake.

Jared glared at him. "Ruby is not my mother. You divorced my mother, remember?"

Ruby blotted her lips as though she'd actually eaten a bite when clearly her plate of food sat untouched. "Don't be vulgar, Jared. And Quentin, don't tease the children. If you have something to say, please say it, dear. We're all listening."

That was one thing he loved about Ruby, her ability to get straight to the point. "You're absolutely right. I thought it might be good to discuss what could happen now that we know Melender's in the area."

He studied his children to gauge their reaction to the topic. Jillian merely toyed with her mashed potatoes while Jared cut his meat into ragged chunks.

"What's to discuss?" Jared finished cutting his prime rib and set his knife down. "You said she'd never get out of prison, and yet, she's been out for months. What's that to us?"

Ruby gripped her now empty wine glass, fingers white with tension. "You're forgetting that she hasn't told us where your brother's body is."

Quentin started to respond, but Jillian beat him to it. "Mom, we all miss Jesse, but it's time to move on."

"I can't." Ruby's voice held a fierceness Quentin had grown to hate. "She knows where Jesse is, and she has to tell me."

"Why?" Jared's question exploded across the room like a bullet.

Ruby whipped around toward Jared and glared at him. "How dare you ask such a question. To bring him home, of course. How can we leave him out there, God knows where?"

"You didn't seem to mind leaving Melender." Jared took a bite of beef.

Quentin winced at Jared's caustic tone. His son rarely let an opportunity pass to needle his stepmother. He started to reply but his wife beat him to it.

"That was different. She's not my child." Ruby picked up her wine glass, noticed it was empty, and replaced it on the table.

"You're the only living family she had left." Jared pushed back a bit from the table. "For all your talk of family, you weren't interested in helping your dear niece at all."

"Who made you an expert on family? What about your mother?" Ruby's eyes glittered.

Quentin wished his son hadn't opened this particular can of worms. "She…"

Jared tapped his fingers on the table. "She left me with dear old Dad, but at least she calls, and she sends presents for my birthday and Christmas. And in case you've forgotten, I spent weeks with my mom during the summer. While you, on the other hand, left your family and never looked back. You didn't even know that your grandmother had died until social services called about Melender."

Quentin stepped in before things got any uglier. "That's enough, Jared."

"Is it?" Jared stood. "I think it's more accurate to say I've had enough with pretending we're one big happy family. Melender didn't destroy this family. It was already rotting on the inside." He snatched his phone from beside Quentin's plate and stormed out of the room.

"If he can go, I can too." Jillian rose, her hand hovering toward her phone, but Quentin pulled it out of reach.

"Not so fast." His daughter's expression darkened, but he held her gaze. "A reporter's on the trail of what happened to your younger brother."

Jillian huffed. "Mom told me. What has that to do with me?"

"He will likely contact you." Quentin's calm voice played counterpoint to his roiling insides.

"So?" Jillian wrinkled her brow. "I don't have to talk to him."

"Melender might contact you as well," he said.

Jillian backed up a step from the table, her expression one of outrage. "Why would she want to talk to me? She knows I want nothing to do with her."

"Because she's maintaining her innocence and she has convinced that reporter to look into the case," Quentin told her in measured tones. He couldn't afford to believe Melender was anything but guilty.

"She's guilty." Ruby's eyes blazed. "She always was a liar. Some of the things she said to me when she first came to live here were so outlandish. I blame it on Sudie. My grandmother made up more stories than Dr. Seuss."

"The fact remains that Gilmore is likely to attempt to take a fresh look at the case." Quentin didn't bother to mention he would be orchestrating the direction Gilmore would take without the reporter even noticing.

Jillian shrugged. "So what?"

"Be careful if Gilmore does call you," Quentin warned.

"I don't know what you're so worried about. It's not as if I remember anything from that night. I was only three at the time." She held out her hand. "Now can I have my phone back?"

Quentin gave her the device, and she flounced out of the room.

"That went superbly well, dear." Ruby pointed to her wine glass. "I need a refill, but something more potent than a California red."

Quentin walked to the liquor cabinet. There wasn't enough booze in the world to dull the pain of losing a child. He only hoped that by the end of this, he wouldn't lose more than one.

CHAPTER
ELEVEN

Brogan straightened his tie as he rode the elevator to the eleventh floor in the Arlington, Virginia, office building owned by Thompson Energy. After exiting the elevator, he made his way through the double glass doors into a plush waiting room. Water bubbled down a small rock waterfall, and numerous green plants created an atmosphere of peace.

After giving his name to the young male receptionist wearing an aquamarine dress shirt, he moved to view the framed photos lining one wall. Each image featured Quentin Thompson poised with federal and state senators and representatives, as well as numerous celebrities and even a former president of the United States. Impressive.

Brogan had done his homework on Quentin and Thompson Energy, which had been founded by Quentin's great-great-great-grandfather, Charles Thompson, in the 1820s with a coal mine that straddled what became the West Virginia-Virginia border. Charles had expanded his coal empire to include some twenty mines in Appalachia stretching from Virginia to Pennsylvania. Each generation had at least one son who carried on the family tradition of carting the black fuel out of the depths of the earth. Quentin's father, Richard Thompson, expanded the family holdings to include permits for fracking and natural gas, along with precious mineral deposits. By all accounts, Quentin continued the family practice of taking no prisoners when it came to prying energy from the bowls of the earth. A man used to getting his own way by any means, even those on the wrong side of the law. While Brogan managed to track the scent of potential scandal related to some of Quentin's business dealings, he'd not had time to find concrete proof the man had crossed any unethical lines.

"Mr. Gilmore?"

Brogan turned to a middle-aged woman wearing a stylish tailored skirt suit standing beside the receptionist's desk. "Yes?"

"I'm Ms. Budner, Mr. Thompson's executive assistant. If you'll come this way?" She didn't give him a chance to respond but started walking.

Puzzled by her frosty greeting, Brogan followed her down a short hallway. But it wasn't Ms. Budner's opinion he needed to worry about, it was her boss's. She paused at a door and pressed her thumb against a pad, then pushed the door open, holding it for Brogan to walk through.

"Right this way." With a sweep of her hand, she indicated another hallway. He obediently followed her, taking in the muted sounds of a busy office. No one looked up as he passed offices on his right and cubicles on his left. Finally, Ms. Budner opened a door on her right.

He went after her into a large anteroom with a comfortable seating group off to one side surrounded by more plants and a desk with a laptop and phone. Ms. Budner marched straight to a frosted glass door, knocked once, then opened it.

"Mr. Thompson, Mr. Gilmore is here for your eleven-thirty appointment."

Brogan stepped into the office as Quentin moved from behind his desk.

"Thank you, Anna. Please buzz me a few minutes before noon." As his assistant nodded and left the room, Quentin held out his hand to Brogan.

Brogan shook the older man's hand, then took the chair indicated as Quentin returned to his seat behind the desk. "I appreciate your making the time to see me."

Quentin smiled, but Brogan detected a calculation behind his expression. He had prepped for the interview fully expecting Quentin to have done the same. By all accounts, the businessman was formidable in pushing his own agenda, and Brogan had no doubt Quentin would attempt to control the interview—and the direction of Brogan's story. Which likely meant Quentin would know about Brogan's past missteps and try to use it to his advantage.

"I apologize for the incident the other evening. That can't have been pleasant for someone unfamiliar with our family tragedy." Quentin relaxed into his plush leather executive chair.

"It was interesting." Brogan crossed his ankle over his knee and pulled out his notebook and cell phone. "Do you mind if I record our conversation?"

Quentin narrowed his eyes for a second before smoothing out his countenance. "What exactly is your story about?"

"At this point, I'm just gathering background information." True as far as it went. No need to tell Quentin that Brogan suspected there was a chance justice hadn't been served in the disappearance of Jesse.

"I see. I'll answer some of your questions with the understanding that this is for background information only."

The words, though courteously spoken, carried an undertone of warning. Brogan nodded his agreement. He hit the record app on his phone and crisply related the date, time, location, and his and Quentin's names. "How did Melender come to live with you and your wife?"

Quentin didn't answer right away, as if considering how he should respond. "My wife, Ruby, was the younger sister of Melender's father. Bobby Ray died when Melender was fifteen. Melender went to live with her great-grandmother, Sudie Harman, who was Ruby and Bobby Ray's grandmother. When Sudie died a year or so later, social services contacted Ruby about taking in Melender."

Brogan had learned all of that from newspaper accounts of the trial. "How did Melender fit into your household?"

"Not very well."

Brogan's curiosity piqued by the clipped response. "Why was that?"

"For one thing, her father had turned over the raising of Melender to Sudie, who allowed Melender to run wild with very little supervision or restrictions. Then there was the obvious disparity between Melender's upbringing in the mountains and life here in McLean." Quentin swiveled his chair slightly away from Brogan. "To say she experienced culture shock is an understatement."

"In what way?"

"When she first came to live with us, it was early spring, and we often found her sleeping on the deck wrapped in a blanket. She was always climbing trees and staying outside. Plus, she rarely wore shoes, even in the wintertime."

That jived with what Tim Nash had told him. Brogan looked up from his notebook. "How did she get along with the other members of your household?"

"Ruby left when Melender was only a preschooler, so they had no relationship prior to the girl's arrival. We only took Melender in because she literally had no place to go. Besides, at sixteen and a junior in high school, the arrangement wouldn't be for long."

The coldness of that statement shouldn't have shocked Brogan, but it did. Melender, grieving for the recent loss of her father and grandmother—and the only home she'd ever known—tossed into a foreign household where no one wanted her. Pity for the uprooted teenage girl stirred in his heart. "How did Melender get along with your kids?"

Quentin tightened his jaw. "Jared was nineteen at the time and attending community college. Jillian was a baby when Melender came."

Unspoken was Jesse's name, with whom Ruby must have been pregnant around the time of Melender's arrival. "And what did Jared think about her?"

"I doubt he thought much about her at all." The phone on Quentin's desk buzzed, and he hit a button. "Yes?"

"Mr. Thompson"—his assistant spoke crisply—"five minutes until your lunch appointment."

"Thank you, Anna." Quentin released the button, then stood, signaling the interview was over.

Brogan closed his notebook, hit the stop button on his phone's recording app, and got to his feet. He held out his hand to the older man. "Thank you for seeing me on such short notice."

"My pleasure." Quentin gripped his hand hard before releasing it, the tone in his voice indicating anything but pleasure. "Mr. Gilmore, I strongly encourage you to be very careful. This story is old news, and raking up the past generally isn't a good idea."

Brogan stayed silent, sensing the man had something else to add.

"I've read your work. You're a talented writer. I'm golfing with the publisher of the *Washington Leader* later this week. He's always on the lookout for reporters."

"The *Leader* is a fine newspaper."

"I'll mention that we chatted." Quentin picked up his smartphone from his desk. "Anna will see you out."

Quentin's last comment echoed in Brogan's ears as he left the man's office. He understood perfectly what was being offered—a chance to work for the *Leader* if he dropped looking into the disappearance of Jesse. The fact that Quentin had made such a statement quickened Brogan's interest in digging deeper. A man like that didn't do favors without strings attached. There must be something about the case Quentin didn't want to come to light. Might be something that would embarrass the family. But it might be something that would point to another culprit in what happened to Jesse.

～

"WHAT DO YOU MEAN THERE'S ONLY A HUNDRED DOLLARS IN THE ACCOUNT?" Melender stared at the bank teller as a knot hardened in her stomach.

The teller, a young man wearing a powder-blue dress shirt with a magenta tie whose name plate identified him as Marvin Demaris, visibly wilted at her question, making Melender realize that she'd shouted at him.

"Sorry." She rubbed her forehead, then reached into her purse. "Here's the last statement I received from the bank." She handed him the paper.

Mr. Demaris glanced at it, then back up at her. "This is dated six months ago."

"And it shows I should have a little over twelve thousand dollars in the account." Ruby had suggested opening a savings account with the insurance money her grandmother had bequeathed to her. Melender had readily agreed, too grieved over Sudie's death to marvel that her grandmother had taken out a small life insurance policy on her son with the intention of leaving it to Bobby Ray's only child.

Mr. Demaris frowned. "Let me check." He turned to his computer.

As she waited, Melender stifled a yawn. She hadn't slept well, her nightmarish dreams tangling her mind with images of the past. Jesse reaching his little hands toward her, a huge smile on his toddler face. Jillian and Jesse nestled against her on the porch swing as she sang mountain folk songs to them. The last time she saw Jesse, mac-and-cheese smeared on his cheeks as he sat in his highchair.

"Ah, I see what happened." Mr. Demaris swiveled his computer screen toward Melender. He pointed to August 26. "You transferred $12,850 on Monday."

Melender gasped. "No, I didn't."

"That's what happened."

"Where did the transfer go?" Her head began to ache as her stomach clenched tighter.

"Let's see." The teller moved the monitor back into place in front of him and clicked a few keys, then narrowed his eyes.

She crossed her arms on the ledge and leaned her weight forward. The wall clock read 4:15. Maybe she should try to take a quick nap before clocking in at seven. Her mind drifted to Brogan. He'd texted her yesterday that he would be meeting with Quentin this morning but hadn't indicated when he might call her with any updates on his progress.

"Ms. Harman, your account co-owner made the transfer."

"Co-owner!" She lowered her voice. "The account's only in my name."

The teller pointed to his computer monitor. "Actually, Ruby Harman Thompson is listed as the co-owner on this account."

Now the missing money made perfect sense. Ruby was waging an all-out war in the hope that Melender would reveal the whereabouts of Jesse's body.

Melender drummed her fingers against the counter. "Please show me when Mrs. Thompson was added to the account."

The teller accessed another screen. "You opened the account as a minor and therefore needed an adult to be designated on the account."

"Why didn't her name show up on my statements?"

Mr. Demaris clicked on his keyboard for a few minutes. "Looks like she's only listed with her initials. May I see your statement?"

She handed it to him, and he pointed to the letters RHT underneath her name with the word "custodian" next to them. Melender didn't say anything for a moment as she digested the information. She vaguely recalled accompanying Ruby to open the bank account for the insurance money but hadn't realized her aunt's name would stay permanently attached to the account. "But I didn't authorize her to take my money."

The teller averted his gaze. "I'm sorry, but since Ms. Thompson is a designated user on the account, she could enact the transfer. You'll have to ask her to return the funds."

She could, but she might as well save her breath. "There's nothing else I can do to get the money back?" Melender tried not to let panic creep into her voice.

Mr. Demaris shook his head. "She had full authority to transfer funds from the account."

"How do I remove her from my account?" Not that it would help her recover the money, but she didn't want Ruby to have access any longer.

"You both have to come to the bank."

As if her aunt would agree to that. "That's unlikely to happen. Can I just close the account?"

"Yes, you can certainly do that." The teller tapped his keyboard. "Do you want the one hundred dollars in cash or cashier's check?"

"Cash." Melender shifted her feet. Ten minutes later, she walked out of the bank. The heat and humidity greeted her with a sticky embrace. After starting the car and blasting the air conditioning, she sat motionless. *Dear God, please help me. I've struggled for so long on my own, and every time I think I see a little bit of light, everything goes dark again.*

Her ringtone startled her. Brogan's number flashed on the screen. Her heart suddenly lighter, she answered. "Hello?"

"Melender, it's Brogan."

At the sound of his strong, male voice, the words of greeting stuck in her throat. She swallowed hard. She still wasn't sure she should trust a reporter, but Brogan was her best bet for getting to the bottom of what really happened the night Jesse disappeared.

"Are you okay?"

"It's not been a good day." Rotating her shoulders, she attempted

90

to ease tension from her body—and hopefully, her voice too. The words came out more sorrowful than she had meant.

"What happened?"

The bank visit tumbled from her lips. "Ruby nearly drained my savings account. It's not only that the money is gone, it's, I feel..."

"Like someone kicked you in the gut."

The succinct phrase resonated. "Exactly." She blew out a breath. "I don't expect Ruby to invite me over for family dinners, but I didn't expect this level of, well, I'm not sure what to call it."

"Vindictiveness." The matter-of-fact way he spoke soothed her tattered nerves. He might not be one hundred percent in her corner, but he wasn't fighting hard for her opponent either.

"I suppose it is. Not that I blame her. She's still grieving for the loss of her son. I can't imagine how that feels." She eased on her sunglasses. "But you didn't call to listen to me have a pity-party."

"It's okay to be upset." Brogan paused. "But that might change when I update you on my interesting meeting with Quentin this morning."

She lowered the A/C. "Learn anything?"

"More than I think he meant to reveal."

"That sounds cryptic." Her dashboard navigational screen dissolved from the outside temperature reading—a sultry ninety-one degrees—to the time. 4:53.

Brogan laughed. "I didn't mean to be. Are you working tonight?"

"Yes, seven to seven."

"That's a long shift."

"Just on Wednesdays. I work Mondays, Tuesdays, Thursdays, and Fridays nine to five. The extra hours on Wednesdays means twice a month, I have an extra day off." Melender rolled her eyes at her babbling. The man hadn't asked for her work schedule, for goodness' sake.

"How do you feel about breakfast?"

"Breakfast?" She wished she hadn't parroted him.

"Bacon, eggs, pancakes. Breakfast."

"You had me at bacon." Was he asking her out? *Brogan's only interested in you as a story.* Repeating that phrase in her mind a few times calmed her racing heart.

He chuckled. "A woman after my own heart." The faint sound of a keyboard clacking captured her attention. "Would you be available to meet me tomorrow morning at seven-thirty at the 29 Diner on Fairfax Boulevard?"

Since her social calendar had no engagements whatsoever, it was an easy answer. Whether this was solely for a story or because he wanted to see her personally, she didn't care. Meeting a man for a meal would be a novel experience either way. "Sure."

"Great, see you then."

Melender said goodbye. As she disconnected the call, her stomach fluttered. This was most certainly not a date, but that didn't mean she couldn't make sure she looked her best.

CHAPTER

TWELVE

When his intercom buzzed, Quentin swore under his breath. He'd given Anna explicit instructions not to disturb him as he marked up a proposal from his chief lobbyist to pitch to a Virginia congresswoman. Gilmore's visit earlier had disrupted his morning, and this interruption only fueled his foul mood. The intercom buzzed again. Quentin hit the talk button with more force than necessary. "Anna, this better be a true emergency."

Anna ignored his clipped tone. "I'm sorry to disturb you, but Mr. Raines is on line two."

His irritation grew. Raines knew better than to contact him at the office. Quentin disconnected without a word to his admin, then punched line two. "Make it quick."

"There's been a slight complication."

Quentin tightened his grip on the receiver. In his experience, that meant something he wasn't going to like. "And what might that be?" His voice took on the harshness that usually sent associates scrambling out of his way.

Raines didn't miss a beat. "The FBI is handing over copies of the original kidnapping investigation."

An oath escaped his lips before Quentin could gain control of his emotions. "How is that even possible? The case was solved nearly two decades ago."

"That reporter submitted a Freedom of Information Act for the file."

"What are our options?" Quentin learned over the years that there was always a way around bureaucracy.

"The request has already been rubber-stamped."

"I don't want that nosy reporter reading those files."

"I understand. However, the new FBI director has initiated a policy of quickly complying with FOIA requests. If the case is solved, is more than ten years old, and the perpetrator is either deceased, has been sentenced, or has served—or is serving—his or her time, it's expedited. This case ticks all of those boxes." Raines drew in a breath. "I discreetly inquired as to what could be done to slow or halt the process in this particular case, and my source emphatically told me not a thing. The director is, and I quote, 'not going to make the same mistakes as her predecessor did by antagonizing the press,' end quote."

Quentin digested the information as if it had been a sour apple.

"As for the FBI files, anything we do to try to prevent Gilmore from acquiring that information will likely trigger bureau interest, which I know you do not want."

He most certainly did not want the FBI nosing around again in the disappearance of his son. The first time had been bad enough.

"Do you want me to put someone on the reporter?" Raines asked.

If the FBI hadn't uncovered what happened to Jesse, a journalist certainly wouldn't either. "No, just keep an eye on the girl." Quentin ended the call. His hand hovered over the speed dial to his wife's cell phone number, then he replaced the receiver. Better to tell Ruby in person. She'd be angry, but he would be sure to have something on hand to sooth her nerves. Not for the first time, Quentin cursed the day Melender Harman came down out of the mountains and into their home.

IN THE GROWING DARKNESS, JARED KEPT HIS HEAD DOWN BUT HIS EYES ALERT as he scanned the park while making his way to the paved path that led around the soccer field. After hours, an eeriness blanketed the playground as the swings hung motionless. Maybe the word on the street had been wrong and Snake was still in jail. That would make things so much easier. Then he brushed past a trio of whispering college girls, one of whom covertly tucked a plastic baggy into her purse. The trio then moved quickly toward the parking lot. A familiar longing for a high coursed through his veins. Snake always had the good stuff that made you forget your troubles, at least for a little while.

Jared clenched his fists. No way he was heading down that road again. He'd been clean for three years, and he had no intention of becoming a slave to the pills again.

Moving off the paved path and into the tree line, he spotted a wisp of smoke to his right. The sweet scent of marijuana teased his nostrils with its seductive promise of relaxation and peace. He'd drawn in a deep breath before he even realized what he was doing.

"It's been a long time, Jared." Snake's voice drifted along with the smoke from his joint.

As his eyes adjusted to the gloom that enveloped the small patch of wilderness on the edges of the park, he saw Snake stood with his back against a tree. "I heard you were out." Jared turned his head away from the wafting smoke to avoid as much of the intoxicating aroma as possible. He didn't need to get a buzz just from talking to his former drug dealer. The man hadn't weathered this last bout in prison too well. He'd been slim before his incarceration six years ago, but now his frame was even bonier. His skin hung on his body like a

95

second suit of clothes. The snake tattoo that encircled his neck sagged, losing its menacing appearance.

"I heard you kicked the habit." Snake drew deeply on the joint and blew the smoke in Jared's direction.

It took every ounce of Jared's self-control to not wave his hand to push the smoke away. Snake would interpret the motion as weakness on Jared's part, like he couldn't handle a little smoke. "Yeah, I decided to move on."

Snake pinched the joint with the tips of his fingers, then pocketed the stub. "So it had nothing to do with your daddy threatening to cut down the money tree unless you quit."

He's baiting you. Jared should have expected Snake to have picked up on the gossip about his former client. "That was definitely a consideration in my decision."

Snake laughed. "You always were a cool customer." He stepped closer to Jared. "My sources tell me that your cousin is out of jail."

A chill swept over Jared even in the August heat. "What else?"

"That your stepmom lost it with Melender in a convenience store in front of some reporter." Snake leaned closer, his hot breath fanning Jared's face. "Don't worry, I remember our deal."

"Good to know." Some of the tension eased from his shoulders. Still, the intel meant Snake must keep up with local news. And with anything to do with the Thompsons. This was not good.

"But I think another payment will ensure I don't forget our little arrangement and say the wrong thing to the wrong person, if you know what I mean."

Scum like Snake always wanted more. For now, he'd give him what he wanted. Reaching into his back pocket, Jared withdrew a battered envelope. "Consider this my stay-out-of-jail donation."

Snake took the envelope, opened it, and fingered the currency. "Now if you're not here to buy, then get along. I have business to conduct."

As Jared walked away, he couldn't help but wonder if he'd done the right thing. Maybe he shouldn't have... Well, too late now. He'd have to play it out to the end and hope his stupid mistakes didn't come back to swamp him.

⁓

IN THE GRAY DAWN, A LIGHT BREEZE TOUSLED RUBY'S SHOULDER-LENGTH blonde hair as she climbed from her Mercedes convertible. She adjusted the Velcro band that held her iPhone snug against her upper arm, then inserted her wireless ear buds. Like she'd done hundreds of times before, she turned left to start her circuit of Burke Lake Park's crushed gravel path. Only this time, she had a different agenda in mind than exercise.

As she pumped her arms to an upbeat playlist pulsing in her ears, she picked up her walking pace. Her thoughts drifted to an image of Melender as a chubby-cheeked six-month-old. With Bobby Ray being older by a dozen years, he'd been married and had Melender by the time Ruby had turned thirteen.

Ruby pushed herself to walk even faster, nearly jogging, but the pace didn't stop the memories playing in her mind's eye like a movie. Melender as a toddler, calling after her Aunt "Wuby." Melender as a three-year-old, clinging to Ruby after her mother's early death. Melender as a four-year-old, tears trickling down her cheeks while Ruby packed her bag to leave the hollow. The sadness in Bobby Ray's eyes as he handed Ruby a sack of sandwiches at the bus station. The letters Sudie wrote once a month on notebook paper until Ruby moved one time too many and hadn't bothered to tell her grandmother the new address.

A pair of squirrels darted in front of her across the path, their furry figures blurred by sudden moisture in her eyes. Dashing away the tears, Ruby jacked up the volume in an effort to drown out the memories. But the increased noise did little to stop the flow. The brown-wrapped parcel she received from Sudie upon her return from their European honeymoon. Inside the package, she found her parents' wedding quilt that Sudie had made years ago. Holding the bedspread with its mountain flower pattern and two doves in the center against her chest, she'd breathed in the sweet, clear scent of the mountains.

Pregnant with Jillian, she'd hidden her tears when Sudie had sent news of Bobby Ray's death from a fall down an abandoned mineshaft. Her shame in not wanting Melender when social services contacted her after Sudie's death nearly two years later. She'd worked too hard to have a daily visual reminder of all she'd left behind on the mountain.

Sweat soaked her shirt as she rounded another bend in the path, still alone as the sun inched over the horizon. She should have listened to her instincts and not let that viper into their midst, but she had bowed to the pressure from social services and her husband and brought Melender home. No good deed goes unpunished applied in spades to that decision.

As she caught a glimpse of the paddleboat dock, she slowed her pace. No sense arriving out of breath. By the time her sneakers hit the wooden boards of the dock, her breathing had steadied and her reminiscences about the past had been firmly shoved back into her mind's locked box. Her gaze focused on the ripples across the lake as fish nibbled at the surface and ducks dove for their breakfast.

The dock shuddered as another person approached on the weathered boards. Ruby turned off her music and faced the individual. The young man wore a Nationals baseball cap pulled low, shielding his eyes, while a scruffy beard hid the lower half of his face. What was up with the youth of today and beards anyway? Reeling in her thoughts, she took a step toward him, causing the dock to sway. "I want her harassed as much as possible."

"So you said." The man sounded bored, but Ruby resisted the urge to correct his dismissive tone. "Physical contact?"

Ruby considered which approach would hurt Melender more—psychological torment or physical punishment? "Nothing physical right now."

The man nodded.

"You'll find a bag with everything you need under the passenger's seat in the Mercedes convertible parked near the ice cream stand." She gave the man a hard stare. "I expect daily reports."

The man touched the brim of his hat with slim fingers, then slouched away down the dock.

Ruby returned her gaze to the water as the sun burst over the horizon, shedding red, orange, and yellow rays across the lake's surface. Watching the sunrise used to thrill her as a new day unfolded, but that was before the nightmare of Jesse's disappearance.

CHAPTER

THIRTEEN

Brogan thanked the waitress for his coffee and settled back into a booth at the 29 Diner. Melender texted that she was on her way, so he organized his thoughts on the story at hand. Usually, he had no trouble focusing on an article, but a certain blue-eyed woman who was running late this morning had become a distraction. Sure, he hadn't dated much in his exile, but only because he hated seeing pity or disgust in a woman's eyes when she found out he wasn't a hot-shot journalist, or worse, had read about his inglorious fall from grace. He resisted the urge to smile as he recalled getting up well before his alarm clock to work out, then shower, shave, and dress in a pair of khaki pants and a new button-down shirt.

"Sorry I'm a little late." Melender slid into the booth opposite him. "I decided to stop by my house to clean up a little bit after work."

A subtle floral scent tickled his nose, and he breathed in deeply. Melender's long hair, tightly braided and wound in a single bun at the crown of her head, appeared damp. So he wasn't the only one wanting to make a good impression.

She smiled as the waitress stopped at the booth holding a mug and a coffee pot. "Would you like coffee too?"

"Yes, please."

As the waitress refilled Brogan's cup, Melender picked up the menu.

"You folks ready to order?" The waitress poured coffee into Melender's mug.

"I always order the same thing," Melender said. "Are you ready, Brogan?"

He nodded.

Melender turned to the waitress. "Biscuits and gravy with two scrambled eggs."

Brogan ordered the Farmer's Wife platter with two eggs over easy, two strips of bacon, and two pancakes. When the waitress left, he smiled at Melender. "Do they make good biscuits and gravy here?"

"Not as good as Sudie did, but this is one of the few places that comes close."

Her wistful tone tugged at his heart, but he tamped that down. He needed to approach this—her—with as much objectivity as he could. Otherwise, his story would be compromised. But instead of asking her a question related to the kidnapping, he wanted to know about her upbringing. "Sounds like you were very close with your grandmother."

"Sudie was my great-grandmother." A smile graced her face. "Growing up, I saw Sudie every day. I don't remember my mother much at all, only bits and pieces." Her smile faded. "She died when I was three."

"I'm sorry."

"It's okay. Sudie was like a mother to me, so I didn't mourn the loss as much as I might have if my mother had lived longer." Melender picked up her coffee with steady hands, but he caught a glimpse of tears in her eyes before she blinked the moisture away. "What about your family?"

These days, Brogan rarely spoke with his parents. After his disgrace, they had even less interest in their middle son, preferring to spend time with his older brain surgeon sister and younger lawyer brother. His father put a premium on success, while his mother only wanted to talk about positive things, not Brogan's struggles. Brogan had been a close part of the family circle until his journalistic life imploded in such a public manner. "It's complicated."

"Families generally are."

Her wry observation loosened his tongue, and he sketched a basic outline of his parents and siblings without conscious effort. "I haven't seen them in a couple of years."

"Not even for the holidays?" Her incredulous look sharply reminded him that she had spent every special occasion away from her family while in prison.

"It wasn't on purpose, at least not on my part. Two years ago, my parents and brother flew out to visit my sister and her husband in San Francisco for Christmas. I was invited, but plane fare around the holidays was out of my budget. Last December, they all decided to spend the last two weeks of the year on a cruise around the Hawaiian Islands, but again, the cost of the cruise and airfare was more than I could afford to spend."

A sharp stab of pain hit him at the memory of telling his mom the cruise was out of his financial reach. His well-to-do parents hadn't offered to help. It was like she'd barely heard him, her voice rolling on about the challenges of packing for a cruise in the dead of winter. When he'd jumped in to ask when he could stop by to visit them before or after their trip, she put him off with a "We'll get back to you on that, darling. You know how hectic things can be before a trip, and how tired we'll be when we return." In the end, he'd received a photo card featuring pictures of his siblings and parents against the backdrop of touristy Hawaiian settings and a pre-printed message. "Our family vacation."

Melender touched his hand, yanking him back from those memories. "Now it's my turn to say I'm sorry."

103

He didn't pull back but turned his hand over to lace his fingers through hers. For a second, he thought he'd scared her off. But she didn't move. The warmth of her fingers countered the roughness of her skin. Without looking at her, he concentrated on their joined hands.

"Nothing to be sorry about. I sometimes feel like I was born into the wrong family. My mom, my dad, my brother, my sister, and even my brother-in-law all seem to be focused on climbing to the top. Of what, I haven't figure out." He rubbed his thumb along the top of her hand. "When I look back at my own mistakes, I think part of why I took those shortcuts was to earn my parents' approval. To show them that I could find real success in journalism. But of course, that didn't turn out so well."

The waitress stood by their booth, steaming plates of food in her hands. "I have biscuits and gravy with scrambled eggs and the Farmer's Wife platter."

Brogan released Melender's hand as the waitress set the plates on the table. After the woman inquired about them needing anything else and they declined, she left the booth.

He snuck a glance at his beautiful companion. Talk about good timing. If the waitress hadn't arrived when she did, he might have spilled even more of his guts.

"I'm starved. How about you?"

"Me too."

She bowed her head. These days, prayer was something Brogan did more frequently. The faith of his childhood—instilled during his summer visits with his aunt and uncle—had become much more real to him in the dark days after his exile. He might not talk about it, but it was ever present.

He had to find out if Melender was blessing the food. "Would you like me to ask the blessing?"

Her head came up, surprise written in the wide eyes. "Are you a Christian?"

No one ever asked him that directly. "Yes, I am. Are you?"

She nodded. "I would be glad for you to pray over our meal."

"Dear God, please bless our food and our conversation. In Jesus's name. Amen." He picked up his fork. He'd wanted to grill her about her faith and if it was a jailhouse conversion. Instead, he told her about the FBI files. "I hope to hear back from the bureau this week."

"That's fantastic."

The hope in her eyes made him inwardly wince. "Melender, the FBI conducted a very thorough investigation into the kidnapping. If they concluded you were guilty, then I seriously doubt the files would have anything that would prove otherwise."

To her credit, she didn't flinch at his words. After putting her fork down, she leaned toward him. "You read the transcript. The evidence was only circumstantial. It was the testimony of my aunt and others who convinced the jury of my guilt."

"That might be true, but that doesn't mean the FBI files will have anything that would exonerate you." He crunched on a piece of bacon.

"Will that be everything the bureau had relating to the case?"

"As far as I know."

"That means we'll be able to see who else was on their suspect list before they zeroed in on me." She took another bite.

He hadn't thought of that. "I suppose that could be true."

"Will you let me know when you have the files?"

Ah, there was the rub. To stay objective, he should keep her well away from his investigation. But Melender's statement of faith tipped the balance in her favor. "I'll give you a call."

Brogan wasn't sure that was the right thing to do, but to get a clear picture of the players involved, he needed her input. He only hoped it wouldn't compromise the investigation.

MELENDER PULLED INTO THE PARKING LOT OF FOX'S MUSIC AND CUT THE engine, thankful once more for the We Are His Hands ministry that taught her to drive and gave her a good used car to help her get back on her feet after her release. Jazzed from her breakfast meeting with Brogan, she stepped into the humid morning. She wiped a bead of sweat from her forehead and hustled to the door.

In her wildest imaginings, she had never once considered that Brogan would turn out to be a fellow believer. Maybe that's why she instinctively felt he could be trusted. His avowal of impartiality was exactly what she wanted. She needed someone to look at the evidence and the facts without a bias toward her guilt or innocence. Perhaps his faith would ensure a fair rendering of his ultimate verdict.

A blast of cold air brushed over her as she opened the door, the sudden cooling of her moist skin giving her shivers. She hurried to the back of the shop where the owner displayed instruments for customers to try.

Jimmy Stork stood talking with Mr. Trent, but her eyes immediately strayed to the instrument on the tabletop. Mr. Trent's dulcimer had undergone a metamorphosis since Monday with the addition of new strings and a thorough cleaning. Now that the dirt and grime had been removed, two delicate cutouts near the bottom of the tear-shaped body were more visible. Her heart pounded.

"Mel, I'm glad you could join us." Mr. Jimmy nodded as she stopped by the table. "You remember Nolan Trent?"

"Yes. Good morning, Mr. Trent." Melender smiled, but the man didn't reciprocate. In fact, she would have labeled his posture as defensive with his arms tightly folded across his chest, but she figured it had nothing to do with her and returned her gaze to the dulcimer. "It cleaned up nicely."

Mr. Jimmy laughed. "That's an understatement."

Her fingers itched to touch it, to look inside the body for the mark she was beginning to believe would be there. Somehow, she managed to refrain. "Did you figure out how old it is?"

"Once we got the grimy buildup removed, we could see more clearly the marks inside the body." Mr. Jimmy paused.

Melender gazed at him, dead certain she knew what he would say. "John Scales of Floyd Co. Virginia, 1843," she volunteered.

"How did you know that?" Mr. Trent's voice had an edge to it.

She drew in a deep breath and laid her hand gently on the instrument's body. "Because I'm nearly certain this was my great-grandmother's dulcimer."

"Your great-grandmother's." Mr. Trent shook his head. "Sir, I think you have some explaining to do." Anger tinged his words. "Is this some kind of set up? Is she about to accuse me of stealing her dulcimer?"

Melender staggered back from the table as memories of the police snapping handcuffs around her wrists and the humiliation of a body search flooded her senses. The shop receded as the images flashed through her mind like an old-fashioned flip book. A booking photo, followed by pressing her fingertips on a screen, and ultimately the clang of the cell door as the booking officer walked away.

"Mel?" Mr. Jimmy's voice broke through the chaotic scene in her mind. "Sit down. It's okay." He guided her into a chair, then placed gentle pressure on the back of her neck, directing her head between her knees.

She squeezed her eyes shut. She wasn't going back to jail. She wasn't being arrested. It was all a misunderstanding that she could clear up as soon as she got her breath back. Her breathing slowed, and the memories faded. After blinking, she raised her head.

Mr. Jimmy, his brow furrowed, held out a bottle of water, which she took between both hands. Good, her hands had stopped shaking. She drank half the contents, then sat up all the way.

"Better?" Mr. Jimmy pulled up another chair and sat down, waving Mr. Trent to a third chair on the other side of the table. While Mr. Trent brought the chair around, Mr. Jimmy patted her shoulder. "It's okay."

Melender stared at the owner, his words tumbling in her mind. In his eyes, she saw he knew her true identity, had maybe always known her background, and had still welcomed her into his shop.

Tears threatened to spill from her eyes, and she furiously blinked them back.

"Is she okay?" Mr. Trent sounded a bit less angry now, but one look at his face showed that he still wasn't convinced he hadn't been had.

Mr. Jimmy turned to his client. "You've been coming to my store for going on six years now. Do you think I would be involved in anything underhanded?"

Mr. Trent leaned back in his chair. "Not intentionally. But maybe she's the instigator." He looked at Melender. "I did some research on Mel Harman. With a voice like yours, I figured you couldn't possibly be an unknown singer. Didn't find any recordings, but I found plenty about a Melender Harman, who came from the Appalachian Mountains and who spent seventeen years behind bars for killing of her one-year-old cousin."

"I served my time."

"What are you trying to pull now with claims that this dulcimer is your great-grandmother's?" Tension rolled off Mr. Trent like water from a duck's back.

"You've got this all wrong, Nolan," Mr. Jimmy said, but Melender laid a hand on his shoulder briefly.

"It's okay, Mr. Jimmy." She laced her fingers tightly together. "That dulcimer has been in my family for generations, ever since one of my maternal ancestors bought it new from John Scales. There's another mark inside, to the right of the Scales mark. It's the outline of a small wood anemone blossom, a wildflower native to the Appalachian Mountains."

Mr. Trent glanced at Mr. Jimmy, who nodded his agreement.

Melender continued. "I brought the dulcimer with me after Sudie, my great-grandmother, died, and I came to live with my Aunt Ruby and her family in McLean. I hoped my aunt would keep the dulcimer—after all, it was her heritage, too—but I suspect that she found it and took it to a pawn shop after I went away." She drew in a deep breath to distill the pain building from yet another example of her aunt's hatred of her. "Where you found it."

She looked Mr. Trent straight in the eyes. "I'm not accusing you of stealing it, nor am I asking for it back, Mr. Trent. To be honest, I'm thankful that it will have a good home because I feared my aunt had destroyed it."

She might have said the right things, but her heart ached with a sorrow that ran deeper than a mine shaft at seeing Sudie's dulcimer again in the hands of someone else.

Mr. Trent's shoulders had relaxed a fraction during her explanation. "I see." He turned to Mr. Jimmy. "Did you know this touching story?"

Melender detected a slight emphasis on the word touching but kept her face impassive, although inwardly, she flinched at the tone. Her time in prison had taught her to master the art of appearing indifferent and unaffected by what was happening around her, and it served her well in situations where emotions could tip her hand too much.

"I knew Mel played the dulcimer and her fondness for folk songs, but not about this particular instrument," Mr. Jimmy replied in an even tone. "That's why I arranged for the two of you to meet."

"Because she played the dulcimer." Mr. Trent didn't sound as aggravated.

"Yes, and because I knew you were always on the lookout for rare folk songs." Mr. Jimmy nodded to Melender. "She knows some I've never heard."

So Mr. Jimmy wasn't just encouraging her to sing for his own benefit. He had Mr. Trent in mind all along. Melender didn't know whether to be upset or grateful at the shop owner's idea to bring her and someone who collected folk songs together.

Mr. Trent unfolded his hands and stood. "Now that this matter has been resolved, I must be going."

Mr. Jimmy got to his feet. "I'll pack the dulcimer in its case." He drew a leather case from under the table and nestled Sudie's dulcimer inside.

Melender fought back tears at seeing the beloved instrument disappear from view as Mr. Jimmy lowered the lid. It was silly to feel such pain at being separated from a piece of wood and some strings, but it was almost like losing Sudie all over again.

If she didn't leave now, she would break down. On her feet, she choked out, "Thank you for letting me see the dulcimer."

Melender rushed for the exit, not looking back at the two men or the beautiful instrument that had been such an integral part of her mountain upbringing.

FOURTEEN

"Are these all the files related to the Thompson kidnapping case?" Brogan eyed the three file boxes stacked on top of one another on the floor of Tim's office at FBI headquarters. It was going to cost him a pretty penny to pay for the copies, but reading the transcript had given him enough doubts that he was beginning to believe Melender's side of the story. If she was innocent, the story would be worth the investment of his time and money.

"That's all the documents the FBI collected on the case."

The way Tim emphasized FBI caught Brogan's attention. "Who else has documents on this case?"

Tim raised his eyebrows. "You must be slipping in your reporter's instincts. Maybe the time away from keyboard has dulled your senses."

Brogan narrowed his eyes. Tim had always loved to pull his chain, but he wouldn't take the bait. "That's definitely possible."

A puzzled look crossed the other man's face, as if surprised Brogan let the dig go without comment. "Until the ransom note had been discovered, it was only a missing persons case, which was handled by local authorities at first."

Brogan tapped the top box with his forefinger. "The Thompsons lived in McLean, Virginia, at the time of Jesse's disappearance. Still do."

Tim nodded.

"Which means the Fairfax County Police have files related to the initial investigation into the disappearance." Getting access to the police files might uncover other suspects or avenues to explore.

"Exactly."

"But wouldn't those papers, or at least copies of those documents, be included with the agency's notes?"

The other man shook his head. "You remember who was chief of police for Fairfax County at the time of the arrest?"

"No, I wasn't around here then."

"That's right, you were off in New York making your mark in the world of journalism." Tim paused, but again, Brogan resisted the urge to bristle at the other man's comments. Tim would only tease him further if Brogan reacted negatively. "I'll help you out. It was James Chatham, who had been chief since 1988."

"James Chatham," Brogan repeated slowly, as the name faintly rang a bell deep in his memory. He shrugged.

"What about a certain incident back in the mid-1990s involving the attack on a U.S. senator's maid by Georgetown University's chancellor?" Tim asked. "It was during a party held at the senator's McLean home."

Brogan cast his mind back but couldn't bring up the event. "No, I don't recall it."

"In short, the brouhaha over the FBI's muscling out the Fairfax County detectives who had done the majority of the legwork and evidence gathering on the maid's attack irked Chief Chatham to no end. From then on, he only shared the bare minimum of their files with the FBI."

Tim pointed to the top box. "So, while that has a couple of

summary sheets from the county's case paperwork, there's probably a box or two in their archives gathering dust with the original interviews from the missing persons case."

"It shouldn't be a problem to get those files now, since Chief Chatham has been long gone from the department."

"Probably not. I hope you know what you're doing."

"I'm looking into inconsistencies in an old case." Brogan didn't like the direction he suspected Tim was heading with that comment. "I'm doing everything strictly by the book, no shortcuts."

"That's not what I meant. I mean with Melender Harman."

Brogan's heart kicked up a notch. "She's only a source for a story."

"You keep telling yourself that, and maybe, just maybe, you'll convince yourself it's the truth." Tim's eyes never wavered from Brogan's. "I can still tell when my buddy's interested in a girl, and you've got it bad for Melender."

"I've hardly mentioned her name."

"That tells me all I need to know."

"I admit she's an attractive woman, but this isn't becoming personal." Brogan ignored the little voice that said he was lying.

Tim shrugged. "If that's how you want to play it, fine. But remember the last time you got personally involved with a source, it didn't turn out so well for you."

MELENDER JUGGLED HER FRAPPUCCINO AS SHE SEARCHED FOR HER KEYS IN her messenger bag. She had meant to put them in the outside pocket like always but somehow had dropped them inside.

Stopping in front of her door, she focused her attention fully on finding the missing keys.

"I've already called the police."

Melender jerked her head up to meet the gaze of Mrs. Horner, who nodded toward Melender's apartment.

"The police?" Melender's gaze darted from the widow she occasionally exchanged pleasantries with to her front door that now sported a busted lock. Then she noticed the words spray painted in ugly red letters on the outside wall beside her door.

Baby Killer

She turned back to Mrs. Horner. "When?" Her voice failed her, and she gulped her iced drink to clear the clog in her throat. "When did this happen?"

"I heard a ruckus about twenty minutes ago. I peeked out my window to see three men wearing ski masks and gloves leave your apartment." Mrs. Horner crossed her arms. "I wouldn't have bothered to call the police had I known who you are."

Sirens sounded louder. Melender swallowed hard as she struggled to retain her outward composure. She couldn't fall apart now. It would only give whoever had done this the satisfaction of seeing her gut reaction. Her gaze returned to the letters, the fresh paint running down the side of the wall like blood. "I'm not a killer," she muttered.

Mrs. Horner snorted. "I called my son after I phoned the police. He Googled you, then told me all about what you did to your poor little cousin. To think I shared my banana bread recipe with the likes of you." She went back insider her apartment and slammed the door.

A pair of police cars roared into the parking lot. Melender peered over the railing into the courtyard, shoving the fear aside and praying that the officers would keep an open mind when looking into the break-in. But once they found out about her record, they might not be as motivated to investigate.

Squaring her shoulders, she recited Philippians 4:13 in her mind. *I can do all things through Christ who strengthens me. Strengthen me, Lord!*

"Mr. Simpson, I didn't cause the break-in." Standing in the middle of her destroyed living room with her burly landlord four hours later,

Melender put as much steel into her words as possible, yet she sounded as weak and tired as she felt. If the man continued to refuse to have her door fixed today, there was no telling when she could finally get some sleep.

"You talked with the police, Mr. Simpson. All I'm asking is that you have someone come over and repair my front door as soon as possible." Melender had been grateful that the responding officers took the break-in seriously and gathered forensics evidence. A detective, Rich Delaney, had even shown up to interview Mrs. Horner and Melender.

Mr. Simpson crossed his beefy arms. "I got complaints about you."

Cradling her cat close to her chest, Melender couldn't stop the groan that escaped. "From who? And when?"

"I don't gotta say, but we don't need residents like you living here. Get your stuff and get out."

"You can't just kick me out because someone broke into my apartment." Surely her landlord wouldn't fabricate evidence to kick her out. She drew in a breath to regain control of her emotions. "I signed a year's lease."

"I found evidence that you were smoking in the apartment." He pointed a finger at her. "Your lease clearly states no smoking and that if there is evidence of smoking, your lease will be terminated immediately."

"I don't smoke, so what evidence are you talking about?"

With a snort, he pointed to a saucer near a broken lamp and two spent cigarettes. "Before you try to pin that on whoever broke in here, don't. It's absurd to think someone would break in and plant smoked cigarettes. That's crazy talk."

He maneuvered around the debris to the front door. "You have until midnight to get your stuff out of here."

Melender barely registered his departure, just stared at the mess of broken and ripped objects.

"Melender?" Brogan called from the entrance doorway.

She turned to see him surveying the destruction, her cat still in her arms. "Why are you here?" Not quite what she meant to say.

"Colleague heard about the break-in on the police scanner, so I thought I'd stop by to see how you were holding up." He did another visual sweep of the living-dining room combination. "They did a pretty thorough job of it, didn't they?"

She only nodded, her throat clogging once again with emotion.

Brogan scratched Goliath under his chin, eliciting a purr from the feline. "Your cat's okay?"

"As far as I can tell. I think he probably hid under the bed while they rampaged through the apartment."

He stepped around an overturned kitchen chair and glanced into the small kitchen. She followed his gaze, once more taking in the scene. Cupboard doors had been ripped from their hinges, their contents tossed about as if the kitchen had been in a shipwreck.

"What did the police say?"

"Not much." She shifted Goliath to wipe at her wet cheeks with the back of one hand. "They sent out a forensics team to gather evidence, but the place had no discernible prints but mine. Once they learned my prints are in the system, well, things got awkward."

He walked down the hallway to the bedroom and bathroom. After several minutes, he rejoined her, but Melender couldn't read the expression on his face. Disappointment? Anger?

"They photograph the bedroom wall?" Brogan locked eyes with her.

"Yes." As if she would ever need a picture to remember the vile, spray-painted words. BABY KILLER had been kind compared to the filth decorating the wall above her headboard.

"Do you have a place to stay until your landlord fixes the door?"

Goliath squirmed in her arms. Time to return him to his cat carrier, which had been down in her storage locker and therefore spared destruction. After securing the feline, she massaged her throbbing temple. Having been up all night cleaning, she desperately needed a few hours of sleep to power her through the coming evening shift. Her renter's insurance would provide funds to replace her furniture and possessions, but that would take weeks to resolve. She highly doubted her landlord would give back her security deposit in light of the apartment's destruction. Even if she fought it, it wouldn't help her immediate need of lodging.

Brogan touched her arm. "Are you okay?"

A giggle escaped her. Totally inappropriate for the dire situation, but pent-up emotions sometimes spilled out in weird ways. "No, I'm not." She shoved a fist to her mouth to stop the laughter or sobs—she wasn't sure which emotion would win—from escaping. "I can't go through this again."

"Go through what?"

"The harassment." She sucked in a deep breath, willing the motion to calm her shattered nerves. "When you're a convicted baby killer, you're at the very bottom of the prison hierarchy. Everyone bullies you constantly, and there's always the very real danger that an inmate will kill you."

Melender closed her eyes and tried to think of something uplifting in spite of the prison memories raging in her mind. Only God had helped her survive in the abyss of incarceration.

She opened her eyes and didn't bother to hide the tears streaking down her cheeks. "Many people think I deserved to be locked up forever as justice for what I did to Jesse. There will be plenty who think this is also what I deserve." She swept her hand around the room.

"I'm so sorry someone destroyed your home." Brogan gently wiped away her tears.

Melender didn't move as the pads of his fingers brushed over the soft skin. No one had touched her face in years. Her eyelids drifted shut, and she simply allowed herself this moment to feel the kindness of another human being. Touches most people took for granted had been denied to her.

He brought up his other hand to cup her face, his fingers skimming the nape of her neck before settling at her hairline while his thumbs lightly caressed her damp cheeks. Fresh tears spilled from her closed eyes, but she couldn't stop them. Brogan continued brushing the wetness away as she remained stock still and cried.

Grandmother Sudie's voice echoed in her head. *Child, just when you think the Almighty has forgotten about our needs, He sends someone or something to remind us of His provision and His promise to never leave us nor forsake us. You remember that when you feel abandoned by Him.*

FIFTEEN

"Uncle Nolan, how are you?" Brogan repositioned the phone as he waited in his car. From the back seat, Goliath meowed in his carrier.

"Good. Colleen was just saying it's been too long since our favorite nephew came over for dinner."

"I won't tell my brother you said that."

Nolan laughed. "Don't worry, I tell him the same thing."

Brogan chuckled. "Why am I not surprised?" Brogan tapped his fingers on the steering wheel as he considered and rejected several ways to approach his request.

"How about you come over Saturday for dinner?"

"That would be great." Brogan loved spending time with the Trents and their low-key family. Nolan might be a well-respected musicologist with several popular histories of folk songs, but he wasn't stuffy or pretentious. Aunt Colleen mothered Brogan more than his own mom, always giving him a safe haven to relax when the world pressed in too tightly. After his downfall, he'd spent a few months living in their basement apartment. They hadn't asked questions or hounded him to explain his action. They'd simply given him space to come to terms with what he'd done.

"Wonderful. Colleen will be thrilled. Now tell me what's on your mind."

"You know me too well."

"Well enough to know that my favorite nephew is a busy reporter and he doesn't call out of the blue for no reason."

After drawing in a deep breath, Brogan plunged in. "I have a favor to ask. It's a big one, and I'd understand if you said no."

"Hmm. That sounds mysterious. What's the favor?"

"Someone I know—and her cat—needs a place to stay." Brogan scanned the Walmart parking lot for Melender, who'd needed to pick up a few necessities since not much had been salvageable from her apartment.

"We're always willing to help."

Brogan had expected his uncle's quick response, but Nolan should hear the entire story first. "I know, but this one has special circumstances."

"Okay, tell me."

"First of all, I'm not sure for how long she would need a place. She works nights for a cleaning company and came home this morning to find her apartment had been vandalized and all her stuff completely destroyed. Her landlord kicked her out on some pretense, so she can't move back in even after the place is repaired."

"That's terrible," Nolan interjected when Brogan paused.

"Yes, it is. The police hold out little hope of finding whoever did this, but I'm not sure they will look very hard."

"Why's that?"

Brogan gripped the steering wheel. Now for the hard part. "She's a former convict."

"What was her crime?"

"Murder. She was convicted of killing her one-year-old cousin."

Nolan didn't say anything for several seconds. His aunt and uncle loved God and attended church regularly. They had a heart for the downtrodden, with Colleen working for a local charity that helped single mothers acquire training and skills to get better jobs. While having no children of their own, they had been foster parents for numerous children over the years. But for all that, asking them to take in a convicted child killer might be more than they would want to take on.

"God indeed has a sense of humor." Nolan finally broke the silence.

Whatever Brogan had expected his uncle to say, it wasn't that. "What do you mean?"

"I've always known that an Almighty hand directs my path, but there are times in life when that becomes clearer. This is one of those times."

"I don't understand."

"I'll explain it all when you bring Melender Harman over."

SITTING POOLSIDE ON A CHAISE LOUNGE IN THE SHADE OF AN UMBRELLA, Ruby flicked through the photos on her phone with her freshly mani-cured fingers. The before-and-after shots of Melender's apartment would never make a glossy home-and-garden magazine spread, but she couldn't be more pleased. Her contact had done a superb job of methodically destroying the place. Absolutely nothing remained intact, from shredded pillowcases to a decimated box of cereal.

Again, Ruby went through the photos, more slowly this time to savor the scene. She imagined the look of horror and surprise on her niece's face. If only the man could have stuck around to photograph Melender's reaction. For she had been very clear in her instructions to the man on what words to scrawl on the bedroom wall. To an outsider, it would have simply been read as a typical, foul-mouth rant against a convicted baby killer. But Melender would have imme-

SARAH HAMAKER

diately recognized the phrasing as one Ruby had said several times over the course of her niece's arrest and trial.

Ruby's conscience piped up that maybe she was taking her need for vengeance too far, but she ignored the nagging voice, much as she had done since leaving Maple Hollow. Uttering a word Sudie would have washed out her mouth with soap for saying, Ruby exited the photo gallery. She would enjoy looking at them again. But Quentin would be arriving home soon, and she had to be ready to pretend like everything was as usual. It wouldn't do to have him suspect she was harassing Melender.

"Ruby?"

She froze as her husband came out onto the pool deck, loosening his tie. He wasn't supposed to be home for another hour.

Quentin paused by her chair. "Darling? Are you okay? Consuela said you have been sitting out here all afternoon."

Always careful of too much sun exposure, she'd only been poolside for half an hour. With a smile, she reached out a hand toward her husband. "I'm fine, but why are you home early?"

He sat on end of her lounge. "I'm not home early. It's after six."

Ruby blinked. She'd come outside at two-thirty after receiving the text with the photographs. Had she really lost track of time for that long? Quentin's worried expression made her scramble for an acceptable excuse for her time lapse. "I guess I must have fallen asleep."

Her explanation smoothed the lines from his forehead. "I'm glad you were in the shade and didn't get a sunburn." He leaned forward and kissed her gently on the lips. "I heard someone broke into Melender's apartment and trashed it."

A tightness gripped her throat at the steady look in his eyes. He knew. Somehow, he knew she had instigated the break-in. "Is that so?"

Without breaking eye contact, Quentin continued. "Yes, there's nothing left intact, and they left a pretty vile message spray-painted on the bedroom wall."

Indignation rose in her like an erupting volcano. "She has no right to be walking around, living like a normal person. Not when our Jesse is still out there, somewhere."

"I understand those feelings." He cupped her cheek with his hand. "I miss our son every day too."

Ruby stared at him. He rarely spoke of Jesse, didn't cry on his birthday or Christmas like she did. As the years slipped by, she had begun to think her husband didn't care that their son had no final resting place. But looking into his eyes, the depths of his own pain and loss became visible again, sharply reminding her of how she'd chosen not to notice his own pain.

Her hand over his, she turned her head and kissed his palm. "My darling, I'm so sorry." Hers had simply been the more vocal, the more public grief. His had been more private, and therefore, less conspicuous.

Quentin scooted back on the lounge and drew her into his arms. Ruby nestled closer, laying her head on his shoulder. She would confess what she had done since he seemed to already know.

Together, they would come up with a plan to force Melender to tell them where Jesse was, and they could bring their little boy home. At last.

MELENDER CUT THE ENGINE AND UNBUCKLED HER SEATBELT. BROGAN HAD insisted on following her to Walmart, then having her follow him to his aunt and uncle's house. Since he offered to take Goliath in his car to keep the cat cool while she shopped, she'd agreed to the plan. The rambler tucked into an older neighborhood in Fairfax City was worlds away from the Thompsons' McLean mansion, but the neat landscaping spoke of care. She still wasn't sure about staying with Brogan's aunt and uncle, but he had insisted they were willing, even after knowing her background, so here she was. He'd told them she needed to catch a few hours of sleep before her night shift, so she hoped it would be a quick introduction.

She had no sooner grabbed her bag of hastily-purchased clothes and minimal toiletries and climbed out of the car when the front door of the home opened. A plump older woman stepped onto the porch. The woman's hand planted on her hip reminded Melender of the nursery rhyme about a little teapot short and stout. Melender stifled a chuckle.

"Brogan!" The woman threw her arms up for an embrace. "You've finally decided to come visit your aunt and uncle."

"Aunt Colleen, it's good to see you, too." Balancing Goliath's carrier in one hand, Brogan bounded up the short flight of steps and enveloped the woman in a one-armed hug.

Melender paused at the bottom of the steps leading to a covered porch that stretched down one side of the house.

Brogan released his aunt and turned to Melender. "Aunt Colleen, this is Melender Harman. Melender, this is Colleen Trent."

Trent. Surely, it would be too much of a coincidence if Brogan's aunt was married to the Nolan Trent from the music store. Melender pushed away that thought as she came up the steps and held out her hand. Mrs. Trent took Melender's hand in hers and gave it a little squeeze before releasing it. The touch was over before it had barely began, leaving Melender feeling bereft and not quite knowing why. Mrs. Trent gazed straight into her eyes. "Welcome to our home, my dear."

The kind words nearly undid Melender's composure, but she hung on to her emotions by a thread. "Thank you for letting me and Goliath crash here."

Mrs. Trent patted her arm, then moved to open the front door. "Let's get inside out of this heat. I swear, August gets hotter and more humid every year."

Brogan held the door for Melender. "Is Uncle Nolan home?"

"Nolan Trent, the musicologist?" The question burst out of Melender before Brogan could close the screen door behind her.

"Yes, that's right." Brogan frowned. "Do you know him?"

"We've met at Fox's Music store," Nolan Trent called from the top of the basement stairs to the right of the front door. He handed his wife a light bulb. "I can't remember where we put these to recycle."

Melender nodded when Brogan turned her way and raised his eyebrows. "I like to talk about music with Mr. Jimmy, the owner."

"I see." Brogan probably didn't see, but the strange coincidence of Nolan Trent being Brogan's uncle made Melender a little uneasy, especially after the way Mr. Trent had practically accused her of extortion over her grandmother's dulcimer.

"Miss Harman, when Brogan told us about your situation, we were delighted to provide a place for you to say. And, Goliath, of course." Mr. Trent offered her a slight smile as her cat meowed from the carrier. "It's the least I can do after jumping to unfounded conclusions the other day at the music store."

Melender pinched the bridge of her nose, a headache forming. She couldn't deal with this right now. She desperately needed a few hours of sleep before she collapsed. "I appreciate it, but I only have a few hours before my evening shift, and I've been up since yesterday afternoon."

"Of course." Mrs. Trent bustled forward, touching Melender's arm. "Just follow me, and I'll show you the basement apartment. We took the liberty of setting up a litter pan, food, and water in the bathroom for Goliath."

With a quick smile of thanks to Brogan, Melender followed the woman down the stairs to a compact apartment that boasted a bedroom, a full bath with shower and tub combination, a small kitchenette, a and larger living/dining room space, all separated from the rest of the house by a sturdy door with a deadbolt. Melender released Goliath into the bathroom and closed the door.

"There are clean sheets on the bed and fresh towels in the bathroom." Mrs. Trent smiled. "I'll leave you to your nap."

Alone at last, Melender threw the deadbolt, set her phone's

alarm, then tumbled, fully clothed, on top of the bed. Her last conscious thought centered on the fact that she didn't believe in coincidence, so what was she to make of finding herself in the home of Nolan and Colleen Trent?

CHAPTER

SIXTEEN

Brogan accepted a glass of unsweetened iced tea from his aunt, then followed his uncle out onto their enclosed back porch. A ceiling fan made a decent attempt to circulate air, with a little help from a light breeze through the open windows.

"You wanted to explain how you met Melender?" Brogan sipped his tea, then placed the glass on a coaster on a nearby table.

"Yes." Nolan swirled the ice and liquid around in his half-full glass. "A few months ago, Jimmy Storks told me about a woman who'd been stopping by his music store once a week, never on the same day but always near closing time when the store had very few customers."

"That was Melender?" Brogan asked.

"Yes, only Jimmy called her Mel." Nolan drank some tea. "Jimmy kept mentioning her until I finally asked him why."

Brogan hobbled his impatience with effort. His uncle would tell this story in his own time. Rushing him would only delay the tale.

"Jimmy said that she was from the Appalachian Mountains, and he suspected, given their conversations, she knew some folk songs." Nolan sighed. "Jimmy knew he'd pique my interest. I've been mining the American folk song shaft for a long time, and the vein has run dry. But I've always suspected there are more unknown songs and older versions of songs out there just waiting for discovery."

"You thought Jimmy might have stumbled upon someone who might know some of those songs."

Nolan nodded. "I didn't think Melender herself knew any songs, given how old Jimmy estimated her to be, but I thought perhaps she would know older members of her mountain community, who might be persuaded to sing."

"What happened?"

"Jimmy would text me when he saw Melender come into his store. This past Monday afternoon, I happened to be close to the store, so I dropped by. I'd found an old dulcimer at a pawn shop, and Jimmy was restoring it for me. When I arrived, Melender was gazing at the instrument like it was a long-lost relative." Nolan reached for his tea and took a sip. "I nearly didn't say anything for fear I'd break the spell."

Brogan leaned forward, not wanting to miss anything. This fresh insight into Melender's character intrigued him beyond the story.

"When she said she knew how to play the instrument, Jimmy encouraged her to try, with my permission." Nolan directed his gaze directly at Brogan. "To be honest, I thought she was exaggerating, as hardly anyone plays the dulcimer anymore, and certainly no one her age. I expected her to pluck a few strings, but she tuned the instrument, then started singing a version of 'Forsaken Love' that I'd never heard. And her voice..."

"What about it?" Brogan prodded when the older man didn't continue.

"She'd had no formal vocal training, that was obvious. But the purity of her phrasing, the way she sang the words—I've been listening to folk music my entire adult life, and I've never come across anyone who sang like her. It's almost like discovering a new genre of music."

Brogan frowned. "But you said you'd heard that song before."

"A version of it, yes. But that's what makes this even more interesting." His uncle leaned in. "The lyrics are very similar, with only slight changes that are normal for an oral tradition like folk songs. But it's the melody that caught my attention. She used a melody that has only hints of the one associated with 'Forsaken Love' today. It's basically a different melody."

"The lyrics are familiar, but the tune is not." Brogan attempted to sum up what his uncle was saying. He liked folk songs okay—one didn't grow up as the nephew of a musicologist without hearing a fair number of them—but he didn't quite get Nolan's passion about some old music.

"Exactly." Nolan sat back, crossing an ankle over the opposite knee. "But she refused my request to have her come sing for a few of my colleagues, and I thought might be the end of it."

"This happened on Monday afternoon?"

Nolan agreed. "I stopped by this morning to pick up the dulcimer Jimmy had cleaned up and chanced upon Melender there as well. With the instrument restored to its former glory, she thought she recognized it as belonging to her grandmother."

"Great-grandmother," Brogan corrected, his mind replaying the conversation he'd had with Nolan earlier, which was starting to make more sense to him now.

"It turned out she was right. There's a small flower etched inside the instrument next to the maker's mark." Nolan paused. "I had looked up the name Mel Harman after our encounter on Monday and discovered Mel Harman was Melender Harman."

Brogan met his uncle's gaze. "You were suspicious that Jimmy didn't know her true identity and she might be taking advantage of him in some way."

"That's about the gist of it. When she said that about the dulcimer's provenance, I accused her of trying to extort money by accusing me of stealing it because she was an ex-con."

That must have cut Melender to the quick.

Nolan continued, "She nearly collapsed, and then Jimmy informed me that he'd known her identity all along."

"What did Melender do?" Brogan's heart ached at the thought of her going from such a scene to find her apartment had been trashed.

"She said she wasn't accusing me of anything, and her aunt must have sold the dulcimer to the pawn shop. Then she ran out of the store." Nolan finished his tea. "That's why when you called, I realized God was giving me a second chance to do the right thing, to show Melender kindness and forgiveness rather than the rush-to-judgment I'd done."

"She could use more friends." Brogan didn't want to contemplate why God had brought Melender into his life because that would mean he might have a bigger role to play than to merely write her story. His cell buzzed with Fallon's name on the screen. "Excuse me, it's my boss calling." He accepted the call. "Brogan speaking."

"Where are you?" Fallon barked without a greeting. Typical.

"I'm near Ratcliffe Park in Fairfax City."

"There's a five-alarm fire over at the courthouse. I expect a story by ten." Fallon clicked off before Brogan could response.

"I hate to rush out of here, but I've got to go cover a fire." Brogan rose, as did his uncle. "You'll take good care of Melender, won't you?"

Nolan laid a hand on his shoulder. "Don't worry. She'll be safe with us, and, if I know my wife, she's already convinced Melender to stay with us for a while."

Brogan thanked him, then exited the porch by the back entrance. As he walked to his car, he sent up a quick prayer of thanks for Melender's safety and a petition that they could figure out who was targeting her.

THE SUN PEEKED OVER THE HORIZON AS MELENDER WALKED TO HER vehicle. Somehow, she'd managed to make it through her shift without collapsing from exhaustion. She rotated her shoulders, but

JUSTICE DELAYED

it did little to relieve her overall fatigue. She hadn't felt this weary since her arrest eighteen years ago. Back then, she hadn't been able to sleep in the crowded jail and wore a cloak of perpetual tiredness. After her sentencing, she eventually got used to the constant noise and lack of privacy in prison and was able to sleep most nights.

After being forced into close proximity with dozens of women in her prison pod, she enjoyed the solitude of this work and lifestyle. Adjusting to working nights hadn't been too difficult. In fact, after the first few weeks, she'd fallen into the rhythm of sleeping during the daylight hours.

After chirping her car door unlocked, she reached for the handle.

"Melender Harman?"

The unfamiliar male voice caught her off guard. Usually, she paid more attention to her surroundings, but lack of sleep had dulled her senses. She turned. An audible sigh escaped her lips at the sight of an older man in a short-sleeve dress shirt and rumpled khaki pants who stood near her car's back bumper. A woman stood beside him. Cops.

"May I see some identification?" Melender didn't move closer, wanting to keep her distance from the pair of them.

Surprise flickered across the woman's face, yet she flashed her badge. The man removed his credentials from his back pocket. Each held up their IDs, forcing Melender to step closer to read their names and affiliation. Fairfax County Detective Lauren Collier and Fairfax County Detective Mark Livingston.

Melender threw a glance at Detective Livingston's lined face, recognition flaring in her memory. "You investigated Jesse's disappearance." The declaration burst out of her before she'd weighed the consequences.

"I was part of the team." Livingston pocketed his badge.

Her fingers tightened on the key fob. "Why are you here?"

"You're Melender Harman?" Detective Collier pressed.

Melender ignored the question, and instead repeated her own. "Why are you here?"

131

"Yesterday afternoon, a body was found." Livingston clipped tone didn't faze her.

Melender's heart kicked up a notch "A body? Was it..." She swallowed hard. "Was it Jesse?"

"What makes you say that?" Collier shifted closer to Melender.

Melender didn't budge. She would not be intimidated by them and refocused her attention on Livingston. "Have you identified the body?"

"The victim was an adult male, TJ Williams, who had been murdered by a blow to the head," Livingston said.

"That's terrible, but I don't understand what that has to do with me." Melender glanced from one detective to the other but couldn't read anything on their impassive faces. Her heart went into overdrive. "You don't think I had anything to do with it?" Panic tinged her words, but she couldn't help herself. *Please God, don't let the nightmare begin again.* Livingston said something, but Melender didn't track it. "I'm sorry, what did you say?"

"Williams had twenty thousand dollars in cash on him when he died." Livingston met her gaze.

Melender drew in a deep breath, letting it out slowly to calm her galloping pulse. Misery colored her voice as she put into words the reason for their visit. "It's part of the ransom money, isn't it?"

"Why would you assume that?" Collier jutted her chin out, her tone combative.

"I didn't assume, I asked because you're telling me about the murder of a man I don't know who had a lot of cash." Melender rested her hip against the rear door of her car to steady her wobbly legs. The warm metal pressed against her thigh, helping to keep her grounded. "I don't know anyone named Williams, and I certainly never collected any ransom money."

"But you did kill Jesse Thompson."

She winced at Collier's bald statement. In the eyes of the world, she was a convicted murderer. It didn't matter that she didn't do it, and saying so would only heighten their suspicion of her in connection with this new crime. "I've got nothing to hide."

"Then you won't mind if we search your apartment?" Collier raised her eyebrows in a challenge.

Melender gave a weak chuckle. "Knock yourself out. If you find anything salvable that I overlooked yesterday, let me know."

"Salvable?" Livingston said.

"Oh, didn't check with your colleagues in robbery before coming here? Someone—or, more accurately, according to one of my neighbors, several people—broke into my apartment yesterday while I was out and completely destroyed all of my possessions. There's not a dish, picture frame, sofa cushion, or item of clothing that isn't smashed or slashed to shreds."

Melender pushed off from her car, adrenaline spiking her words. "Please, search away. Now, unless you have a warrant for my arrest, we're done here."

CHAPTER

SEVENTEEN

This wasn't supposed to happen. Jared cradled his head in his hands. How could Snake be dead? The craving for a hit roared through his body like a runaway train. He rocked back and forth, pressing his hands against his temples in an effort to banish the desire.

No, he wouldn't succumb. He wouldn't go back down that path. He'd been clean for months and liked the way his brain completed thoughts and his body didn't vibrate when he needed a fix.

But Snake's murder shook him to the core. The cops wouldn't come knocking on his door, not when he'd cut ties to the drug community three years ago. No one had seen him visit Snake on Wednesday night. He'd carefully wiped his fingerprints from the bills and plastic bag before handing the bundle to Snake.

His grand scheme to cast suspicion about Melender's involvement with the kidnapping by slowly leaking some of the ransom money out through a drug dealer had imploded. Jared slumped against the back of his leather couch, closing his eyes. If only his dad hadn't severely curtailed his allowance after learning about his drug habit. Back then, Jared needed money, and the opportunity to make some quick cash when Jesse disappeared had won out. But after the ransom pickup, Jared had overheard an FBI agent discussing how the bills could be traced through special markings and serial numbers. Which meant he'd ended up with a million dollars he couldn't spend.

A rapid knock on the door broke into his thoughts. Jared wasn't expecting anyone. Maybe he hadn't completely removed his prints from the bills. The person knocked again, harder this time.

"Jared, I know you're home. Open up."

His father, not a man you ignored. Jared pulled open the door. Quentin pushed past him into the condo, fury stamped across his taut features. His dad didn't give him a chance to speak before he exploded.

"What on earth were you thinking?"

No way Quentin knew about Snake and the ransom money. Best to stay quiet until Jared figured out what had gotten his father all riled up.

"Don't just stand there, acting like you don't know what I'm talking about." Quentin's voice dropped to a controlled tone, which scared Jared more than his first outburst.

Before Jared could decide whether to agree or bluff his way out, Quentin continued.

"Ruby showed me the photos of Melender's apartment."

Jared's body nearly sagged with relief. This wasn't about Snake's death. This was about Ruby's request. "Dad, she begged me for the name of someone to harass Melender. You know how Ruby can get. She wasn't going to let this go."

"You thought giving her a criminal's contact info was the right choice?" Quentin paced across the living room and peered out of the window.

"If I hadn't, she would have found more trouble trying to do it on her own." His father's loud harrumph revealed he still needed to be convinced. "She called me the day after our family dinner, crying about how much she missed Jesse. Then she asked me for the name of someone who could—and I'm quoting her exact words—'put enough pressure on Melender to make her reveal where she hid Jesse.'"

Quentin didn't turn around.

"I gave her the name of someone I knew would treat it like a business proposition. After all, I didn't want her asking the wrong person for the job."

"A business proposition." Quentin turned to face Jared. "Your stepmother has agreed to not contact this person again. I want you to tell this individual that he is not to accept another job from my wife. If Ruby does contact him, he's to come directly to me."

Jared nodded, catching a glint of moisture in Quentin's eyes before he bowed his head. For the first time, Jared realized his dad keenly felt the loss of Jesse and the turmoil it had created in their family. All these years, Jared had only seen Ruby's outward grief in her rage and crying bouts, not his father's inward sorrow. That his father cared deeply about what had happened surprised him, but shouldn't have. The signs had been there, had Jared been self-aware enough to read the map. He took a few tentative steps toward his father. "Dad?"

Quentin raised his head, his eyes meeting Jared's.

"I'm sorry." That didn't cover everything he wanted to say, but Jared couldn't put into words how much in this moment, he regretted being blind to father's grief.

Quentin laid a hand on Jared's shoulder. "I know, son." He squeezed his shoulder, then turned toward the door.

Jared clicked the deadbolt after his departure. He flopped onto the couch, resting his head against the back cushion. His father could never find out about the ransom money. It would kill him to lose another son.

∼

"Hey, Brogan, what are you doing here?" Seth Whitman leaned over the cubicle wall.

"Just a sec." Brogan finished typing the final sentence on his story about next week's upcoming debate between candidates for Fairfax County Commonwealth Attorney. "Trying to finish this story."

"I figured you'd be down at the police station." Seth unwrapped a piece of butterscotch candy and popped it in his mouth.

"That's your beat." Brogan wasn't up to playing twenty questions with the younger reporter and photographer. He hadn't slept well last night. Thoughts of Melender had intruded long after his head hit the pillow.

"Yeah, but I thought you'd have heard by now." Seth glanced at his phone. "It's been more than twelve hours since the discovery."

A part of him wanted to tune Seth out, but his reporter's antenna rose enough that he'd hear Seth out. The beefy young man had taken a shine to Brogan, often dropping by his desk to chat. He'd once asked Seth why he hadn't been snapped up by a larger, more prestigious paper given his stellar academic background. Seth replied that he'd chosen to pay his dues the old-fashioned way. Personally, Brogan thought Seth was nuts, but he didn't say that.

"Just tell me, already." Brogan picked up his empty mug. "I know you're dying to."

Seth stepped back as Brogan rose, then trailed him to the breakroom. "It has to do with the Jesse Thompson kidnapping."

Brogan whirled around to pin Seth with a hard stare. "What did you say?"

Seth took a step back. "Whoa, don't shoot the messenger."

"Sorry." Brogan continued to the breakroom. He sniffed the pot of caffeinated coffee sitting on a warmer and decided it was fresh enough. "Tell me everything."

"There was a homicide last night, some drug dealer named TJ Williams, but everyone knows him as Snake." Seth hoisted himself onto the opposite counter as Brogan poured coffee into his mug. "I was asking the regular questions, trying to see if there was a bigger story than a garden-variety murder."

Brogan dumped one single-serve coffee creamer into his mug, then stirred as he listened to Seth.

"On the surface, it appeared to be nothing more than a drug deal gone bad. But then one of my sources revealed that a packet of money had been found. A bundle of tens and twenties that added up to twenty thousand dollars."

Brogan straightened. "Part of the ransom money paid in Thompson kidnapping case?"

"That's what my source says, but, of course, no one will confirm it." Seth hopped down. "Not yet, anyway. I know the two detectives assigned to the murder visited Melender this morning when she got off work to ask her about the cash."

"What happened?" Part of the ransom turning up now could mean their questions were making someone uncomfortable enough to try to pull Melender back into the frame for the ransom.

Seth shrugged. "I haven't been able to find out. The detectives aren't talking, and my source doesn't know anything more."

"Thanks for telling me." Brogan moved toward the breakroom door.

"Hey, you'll let me know Melender's reaction?"

Brogan turned back. He met Seth's cocky grin with a smile of his own. "Perhaps. But I'm after a much bigger story than a drug dealer's murder."

Seth became serious. "I know, but if this murder is connected with whoever's responsible for the ransom..." He didn't have to finish the sentence. Brogan heard the warning behind the unspoken words.

"I'll be careful." He considered what to do next. "Any chance your source knows where the detectives in charge of the murder typically eat lunch?"

SARAH HAMAKER

"I think my source can find out. I'll text you the info."

"Appreciate it." Back at his desk, Brogan sipped his coffee. Ambushing the detectives at a restaurant might not put him in their good graces, but since he didn't want to officially request an interview, it might work. The fact of their visit to Melender already told him the money had indeed been traced to the ransom bills. He'd have to get her side of the story later, but for now, a chat with the detectives might prove fruitful. If nothing else, it would alert them someone was seriously looking into the case again.

At Anita's Mexican Restaurant, Brogan settled into the booth with a clear eye of the door. At one o'clock, the small eatery on Fairfax Boulevard was fast filling up with the lunch crowd, which included numerous members of law enforcement. He counted several police officers and fire personnel among the uniformed patrons. By 1:15, not a seat remained open when Detectives Lauren Collier and Mark Livingston walked in.

The hostess greeted them, then pointed to Brogan's booth. He'd slipped her a twenty to seat the pair with him should the restaurant be full when the detectives—who ate at Anita's every Friday like clockwork—showed up. Brogan raised a hand in greeting.

The detectives exchanged glances, then Livingston shrugged, and they walked to his booth. Brogan stood as they approached. "Detective Collier, Detective Livingston. I'm Brogan Gilmore with the *Herald*."

At the mention of his affiliation, Collier firmed her lips.

"What a coincidence to run into the two people I had on my list to call today." Brogan smiled.

"A coincidence." Livingston glanced around the restaurant that had no empty tables. "What tune do you expect us to sing for our lunch?"

Brogan raised his hands. "I just need some background. Strictly off the record, I promise."

"In that case, let's order." Livingston slid into the booth opposite where Brogan had been sitting. "I'm starving."

His partner eased in beside him, her demeanor that of an animal not sure if the situation warranted fight or flight.

Brogan retook his seat as a waitress approached.

"What can I get you to drink?" She addressed the question to Brogan, who gestured toward the detectives. "I already know what they want. Iced tea and a Diet Coke."

"In that case, I'd like a bottle of Perrier poured over ice, please. I'm guessing you two don't need a minute to look over the menu."

Collier smiled. "Benita knows our orders."

Brogan handed Benita his menu. "I'll have the carnitas enchilada with a side of guacamole."

"Now tell us what you want to know, 'off the record.'" Livingston made air quotes as he spoke.

From Seth's source, Brogan had heard that Livingston, a twenty-year veteran on the force, had a no-nonsense style, while his partner of five years had a reputation of being thorough and fair. As a team assigned to Fairfax County's homicide division, Collier and Livingston had racked up an impressive record of closing hard cases.

Benita set down their drinks, two complimentary salsa dishes, and a large basket of warm tortilla chips.

Brogan slipped a straw into his drink. No sense beating around the bush. "I heard you found some of the ransom money from the Thompson kidnapping on a murder victim."

"Where did you hear that?" Collier said, her eyes spitting fire.

"He's a reporter, so he's not going to reveal his sources." Livingston dipped a chip into the salsa and ate it, as calm as if they were all relaxing poolside with frozen drinks in their hands. "Let's go on the assumption that what Gilmore heard is correct. What is your interest?"

"Melender Harman's out of jail and in the area, but you already know that because you visited her this morning to ask about the money." Brogan resisted the chips, concentrating instead on trying to get a read on the detectives sitting opposite him. "What you might not know is that her aunt, Ruby Harman Thompson, accosted Melender last week."

"Accosted?" Livingston sounded only mildly interested, but Brogan sensed tension coiling inside the man.

"Mrs. Thompson screamed at Melender and tried to physically attack her while Melender was working." Brogan sipped his sparkling water.

"And you know this how?" Collier's turn to ask a question.

"Because I witnessed the exchange." Brogan succinctly recapped that encounter.

Benita returned, balancing a tray with steaming plates of food, placing Brogan's enchilada and side of guacamole on the table, then putting down a trio of tacos in front of Livingston and a massive chimichanga in front of Collier. Service was quick at Anita's, which added to its popularity with law enforcement. With a quick glance at their still-full beverages, Benita left.

Livingston picked up a taco and took a bite. Brogan followed his lead and dug into his enchilada after adding a large dollop of guacamole on top. For a few minutes, nobody spoke as they ate.

Two tacos down, Livingston wiped his mouth. "You're looking into the Thompson case."

The statement didn't surprise Brogan. He chewed, then swallowed his mouthful slowly to give himself time to consider how to answer. Simplicity seemed the best course. "Yes."

"Why? It's a closed case." Collier had made short work of her lunch. "The ransom money turning up now is simply a loose end. Melender Harman's out of jail and was trying to launder the ransom. She can't be tried twice for the same crime, so she figured it was worth a shot. A million dollars is a lot, especially for an ex-convict."

"You were looking into this before the ransom money came to light." Livingston tossed his napkin onto his clean plate. He appeared to study Brogan for a moment, then nodded. "She's a beautiful woman. Prison life doesn't seem to have taken a toll on her."

Brogan schooled his face with an effort. Melender's outward beauty had nothing to do with his interest in her case. Maybe if he kept telling himself that, he'd actually believe it. "It's an intriguing case that has a lot of anomalies."

"Such as?" Collier said.

"The missing ransom money and the lack of a body top the list." Brogan finished his own meal just as Benita stopped by their table.

"All finished?" She didn't wait for a response as she picked up empty plates. "Be right back with your checks."

Livingston drained his Diet Coke. "I admit that not finding anything to place Melender with the ransom is a loose end I would like to tie up. The missing body is another."

Brogan leaned forward. "I've got the FBI files from the kidnapping. Any chance I could have copies of the police files related to the case?"

Benita dropped off the checks, reminding them to pay at the cash register on their way out. Brogan grabbed all three, but Livingston responded that department policy forbade comped meals.

Check in hand, Collier moved to exit the booth. "You'll have to file a FOIA request with our media relations department."

"I already did, but they said it could take weeks to process." Brogan switched his attention to Livingston. "Look, I'm not on a crusade to prove the police or FBI dropped the ball with this case, but I do think there are some things that don't add up."

Livingston stood beside his partner. "Do you have a business card?"

Brogan dug out his wallet and extracted one. "Here you go."

The detective shoved it into his pocket. "We'll be in touch if there's anything we can do to expedite the request."

"Thanks." Brogan joined them beside the table, then shook hands with each detective. "I appreciate your talking with me."

"As long as what we discussed stays off the record." Livingston

SARAH HAMAKER

and Collier walked to the cash register. Brogan retook his seat, pulling out his phone to check for messages. The impromptu meeting had gone better than expected, and he had learned one very important thing.

Detective Mark Livingston still had unresolved questions about the closed case.

CHAPTER

EIGHTEEN

Melender paused at the top of the stairs, unsure whether to approach Mrs. Trent as she stirred of pot on the kitchen stove.

The older woman turned, a smile on her face. "Good afternoon, Melender."

"Hello." Melender had yet to master the art of small talk. In prison, you kept your mouth shut and avoided eye contact with the other inmates. She still defaulted to what had kept her safe for so many years.

"Brogan called a little while ago to see if you were still sleeping," Mrs. Trent said. "When I told him you were, he asked me to say he would be by around six."

"Thank you." She moved a little closer to the stove. "Something smells good."

"Beef stew. I told Brogan to stay for supper, and you're welcome to join us as well." Mrs. Trent gestured toward the pot. "As you can see, I've made more than enough."

Mrs. Trent replaced the lid on the tall pot. Sudie had had a battered version of that same cook pot. If Melender closed her eyes, she could almost swear she was in Sudie's tiny kitchen, standing on a stool to stir the contents of a stew made with chunks of squirrel meat, chestnuts, wild onions, parsnips, and carrots.

"That's very kind of you, but I don't want to impose." If there was one thing ingrained in her from prison, it was that no one offered you anything without a very long, very barbed attachment.

Mrs. Trent wiped the spotless counter with a sponge. "Do you believe in God?"

"Yes, I do." Her faith had grown stronger throughout her incarceration, given that most of the time, it was just her and God against the world. But living that faith on the outside had proved to be harder than she anticipated. Not everyone proclaiming to be a Christian welcomed ex-cons with open arms.

"Nolan and I do as well. We believe our faith compels us to live our life everyday as if Christ could return at any second."

Mrs. Trent eyed her with a thoroughness that Melender hadn't encountered since her grandmother died. Sudie had the same penetrating yet compassionate gaze that looked beyond facades and into a person's soul. "To us that means opening our home to those in need. You have no place to stay. We have space to offer. Stay with us, Melender. Break bread with us. Let us come alongside you for a time on your journey."

Melender swallowed a lump in her throat. She didn't doubt the sincerity in the other woman. "Do you know why I was in prison?"

"Yes, but Brogan says you're fighting to prove your innocence."

The bluntness of the reply surprised Melender. No one had given her the benefit of the doubt. She'd learned early on in prison that few were truly innocent, but most everyone claimed to have not committed their crime. She'd stopped saying she wasn't guilty of the kidnapping or murder long ago when she'd realized no one cared. Now, looking at Mrs. Trent, she managed to get the words out. "I never hurt Jesse."

The older woman nodded once. "We don't think otherwise. Now, I expect you could use some more personal things."

Melender blinked back tears She wanted to hug the other woman for believing in her. To regain control of her emotions, Melender focused on the second part of the statement. "I was going to pick up a few more outfits before my shift tonight."

"I hope you don't mind, but I called some of the younger women in my Bible study to help gather some clothes and other necessities." Mrs. Trent extracted three department store bags from underneath a counter opposite the kitchen island that served as a workstation. "We guessed on the sizes, so if something doesn't fit, we can exchange it."

Staring at the bags, Melender tried to process what Mrs. Trent was saying. "This is for me?"

"Brogan told us that everything you owned had been destroyed." Mrs. Trent pushed one of the bags into Melender's hands. "I told them to start from the ground up in the way of clothing."

Melender set the bag on the floor, then squatted and opened it. Rifling through the contents, she noted t-shirts, shorts, skirts, sundresses, undergarments, and socks. Most appeared to be in her size too. Mrs. Trent placed the other bags next to the first one. In one, Melender found more clothing similar to the first bag. In the third bag, a pair of sneakers, flip flops, and sandals, plus several hair-brushes, hair accessories, shampoo, conditioner, feminine products, and a small box holding a generous gift card to a local discount store.

"This..." Melender cleared her throat as a warm feeling of being loved wash over her. "This is too much."

Mrs. Trent laid a hand on her shoulder. "Please don't feel you can't accept it. These young women were delighted to do this for you."

Melender stood, her head bowed in an attempt to hide her tears. "But if they knew who I was..."

"They do." Mrs. Trent spoke softly. "Ever since Brogan called yesterday, the ladies and I have been praying for you and your diffi-cult circumstance."

This outpouring of God's love on her life came just when she needed it the most. Mrs. Trent enfolded her into her arms, holding her close as Melender let herself cry, releasing emotions she'd kept bottled up for years. Knowing her heavenly Father used his people here on earth to minister His love surrounded her in peace that passed all understanding.

She wasn't alone.

~

BROGAN STRUGGLED TO SEE OVER THE THREE COPIER PAPER BOXES AS HE mounted the steps to the Trents' home. He should have texted his aunt to meet him at the door before grabbing the boxes from the back seat of the SUV. Now he tried to shift his load to one side in order to use an elbow to push the doorbell. But before he could attempt that, the front door opened, and he saw a pair of bare feet on the threshold.

"Need some help?" The laughter in Melender's voice warmed him more than the heat of the August day.

"Yes, please." Brogan twisted sideways to maneuver into the house without dropping his load.

"Brogan, dear, I've set up space for you in one of the back rooms," Aunt Colleen said. "This way, down the hall."

He moved by memory more than sight behind her and into a room on the right.

"You can set the boxes on the table."

After putting down his load, he straightened to see she'd outfitted the small space with a long folding table and a couple of straight-backed wooden chairs with padded seat cushions. "This will work out great, thanks."

"It's no problem." She eyed the trio of boxes. "Now, can you tell me what this super-secret project of yours is? You were rather cagey on the phone when you asked about space to go through some files."

"Is that everything?" Melender said from behind him.

148

Brogan turned to see her just outside the door. He looked back at his aunt. "All the FBI files from the kidnapping of Jesse Thompson."

"Any word from Fairfax County Police about those files?" She came into the room and touched one of the lids.

"I've filed an FOIA but haven't heard back yet." Brogan flexed his fingers to get the blood circulating again. "That could take weeks, so for now, we'll start with this."

"Not until after dinner." Colleen squeezed past him to exit the room. "It'll be ready in about ten minutes."

"Is there anything I can do to help?"

"I've got it under control," she said, then went down the hallway to the kitchen.

"Your aunt is very nice." Melender took the lid off one of the boxes and riffled through the stack of papers. "You're blessed to live so close to the Trents."

"In some ways, they've been more like parents to me since I moved here just over a year ago." Brogan had stopped hoping Mom and Dad would help him pickup the pieces of his shattered career, but he had been grateful to the Trents for their generosity in opening both their home and their hearts to him.

His phone signaled an incoming call. An unfamiliar number with a local area code flashed on the screen. "Excuse me while I take this call."

"I'll go see if Mrs. Trent would like the table set." Melender slipped out of the room as Brogan answered the call.

"Gilmore."

"Good evening. Detective Livingston here."

Brogan stifled his surprise at hearing from the detective so soon after their impromptu lunch meeting, but decided the other man's greeting didn't warrant a response from him.

"I pulled a few strings and had copies made of our files related to the Thompson case."

"Thank you, I appreciate that."

"The boxes are with the on-duty sergeant at the front desk under your name. I had the bill for the copies sent to your *Herald* office email address."

A small price to pay for getting the information quicker than he had anticipated. Curiosity nibbled around the edges of his elation. "What made you change your mind from lunch?"

Livingston didn't answer for several seconds. Just when Brogan thought the other man must have disconnected the call, he spoke. "We couldn't definitively link Melender Harman to the ransom."

"You think something might have been overlooked in the original case?"

"Let's just say that I've never liked convictions based solely on circumstantial evidence."

"I see." But Brogan wasn't sure that he did.

"But that doesn't mean I think there's been a miscarriage of justice in this case. Since it's a solved case, I don't see the harm in having you take a look through the files."

"I appreciate your expediting my request." Brogan itched to get started on the boxes he already had, but it might be wise to include the files from the police station. He could leave after supper to retrieve them, in case Livingston had second thoughts.

"All I ask is that if you do manage to open a new avenue of inquiry related to the ransom, you'll do me the courtesy of a phone call before you print the story."

Brogan wasn't surprised at the request. Law enforcement always wanted to be kept apprised of anything that popped up related to open or closed cases. "Aren't you looking into the ransom aspect now that some of the money was found?"

"We are, but, as we both know, people are usually more forthcoming with a reporter than they are with the police." Livingston said something Brogan couldn't catch but that sounded like it was addressed to someone else. "One more thing you ought to consider."

"What's that?" Brogan moved to the doorway after his aunt called out that dinner was ready.

"Melender Harman might have been involved in the ransom after all. I doubt it's a coincidence some of the money turned up now when she's out of prison." Livingston disconnected the call without a formal goodbye.

Brogan slipped the phone back into his pocket and left the room. He didn't want Livingston's warning to be true because he had begun to think of Melender as being more innocent than guilty. He needed to stay impartial in order to write a good investigative piece, but his interest in the case had started to tilt more into helping her prove her innocence than discovering what really happened to Jesse.

CHAPTER
NINETEEN

L ater Saturday afternoon, Melender sipped the large coffee Brogan had thoughtfully brought for her, willing the caffeine to work its magic and revive her sluggish brain. He settled into the chair opposite as she stifled an unwelcomed yawn.

"This is everything from the FBI and Fairfax County Police." Brogan flipped the lid off one of the boxes. "While you were sleeping, I organized them into folders under each person's name to make it easier for us to go over."

"Wow, you must have been up here for hours." She peeked into the open box stacked with labeled file folders.

"I did have a little help from my aunt and uncle."

"I'll have to thank them." Her heart clenched at the reminder of how sweet the support of family could be—and what her own family refused to offer. The laughter, inside jokes, and affection between the Trents and Brogan during last night's dinner had only increased the ache in her own heart for what she had missed. "Will they be back soon?"

Brogan shook his head. "They have tickets to a concert at Wolf Trap and took a picnic to enjoy the grounds ahead of time."

"That sounds lovely." She'd been wanting to attend a concert at the popular local indoor/outdoor theater, but her work schedule didn't afford many free nights, nor did her bank account allow for the price of a ticket.

He tapped the box, redirecting her attention. "Apparently, there was a bit of a tiff between the Fairfax County Police Department and the FBI around the time of Jesse's disappearance, so the county only shared the bare minimum with the feds on the case."

"The FBI files were incomplete?" That didn't sound right.

"The agency only had summaries of the county's interviews, so I don't know if any agent asked the police for more or not."

"Doesn't that seem strange to you?" Melender set her coffee down, then reached in and plucked a thick folder from the stack.

Brogan shrugged. "I don't think we should read too much into it. The FBI focused on the kidnapping aspect, but once you were arrested, their investigation didn't continue with as much force."

"I guess when you have a suspect in custody, there's not much incentive to look for additional suspects." Melender eyed the label on the folder. *Jared Thompson.* Inside, the heading on the first piece of paper read: *Fairfax County Police Interview with Jared Thompson.* Her hand shook, but she steadied her grip. After all this time, she would finally discover what her cousin had to say about the night of Jesse's disappearance. His testimony at her trial hadn't tallied with what she'd remembered from that night.

Brogan slid a yellow legal pad and pen across the table to her. "Jot down anything that doesn't jibe with what you remember about the event and the days that followed. I'll write down notes that don't seem to match up with the trial transcript."

She picked up the interview transcript and read.

Jared Quentin Thompson, age 19, attends Northern Virginia Community College
Resident address: 23014 Crescent Moon Drive, McLean, Virginia
Mother: Sandra Evans Thompson of San Jose, California

Father: Quentin L. Thompson of McLean, Virginia
Siblings: half-sister Jillian, half-brother Jesse
Location: Fairfax County Police Station in McLean, Virginia
Present: Detective Mark Livingston, Detective Richard Delaney

LIVINGSTON: Walk us through last night.

JARED: You want me to start when Jesse went missing?

DELANEY: You know when that was?"

JARED: Nah, man.

DELANEY: Where were you last night?

JARED: At home.

LIVINGSTON: All night?

JARED: Define night.

LIVINGSTON: Your stepmother states that you came home around 1 a.m.

JARED: Yeah, I meant, I wasn't in the house when he went missing.

LIVINGSTON: How do you know you weren't in the house when he went missing?

JARED: Ah, man, don't try to trip me up. You know who my father is?

DELANEY: Of course we do. But you want to help us find your little brother, don't you?

JARED: Half-brother.

LIVINGSTON: What did you think of him?

JARED: He was okay, cried a lot when he was born, but he didn't do much. Just crawled around and whined. Only time Jesse and Jillian were quiet was when Mel sang.

DELANEY: Melender Harman, your cousin?

JARED: I guess.

DELANEY: Did she sing to your younger siblings a lot?

JARED: All the time. There's something about her voice.

DELANEY: What do you mean?

JARED: I tried to get her to sing for a buddy of mine who knows some people in the music industry, you know, but she said her voice wasn't for sale. Crazy. I brought him over one time, and we hid behind the pool shed when we saw her go into the wooded area in

155

the back of the lot. She used to climb this oak tree and sing when she thought no one was around. When my buddy heard her sing, he wanted to come back and record it. But then Jesse went missing, and that ended that.

LIVINGSTON: Where did you go that evening?

Melender played with the tail of her braid when she finished reading the rest of Jared's police interview. Not once did her cousin mention that Ruby and Quentin left him in charge of his half-siblings the night Jesse went missing. Melender had been at a graduation party hosted by one of her classmates, who happened to live a few streets over from the Thompsons. Funny how Melender had never considered her aunt and uncle's home her own. In her mind, it was always "the Thompson house." Her home was a little log cabin tucked into a hollow with a breathtaking view of the Blue Ridge Mountains.

A longing to return to her roots, to forget about clearing her name and allow the mountains work their restorative magic on her battered soul welled up so strongly, tears sprang to her eyes. Melender allowed herself to picture the kitchen and living area, the small bedroom, and—her grandmother's pride and joy—a tiny bathroom with a clawfoot tub, sink, and toilet. While power lines to the cabin's remote location was impossible, Sudie loved having running water, albeit only cold water.

"Melender?"

Brogan's voice jolted her back to the present. Swiping away the wetness from her cheeks, she met Brogan's gaze.

"Are you okay?" He reached across the table and grasped her hand in his.

The warmth of his touch sent a shudder through her body, like water pushing against a weak spot on a dam.

"What's wrong?" His soft-spoken question, accompanied by the tender movement of his thumb across the top of her hand, pushed the water over the dam in a whoosh of emotions.

Tears streamed down her cheeks. Withdrawing her hand from his, she bowed her head and wrapped her arms around her middle, but the pent-up emotions wouldn't be contained. Sobs shook her frame. She cried all the tears she couldn't shed in prison. Her crying yesterday with Mrs. Trent had loosened something inside her. The grief over what happened to Jesse and the loss of being totally alone in the world broke her down.

"Shh. It'll be okay." Brogan gently tugged her up and into a strong embrace.

Melender encircled his waist for support. Brogan stroked her hair and murmured comforting words she didn't quite catch. For once, she didn't try to reign in the floodgates of tears but let them fall, soaking his t-shirt. She didn't know how long they stood like that, but when the tears slowed, she raised her head.

He smoothed back a strand of hair from her wet face. "Better?"

She seriously considered the question, then decided her crying jag had released some of the tension and grief bottled up inside her. "Yes."

Brogan smiled, his eyes holding a tenderness that sent a different sort of tingle throughout her body. "You must have carried that weight around for a long time."

That was the understatement of the year. Now that the tears had been spent, she became more aware of how tightly he held her, how snugly she fit into his embrace. Embarrassment crept over her like a vine. She stepped away only to find her back against the wall. "I'm, um, sorry about getting your shirt all wet."

"Don't worry about it."

His nearness, coupled with the intensity of his gaze, heightened her senses. Drawing in a ragged breath, the scent of cedar mixed with what she was beginning to associate with Brogan. A desire to place her hand along his jawline to see if the five-o'clock shadow felt as scratchy as it looked zoomed through her. This was madness. She needed to remove herself from his vicinity pronto before she did something truly stupid, like throw herself back into his arms. He was only being kind, much like a person would comfort a small, wounded animal. Brogan had made it clear he was keeping an open mind about her guilt and that he was only in it for the story.

She slipped out of the door and into the hall bathroom a few steps away. After using the facilities, she washed up, blew her nose, then examined her face in the mirror. The tears had turned her nose red and made her eyes a little puffy, but a few splashes of cold water helped to sooth both her face and her tattered emotions. In her heightened emotional state, she clearly had misread his kindness for something more. *Dear God, please help me to focus on the task at hand. Help us to find out the truth.*

BROGAN PRESSED THE HEELS OF HIS HANDS TO HIS EYES. HAD HE REALLY BEEN thinking of kissing Melender? Seeing her cry had touched something deep inside him. He remembered how alone he'd felt after his disgrace, how his former friends wouldn't return his calls, and how his own family expressed their disapproval by withholding contact for a time. Those memories had driven him to rise and pull her into his arms. No one should cry alone. But his comfort had turned to something else.

As he'd stroked Melender's hair, the silkiness of her braid redirected his thoughts to how long her hair might be when undone. He'd itched to slip the tie off and run his fingers through the silvery-blonde strands. When she pulled back and gazed at him, the lingering sadness in her dark blue eyes heightened the impulse to kiss away her pain.

Thank goodness she'd slipped away before he could act on that impulse. He needed to get hold of himself. He wasn't involved with Melender to romance her but to find out if the real murderer of Jesse Thompson was still out there.

The best remedy for wayward thoughts was work, so he resettled in his chair and picked up the folder labeled *Ruby Harman.* He selected the initial interview with Fairfax County Police mere hours after she and her husband had reported Jesse missing.

Ruby Harman Thompson, age 46, no profession
Resident address: 23014 Crescent Moon Drive, McLean, Virginia
Spouse: Quentin L. Thompson of McLean, Virginia
Children: Jesse, Jillian, stepson Jared
Location: Fairfax County Police Station in McLean, Virginia.
Present: Detective Mark Livingston, Detective Richard Delaney

LIVINGSTON: Mrs. Harman, where were you the night that Jesse disappeared?

RUBY HARMAN THOMPSON: We were at the McLean Country Club's annual charity fundraiser.

DELANEY: With your husband?

Ms. THOMPSON: Yes. We'd left Jesse and Jillian with Melender, like we'd done dozens of times before.

LIVINGSTON: When did you get home that night?

Ms. THOMPSON: After midnight. I was so tired, I didn't check on Jesse or Jillian, but went straight to bed.

LIVINGSTON: When did you realize Jesse was missing?

Ms. THOMPSON: I didn't know anything had happened until the morning when Isadora screamed. That's when we all realized Jesse wasn't in his crib.

DELANEY: Isadora Alonso is the children's nanny?

Ms. THOMPSON: Yes.

DELANEY: How long had Ms. Alonso been with you?

Ms. THOMPSON: Since Jillian's birth nearly four years earlier.

DELANY: Why didn't Ms. Alonso watch the children during the party?

Ms. THOMPSON: It was her night off.

Brogan skimmed the rest of the interview but gleaned nothing else interesting. Instead of continuing with Ruby's FBI interviews, he rummaged in the box to grab the nanny's folder. The same two detectives had interviewed Isadora. He skimmed past the preliminaries, stopping to read more slowly when the questions centered on the evening of the disappearance.

LIVINGSTON: Where did you go on your night off?

Ms. ALONSO: Night off? I didn't have a night off.

DELANEY: You weren't watching the children the night Jesse disappeared. Mrs. Thompson said it was your usual night off.

Ms. ALONSO: That's what she called it? Sure, I was not watching the children, but I was working just the same.

LIVINGSTON: Working where?

Ms. ALONSO: At the McLean Country Club.

LIVINGSTON: Did you work there often?

Ms. ALONSO: I didn't work at the club. I worked for Mrs. Thompson, and she needed me at the club to help with the fundraiser.

DELANEY: Why was that?

Ms. ALONSO: Someone with the catering company called in sick. Mrs. Thompson insisted that I go to the club to help. She promised to pay me extra.

DELANEY: You worked at the gala that Mr. and Mrs. Thompson went to that night?

Ms. ALONSO: Yes.

LIVINGSTON: What exactly did you do that night?

Ms. ALONSO: I picked up dirty plates and cups, napkins. People leave them all over the ballroom, hallways, porches, and gardens.

LIVINGSTON: So you were in and out of the ballroom all evening?

Ms. ALONSO: Yes.

LIVINGSTON: Did you see either one of them leave the premises at all during the evening?

Ms. ALONSO: Mrs. Thompson danced and danced. She was quite popular with the gentlemen because she was such a lovely dancer. Mr. Thompson spent most of his time talking. He did get a phone call, go outside, then come back, maybe an hour later. I don't know where he went. The weather was very nice for June, so many people went outside to enjoy the gardens at the club.

Brogan tapped the table, then opened up Google Maps on his phone to discover the distance between the country club and the Thompson home.

"Want a snack?" Melender slid a plate with apple slices and a small dish of hummus on the table before settling back in her chair.

"I don't think I've ever had apple slices dipped in hummus."

"I worked in the kitchen for a time, and the cook introduced me to this treat."

Brogan reached for an apple slice, dipped it in the hummus, then popped it in his mouth. As he munched, he traced the route from Crescent Moon Drive to the country club. Google Maps indicated the trip would take 10 minutes by car.

"Find something interesting?"

"I'm not sure." He ate another slice. "According to the nanny's interview, your uncle left the gala for around an hour. She thinks he was talking on the phone outside in the gardens."

"The club is close to the Thompson home." Melender blotted her lips on a napkin. "Quentin could have left the club and driven home."

"Did your attorney look into Quentin's business and finances? He obviously had enough to pay the kidnappers a million dollars in cash." He sipped his iced tea.

"I don't think my attorney did much of anything."

"That was Dan Stabe, right?"

She nodded. "Sometimes, I wish I had used some of Sudie's insurance money to pay for a lawyer other than a public defender, but by the time I realized Stabe wasn't mounting much of a defense, the trial was over."

"Most defense attorneys work with private investigators to dig into the background of the witnesses, key players, and so on. Did Stabe?"

"Not that I'm aware of." She tucked a strand of her hair behind her ear, drawing Brogan's attention back to how her hair had felt so soft, like a fine silk scarf. "Do you think that's significant?"

Yanking his thoughts back to the matter at hand, he made a note to follow up about the PI question. "Probably not, but it's something to ask Stabe. Have you had any contact with him since your release?"

"No. He stopped accepting my calls and letters years ago." She polished off the last apple slice. "Right around the time he joined the firm of Davis, Ramsey, and Stevens." Her eyes met Brogan's. "That's the firm—"

"—that represents Thompson Energy."

CHAPTER
TWENTY

Melender spooned sour cream on top of her chicken, peppers, and onions, then sprinkled cheese over it before wrapping up the tortilla. She'd grown to love fajitas since her release from prison because she could pick and choose what to put on them as opposed to simply getting whatever the cafeteria was serving.

Beside her, Brogan assembled his own meal, while Mr. and Mrs. Trent chatted about the sermon. Before she left for church, the Trents had invited Melender to lunch. To Melender's surprise, Brogan had shown up at the house as well, looking entirely too handsome in a bright green polo shirt and pressed khaki pants.

"Melender, what passage did your pastor preach on today?" Mrs. Trent passed the salsa to her husband.

Melender swallowed her bite. "He's preaching through Ephesians. Today's passage centered on Ephesians 4:32. 'Be kind to one another, tenderhearted, forgiving one another as God in Christ forgave you.'"

"You memorized that since this morning?" Brogan asked.

She laughed. "No, that was a favorite verse of my grandmother's.

She made me memorize it one summer when I kept getting into fights with my best friend, Robyn. Anytime we were bickering within earshot of Sudie, she would march up to us, plant her hands on her hips, and say, 'Ephesians 4:32, girls.' Then we had to repeat the verse. That usually cooled us off enough to forget what we were tussling about and move on to something else."

"She sounds like a wise woman," Mr. Trent said. "You must miss her."

Melender fought off the melancholy that nearly always accompanied memories of Sudie. "She was, and I do." She drew in a breath to hold the tears at bay. Since shedding so many yesterday all over Brogan's shirt, she had struggled to recover her equilibrium. Now she wanted to weep constantly. "That's why I'm glad you found and restored her dulcimer. Sudie said an instrument longs to be played and loved. If it is left to gather dust, forgotten on the shelf, it's like leaving its heart unsung."

"That's a beautiful way to put it," Mrs. Trent said in a soft voice. "There is something sad about an unwanted and unused instrument. Did your grandmother teach you to play the dulcimer?"

Melender nodded, bracing herself for Mr. Trent to make his request for her to sing at his gathering next month, but the older man took the conversation into another direction. "Do you happen to know where your ancestors came from before settling in Appalachia?"

"Sudie talked about our ancestry a lot, but I was young." She shrugged. "I didn't pay as close attention as I should have when she told her stories. But I do remember that the first of the Harman line —called Harne back then—were Ulster Scots, who migrated from Ireland to Pennsylvania, then down into the Appalachians in Virginia."

"Why would the Scots be in Ireland?" Brogan piled cheese on his second fajita.

Mr. Trent leaned forward. "The Ulster Scots, also called the Scots-Irish, came from lowland Scotland. They migrated to Ireland's

Ulster as part of a government-sanctioned planned colonization under James VI of Scotland and I of England." Mr. Trent filled another tortilla. "Eventually, the Scots-Irish emigrated to America, bringing with them their traditions and folk songs."

"And thus ends our history lesson for today." Mrs. Trent laughed as she winked at her husband.

Mr. Trent held up his hands. "I wasn't going to launch into a full discourse on the Ulster Scots, my dear."

"I didn't say you were," she rejoined, "but just in case, I wanted to forestall you." She turned to Melender. "Nolan has a tendency to think everyone's as fascinated by the history of American folk songs as he is and can sometimes forget he's not in a classroom."

The normalcy of the banter touched Melender deeply. She scrambled for something to add to the conversation before she started bawling. Again. Her emotions seesawed between elation about the progress being made on her case and sorrow for everything she had lost. Add in her struggles to readjust to life outside prison, and no wonder tears threatened to fall at the most inopportune times. Like last night, when Brogan had held her so gently. If she closed her eyes, she could recreate the sensation of his arms around her, one hand stroking her hair, his lips against her temple as he whispered words of comfort. But she wouldn't allow herself that luxury.

Returning to the table conversation, she said, "Sudie had an old Bible with the births, deaths, and marriages of our family going back generations. I brought it with me when I moved in with Ruby and Quentin, but I don't know what happened to it." She hadn't thought about the Bible in years. A sudden longing to hold it in her hands, to read the old King James verses and to know that centuries of Harmans had done the same overwhelmed her.

Mr. Trent leaned forward. "Do you happen to remember the earliest date in the family tree?"

Melender stared down at her plate as she concentrated on picturing the page in her mind. The funny lettering that turned "s" into "f" came into focus in her memory, then the first entry. "I think it was 1752 or 53." She squeezed her eyes shut, trying to dredge up the names. "The marriage of Clyde Harne to Mary Ewing, I think."

"Ah, that's the first wave of emigration to America by the Ulster Scots." Mr. Trent wiped his fingers on his napkin. "Your family has a rich heritage, if you have a Bible that records its history that far back."

"Sudie would tell stories about our ancestors. But I remember the songs more." She held her breath, wishing she hadn't mentioned the music. Mr. Trent would ask her to sing again, and she would feel obligated to comply, since she was staying at their house. She should have spent part of yesterday searching for a place of her own but had been focused on reading through the files instead.

"Melender, while you're staying with us, if you want to play your grandmother's dulcimer, you're more than welcome to." Mr. Trent exchanged a glance with his wife. "In fact, my wife and I have talked it over, and we'd like you to consider staying with us indefinitely. Frankly, after what Brogan told us about the break in, we're concerned about you being on your own. We'd like to help, and you could work on your files with Brogan anytime."

For a moment, Melender couldn't say anything. The generosity from near-strangers wrapped her like the hug from an old friend. "Thank you. I don't know what to say."

"Say yes," Brogan prodded, a twinkle in his eye.

With another glance at the Trents, Melender decided that using her free time to review the files would be better than finding a new place to stay, at least in the short term. "Thank you."

Mrs. Trent clapped her hands. "Wonderful. Now who wants peach pie with ice cream?"

BROGAN STARED DOWN AT THE POLICE INTERVIEW WITH ISADORA ALONSO, but he didn't read the words. Across from him, Melender bent her head to study another file. A tendril of hair had escaped her braid to rest on her cheek. His fingers itched to tuck it behind her ear just to feel the silkiness of the strand again. He needed to get a grip and concentrate on reading the files. At this rate, it would take them weeks to weed through all the interviews and other case notes. Mentally shaking his head, he returned to finish reading the police interview with the nanny.

DELANEY: Who was at the house when you left for the club?

Ms. ALONSO: Jared, Jillian, and Jesse.

DELANEY: What about Melender?

Ms. ALONSO: Miss Melender wasn't home that evening.

DELANEY: Mrs. Thompson said she left her niece in charge of Jillian and Jesse.

Ms. ALONSO: I don't know why she said that because Miss Ruby knew Miss Melender had a party that night with some friends from school.

LIVINGSTON: Mrs. Thompson said Melender didn't go out much.

Ms. ALONSO: She didn't usually, but she went to this one.

LIVINGSTON: What party was this?

Ms. ALONSO: It was the senior class party at the Rice house, the one on the street behind the Thompsons with the fountain in the front driveway.

DELANEY: You're sure this party was on the evening of June 14?

Ms. ALONSO: Yes. I helped her pick out a dress and fix her hair before I left for the club.

LIVINGSTON: Then who was watching the kids? Surely the Thompsons didn't leave a three-year-old and a one-year-old home alone.

Ms. ALONSO: Of course not. Miss Ruby told Jared that he was in charge until Melender came home.

Brogan jotted down the questions that flooded his mind after reading the transcript. Had the police followed up on the party to see if Melender had attended? What did Jared say about what unfolded earlier that evening? He decided to read Jared's statements next and reached into the box holding the transcripts. After flipping through the folders, he couldn't find Jared's. "Are you reading Jared's file?"

Melender glanced up. "Yep, I've got it here."

"The nanny says Ruby told her Jared was in charge of his siblings while you were at a graduation party. Did the police ask him about that?"

She shook her head. "Jared told the police he was home all night, but apparently Ruby said he came in around 1 a.m. Jared never said he was left in charge of the kids." She shuffled through some papers. "I'm about to read the FBI interview. Do you want me to read it out loud?"

"Sure." Brogan sat back to listen as Melender cleared her throat.

"This is with FBI Special Agents Theresa Reardon and Sheldon Martinez, who noted they interviewed Jared at home." She flipped a page. "They asked a bunch of the same questions the police did. Ah, here they ask about the disappearance."

AGENT MARTINEZ: Who do you think kidnapped Jesse?

MR. THOMPSON: How should I know? I certainly didn't.

AGENT CANE: How well did you get along with Jesse?

MR. THOMPSON: He was a toddler. You can't have much of a relationship with a toddler who can't even talk.

Melender skimmed through a couple of pages of background as the agents probed Jared's relationship with Jesse. On the top of page three, she slowed down.

AGENT CANE: He was your half-brother. Wouldn't that mean you'd have to share your inheritance?

MR. THOMPSON: You know how much money my father has?

AGENT MARTINEZ: Why don't you tell us?

MR. THOMPSON: He has millions tied up in property and businesses and has more money in overseas accounts than you'll ever see in your lifetime.

AGENT CANE: So you think the kidnappers knew that when they snatched Jesse?

MR. THOMPSON: It's not exactly a secret, although he's so stingy with money, you'd think he was flat broke.

AGENT MARTINEZ: Your father told us that he gives you a very generous allowance.

MR. THOMPSON: Generous by his standards, maybe, but me, I got expenses.

AGENT CANE: What kind of expenses?

When Melender stopped reading, Brogan leaned forward. "Is something wrong?"

She flipped the page over. "It just abruptly ends. There's a note. *Interview terminated by arrival of Mr. Thompson's attorney. No further questions permitted at this time.*"

"Is there another transcript in the file?" He tapped his fingers on the tabletop as Melender sorted through the papers.

"No, that's the last interview with Jared in these records." Her eyes met Brogan's. "Wonder why they didn't continue the interview later with the attorney present."

"A very good question." He pushed back from the table. "Interested in finding out?"

She closed the folder. "What did you have in mind?"

He checked the time on his phone. Three o'clock. "With any luck, he'll be home."

"Who?" Melender rose as well.

"Jared."

CHAPTER
TWENTY-ONE

M elender snapped the seatbelt buckle into place, trying not to let her excitement with a tinge of fear show. She hadn't seen her cousin since Jared's courtroom testimony. Then, she'd wanted to scream at him to tell the truth instead of the lies he spewed about Jesse's last night in the Thompson house.

Brogan touched her hand. "Are you sure you want to come?"

Drawing in a deep breath, she let it out slowly to calm her racing heart. "Yes." She met his gaze. The compassion in his eyes tipped the balance for her to share her thoughts. "I've read the court transcript so many times over the years, it began to feel like it wasn't my story, like it happened to someone else. Here, now, on our way to confront Jared face-to-face makes it real, and all the feelings from the arrest and trial have come rushing back."

"But this time, I'll be right beside you." His quiet words lifted some of the fear threatening to take hold of her again.

With a mental admonishment, she reminded herself that he wasn't truly on her side. She needed to keep that foremost in her mind before she started spinning stories of a happily ever after that could only reside in a fairy tale. "For the story."

Brogan cranked up the A/C to ward off the sticky afternoon heat but kept the vehicle in park. "For the story." He entered in an address to the car's GPS system. "But also because I believe there's more to what happened that night and after than the official version played out in court."

To avoid letting him see how much his agreement with her statement hurt, she focused her attention on the map now showing the location of 1816 N. Queens Lane, Arlington, Virginia, within the community of Colonial Village. She tightened her hands together on her lap.

"Melender."

Keeping her gaze on the screen even though the blinking blue dot wasn't moving along the outlined route, she didn't answer, unsure if her voice would be steady or not.

Instead of putting the car in gear, his hand covered both of hers. Such strong hands. The memory of Brogan stroking her hair yesterday while she cried brought a wave of desire to be in his arms again. But that was foolishness. He was a journalist looking for a story to bring him back into favor. She was using him just as much as he was using her. Hadn't she learned that lesson over and over in prison? That was how you survived—by making sure the balance of favors stayed as even as possible.

Brogan removed his hand, but before she could miss the contact, he cupped her chin to tip her head toward his. "That's not the whole truth."

The intensity of his gaze had her heart racing in an entirely different way. Not of fear, but of anticipation. The interior of his SUV suddenly shrank, his face mere inches away from hers. With difficulty, she tried to catch hold of the conversational thread. Something about not being the entire truth. Since he seemed to be waiting for a response, she queried, "It's not?"

"No." He slid his hand from her chin to the back of her neck, his fingers tangling with the hairs that had escaped her ponytail.

She licked her suddenly-dry lips to voice another question. "What did you leave out?"

His gaze dropped to her lips, lingering there. He shifted closer, so near his breath brushed against her face. "That it's not just the case I find fascinating."

"It's not?" Good grief, couldn't she think of something else to say? But her thoughts jumbled together at the sensation of his fingers massaging her neck and his darkening irises. She could barely remember why they were in the car, much less what they were talking about.

"You." He exerted slight pressure with his hand to draw her face toward him.

She willingly came, stopping right before their foreheads collided. Only a hair's breadth existed between them. "Me?"

"I've never met anyone like you." Passion dominated Brogan's deep blue eyes, turning them darker. She should identify the other emotion swirling in their depths but couldn't seem to care what it might be. "You're so different from other women your age."

His words slammed into her, pulling her back from the brink of whatever they might have fallen into as they reminded her of why she wasn't like women her age. "Being in prison for nearly two decades will do that to a person." She broke his hold on her, sitting back and away from him.

For a moment, Brogan didn't move, only let his hand drop to his side. "That's not what I meant at all." He closed his eyes and clenched his hands into fists, as if wrestling with himself. Several minutes passed with neither of them speaking.

Melender tried to regain her own equilibrium after the near kiss. For if she hadn't doused their emotions, she had no doubt Brogan would have touched his lips to hers. And while she ached to know the feel of his lips on hers, she had to keep her eye on the purpose for their collaboration. If she had any hope for a future, she had to solve the mystery of her past. Only then could she turn her thoughts to things like romance.

Wordlessly, Brogan put the car into gear and pulled away from the curb, the only sound being the GPS voice guiding them toward their destination.

~

BROGAN FOLLOWED THE GPS DIRECTIONS ALMOST ON AUTOPILOT, HIS BODY and mind still reeling from nearly kissing Melender. What had he been thinking? Even when he had been fudging sources to gain more notoriety as a reporter, he had never been tempted to cross that particular line. But a week after meeting Melender, he had trouble remembering she was a convicted felon, much less a source to a story that had the potential to catapult him back into favor in the journalism world.

When he turned right onto Rhodes Street, he scanned for a parking spot. After slipping into an open space, he cut the engine. When he'd found Jared's address, he had not been surprised the scion of Quentin Thompson lived in the Colonial Village complex. The location offered easy access to Northern Virginia and Washington, DC, as well as a vibrant nightlife. He had no doubt Quentin had footed the bill for the condo, considering his son's lack of work history.

"Are you ready?" Melender had her hand on the door handle.

"Yeah, let's go." He joined her on the sidewalk in front of a tall brick privacy wall that ringed six two-story red brick buildings. On the brick wall near the open entrance to a resident-only parking lot, a plaque proclaimed: "Colonial Village I is an historic landmark."

Melender fell into step beside him as they headed through the parking lot to the buildings on the far side. "Do you know what makes it historic?"

"Uh, actually, I do." Brogan cleared his throat, grateful for a safe topic to discuss. Maybe some small talk would diffuse the tension between them. It wouldn't do to have Jared pick up on that. They needed to be on the same page to be more effective in learning something new from her cousin. "This was part of a much bigger development built in the early 1930s as the first Federal Housing Administration-insured multi-family complex in this country. The buildings were also used as housing for many federal government workers during World War II."

Melender clapped her hands. "I'm impressed."

He kicked a stone off the sidewalk, grateful that the warmth in her tone suggested her willingness to move beyond what nearly happened in the car. "I read about it online when researching Jared's residence." Brogan glanced at his companion, noting how the light played off the silvery blonde of her hair. Without thinking, he raised his hand to touch a wayward strand.

She halted, and he stopped as well. "Brogan, what's going on?" Her eyes focused on the ground.

A denial sprang to his lips that nothing was going on, but he swallowed the lie. "I don't know."

The admission brought her head up and their eyes met. "Then I'm not wrong that you wanted to kiss me yesterday and just now in the car?"

The misery and hope in her eyes wrenched his stomach. The truth would complicate things, but he wouldn't let her think she was imagining his interest. "No, I admit I thought about kissing you. You are very tempting."

She blew out a breath, then ducked her head. "I have no experience with flirting or dating, so I'm sorry if I led you on or something."

Her words jabbed his heart. "Hey. Look at me." Melender slowly raised her face so he could search her eyes, now swimming with unshed tears. "You didn't do anything wrong. Okay?"

She nodded, but not before he caught of glimpse of the hurt she quickly masked before she headed toward the sidewalk that led away from the parking lot and into the complex. He hurried after her, catching up as she reached a junction on the path.

"Melender, wait."

She didn't move forward but didn't turn to face him.

He was making a hot mess of this, maybe because he'd been out of practice for so long. He'd dated regularly when he had been climbing the journalism ladder, but since his disgrace, he'd not had more than a handful of dates. Online dating held little appeal to him, and although he and Seth occasionally hit the bar scene, he never felt comfortable in the boozy, flirtatious atmosphere. "I'm sorry. I'm out of practice myself."

She swiveled to face him. "You are?"

He smiled sheepishly. "Believe it or not, I don't date much. In fact, I can't remember the last time I asked a woman to anything more than a causal coffee."

Melender didn't respond, only stared at him with those gorgeous blue eyes.

"The thing is, I don't want to hurt you." He shoved his hands into his pockets to keep from reaching for her. "I do find you very attractive, but, well..." He floundered to put into words why he felt the fierce need to protect Melender, even from himself.

"You're not sure if I'm guilty or not."

The statement jarred him into action. He grabbed her hand before she could turn away. "No, that's not it." As he rushed to convince her, he realized the truth behind the words. Somehow, he'd moved from thinking her guilty to innocent, even though the evidence had yet to firmly convict or exonerate. He opted for simplicity. "I believe you."

CHAPTER

TWENTY-TWO

Melender blinked rapidly, trying to process Brogan's words. "You do?"

Hope replaced the knot that had tightened in her stomach after the aborted kiss. She'd tried to act like it hadn't affected her but couldn't move past it to discuss architecture as if nothing had happened. Given her limited interactions with men outside of prison, she had no idea how to handle her attraction to Brogan. All she knew about dating she'd learned from sitcoms, movies, and books, which didn't exactly parallel real life.

He squeezed her hand. "I believe you."

For a moment, she basked in the knowledge that someone believed her innocent of Jesse's disappearance. Then she leaned forward and kissed his cheek, a quick, soft brush of her lips. "Thank you."

Melender's heart kicked up a notch as his eyes widened. A barking dog broke the spell as a panting Labrador retriever bounded past them after a Frisbee. Brogan stepped back, letting go of her hand. "I think building 1816 is to the left."

Melender shook off her disappointment at the dog's interruption and kept pace with Brogan as they approached the common, ground-floor entrance to 1816. They were here to question Jared, not canoodle, as Sudie used to say about courting couples. She needed to remember that proving her innocence would be the only way she'd have a chance at a normal life.

Brogan pulled open the main entrance door, then scanned the four downstairs units. "Number seven should be on the second floor at the back."

Following Brogan up the stairs, Melender mentally reviewed the interviews with Jared. On the landing, rock music permeated the walls of a condo.

"Someone likes to play their heavy metal loudly," Brogan said.

Melender stopped short. The notes formed a familiar song. Blue Oyster Cult's "Don't Blame the Reaper" thumped behind the door to number seven, but even without the confirmation, she'd have known the sound was coming from Jared's condo. He used to play that particular tune in his room with his buddies.

"Are you okay?"

She gave a jerky nod. She wasn't seventeen anymore. Brogan was with her. Nothing would happen. Blowing out a breath, she squared her shoulders. "I'm fine."

Before he could question her further, she marched up to number seven and knocked on the door. The music was even louder now that they were standing in front of the source. She pounded harder on the door.

The music ended abruptly, then the door flew open. "Whattya want?" Dressed in a threadbare tank top and baggy shorts, Jared stared at Melender. "You." His expression hardened.

Melender merely stared back, refusing to let her cousin intimidate her. "Hello, Jared. It's been a long time."

Jared grunted. "You've got some nerve showing up here."

Beside her, Brogan crowded near, his solid frame giving her strength. "Not as much nerve as you did when you lied to the police."

"What are you talking about? I haven't had any trouble with the police in years." Jared flicked his gaze from Melender to Brogan and back. "Who's he?"

"A friend. Can we come in? Or do you want your neighbors listening in on our conversation?" Melender had segued into the calm, cool, and collected persona she'd practiced over and over again in her cell. She'd imagined this encounter so often that it was almost like playing a part in a play she'd rehearsed a thousand times.

"Sure, why not." Jared pulled the door open the rest of the way and stepped aside.

Melender entered the condo, Brogan at her heels. Jared closed the door and stalked into the living area where a leather sectional sat in front of a huge flat screen television. A war-themed video game on pause. Jared hit the power button, and the image faded. Chin-cocking toward Brogan, he asked Melender, "Are you gonna introduce your friend?"

"Brogan Gilmore." Brogan extended his hand to Jared, who didn't even acknowledge the gesture. "I'm a reporter with the *Northern Virginia Herald.*"

Jared turned his attention back to her. "What do you want?"

"The truth."

"What truth?" Jared flopped down on the couch, stretching one of his arms across the back of the cushions. His right leg jiggled up and down.

"About what really happened to Jesse."

"You're the only one who knows that." Jared shook his head. "Why don't you own up to the truth and tell us where you buried Jesse?"

"Lying in court is a crime." Melender ignored his question.

Jared snorted. "I don't know what you're talking about."

"You said you weren't home the night Jesse went missing, but the nanny told the cops Ruby left you in charge of Jillian and Jesse." If Melender hadn't been watching Jared so closely, she might have missed the anger that passed over his face in a flash.

"If that was the case, why didn't they follow up?" Jared held up his hand in a motion that said he really didn't want her to answer. "I'll tell you why. Because they knew you killed Jesse."

Melender had been expecting Jared to lash out if she questioned his recollection of that night, but it still hurt to have those who had known her believe she'd hurt Jesse. While incarcerated, fellow prisoners, anonymous letter writers, and the press had called her a baby killer, but she'd been able to largely brush off their words. Now she schooled her face to betray none of her inner turmoil.

"What about the ransom money?" Brogan spoke in a casual voice. "They didn't tie that to Melender." He leaned forward, his gaze fixed on Jared. "I wonder who sent the kidnapping note and picked up the ransom?"

Jared wiped his hands down his shorts. "Got me."

"Some of it turned up, you know." Brogan continued in a conversational tone.

"Really? I hadn't heard." Jared tried to sound bored, but Melender detected a thread of fear inching into his voice.

"Twenty thousand dollars of the ransom money," Brogan said. "In the possession of a dead drug dealer called Snake."

Jared's expression didn't change. *He knows about Snake's death.*

"What's that got to do with me?" Jared shrugged.

"You knew Snake." Brogan's eyes narrowed. "In fact, I heard you and Snake were very close, that he was your supplier for a rather nasty drug habit."

Jared leaped to his feet. "I don't know what you're talking about. I don't know where you got your facts, but they're wrong. It's time you left." He went to the door and threw it open. "Now."

Melender stood. "You seem rather upset, Jared."

Brogan rose beside her.

"Yeah, I'm upset." Jared pointed a finger at her. "You have no right coming here, stirring up trouble. It was bad enough when Dad married Ruby and those two little brats came along. But you. You spoiled everything."

~

"WHY WOULD JESSE AND JILLIAN MESS THINGS UP FOR YOU?" THE SLIGHT tensing of Melender's shoulders told Brogan she wasn't as calm as her tone portrayed.

"How do you think?" Jared huffed. "The trust my grandfather put in place for any grandkids was now going to be split three ways."

"That must be a lot of money. You must have been angry." Melender sounded sympathetic to Brogan's ears.

"Yeah, I was." Her cousin threw her a sly look. "But not enough to kill Jesse, if that's what you're after."

"I've often wondered why you lied to the police about not being home that night." Melender continued.

"What do you mean?" Jared clenched and unclenched his hands.

Brogan shifted slightly in case Jared did more than posture his displeasure.

"You know exactly what I mean. I was at a graduation party down the street. Ruby left the kids in your care. You told me they were both asleep when I got home at eleven. Then the next morning, Isadora started screaming Jesse was gone." Her hands tightened slightly, the only sign she was agitated.

Brogan was so busy watching Melender and Jared's body language that he nearly missed the significance of her words, which fit with what the nanny had said in her interview.

Jared rolled his eyes. "Who did they believe when I told them you were left in charge of the kids all night long? Ruby and Quentin backed me up. You were the odd man out, little cousin. No one cared what happened to you."

Melender didn't flinched at the harsh words. Brogan didn't know whether to be impressed by her self-control or saddened that she must have endured far worse verbal abuse during her incarceration. "You admit you lied about being left in charge of Jesse and Jillian?" She pressed Jared.

"Sure, if it makes you feel better, I admit it." He leaned towards her. "So what? Not as if it matters anymore." He averted his eyes from hers.

"What was Jesse wearing that night?" Melender shifted the conversation.

Jared glared at her. "Woman, you are getting on my last nerve. How should I know that? It's been nearly twenty years ago."

"Surely you've thought about what your little brother was wearing the last time you saw him." Brogan interjected to divert Jared's attention from Melender.

"I haven't a clue what the kid was wearing, okay?" Jared swept his arm toward the open door. "Leave. Now."

Brogan moved to stand by Melender, who had gone stock still, her eyes focused not on Jared but on something past his shoulder. "Come on, let's go." He touched Melender's arm, but she shook off his touch.

Pointing a finger at Jared, she said, "You were doing drugs that night."

"What? No way." Jared shook his head.

Melender didn't give up. "You left the kids alone to meet Snake. He'd never come to the house. I heard you begging him to come once, but he was afraid of Quentin. So you used to meet him at the end of the driveway."

"That's old news." Jared linked his hands on top of his head. "I've been clean for years."

Brogan took a chance and asked the question building in his mind. "Then why were you meeting Snake the night he was killed?"

CHAPTER

TWENTY-THREE

"I told you to leave." Jared pulled out his cell phone. "I'm calling the police if you don't get out of my place in five seconds."

Brogan gripped Melender's arm. "We're going." He didn't like the fear in Jared's eyes. He hustled Melender down the stairs, ignoring her protests. They weren't likely to get anything else of use from Jared anyway.

Outside the building, Melender wrenched her arm away and whirled on him. "Why did you drag me out of there? He didn't answer your question about seeing Snake."

"He wasn't likely to." He nodded toward the parking lot. "Let's go to the car. No sense giving Jared and his neighbors a show."

"Fine." She stormed down the path, leaving him to catch up to her.

Once in his SUV with the AC running, he turned to her. "Listen, I'll call the detectives investigating Snake's murder and let them know about our conversation with Jared."

"Do you think they'll ask him if he saw Snake before the

murder?" Melender clicked her seatbelt into place, some of the anger draining out of her voice.

"I don't know."

"Will you tell them Jared lied about the night Jesse disappeared?"

The hope in her voice touched him, but he couldn't let her keep wishing for something that wasn't likely to happen. "Jared's story does differ from what he said eighteen years ago, but that doesn't constitute new evidence in the case."

"He lied." Melender folded her arms, her voice regaining strength. "Jared probably killed Snake because the dealer could confirm Jared left the house to buy from him."

"It doesn't mean Jared had anything to do with Jesse's—or Snake's—death."

"But it proves I was telling the truth about not being left in charge of the kids."

"Look, I know you see this as a big step in proving your side of the story." When she started to object, Brogan held up a hand. "I grant you it's significant no one followed up on the inconsistencies of his and the nanny's statements, but the fact remains a jury convicted you based on the evidence presented by the prosecutor. It will take more than a witness lying on the stand to officially re-open the case."

Melender blew out a breath, tension radiating from every line of her taut form. "Jared knows something he's not saying." She whipped around to face him, her blue eyes intent on his face. "And it's not that he slipped out to meet Snake. There's something else."

Brogan had also pegged Jared as hiding something. "What makes you think that?"

"He seemed very agitated about our asking about Jesse."

"It could be a normal reaction."

"Yeah, maybe." She didn't drop her gaze from his. "But the way he related those facts sounded rehearsed, like he practiced it. Besides, I noticed he had tiny beads of sweat on his upper lip and his micro-expressions showed fear."

"That's a lot of detail to notice." Brogan didn't bother to hide his amazement at her perception. Even he hadn't pinpointed exactly what made him think Jared was withholding something. He relied more on his gut and experience of interviewing hundreds of people over the years than science.

"You mean because I'm not a trained law enforcement agent, it's amazing I could pick up on such subtle changes in a person's behavior?" The words, while spoken in a light tone, carried the weight of steel.

"Whoa." How an innocent observation on his part triggered such an outburst, he hadn't a clue. "I wasn't—"

"Weren't you?" She cut across his words. "I might not have had all the educational advantages of a traditional college, but I didn't twiddle my thumbs behind bars either. I took whatever courses I could, and I studied hard."

"Hey, I didn't—"

"Yes, you did." A becoming flush dotted her cheeks, but the spark in her eyes doused any tender feelings he had in the moment. "You said you believed me, but that could have been a ploy to get me to open up. Maybe you're just like all the rest of the journalists who have hounded me over the years, after a sensational story to propel you to fame and fortune."

Brogan's own anger rose to the surface, fueled by the contempt in her voice. Ignoring the nudge that warned him against impetuous rebuttal, he plunged in. "I've been upfront with you from the start. If anything, you've been using me to further your own ends."

"And what ends would that be?"

Her voice had dropped, along with her head. Something about her posture spoke of loneliness and uncertainty. Still he let frustration with the case and conflicted feelings for Melender override the voice that cautioned him to respond with gentleness.

"I understand you want to prove your innocence, but to find someone else to blame for Jesse's kidnapping and death so you won't have to own up to any part in it is wrong."

185

For a long moment, Melender just stared out of the windshield. She didn't say a word, the whiteness of her face a stark contrast to its earlier flush of anger. She sucked in a deep, shuddering breath, and squeezed her eyes closed. A single tear edged out as if wrung from a washcloth.

In the growing silence, his words hung between them like a chasm too big to bridge. He'd regretted the words as soon as he had uttered them. *Lord, forgive me.* An apology formed on his lips, but he couldn't find his voice because part of him still wasn't sure she was completely innocent in the case. He did believe her, but he was beginning to wonder if she had repressed the memories of what happened that night and truly thought she had nothing to do with Jesse's disappearance.

"I'd like to go back to your uncle's now, please." The request seemed to come from a different person than the one who minutes before angrily demanded he see her side of things. Now her voice hesitated, and she sounded tired, as if someone had deflated her like a tire losing its air.

At a loss as to how to verbally respond, he pulled out of the parking space, driving back to Fairfax in silence. An eighties music station on Sirius XM filled the void of conversation and kept at bay his insistent heart commanding him to make things right with her.

BROGAN FOUND SPACE AT THE CURB NEAR THE END OF THE TRENT'S BLOCK TO park. Although incensed by Melender's demand to get out of the vehicle once she'd spotted the house, he refused to be sucked into another conflict with this beautiful but headstrong young woman.

After responding to a couple of work-related texts and calls on his cell phone, he dialed into his desk phone. Fallon insisted all reporters have a published number that rang to the *Herald* offices. Brogan had only one phone message, time stamped at eleven a.m.

that morning from former FBI Special Agent Stanley Presley, who simply stated his name and asked for a return call.

Puzzled, Brogan punched in the number Presley had given. The call was answered on the second ring. "Stanley Presley."

"Hi, it's Brogan Gilmore with the *Herald* returning your call."

"Mr. Gilmore, I hear you're looking into the Jesse Thompson case."

"How did you know that?"

"Let's not waste time with superfluous questions. I think you might like to hear what I have to say about the matter."

Brogan hadn't considered his query gratuitous but let it go in favor of setting up a meeting with Presley. No sense in antagonizing the man beforehand by pressing how the agent found out about Brogan and Melender's actions. "I'm free now. Where would be a convenient place for us to meet?"

"The Starbucks in Kamp Washington near the HoneyBaked Ham store. Can you be there in fifteen minutes?"

"I'll be there." Good thing Brogan was less than ten minutes away from the location. As he drove to the destination, he tried to tamp down his excitement over whatever Presley had to say and whether it would be another chink in the case against Melender or drive another nail of guilt in her coffin.

"She came to see you?" Quentin held the phone tightly to his ear and angled his body away from Ruby, who reclined on a chaise lounge beside their pool.

Jared mumbled something his father didn't catch, then said more clearly, "She and that reporter, Brogan something. She asked me why I'd lied in court, pointing out that what I said differed from what was in the police transcript."

Quentin firmed his jaw as Jared berated Melender in colorful language. Underneath his son's tirade, he smelled fear. "No one's going after you, not on a case that has gone to trial with a successful conviction. Melender's served her time, so now she's free to stir things up. She's probably nitpicking these kinds of anomalies to deal with what she did."

Jared exhaled into the phone. "I checked one of those Virginia law sites online, and there's no statute of limitations on perjury. I could be sent to prison."

"That's only if a prosecutor brought charges against you." Quentin didn't want to reveal to his son why he knew that tidbit but doubted Jared would even ask.

"Is everything all right, Quentin?"

Quentin turned to see Ruby, her large sunglasses hiding her expression. He placed the phone on his chest to reply. "Just a business matter, my love. No need to worry."

"I'm going inside. It's too hot today." She rose and walked into the house.

All he had done had been to protect his wife, to give her a life of ease after her impoverished upbringing. And she'd repaid him with loyalty, love, and two beautiful children.

Replacing the phone to his ear, he reiterated, "The district attorney's office isn't going to bother with perjury charges. Not after all these years and definitely not on a closed case."

His words must have mollified Jared, who merely grunted, then said a quick goodbye. Quentin tapped the phone against his hand as he reviewed the conversation in his mind. His gut screamed that Jared's uneasiness went beyond a fear of being charged with perjury, which meant something else about Melender's asking questions had frightened his son. As he punched in a number, he moved off the pool deck and onto the covered patio to escape the sun's brutal rays.

"Raines," the man barked.

"I have someone else I want you to follow."

"Name?"

"Jared Thompson, my son." Quentin didn't like spying on his firstborn, but he had to find out more about what was troubling him.

"Address?" If Raines was surprised that Quentin wanted his son under observation, his tone didn't show it. Family members asking for surveillance on other family members was likely a large part of a PI's business.

Quentin provided the information, then hesitated before asking his final request. As he disconnected the call, he questioned whether he wanted to know what Raines might uncover. Quentin headed to the house, certain that whatever the private investigator might find out couldn't hurt his family as much as Jesse's disappearance.

"So the last time you saw Melender was nearly four years ago?" Brogan sat across from former FBI agent Stanley Presley, thankful to have snagged a corner table at the busy Starbucks.

"Yes. At that time, she'd been in prison fourteen years, with at least three more to go to fulfill the rest of her sentence." The older man leaned forward. "Did you know she turned down parole?"

"What?" Brogan wasn't sure he'd heard the man correctly. No prisoner in her right mind would ditch a chance for freedom.

"Yep, she sure did. My partner and I talked to the warden before we interviewed Harman. The warden—this was at Fluvanna Correctional Center in Troy, Virginia, before Harman was moved to Deep Creek Correctional Facility—said Harman had been eligible for parole a few months before. The warden figured Harman would get it, too, what with her model behavior and exemplary record. Not one fight with fellow prisoners, which, considering the company she'd been keeping, was rather impressive. But when the parole interviewer asked her if she was ready to be released, Harman replied she wanted to serve her full sentence. The interviewer wrote her exact words. 'I'd rather finish my sentence and be beholden to no one than be freed early and have to report to someone.'"

Brogan shook his head and took a sip of his coffee. "That's quite an amazing statement."

"I figured it was also smart. Once she's served her time, with no parole hanging over her, there would be no leverage to make her tell where the body's buried, now is there?" Presley leaned back in his chair. "She couldn't be tried for the same crime and couldn't be compelled to give up what she knew."

Brogan still struggled with picturing Melender in a prison garb.

"My boss worked the original kidnapping case, and the missing body still bothered her. Whenever she had a couple of agents in her division between cases, she would authorize a trip to see Harman. My boss figured there was always a chance Harman might spill her secrets."

Brogan stayed silent as the other man picked up his coffee.

Presley met Brogan's gaze. "But as soon as Harman walked in the room and pulled out a chair to sit across from us, I knew she was a tough cookie and wouldn't giving up anything."

"You sound as if you admire her moxie." Admittedly, Brogan had been taken in by her dark blue eyes, but he wasn't a trained law enforcement officer.

"You've met her. Melender Harman was a beautiful woman even in prison."

"Is that your professional opinion?" For some reason, hearing the older man describe Melender as beautiful got under Brogan's skin.

Presley chuckled. "Yes, and before you get worked up, I wasn't attracted to her. I've been very happily married for thirty-five years, and my missus would have my head on a platter if I even looked at another woman with lust in my heart."

Brogan wasn't sure he believed the former agent or not, but he let it go. "Did anything about her surprise you?"

"That one of the inmates hadn't taken a knife to her mane of hair and sliced it clean off. After all, inmates don't look kindly upon prisoners convicted of crimes against children."

Brogan suppressed voicing his concerns over what Melender had experienced behind bars. To recover his emotional balance, he steered the conversation back to the actual interview. "What happened when you saw her?"

"Nothing."

"What does that mean?" He should have sprung for a larger coffee. Maybe the extra caffeine would sharpen his brain and help to make sense of the information from Presley.

Presley smiled. "It means she studied our badges, gave a little half smile, folded her arms, and simply waited us out. It's rare to come across anyone who could keep quiet for a solid hour. My partner, Belinda Carlisle, tried to engage her in girl talk, but Harman ignored her."

Brogan considered what little information Presley had given him. "All you've told me is Melender's reaction to visits from the FBI during her incarceration. If you don't mind my asking, why did you want to meet with me?"

"I heard you were looking into the case."

"So you said when you called me." Brogan's impression that this was a wild goose chase growing with every minute.

The other man regarded him steadily. "I've read the entire FB file of this case more than once because I thought justice hadn't been served."

"You think Melender's innocent."

"Despite the circumstantial evidence, my gut tells me that Melender Harman had nothing to do with whatever happened to that little boy." The other man drained his coffee. "If I were looking into this again, I would start with the family."

"You think someone in the Thompson household is behind Jesse's disappearance?" Brogan wouldn't be surprised if a relative—father, mother, sister, brother—harmed their own flesh and blood. He'd written too many stories over the years about the awful things family did to one another.

The former agent shook his head. "That I don't know. What I do know is that Quentin is protecting someone. Whether it's because that someone was directly involved with whatever happened to Jesse..." He let the thought trail off.

"That's what you want me to find out."

Presley stood, his gaze on Brogan. "I think it's high time Ms. Harman had someone in her corner who will fight for her."

CHAPTER

TWENTY-FOUR

As Melender entered the Trent home, she breathed in the aroma of fresh bread and chicken with a hint of rosemary and thyme. The scent took her back to her childhood, standing on a stool in front of the old wood-burning cook stove in Sudie's kitchen to stir the simmering soup. Tears pressed her eyelids as a fierce longing for her grandmother's warm embrace shuddered through her. In the kitchen, Mrs. Trent wiped her hands on a towel. A large pot bubbled on one of the burners and bread cooled on the counter.

"Melender, I thought you'd be gone all afternoon." Mrs. Trent greeted her with a smile.

"We finished earlier than expected." Melender left out that she'd spent the past forty-five minutes walking around the neighborhood to settle her thoughts about Brogan before entering the house. Now, to avoid more questions about her outing with Brogan, she redirected the conversation to safer ground. "Something smells good."

"My grandmother's chicken soup recipe, guaranteed to sooth away any sickness in one mouthful." Mrs. Trent lifted the lid and stirred the pot's contents with a long-handled wooden spoon.

Melender inhaled deeply. "Too bad it doesn't provide a balm to the soul as well."

Mrs. Trent replaced the lid and set the utensil on a cat-shaped spoon rest. "It's been known to calm the mind." She shot Melender a knowing glance. "Is my nephew giving you a hard time?"

Melender ducked her head at the straightforward question. How on earth did she answer that without revealing more than she wanted to?

"Ah, I can see by the look on your face he has." Mrs. Trent chuckled as she wiped up a spill by the stove. "I'm not surprised. You're as nervous as a cat on a hot tin roof and Brogan, well, he's as jumpy as a caged tiger."

That was one way to sum up the situation. Curiosity compelled her to question Brogan's aunt. "What has he told you?"

"About you?"

Melender nodded as she leaned against the counter.

"Not much, beyond the basic facts." Mrs. Trent plugged in the electric kettle. "How about I make us a cup of tea?"

"That sounds lovely. Let me wash up first." Melender ducked downstairs, glad for a few minutes to regain her composure. She had been so sure that catching Jared in a lie about the night Jesse disappeared would be enough evidence to propel a deeper look into the case. But now that she thought about it, Brogan was right. She needed hard proof that someone else committed the crime before law enforcement would take another look at the kidnapping.

When she came back upstairs, Mrs. Trent was pouring boiling water into a tea pot.

Not sure she was ready for a tête-à-tête with Brogan's aunt but wanting to hear more about Brogan, Melender seized on a diversion. "I noticed you have a lot of what look like journals on the shelves of the bookcase at the foot of the stairs. Are those family writings?"

"Oh, no." Mrs. Trent smiled as she set sugar and cream on the counter. "As you know, my husband's work is collecting and studying American folk songs. That's part of his collection of diaries written by Appalachian women."

At the mention of Appalachia, Melender pictured the soaring cliffs of the majestic mountain range. All these years later, she could still tick off the states the range touched after memorizing them in school: Kentucky, Tennessee, Virginia, Maryland, West Virginia, and North Carolina. Homesickness washed over her like a breeze on a peak.

"Brogan said you grew up in the mountains."

She nodded. "Every morning, I'd greet the sun rising slowly over the top of a peak. In the glooming of the day, I could hear the nightingale's song. It was my home until Sudie died."

"You must miss her very much."

The soft acknowledgement of her still-sharp grief nearly loosened Melender's hold on her emotions. "I do." She cleared her throat. "Sudie left school at age nine when her father was killed in a mining accident, so she never read or wrote well. But she could tell stories like no one else in the hollow. I loved to listen to her as we shelled peas on the front porch or canned a batch of her famous huckleberry preserves."

"She raised you?" Mrs. Trent passed Melender a mug, steam wafting up like fog on a mountain.

Melender held the cup as the memories flooded her mind. "My mother died when I was three. Complications from childbirth. My little brother died too."

Mrs. Trent asked other questions, drawing out Melender's family history and upbringing. Sudie had schooled Melender well in their family heritage. During the early years of the nineteenth century, her family had settled in the foothills in the Blue Ridge section of the range. Some of her ancestors had even been displaced when Shenandoah National Park had been cobbled together. Her home sat deep in Maple Hollow just outside the park borders.

"When Sudie died, my only living relative was my aunt, my father's younger sister," Melender said. "At sixteen, the Commonwealth of Virginia didn't deem me old enough to be on my own. I didn't realize until later that I could have petitioned the court for emancipation, but by that time..." She didn't want to reveal she learned that tidbit of information in the prison library.

"Have you gone back to visit since your release?"

Melender shook her head. Even though the mountains called, were a part of her, she hadn't dared venture back. Her years in prison had not diminished the burning need to return to her heritage or her longing for the quiet stillness of the forest.

Staring at the dregs of her tea in the bottom of her cup, Melender struggled to put into words why she couldn't go home, not yet. "There's something pure and clean about the mountains that I can't contaminate with a felony conviction."

She shook her head. "Until I find out the truth of what happened to Jesse, I can't go home. The mountains should be used as a sanctuary, as a resting place, not as a hiding place. If I go back before this is completely resolved, the peace that the mountains give won't be mine. It'll be a facsimile of the rest I'm longing to have."

Looking Mrs. Trent square in the eye, she added, "That's why I won't stop until I untangle the lies and bring Jesse home. Only then can I return to the mountains."

Brogan's heart sank as Fairfax County Police Detective Mark Livingston exhaled loudly into the phone.

"Can't do it," Livingston said. "The district attorney will not want to press charges against Jared Thompson for perjury. His testimony supported what others said, but it wasn't crucial to the conviction."

"That's what I thought." Brogan held the phone to his ear with his shoulder as he opened the car door. "But that's not the only reason I called you."

"If it's related to the closed Thompson case, I don't have time."

"Jared knew Snake."

Silence. Believing the detective hadn't hung up, he went on. "Snake was Jared's supplier around the time of the incident. On a hunch, I asked Jared why he met with Snake the night the man was killed."

"What did Jared say?"

"He insisted we leave. Cleary the question scared him. A lot." Brogan started the car. "Given some of the ransom money was found on Snake, I thought you might like to know."

"Thanks for the tip. Gotta go."

He'd planted the seed and hoped Livingston would water it. Jared was hiding something, but it could be nothing more than he had returned to his old drug habit. Brogan laid his phone on the front seat, then maneuvered out of the parking lot.

But his gut screamed that there was a lot more to the Jared's fear, one that had the potential to blow the case against Melender wide open.

BROGAN TUCKED IN HIS SHIRT WITH ONE HAND AS HE SEARCHED AROUND FOR his notebook on his desk. It had to be here somewhere. Fallon had requested an update on the Thompson case pronto, and his boss didn't like to be kept waiting.

Seth rested his forearms on top of the short cubicle wall that separated their workspaces. "Anything new on the ransom money?"

"Nothing concrete yet." When he spied his notebook under a pile of folders, he grabbed and stood. "Can't talk now. Fallon called me in for a meeting five minutes ago."

Outside Fallon's office, his boss's assistant looked up from her keyboard. "You're late. He's waiting for you."

"I know." He held up the notebook. "Couldn't find my notes." Better gauge the boss's mood before entering his office. "Kendra, how's the temperature this morning?"

"Sunny with a chance of isolated thunderstorms." She shot him a smile. "But I'm prepared for all kinds of weather."

"Appreciate it." Brogan headed toward Fallon's closed office door and knocked once before entering the room and shutting the door behind him.

Seated behind his desk, Fallon glanced at his watch, then motioned for Brogan to take the chair opposite him. "Catch me up on the Thompson investigation."

Brogan recapped what they'd gleaned from the files and interview with Jared Thompson, plus his conversations with Quentin, the detectives, and the former FBI agent.

"What's your take on Jared Thompson?" Fallon walked a pencil across his knuckles, flipping the item with causal indifference, his trademark thinking stance.

"Thompson admitted to lying to the police about his actions the night Jesse disappeared, but that's not what concerned him the most. He got agitated when we brought up Snake's murder. I've interviewed enough people to know when I've touched a nerve."

"Snake was Jared's longtime drug dealer, correct?"

Brogan nodded. "When I asked him about seeing Snake before the man's death, Jared sidestepped the question and threw us out of the apartment."

"Hmm." Fallon tapped the pencil on his cluttered desk. "What do you think of Harman?"

Brogan didn't want to touch that, but Fallon's expression warned that his boss wouldn't let him sidestep the question. Fallon had told Brogan his first day on the job that he expected full honesty from his reporters. Given Brogan's own shaky background, he had to be even more scrupulous.

"I, uh." Brogan struggled to find the right words to diplomatically reveal his thoughts about Melender. "She's maintained her innocence throughout everything—her arrest, trial, and incarceration. Now that she's out, she's very determined to find out what happened to Jesse."

"Bottom line. Do you think she's guilty as charged?"

"That's the million-dollar question, isn't it?" Brogan scrubbed his face. "I think she has valid points in favor of her innocence." He picked his way through the words like a soldier clearing a minefield, wanting to give Fallon the truth but not the whole truth of his conflicted feelings for Melender. "Her lawyer did the bare minimum as far as fair representation, and he didn't challenge any of the witnesses or circumstantial evidence presented at trial. Even I could see places in the transcript where her attorney ought to have followed up. Are there enough points in her favor to give a jury reasonable doubt? I couldn't say, but it's odd that a couple of years after the trial, her defense attorney ends up at the law firm for Thompson Energy."

"Have you spoken with this attorney?"

"Not yet. I wanted to finish going through the FBI and police files first."

Fallon leaned back in his chair, steepling his fingers as he regarded Brogan, who tried not to squirm under the scrutiny. Could Fallon see that Brogan had lost his objectivity when it came to Melender?

His boss depressed the intercom call button. "Kendra? Please ask Seth to come to my office right away." He released the button upon Kendra's acquiescence but didn't reveal why he'd called for Seth.

Brogan still didn't have a clue as to what Fallon had in mind when, minutes later, Seth knocked on the door of Fallon's office.

"Have a seat, Seth. I think you know Brogan's been looking into the Jesse Thompson kidnapping," Fallon said.

"Yes. Good timing, too, because it's been in the news again since a chunk of the ransom money was found on that murdered drug dealer," Seth replied.

Fallon looked from Seth to Brogan, as if trying to make up his mind about something. "Right." The editor pointed a finger at Brogan. "As of now, you're off your usual beats."

Brogan's heart sank. Despite his best efforts, it sounded like

Fallon was firing him. He'd fallen in love with journalism all over again, writing about the little moments—and some big ones—in the lives of Fairfax City and county residents. While this job had morphed from a steppingstone back to the big leagues and into a real career move, he was now terminated.

Fallon turned to Seth. "What are you working on?"

His colleague recounted his current assignments to Fallon, while Brogan tried to school his face to not show the disappointment building inside him.

"Brogan?"

At Fallon's query, Brogan snapped back to attention. "Yes?"

"I want you to bring Seth onboard. I think this has potential to be something really big."

"You want us to..." Brogan nearly shook his head. Surely he hadn't heard his boss right.

"Reinvestigate the Thompson case." Fallon finished for him. "Obviously, details were overlooked if ransom money is turning up nearly two decades later. You already have an in with Harman, and with Seth's assistance, you'll be able to go through the material quicker."

Brogan couldn't believe it. He wasn't being fired. In fact, Fallon was giving him carte blanche to dig deep into the case. "Thank you, sir."

His editor dismissively waved his hand. "Don't thank me. Unearth the truth and write the kind of investigative piece I know you're capable of writing."

Brogan swallowed the unexpected complement with gratitude. "I will."

"I expect daily updates. Now get to work." Fallon turned to his computer.

Brogan and Seth moved as one to the door. Brogan had just pulled it open when Fallon spoke again. "The paper can spare you two for a week to work on this assignment. Use your time wisely."

TWENTY-FIVE

"Jared Thompson?"

Jared glanced up from his phone. An older man with slightly familiar features and a woman a few years younger than himself stood beside his table at the De Clieu coffee shop in downtown Fairfax. "Who's asking?"

The woman reached into her pocket and produced a badge. "I'm Detective Lauren Collier, and my partner, Detective Mark Livingston, with the Fairfax County Police Department. We'd like to ask you a few questions about TJ Williams."

At the mention of Snake's real name, Jared didn't react outwardly, keeping his expression puzzled. "Who?"

Livingston pulled out a chair and sat down across from Jared while his partner remained standing. "If you want to play the I-don't-know-anyone-named-Williams game, that's fine. We'll just move what could have been a quiet conversation to the police station." The lines on the detective's face hardened. "What's it going to be?"

Jared fiddled with his phone. He'd rather not be hauled in for formal questioning, but he also wanted to distance himself from Snake.

"Now that I recall, I might have known someone named TJ, but he went by the nickname Snake. Is that the same person you're talking about?"

The expression on Livingston's face didn't change. "One and the same."

"Wasn't this TJ character murdered recently?" Jared was pleased with how casual the question came out. The tension that had been mounting in his neck and shoulders since the detectives introduced themselves dissolved. They had nothing to tie him to Snake recently—he'd made sure of that.

"Yes, he was," Livingston said. "You admit to knowing TJ Williams, aka Snake?"

"Yeah, I did, a long time ago." Jared paused, debating how truthful to be and deciding a partial truth should satisfy their inquiries. "I used to buy drugs from him, mostly prescription pain pills."

"When was the last time you saw him?" Livingston leaned back in his chair, his tone less adversarial.

"I don't know. Maybe fifteen, sixteen years ago?" Jared shrugged. "As I said, it's been a long time."

"So you wouldn't have been at Van Dyke Park's soccer fields last Wednesday?" Collier asked.

Jared's heart rate accelerated. "No, I don't have kids." That was a safe answer.

"This would have been at night, around eight," Livingston clarified.

"I was home at eight," Jared said.

"Can anyone vouch for you?" Collier's tone warned him she already knew what he would say.

"No, I was alone." Jared looked from one detective to the other. "What's this all about?"

A faint smile crossed Livingston's lips. "I'm glad you asked. We have three witnesses who said they saw a man bearing your description pass them as they left Snake on Wednesday about that time."

Jared snorted. "They were probably buying from him, so how reliable is what they say?"

"Reliable enough that we're talking to you." Collier's calm voice grated Jared's nerves.

"Why were you meeting with Snake if you've been clean for years?" Livingston asked.

"I wasn't." Jared had had enough. He didn't have to talk to them, a fact his father's pricey lawyer had hammered into him years ago. "I've got to go." He pushed to his feet.

Livingston stood, his lanky frame filling the space between Jared and the path to the door. "I think that's an excellent idea." He nodded to his partner, who placed a hand on Jared's arm. "We should continue this conversation down at the station."

QUENTIN ENDED THE CALL WITH HIS PRIVATE EYE, THEN UTTERED AN expletive. Raines had contacted Quentin as the detectives escorted Jared from a local coffeeshop to their unmarked vehicle. The private eye had eavesdropped on their conversation with Jared, who would be questioned further about his relationship with a dead drug dealer.

His son had been hiding something when Quentin stopped by Jared's place after Ruby's confession about the break-in at Melender's apartment. Now a sickening feeling washed over him as exactly what that something might be coalesced in his mind. How had one act of mercy spawned such a mess?

"Quentin?"

He whirled to see Ruby standing in the doorway of the kitchen in her tennis whites. "Off to play a set with Alice?"

"Yes. You're home early today."

"I'll be heading back to the office soon." After he called a lawyer for Jared.

His wife came closer. "You look tired." She laid a cool hand on his cheek.

Closing his eyes, Quentin allowed her presence to comfort him.

"I'm not as fragile as you think, you know."

At Ruby's softly spoken words, he snapped open his eyes to gaze directly into hers. Her delicate features hid a core of steel he sometimes forgot ran through her. "You are one of the strongest women I know."

A slight smile played on her full lips. "Yet you still feel the need to protect me."

He encircled her, drawing her close to feel the length of her body pressed against his. "That's because I love you more than life itself."

The cliché didn't make her laugh like it usually did. Instead, she narrowed her eyes. "Then why are you keeping things from me?"

With a forced chuckle, he tried to steer the conversation away from dangerous waters. "Can't a man have a few secrets from his wife? I let you have yours."

"There are secrets and there are secrets. The ones I'm keeping have nothing to do with our marriage, and if you really wanted to know, you'd ask." Rising on her tiptoes, Ruby pressed a light kiss on his lips. "However, I can see that you're not ready to tell me, and I'm running late."

When she'd extracted herself from his embrace, she sauntered to the door, swinging her hips in that way of hers that had driven him insane with desire when they'd first met. The familiar feeling rushed through his body as she paused to throw him a look over her shoulder. Rather than the coquettish glance he'd been expecting, sorrow tinged her face. Then she was gone.

Quentin stayed exactly where she'd left him for a long moment. Would she still love him if she got the answers about Jesse she sought? His phone buzzed, breaking into his reverie, and he answered without checking caller ID.

"I thought you were smart."

The caller sounded puzzled, yet Quentin caught the pulse of anger behind the words. He waited for the man to continue.

"What does your son know?"

Quentin had been half expecting the man to contact him since he'd learned of Jared's encounter with the detectives. "Nothing."

"We're beyond nothing. You told me you had nothing to do with the ransom, and yet twenty thousand dollars of marked money turns up in the pockets of your son's former drug dealer. That's something."

Quentin didn't want to acknowledge even to himself Jared might have sent the ransom note. That his own flesh-and-blood had callously capitalized on Jesse's disappearance.

"Now what are you going to do about it?"

Quentin had the answer ready. "Here's what I had in mind." As he relayed the details, he feverishly hoped it would be enough misdirection to keep his family from disintegrating even further.

"They're questioning Jared Thompson in connection with Snake's murder." Seth propped his shoulder against the edge of Brogan's cubicle. "Looks like your phone call to the detective paid off."

"Good." Brogan had brought Seth up to speed after Fallon's directive. Then Seth checked with one of his police sources to see if Livingston had followed up on Brogan's call about Jared. "Did your contact have any other details?"

"Only that forensics matched Jared's fingerprints to one of the bills."

Brogan stared at his colleague. "That's called burying the lead."

Seth grinned. "Yeah, I know. But it was totally worth it to see the expression on your face."

"Jared must have had something to do with the kidnapping." No evidence had tied Melender with the kidnapping, so the prosecution hadn't brought it up at trial. Neither had her defense attorney, which was strange. With the lack of proof Melender had anything to do with the ransom pickup that had taken place while she was being questioned by police, the kidnapping aspect could have cast reasonable doubt onto her guilt in Jesse's disappearance.

"Which means Harman did not." Seth snagged a desk chair from an unoccupied cubicle and scooted closer to Brogan. "What I don't understand is how, if she wasn't tied to the kidnapping, Harman was convicted of murder. They never found his body."

"I think it boiled down to a couple of things." Brogan rubbed his chin. "First, her court-appointed attorney did squat to help her. In reading the transcript, it's like he was going through the motions to give her the appearance of a fair trial. Second, the prosecutor hammered home the theory that Melender killed Jesse because of jealousy and resentment at being constantly asked to take care of her young cousins. Her aunt, housekeeper, Jared, uncle—they all said she wasn't happy about the arrangement. Jesse could be a fussy toddler who often didn't asleep through the night."

"Where's the attorney now?"

"In a cushy job at the law firm representing Thompson Energy." Brogan let that sink in. "I believe it's time we paid Dan Stabe a visit, don't you?"

Seth grinned. "I was just thinking the same thing."

TWENTY MINUTES LATER, BROGAN AND SETH WALKED INTO THE LOBBY OF the building that housed Davis, Ramsey, and Stevens. Brogan checked his phone for the time. One-thirty. With any luck, most of the office staff would have headed out to lunch, leaving fewer people to observe their entrance. Seth had called Stabe's assistant to ask about an appointment in the afternoon and been told the attorney had no openings. Brogan surmised that meant he was in the office but unavailable.

As they rode the elevator to the eleventh floor, Brogan went over their simple plan of attack in his mind. Seth would try to sweet-talk the receptionist to find out if Stabe might be holed up at his desk. If so, they'd ambush Stabe. Brogan put their chance of success at less than ten percent, but hoped they could catch the attorney by surprise. The elevator doors opened, and he caught sight of the receptionist. "Oh, no."

The middle-aged woman manned her reception desk like the captain of a war ship. Her dark brown hair liberally streaked with grey was pulled into a bun at the nape of her neck. Pearl studs in her ears, a single strand of pearls around her neck, and round wire-rimmed glasses completed the austere picture.

"Oh, ye of little faith," Seth muttered under his breath as he strode toward the desk.

Brogan glanced down at his phone to mime concentration on the small screen while trying to monitor Seth's progress with the receptionist. To Brogan's astonishment, within seconds, Seth had the woman laughing, then shaking her head as she clicked on her keyboard. A few more minutes of conversation, then Seth nodded once. He motioned to Brogan to join him at the desk.

"Brogan, this delightful woman is Audrey Evans." Seth introduced the woman with a flourish.

"Nice to meet you." Brogan offered his hand to Ms. Evans, who shook it with a firm grasp.

"Ms. Evans has graciously informed me that Mr. Stabe is in his office, eating lunch at his desk, and now would be the best time to..." Seth turned back to Ms. Evans. "How did you put it?"

Ms. Evans didn't quite roll her eyes, but she came close. "I believe I said, 'beard the lion in his den.'"

"Ah, right. 'Beard the lion in his den.'" Seth tapped the counter lightly. "I can't thank you enough for helping us out. If you'll point us in the right direction to Mr. Stabe's office?"

As Ms. Evans gave succinct directions, Brogan couldn't wait to grill his companion. Seth led the way to Stabe's office with Brogan at his heels.

Once out of Ms. Evans' earshot, Brogan elbowed Seth. "How did you manage that?"

Seth waggled his eyebrows. "Wouldn't you like to know? I never flatter and tell."

Brogan shook his head. "Remind me not to leave you alone with any female I'm interested in."

"Then I won't be talking to Melender Harman alone?"

Seth's teasing remark hit him in the gut, and Brogan nearly halted in the middle of the hall. He struggled to sound nonchalant in his response. "I doubt you'd be her type anyway."

As they stopped in front of Stabe's office, Seth slapped him on the back. "I knew you had it bad but didn't realize you were that far gone."

Brogan tried to mask his amazement at his colleague's perceptiveness. "What are you talking about?"

"That you're falling for her. Big time." Seth knocked sharply on Stabe's closed door.

Brogan opened his mouth to deny it, but found the words stuck in his throat. Because it was true. He was falling for Melender Harman. And the thought didn't fill him with dread.

CHAPTER

TWENTY-SIX

"Melender? Are you up?"

"Just a moment, please." Shoving her hair from her eyes, Melender tossed back the bedding, then padded to the door to answer Mrs. Trent's query. "Is everything okay?"

"I'm sorry to wake you when I know you have work tonight, but there's someone to see you," Mrs. Trent said.

"Is it Brogan?" Only he knew where she was staying.

"No, it's a young woman. She wouldn't give her name." Mrs. Trent smoothed back a strand of hair. "She seems rather distressed, so I don't think she's a reporter."

If Mrs. Trent didn't think she was after a story, then Melender would see what the woman wanted. "Okay, let me get dressed, and I'll be right up."

Mrs. Trent nodded, then retreated upstairs. Melender hurriedly dressed, splashing water on her face to chase away the last vestiges of sleep and her dream of Brogan riding a white horse to rescue her from the clutches of a shadowy figure wearing a black cape.

As she rounded the stairs, she overheard Mrs. Trent and the

unknown visitor talking about the possibility of a break in the hot, humid stretch of weather that had blanketed the region. Melender stopped abruptly as the young woman dressed in jean shorties and a stomach-skimming black t-shirt locked eyes with her.

"Hello, Melender."

Melender took a step back. "Jillian?" With her mass of dark blonde hair held back from her face with a headband, her cousin bore a strong resemblance to a young Ruby.

"It's been a long time." Jillian held a plastic grocery bag in one hand, her smartphone in the other. Her slender frame stretched as taut as a dulcimer string. "I thought it was time we had a little chat."

"Sure." Melender tried to keep the surprise from her voice and expression, but shock at seeing her cousin coursed through her body. She'd written numerous letters to Jillian over the years, once her cousin had gotten old enough to respond, but had never heard a peep. Melender didn't know whether Ruby and Quentin actually passed along her missives or if Jillian had simply chosen to either not read or response to them.

"With the fan on, it won't be too hot on the back porch for you two to sit and talk," Mrs. Trent interjected.

Melender smiled at her hostess. "Is that okay with you, Jillian?"

Jillian shrugged.

"Do you want something to drink?" Melender asked.

Jillian shook her head.

"Then let's go out there." Melender led the way through the kitchen to the covered porch. With the overhead fan on and a breeze through the open windows, the setting was tolerable.

Melender took a seat on the mustard-colored sofa while Jillian selected a chair at a right angle to her. Setting her phone on a side table, Jillian placed the bag on her lap but didn't say anything.

The adoring three-year-old who followed her around the house begging Melender to play with her had vanished. In her place was a brittle twenty-one-year-old with haunted eyes. But the undercurrent emanating from Jillian's entire being was one of loneliness and abandonment.

Melender allowed the silence to build by counting to sixty as slow as she could. "It's been a long time since I've seen you. You're so grown up now."

Her words galvanized the younger woman, who straightened in the chair. Raising her chin to gaze directly at Melender, she said, "Seventeen years will do that to a person." She ran her eyes up and down the length of Melender. "I must say, I thought you would come out of prison looking older, more worn out. But here you are, appearing happy and healthy."

"Having a clean conscious will do that for a person." Melender smiled, consciously mimicking her cousin's words.

"Mother said despite your conviction and prison term you still clung to your innocence." She cocked her head. "But then Mother was never in your corner, was she? She never has a good thing to say about you."

Melender ignored the taunt and spoke instead to the hurt lurking beneath the surface of Jillian. "Do you remember your favorite song when you were three?"

"No." Jillian narrowed her eyes. "Why on earth should I remember something as mundane as my favorite song as a preschooler?"

"It was the only thing that calmed you when you were scared." Maybe their connection hadn't been totally broken and could be repaired. She'd loved Jillian and Jesse as fiercely as if they'd been her siblings.

"One night when you were a little girl, there was a terrible early summer thunderstorm with lots of lightning and even some hail. You came racing into my room, your eyes as big as saucers, and dove under the covers of my bed."

Melender paused to gauge how the young woman would react to the childhood memory, but the stony face staring back at her gave no indication she recalled the night in question. While she didn't know why Jillian had come to see her, she wasn't going to pass up the opportunity to get Jillian to talk about the night her brother disappeared.

"Is that so?" Jillian checked her smartphone.

Melender pulled her trump card. "Yes. The only thing that would calm you down was my singing."

Jillian barely glanced up from the small screen, her thumbs busy tapping out a staccato rhythm. "What, you think we had some bonding moment over 'Twinkle Twinkle Little Star'?"

Instead of replying, Melender simply sang. "The wind doth blow today, my love."

Jillian froze, her head still down and her hair brushing her cheek as Melender continued.

"And a few small drops of rain, I never had but one true-love."

After that line, Jillian set her phone down on the table, her head still bent.

"In cold grave she was lain, I'll do as much for my true-love."

With her voice, Melender tried to recreate the same peace as she had all those years ago to a scared little girl. She'd sang that song to Jillian the morning Jesse's disappearance was discovered, and every night afterward to lull her to sleep until Melender's arrest.

As the last note drifted off, Jillian raised her head, her eyes clouded with tears, her expression one of such longing and grief that Melender felt intrusive witnessing the look. Without thinking, she rose to wrap the younger woman in her arms. Jillian stiffened immediately, her body resisting Melender's comfort. But as Melender started to remove her arms, Jillian reached up and grabbed her shoulders, relaxing against Melender as sobs racked her body. Melender maintained her awkward position of leaning over Jillian, who stayed seated in the chair, murmuring soothing sounds and rubbing the younger woman's back.

Jillian pulled away, swiping at her tear-stained cheeks with the back of her hand. "I didn't know that was you."

Melender dropped into the chair beside her as Jillian drew in a shuddering breath.

"I used to dream about someone, an older girl who had silvery hair and the voice of an angel," Jillian whispered. "In my dreams, she would sing that song to me, and all my fears would dissipate like the fog on a sunny morning."

"I'm glad." A tightness eased in Melender's chest at Jillian's words. Finally, something from her past had a positive impact instead of a negative one. She hadn't realized how much she'd been longing for such an encounter as a reminder of who she was before she became a convicted murderer.

"Mother never..." Jillian's voice hitched on another sob. "She never told me it was you who sang to me, the one I kept dreaming about after Jesse left us."

Melender patted her shoulder.

"I hated you for taking away my little brother." Jillian slumped against the back of her chair. "A couple of days ago, I heard Dad on the phone tell someone where you were staying, and I had to come see you to tell you that." More tears trickled down her cheeks. "I wanted to make you tell me where you hid Jesse so we could be a real family again."

"Oh, Jilly. I'm so very sorry." The childhood nickname slipped out as if Melender were seventeen again and Jillian three. "I would never harm Jesse. I don't know where he is."

"I think, deep down, I've always known that." Jillian suddenly thrust the bag into Melender's hands. "That's why I kept this hidden for you."

Melender longed to turn the conversation back to Jesse and the night he disappeared but instead reached into the bag and pulled out a tattered notebook. "This isn't..."

"Even as a preschooler, I knew how much this notebook meant to you." Jillian touched the cover. "When you left—I mean, when you were arrested—I took it from your room. I couldn't read it, but it was yours, something you treasured. I used to sleep with it underneath my bed."

Melender opened the notebook with trembling hands. Sudie's childish print proclaimed this book as belonging to her great-grand-daughter, Melender Harman. She could picture Sudie sitting in the fading light on her front porch, singing softly as she labored to write down the lyrics to those mountain folk songs she loved so much. Leafing through the book, she paused to read the first few lines of "I Am a Pilgrim."

I am a pilgrim and a stranger
Traveling through this wearisome land
I've got a home in that yonder city, good Lord.

In her mind, Sudie's lovely alto voice sang the lyrics, the cadence making them come alive with purpose. Brushing back a tear, she turned the page to "Meet Me by the Moonlight."

Meet me by the moonlight, oh meet me
Meet me by the moonlight alone, Lord, Lord
I have a sad story to tell you
All down by the moonlight alone.

She mouthed the words and smiled, feeling her great-grand-mother's presence like she hadn't in nearly two decades.

"Those are your grandmother's songs, aren't they?"

"These are your great-grandmother's songs too." Melender closed the notebook, smoothing the cover with her hand. "I didn't want to forget the sweet memories of her singing them to me. I could see she was becoming frailer, so I asked her to write down the lyrics to as many of her favorite mountain songs as she could. I like to think she understood it was my way of keeping her memory alive and the music of my heart forever."

She looked at Jillian, tears welling inside her. "I can't thank you enough for keeping this safe for me."

Jillian averted her eyes. "Last week, one of my earrings fell behind my dresser, and when I moved it to get the jewelry, I found the notebook. I must have shoved it behind the dresser years ago." She lifted her gaze from her hands and looked at Melender, a tear trailing down her cheek. "I nearly burned it but then thought it might be more satisfying to rip it to shreds in front of you. Can you forgive me for such an awful thought?"

"Yes, of course." Melender touched Jillian's arm. "I'm glad you didn't do either of those things."

Jillian drew in a deep breath. "There's more. That's not the main reason I didn't destroy it. After I found the notebook, a nightmare I haven't had since I was a child came back. Jesse's crying and Jared's shouting at me to give Jesse his stuffed rabbit."

This was probably nothing more than a young girl's hazy memories swirling with her fears, so Melender tried not to let her excitement over the revelation show.

"I used to have it every night after Jesse disappeared. Mom took me to a therapist for years. I eventually stopped having the nightmares. Until last week."

"What else happens in the dream?"

Jillian scrunched up her face. "I'm little again. Jared's watching us, but he's acting funny. I know now it's because he was high."

Melender reached over and took Jillian's hand.

"I'm supposed to be asleep, but Jared let me stay up to watch *Toy Story 2*. Jesse has a cold, so he's congested and not sleeping well. He wakes up and starts crying. Jared yells at me to check on Jesse and give him his stuffed animal. You remember his favorite one? The blue bunny with the missing eye?"

"Yes, I remember." Melender rubbed the back of Jillian's hand with her thumb, just like she used to do when Jillian was little.

"Jesse had thrown it out of his crib. I picked it up for him, but he didn't stand up. He just cried. I touched his face, and it was hot, so I got Jared. He came in, said a bad word, then stomped off."

Melender kept up the rhythmic motion of her thumb, hardly daring to breath as Jillian continued.

"He gave Jesse something liquid in a little cup, then told me I'd better get him to stop crying. I played peek-a-boo with the bunny until he finally stopped crying and went to sleep." She wiped a tear from her cheek, then squeezed Melender's hand. "I went to bed, and that's the last time I ever saw my baby brother."

Melender's heart thudded. Her lawyer should have uncovered this information at the time of her trial. Surely Jillian, even though she was only three, had been questioned at the time. "Did you tell this to the police?"

Jillian shook her head. "No one ever asked me about that night beyond when I went to bed. I didn't tell anyone about watching *Toy Story* or playing with Jesse because I knew I wasn't supposed to be awake that late. And I cried every time someone mentioned Jesse's name, so Mom wouldn't let anyone ask me questions."

"Do you know what Jared did after giving Jesse the medicine?"

"No."

Melender reigned in her disappointment. While this tallied with her story about Jared being in charge of the kids, it still didn't shed any new light on what had happened to Jesse. "You said you used to dream about that night a lot?"

"Yeah. I dreamed about Jesse crying and the medicine and the blue bunny for weeks." She let go of Melender's hand and brushed back a few strands of hair from her face. "Last week, when I had the dream again after so many years, it was a little different."

"In what way?" Melender leaned toward Jillian, her eyes fixed on her cousin.

"This time, I dreamed I got up to get a drink of water after going to bed. You remember my room and Jesse's were connected by a bathroom?"

Melender nodded.

"The door from the bathroom to Jesse's room wasn't closed all the way, like it usually was. I got the drink, but thought I heard Dad's voice in Jesse's room. I put my eye to the crack and saw someone leaning over Jesse's crib."

Melender sucked in a breath. "What was this person doing?"

"Picking up Jesse."

CHAPTER
TWENTY-SEVEN

Brogan knocked on the partially closed door to Stabe's office. At his invitation to come in, Brogan and Seth entered the office.

"Do you have the affidavit from the Reynolds case?" Stabe asked without looking up from the file on his desk.

"No," Brogan said as he and Seth approached the man. Remains of the Stabe's lunch spread across one corner of the desk, while a large fountain drink sat sweating on the opposite side.

Stabe whipped his head up. "You're not Tom. Who are you and how did you get in here?"

Brogan extended his hand while ignoring the last part of the question. "I'm Brogan Gilmore, and this is Seth Whitman. We're with the *Northern Virginia Herald*."

Stabe shook Brogan's hand, his grip soft. While the man clasped Seth's hand, Brogan studied him, judging his age to be mid-forties. Compared to a photo taken during Melender's trial, he'd put on considerable weight. Puffy flesh surrounded his brown eyes.

"We have a few questions about the Jesse Thompson case."

Brogan took one of the two chairs situated in front of the desk, motioning Seth to the other one.

"That's been over a long time." Stabe sank back into his chair.

Not surprised by his evasive answer, Brogan pulled out his phone. "Do you mind if I record our conversation?"

"Yes, I do mind." Stabe's gaze travelled to Seth, then back to Brogan. "In fact, I'm very busy, and I don't have time for unannounced visitors. So if you'll please—"

"This will only take a minute." Brogan didn't budge, deciding to come out swinging to see if he could rattle the other man's composure. "I read through the trial transcript, and I've got to say, you didn't put up much of a defense for your client."

Stabe raised his eyebrows but didn't rise to the bait. "The evidence overwhelmingly pointed to Melender Harman's guilt in the matter."

"It was mostly based on witness testimony, wasn't it? There was no forensic evidence tying Melender to the disappearance at all."

"Look, I don't know what you're trying to imply. I did my job." Stabe pointed his finger at Brogan. "I got the death penalty off the table."

Brogan shook his head. "According to the district attorney's office, the death penalty wasn't even considered in this case, given there wasn't a body."

Stabe shifted his gaze away from Brogan. "I did the best I could given the case I was handed." He stood. "It's time for you two to leave."

Brogan remained seated, keeping his temper in check at the man's obtuseness. "You hardly questioned witnesses, and you certainly didn't put forth a compelling reason as to why your client was innocent." He no longer tried to hide his contempt. "In short, you made it every easy for the prosecution to win."

"You think it's easy defending someone accused of murder?" Stabe asked in a tight voice. "Leave my office. Now."

Brogan rose, making a show of glancing around the office. "This is quite the cushy job. How exactly did you get it, being that you were a defense attorney before?"

Stabe shrugged, but the gesture was anything but nonchalant, given the tenseness in his shoulders. "That wasn't a good fit for me, so I made a change after a couple of years." Stabe picked up his office phone. "I'm calling security."

Brogan held up his hands as Seth moved to the door. "We're going." At the door, Brogan turned back to Stabe, who stood with his arms crossed. "One more thing. I find it very coincidental that this firm represents the interests of Thompson Energy."

Brogan closed the door sharply behind them before Stabe could utter another word. He and Seth walked across the parking lot in silence. Brogan unlocked the doors to his SUV. "That went rather well, don't you think?"

"I don't see what we've gained." Seth buckled his seatbelt.

"He's the weakest link. With any luck, he'll get in touch with the people who paid him to throw the murder trial." Brogan put the car into gear.

"Wait a minute, you think Quentin Thompson is involved in his own son's death?"

"I believe Quentin Thompson willingly allowed Melender Harman to take the blame for Jesse's disappearance," Brogan corrected. "I'm not saying he had anything to do with Jesse's death."

"What's our next move?"

"We're going to see someone who might be willing after all this time to finally tell the truth."

Jillian's revelations that she'd seen a man bending over Jesse's crib in the middle of the night revved Melender's internal engine as questions flooded her mind. Had Jared given Jesse Tylenol or something more sinister to shut him up? Who was the man bending over Jesse's crib in the middle of the night? Was Jillian remembering the evening accurately, or was this all the mixed up emotions of a three-year-old trying to process the loss of her baby brother?

Melender pulled into the parking lot at work. At least her cleaning clients didn't require a lot of brain power, so she'd have plenty of time to think through the possibilities. Hurrying toward the office, she passed the alcove that housed the dumpsters and recycle bins for the building. A man stepped out of the shadows and into her path, his stance taut.

Menace poured off of him like he'd put on too much cologne. With her chin high, she moved to the left to let the man pass. As she'd anticipated, he moved with her, and from the corner of her eye, she spotted a second figure slip into place behind her. Praying for safety, she tamped down the fear threatening to incapacitate her as similar scenes enacted in the prison yard flashed in her mind.

She looked the man in front of her straight in the eye. "What do you want?" Her voice came out strong and steady, despite the hard rock in the pit of her stomach.

"You're stirring up trouble where you shouldn't be." The man spoke causally, but Melender picked up on the iron behind the words. "You didn't heed my warning."

"So you're the person who called to warn me?" The best defense was to go on the offensive. "Who are you working for?"

The man chuckled, the sound worming under her composure, but she held onto her calm front. "You have spunk. I like the spunky ones. It's so much more satisfying when they finally crack."

The words should have scared her, but anger overrode her fear. For her entire adult life, someone had told her what to do and when to do it. Her tired body tensed as anger loosened her tongue. "They say it's important to enjoy your work."

Surprise flickered in the man's dark eyes. Before he could speak, Melender sidestepped him. His accomplice grabbed her arm, whirled her around, and slammed her body into the brick wall of the building. He shoved Melender's head against the unyielding surface, scraping her right cheek along the spiky bricks. Fiery pain radiated throughout her entire being as her assailant kept her immobile.

"You will cease and desist in this Quixote quest to clear your name," the first man hissed in her ear.

The man's literary reference triggered a long-ago memory, but his accomplice smashed her head even harder against the brick, driving the thought far away.

"Do you understand me?"

Before Melender could reply, someone shouted, "Hey! What's going on over there?"

The pressure suddenly lifted, and she sagged to the ground like a deflating balloon. A second later, someone touched her arm. "Mel, are you okay?"

Melender raised her head to see Yancy Simmons, one of her co-workers, gazing down with concern stamped on her face. "I think so. Are they gone?"

"Yeah. Tamika's calling 911." Yancy reached into her backpack and pulled out a folded bandana. "Here, your cheek's bleeding."

Melender pressed the cloth to her face. "Thank you."

"Good thing I came along when I did." Yancy squatted beside her, her warm brown eyes filled with compassion.

"I'm thankful you did too." The man's words ran in a loop in her brain. *You didn't heed the warning. Cease and desist. You didn't heed the warning.* Warning. Melender scrambled for her bag, then plunged her free hand inside to find her phone.

"What happened?" Yancy asked.

"I'm not sure." With one hand still pressing the bandana to her cheek, Melender thumbed up her contacts list. "Would you let Janet know I won't be able to take my shift tonight? I need to check on someone first."

"Sure, I'll let her know right away." Yancy rose and moved away to call their boss as sirens wailed in the distance.

Melender called Brogan's number and lifted the phone to her ear. *Please, let him pick up.*

One ring, then two.

Pick up, Brogan!

The call rolled to voice mail. "Brogan, it's Melender. Please get back to me as soon as you get this message. It's urgent." She disconnected as a police cruiser parked near the alcove.

Yancy leaned down. "The police are here. Tamika asked for an ambulance too. I think that cut might need stitches."

Melender had pushed thoughts about her cheek to the side in her frenzy to warn Brogan, but now she realized the cloth was sticky with blood. Dizziness swept over her. With her eyes closed, she leaned her head against the brick until the world righted itself.

"Miss?"

Melender met the gaze of Officer Gutierrez, the cop who'd come to her apartment last week following up on an alleged nuisance call. Great. That meant his partner, Officer Jones, would be here too. She had no desire to relate her story to Jones, who clearly had something against her for being an ex-con.

"Officer Gutierrez." She craned her neck to see around the cop's legs, not wanting to encounter Jones quite yet.

"Officer Taylor is talking to the witnesses," Gutierrez said. "Looks like a nasty cut on your cheek."

Relief poured over her that Jones didn't appear to be with Gutierrez. "He smashed my face hard into the brick."

"The EMTs are on their way." Office Gutierrez dropped into a crouch beside her and pulled out his notebook and pen. "Do you think you can walk me through what happened?"

"Sure." Melender sketched the details of the attack.

"Do you know what warning the man meant?" Gutierrez asked as the ambulance squealed into the parking lot.

"A few days ago, someone called me with essentially the same message. Stop looking into Jesse's disappearance—or else."

Two EMTs hustled toward them. The officer rose, making room for the approaching emergency technicians.

"Or else what?" Gutierrez asked.

She met Gutierrez's eyes. "Or else someone could get hurt. The caller specifically mentioned Brogan Gilmore, a reporter with the *Northern Virginia Herald*."

CHAPTER
TWENTY-EIGHT

"This high rise has seen better days," Seth said as Brogan turned into the apartment complex where Isadora Alonso lived.

Some residents had tried to brighten the façade with window boxes, but the overall effect only drew attention to the drab exterior. Brogan pocketed his keys as he joined Seth on the pavement.

"What apartment does she live in?" Seth walked beside him into the building.

"1436." Brogan stopped by the elevators. He punched the up button. Nothing. Seth did the same on the adjacent elevator. Again nothing. A second try netted the same results.

Brogan groaned. "You up for a climb?"

Seth shrugged. "I haven't worked out today."

Brogan pointed to the stairwell door. "Me either."

The two of them headed up the stairs. The unairconditioned stairway was stifling, adding to their discomfort.

With a sigh of relief, Brogan pushed open the door for the fourteenth floor. In the cooler corridor, he wiped sweat from his brow with the back of his hand. "I need to hit the gym more."

"In this heat, it wouldn't matter too much." Although Seth's cheeks were flushed, he wasn't breathing nearly as hard as he was.

Brogan paused, wanting to catch his breath before approaching the apartment. The smell of cigarettes and cabbage assailed his nostrils.

"Ready?" Seth smoothed back his hair with the heels of his hands.

"Sure." Brogan used the tail of his shirt to blot his face, re-tucked it into his khakis, then moved down the hallway toward number 1436.

The apartment had a brightly painted red door with a small grapevine wreath that sported dried sunflowers. His knock brought no one to the door. After exchanging a glance with Seth, he knocked harder.

Close to the door, he detected footsteps approaching the door from inside the apartment. The door opened a crack. "What do you want?" The woman kept the security chain firmly in place, allowing only a small sliver of her appearance to show.

"I'm Brogan Gilmore, and this is Seth Whitman. We're with the *Northern Virginia Herald*."

"I don't want subscription." The woman started to close the door.

"We're not selling subscriptions. We're looking for Isadora Alonso." Brogan held his breath that she wouldn't shut the door.

"Why?"

Brogan drew in a deep breath. "I'm looking into the disappearance of Jesse Thompson."

The door slammed shut.

Seth raised his eyebrows, and Brogan shrugged. He lifted his hand to knock again, but the door's chain rattled. He lowered his hand as the door swung open to reveal a woman with jet black hair liberally sprinkled with grey and sharp dark-brown eyes. "Come in."

Brogan entered first with Seth behind him. The small, immaculate apartment had worn carpet and beige walls enlivened by brightly colored prints obviously done by children. The woman gestured toward the gray couch. "I am Isadora Alonso."

"Thank you for seeing us," Brogan began with a smile. "Do you mind if I record our conversation?"

Ms. Alonso regarded him steadily, her eyes boring into his own. "Before I answer your question, I have one for you. Why you want to know about Jesse?"

Brogan stuck to the current facts. "Melender Harman's out."

The former nanny frowned. "Such a sweet girl. She should never have gone to prison."

That statement told Brogan where Alonso's loyalties lay. He gambled that the former nanny would be candid with him. "I agree with you."

Surprise wreathed her face. "It's about time somebody did." She squared her shoulders. "Yes, you may record. What would you like to know?"

Brogan opened the app on his phone and activated it, then stated the date, time, place, and those present. "In your statement to the police, you said Jared had been left in charge of Jesse and Jillian."

"Yes," Isadora said.

"But why didn't anyone question Jared about that?" Brogan asked.

The nanny shrugged. "I don't know. When the ransom note came, so did the FBI. The agents asked me over and over about where Melender was. They ask did she like the kids, stuff like that. I tell them Melender was at graduation party, but Jared was home with the little ones. Those agents think because English is not my first language, I don't understand the questions. But it is them who did not understand me."

Brogan exchanged a look with Seth. "Do you recall if anyone corroborated Melender's story of being at the party?"

"Not that I recall."

"According to Jared's statements to both the police and FBI, he wasn't home that night," Brogan said.

Isadora snorted. "That one was bad news."

"Why do you say that?" Brogan had come to the same conclusion from his own research.

"Jared did drugs. He broke his leg skiing, then he pretended to be in pain after his recovery to get more drugs. The doctor would not give him more, but Jared got them from someone." Isadora spoke so matter-of-factly that Brogan suspected she had first-hand knowledge of such a slide. "My nephew was same, only he overdosed. I tried to tell Mrs. Thompson about Jared, but she said it not my business. I knew Melender. She loved Jesse."

Beside him, Seth shifted on the sofa and spoke for the first time. "What do you think happened to him?"

The nanny stayed silent for a long moment. "I think he died, maybe by accident."

"With the kidnappers?" Brogan asked.

"My family comes from Colombia where kidnappings happen frequently. We still have relatives there and hear the stories." Isadora shook her head. "The kidnapping, it never felt right to me."

She raised a possibility that Brogan hadn't considered. "You think the kidnapping was faked?"

"Yes." She twisted her hands together.

"Who do you think tried to extort ransom money from the Thompsons?" If he started from another angle, the pieces began to form an entirely different picture in Brogan's mind

"Mr. Thompson had had an argument with Jared that morning and said he was cutting his son's allowance significantly. I think his exact words were 'I will not support your drug habit any longer.'" Isadora sighed. "I told FBI that, and they seemed interested. Later, the agents told me both Jared and Mr. Thompson said I had misunderstood. Then Mr. Thompson told me he was letting me go."

Brogan tried to hide the excitement over what might be a big break in the case. "So no one really looked into Jared for the kidnapping at the time?"

"I don't know," she said. "I pray you will find out what happened to Jesse."

"There are times when I think it will take divine intervention." Brogan reached for his phone to turn off the recording. "Thank you for your time."

As Brogan and Seth got to their feet, Isadora stood. "Please tell Melender I've been praying for her all these years. I wrote her a few times, but I couldn't visit, since my documents..."

Brogan didn't pursue it any further. "I will pass along your words to Melender."

At the door, Isadora folded her hands. "Please be careful. Digging into the past is bound to make people mighty uncomfortable."

"Melender can't be convicted for the same crime twice," Brogan said.

The nanny wrung her hands. "This time, they might not be satisfied with her as goat."

"Goat?" Brogan repeated, then got it. "Scapegoat."

"Yes," she said. "No, this time, they might just kill her instead."

BROGAN JUGGLED HIS CELL PHONE AS HE PULLED OPEN THE STAIRWELL DOOR. "Melender, I thought you'd be at work." He held the door for Seth, then followed his colleague down the first flight of stairs.

"You're okay?" Concern laced her words.

"More than okay." He wanted to take the stairs two at time to run off some of the excitement after the fruitful interview, but his loafers weren't conducive to that sort of athleticism. "We just had an interesting conversation with Ms. Alonso."

"The former nanny?"

"Yep, she corroborates your story of the Thompsons leaving Jared in charge of Jillian and Jesse." Brogan rounded the corner as the sound of sirens came through the phone. "Where are you?"

"At the hospital."

"Why? What happened?" Brogan halted halfway down the flight of stairs, signaling with his hand for Seth to wait.

"Two men attacked me—" Static swallowed the rest of her words, but Brogan heard enough to dose his euphoria about the interview.

"Are you all right?" He gripped the phone tight against his ear.

Only static came over the line. He tried again. "You're breaking up. I can't hear you." Frustration riddled his body as he pulled the phone away from his ear to gauge the signal strength. One bar wavered, then vanished, taking the call along with it. Brogan groaned and pocketed the phone.

"Is everything okay with Melender?" Seth asked from the twelfth-floor landing.

"She's at the hospital." He pushed past Seth and pounded down the stairs.

"What happened?" Seth picked up his pace as well, catching up to Brogan as they passed the eleventh floor.

"Two men attacked her." At the sound of a door opening, Brogan glanced up as he went down the next set of stairs.

A man dressed in jeans and a t-shirt with a skull wreathed in flowers stepped into the stairwell. Unease settled down like a scarf snug around Brogan's neck, but the man paid no attention to him or Seth, his gaze fixed on his phone. Brogan continued his hurried descent, the other man's footsteps echoing behind them.

On the ninth-floor landing, a bearded man talked on his cell phone in low tones, nodding at Brogan as he rounded the landing and headed toward the eighth floor. The friendly gesture put him at ease, and Brogan returned to digesting the conversation with Isadora. Why hadn't the FBI followed up on Jared's drug habit? He made a mental note to see how often Jared had met with Snake back when Jesse Thompson went missing.

"Brogan, look out!" Seth's cry nearly came too late.

Brogan gripped the railing hard with one hand as he instinctively dropped into a crouch, but he wasn't quick enough to avoid a kick that landed against his ribs. The impact loosened his hold on the railing, while a second kick sent him tumbling down the stairs to the next landing.

The man with the skull t-shirt rushed toward him. Brogan scrambled to his feet in time for the man to connect with another kick that slammed him against the wall.

On his feet, Brogan swung his fist into his opponent's face with a satisfying crack. But the man recovered quickly and responded with a punch to Brogan's gut, doubling him over. His opponent pressed his advantage by hauling Brogan upright, then wedging his arm across Brogan's throat, nearly choking off his air supply.

"You know what happens to reporters who stick their noses where they don't belong?" The man hissed before shoving his arm tighter against Brogan's throat. Black dots danced along the perimeter of Brogan's vision. "They don't live to write another story."

"Hey, what's going on?" A male voice shouted as Brogan struggled to breath.

"I'm calling 911," a different voice said.

"Melender Harman is certainly a pretty little thing. Or at least she was." His assailant said before delivering another punch to Brogan's stomach. Then the man was gone, leaving Brogan to slump to the floor.

"Hey, are you okay?" Seth touched his shoulder, his breathing hard and fast. Blood oozed from a cut on his lip.

Brogan nodded, still trying to catch his breath. Two teenage boys stood a few feet away.

"Man, those dudes were scary," said the taller one.

"Did you call 911?" Seth asked the boys.

"Yeah, ambulance and police on their way." The other boy peered closely at Brogan. "I thought he was going to choke you to death."

The other teen held up his phone. "I got it all on video."

Brogan recovered enough to pull his own phone out of his pocket. "Would you send me the video?"

"Sure." The teen keyed in the info as Brogan recited his number.

Seth leaned closer to Brogan. "What did he say to you?"

"He warned me away from investigating further." Then Brogan remembered what else his assailant had said. "I've got to check in on Melender."

Without waiting for Seth to respond, he held up his phone to check the reception. Two bars glowed. Ought to be enough to connect with the outside world. After hitting redial, he put the phone to his ear and braced his aching ribs with his other hand.

"Brogan, what happened?" The concern in Melender's voice went a long way to soothing his aches and pains.

"We ran into a little trouble." Brogan succinctly related what happened. "The police should be here soon. How are you?"

"I have a cut on my cheek that the nurse said would need a few stitches. I'm waiting for the doctor now."

"What happened?" Brogan's heart hammered as his assailant's words about Melender's face came back to him.

"Two men attacked me in the parking lot on my way to the office. They warned me off continuing to investigate Jesse's disappearance."

Footsteps clattered on the stairs below and someone called up, "Police!"

One of the teens replied, "Up here."

"The police are here, so I've got to go. You're not going into work, are you?" Brogan hoped she would head back to his aunt and uncle's. He desperately wanted to see she was in one piece with his own eyes.

"No, I took the night off." Melender sighed. "Will you come to the Trents after you get checked out at the hospital?"

"Yes, I'll see you there soon." Brogan ended the call as a pair of cops rounded the bend. Despite the soreness in his ribs and throat, a flash of excitement coursed through him. Someone didn't want them to find out what really happened to Jesse, which meant they were on the right track.

CHAPTER
TWENTY-NINE

Although the prescription strength ibuprofen had taken the edge off, Melender's cheek still ached. She climbed from her car at the Trents' and scanned the assortment of vehicles parked along the curb. Brogan's SUV wasn't among them.

After unlocking the front door, she nearly stumbled over a package wedged between the storm and front door. With the small cardboard box, she entered the quiet house, remembering Mr. and Mrs. Trent volunteered at a recovery meeting every Monday evening. Normally, the emptiness would be welcome, but tonight, she was glad Brogan would be arriving soon. A desire to feel his strong arms wrapped around her nearly overwhelmed her senses. *Get it together. Don't throw yourself at him like a lovesick puppy.*

Setting the package on the kitchen counter, she spotted her name written in thick black letters on the outside. No return address or other information appeared on the plain brown surface. Had Brogan said something about dropping off a package for her? She couldn't recall for certain. Using the kitchen scissors, she slit the tape and opened the flaps.

A knock at the front door distracted her from investigating further. Crossing to the door, she opened it to see Brogan standing there, a puffy pink mark on his cheek. "You're hurt." She stepped aside to allow him to enter the house.

"Not as bad as you." Brogan raised a hand as if to touch her cheek, then dropped it to his side. "Are you okay?"

She tried to smile but winced as the skin pulled at her stitches. "Four stitches, but the doctor thinks it will heal without a noticeable scar."

"Before I came here, I called Detective Livingston and asked him to stop by." Brogan stared at her intently as if trying to gauge her reaction.

"Why did you call him?" She sounded huffy but didn't care. At the time of her arrest, Livingston had been the only one who had attempted to keep an open mind about her involvement. But in the end, he appeared to agree with the conclusion she was responsible, like everyone else.

"Because I think he still has questions about the kidnapping aspect of the case." Brogan crossed to the kitchen. "What's this?" He pointed to the open box.

"You didn't leave it for me?" She joined him at the counter, unease snaking up her spine. "It was wedged between the doors when I came home. There's no postage, but it has my name on the outside."

Brogan angled his head to read the block letters on the open flap.

"I was just opening it when you knocked." Melender reached for the box, but Brogan touched her wrist to stop her.

"In light of what just happened to both of us, let's leave it until Livingston arrives."

His tone ratcheted up her unease. "You think it's connected to the attacks."

In reply, he tugged on her arm to move her away from the counter. "I don't know, but I think given what's happened today we should wait for the detective to proceed."

The events of the day crashed over her, and she swayed into Brogan.

"Hey, steady there." He dropped her wrist and wrapped his arms around her, snugging her against his body.

With a sigh, she gave into the offered comfort and allowed herself to relax. She laid her head on his shoulder as he rubbed her back in a slow, rhythmic motion. After a moment, she lifted her head. The pinkness of his right cheek attested to his own brush with danger. Because of her, this man had been hurt. Without thinking, she laid her hand gently along his jawline right below the mark. "Brogan, I'm so sorry you were attacked today. I never meant for anyone to get hurt. I just want to find out the truth."

"Shh, it's okay." Brogan brought a hand up to brush away the tears that had spilled onto her cheeks, carefully avoiding her bandage.

Her eyes widened at his touch, and she closed her eyes, inadvertently squeezing out more tears. His hand on her face quickened her pulse. How could so small a gesture make her feel so safe and secure?

Then his lips touched her damp cheek, the softness of his mouth teasing a sigh from her. She met his gaze. The banked passion in their depths ignited her own like a match to kindling. *So this was what the romance books meant, this feeling that your world might explode as your blood pumped faster through your body.* She'd never quite understood the passionate feelings described in books, but now, everything made perfect sense.

Brogan's lips tingled from the contact on her smooth skin. The brief encounter made him want to kiss her properly, to place his mouth over hers and taste the saltiness of her lips now dampened with tears.

"Oh. You kissed me." Melender sounded breathless. "Why?"

Why, indeed. How to explain the need he had to protect her, to care for her, to show her the love she'd been missing for years. Instead of answering her question, he addressed the one she hadn't asked. "That wasn't really a kiss."

She wrinkled her nose. "I think it counts."

With a shake of his head, he negated her comment.

"It doesn't?" The slight wobble to her voice coupled with the sweet innocence in her eyes undid the last of his resolve.

"Melender."

She obligingly raised her face to his again. "Hmm?"

"This is a kiss." He slid his hand into her hair, tilted her head slightly to one side, and gently brought his lips down on hers. He'd meant it to be a chaste kiss, a peck really, but once his mouth connected with hers, all thoughts of disengaging fled his mind. The softness of her lips, the responsiveness of her body to his touch fanned a flame within him that threatened to engulf them both. Without considering the consequences, he deepened the kiss, sliding his hand to her back and rubbing her jawline with his other thumb. All his thoughts, his breath, his very being centered on the woman he held in his arms.

With a sigh, he raised his head enough to rest his forehead against hers. Her eyes, dark with passion, gazed into his only inches away.

"Oh, my."

He chuckled and brushed a strand of hair from her flushed cheek. "That's one way to put it." Brogan leaned down to drop a kiss on her forehead, but she pulled out of his embrace and took a step back.

"We shouldn't, this isn't..." She paused before finishing her thought. "It's complicated."

Brogan stared at her as she stood in front of him, her head lowered. His insides churned, and she had to add to his anxiety by telling him something he already knew. He knew all the valid reasons why he shouldn't have kissed her, but rather than articulate those, he agreed with her. "Yes."

The doorbell rang. Probably Livingston. With a sigh, Brogan yanked open the door. The detective stood on the doorstep.

"Thanks for coming by." Brogan waved the other man inside, then shut the door. "Would you like coffee or something cold to drink?"

"Coffee would be great. Caffeinated is fine, with one of those little pink packets if you have them." Livingston paused to peer closely at Melender's bandaged cheek. "Ms. Harman, I heard two men attacked you outside of your work today."

Melender avoided Brogan's gaze, focusing instead entirely on the detective. "That's right."

"Melender, did you want some coffee too?" Brogan asked.

She pointed to a water bottle on the counter. "I'm good."

"I know you've already talked to other officers, but would you mind recounting the incident for me?" Livingston pulled a notebook from his pocket and clicked his pen.

Brogan busied himself with inserting a pod into the Keurig as she went over the attack. His heart hammered. She might have come to suffering even more harm, if not for the timely appearance of her colleague. Isadora Alonso's warning about Melender being in grave danger flashed across his mind.

With the detective's mug on the counter in front of him, Brogan selected a decaf pod for himself. He lost the thread of their conversation as he replayed the kiss in his mind. Never had a kiss affected him as much as this one had. His brain scrambled to make sense of the whirlpool emotions. Then the swirling coalesced into one, crystal-clear thought. He was falling in love with Melender. His growing desire to prove her innocence had less to do with the potential for a blockbuster story and everything to do with freeing her from her past so she could embrace her future. A future he could see himself sharing with her.

The machine signaled the brewing had finished, drawing him back to the present. He mechanically doctored his coffee, his heart lighter but his thoughts heavier. He was falling in love with Melender, and he had no clue what to do about it.

"Brogan?" Livingston's tone alerted Brogan that it wasn't the first time the detective had tried to get his attention.

"Sorry, lost in thought." He picked up his coffee.

"Ms. Harman was telling me about the box." Livingston set down his cup and pulled a pair of latex gloves from his back pocket. "I'm glad you stopped her from further investigation into the contents. With the attacks on both of you today, an anonymously delivered box is likely not a friendly gesture."

Brogan stepped closer to the counter as the detective eased back the flaps to reveal a mound of white tissue paper. Livingston gently removed a handful of paper to reveal a furry blue object still half hidden by the remaining paper.

"Oh, no!" Melender stumbled back from the counter, her complexion pasty, and her eyes huge. "It can't be."

"Can't be what?" Livingston asked.

She wrung her hands together. "It's not possible, it's simply not possible."

Brogan hadn't thought her face could lose anymore color, but the shade dropped alarmingly whiter. He moved toward her.

In her eyes, the misery and pain in their depths punched him in the gut. Without a second thought, he drew her trembling frame into his arms. "Shh. It's okay."

"Ms. Harman. Melender." Livingston removed the object, which Brogan now recognized as a child's stuffed rabbit with floppy ears and a faded blue ribbon tied in a bow around its neck. "Do you recognize this?"

In Brogan's arms, Melender shuddered. She buried her face in Brogan's shirt, her fists clutching the fabric. He rubbed her back and sent up a prayer for her to weather yet another storm. "Hey, I'm here. You can do this."

She raised her head to meet his eyes. "It's..." That's all she could squeak out. With her eyes closed, she rested her forehead on his chest. Then, drawing in a deep breath, she turned her head to look at the bunny with the missing eye Livingston held in his gloved hands. "It's Jesse's blue bunny. He took it everywhere."

~

JARED THOMPSON FIDDLED WITH THE EMPTY PAPER COFFEE CUP AND glanced around once again at the bare walls of the interrogation room. He'd been cooling his heels for several hours. Although he'd been read his rights, Jared hadn't demanded to call an attorney. Better if he handled this on his own without alerting his father to his whereabouts. But as the minutes slipped into hours, maybe he had miscalculated what the police had on him.

The door opened, and the two detectives who had brought him in entered, each carrying a folder. The man, who looked familiar, closed the door, and then each took a chair opposite Jared. The woman crisply stated the names of those present, informing Jared the man's last name was Livingston and the woman's Collier. "Monday, September 2, eight o'clock in the evening."

She stared at Jared. "Do you know why you're here?" She could have been asking if he knew the weather forecast, so bland was her tone.

Jared shrugged. "Something to do with that drug dealer's death, I suppose."

Livingston drilled him with a hard stare. "You don't remember me, do you?"

Again, Jared moved his shoulders up and down. "All you detectives look alike to me, you know?"

"I worked your younger brother's disappearance," Livingston said.

Jared froze. He swallowed hard to regain control over his spiking panic. "That so. I would imagine a lot of people worked on that case. I can't be expected to remember each and every one."

Livingston continued as if Jared hadn't spoken. "Back then, I had pegged you as a lowlife drug user, someone willing to sell out his family for a hit." He tapped the folder in front of him. "Turns out, I was right." After flipping open the folder, he picked up a single sheet of paper. "Twenty thousand dollars in cash was found on your former drug dealer."

In an attempt to appear nonchalant, Jared used his thumbnail to rub at a spot on the metal table. "What's your point?" The question came out shakier than he would have liked, but he repeated to himself that there was no way they could tie the money to him. He had been extra careful in wiping the bills clean of any fingerprints.

"The point is that we've been able to determine the cash came from the ransom for Jesse Thompson," Livingston said.

"How'd you figure that? It's been nearly twenty years." Jared didn't bother masking the surprise in his voice, figuring it was a natural question someone innocent would ask.

Livingston leaned back in his chair. "Your father cooperated with the Feds on the ransom, which meant the serial numbers of all those twenties were recorded. Then those numbers were uploaded to a national database. Whenever we come across money in the course of our investigations, we run it through one of those bank machines that checks for counterfeit bills and scans the serial numbers." The detective raised his hands. "Imagine our surprise when the bills matched the Thompson kidnapping case."

"I still don't know why you think I had something to do with Snake's—Williams'—death or Jesse's disappearance." Jared tried to project an I'm-innocent-why-are-you-bothering-with-me attitude, but one look at Livingston's cold eyes told him he wasn't succeeding.

"You know what I think?" Collier interjected into the silence, but she didn't wait for Jared to answer. "I think you saw a chance to profit from your little brother's disappearance and engineered the ransom note and drop. You had expensive habits and a father who was fast losing patience with your debts."

"You don't know what you're talking about." Jared crossed his arms, not caring if it made him appear uncooperative.

"It must have been quite a blow when you realized you couldn't spend a dime of the money," she continued. "So you had to hide it. Then Melender was arrested and convicted. Must have been a huge relief to you that the search for the ransom money was over."

"It was." For the very reason Collier had said, but he quickly added, "After all, she killed Jesse."

"But you were the one who sent the ransom note." Livingston picked up the interrogation. "And you were the one who planted the money on Williams."

Jared shook his head. "You guys are barking up the wrong tree."

"Three witnesses picked your photo out of a lineup as talking with Williams the night he was killed," Collier said.

"I wasn't there," Jared repeated, unable to stop his leg from jiggling up and down under the table.

Livingston opened a folder but shielded Jared's view of the contents with his clasped hands. "It's time you stopped lying about what happened that night and tell us the truth."

"I'm telling you the truth. I had nothing to do with the murder!" Panic clawed at Jared's throat as he glanced from one to the other.

"And I believe you. We know you didn't kill Williams." Livingston's words should have soothed Jared, but instead, they only heightened his sense of impending doom. The detective extracted a stack of photos from the folder. "But, as we said before, we're not asking you about the murder. We're asking you about the money. We were hoping you would come clean, but since you refuse to do so, well, see for yourself."

He slid one picture across to Jared. "This is you meeting with Williams."

Even in the dim shadows of the trees, Jared easily recognized himself and Snake.

Livingston handed over another photograph. "This is you handing Williams the stack of money."

Jared didn't care that his hands shook as the detective added four more photos to the pile, each one clearly showing Jared talking with

243

Snake. For a long moment after receiving the final photo, Jared stared at the table, the pictures spread out before him. Then he straightened and met Livingston's gaze. "I want a lawyer."

CHAPTER

THIRTY

"Consuela, I'm heading out," Ruby said to the housekeeper, who was arranging a vase of fresh-cut flowers in the foyer. Meeting with nosey friends for a weekly lunch of salad and gossip wasn't at the top of Ruby's things to do list, but she also didn't want to fuel questions about her absence. However, if the women probed too deeply about her current state of mind, she would plead another appointment and bow out early.

"Will you and Mr. Quentin be home for dinner tonight?" Consuela asked as Ruby gripped the doorknob.

Ruby adjusted the strand of pearls around her neck, then turned back to face the housekeeper. "For now, plan on both of us being here."

"And Miss Jillian?" Consuela asked.

A finger of worry traced along Ruby's spine. Jillian had been moody since Ruby's encounter with Melender. "My daughter has other plans for tonight. If that changes, I will let you know."

"Very good, Ms. Ruby. Enjoy your lunch."

"Thank you." She flashed a fake smile.

"You're welcome, ma'am." Consuela gathered up the detritus from the flower arrangement and bustled toward the kitchen.

With a sigh, Ruby pulled open the front door and bit back a yelp of surprise. On her doorstep stood a tall man with silver threading his dark hair and a younger woman holding a reusable grocery bag. Ruby put her hand to her chest. "You startled me."

"I'm sorry, Mrs. Thompson." The man removed his sunglasses, tucking them into his suit coat pocket. Then he took out a small folder and flipped it open to reveal a badge and ID card. "I'm Detective Livingston, and this is my partner, Detective Collier, with the Fairfax County Police Department. May we come in?"

Ruby recovered enough to affect a nonchalance she didn't feel inside. "What's this about?"

"It would be best if we talked inside," Livingston spoke firmly but politely, his eyes never leaving Ruby's face.

"You can have five minutes," Ruby snapped, not caring she sounded ungracious. She led the way into the small sitting room directly to the right of the entrance, then pulled out her phone to check the time. 11:37.

"Ma'am, I'm afraid we have some rather disturbing news," Livingston said.

Ruby's heart rate accelerated. It hadn't occurred to her they could be bringing news of Jesse to her. Something about her demeanor must have alarmed Livingston because he gently took her arm and guided her to sit on the love seat.

"Have you..." Ruby couldn't finish the question.

"No, we haven't located your son." Livingston guessed what she had started to ask. "But we do have new information related to his disappearance."

Ruby tried to process what the detective was saying. "What could possibly be uncovered after all this time?"

"We recovered twenty thousand dollars of the ransom money," Collier said.

Ruby frowned. "You found some of the ransom money?" This

didn't make sense. She'd always assumed the money had been spent by whoever had helped Melender dispose of the body. While the prosecution hadn't brought up the ransom during Melender's trial, Ruby firmly believed Melender had an accomplice who handled the ransom drop and who had spirited the money out of the country to avoid detection. "Where did the money turn up?"

"On the body of a man named TJ Williams, Jared's former drug dealer," Livingston said. "Williams was murdered."

"Murdered? That's horrible." At the mention of Jared, a sense of foreboding invaded Ruby's body. Surely, Jared had nothing to do with this, but in her mind's eye, she flashed back to all the arguments Jared and Quentin had about money in the weeks leading up to Jesse's disappearance.

"Jared Thompson's fingerprints have been identified on the ransom money." Livingston leaned forward. "Early this morning, Jared confessed to writing the note and picking up the ransom. He further said he'd given Williams the twenty thousand in an attempt to throw suspicion away from him."

"Ruby!" Quentin called from the foyer. Her husband appeared in the doorway a moment later, his eyes sweeping past the detectives to meet her gaze.

"Is it true?" Ruby stared at Quentin. "Did Jared kidnap Jesse?" An emotion she couldn't identify crossed her husband's face as he joined her on the loveseat.

"No, my darling. Jared had nothing to do with Jesse's disappearance."

"How do you know?" Surely her husband hadn't known about Jared's involvement with the ransom when it had happened.

"His lawyer just called me." Quentin enveloped her hands in his, but Ruby pulled away, not wanting his comfort at a time like this. "I'm sure Jared took advantage of the situation and pretended to have kidnapped Jesse for the ransom, which he didn't spend after hearing the bills had been recorded and marked."

"That's not entirely true," Livingston said.

Ruby turned to the detective. "What do you mean?"

"You probably don't remember, but I was one of the detectives working your son's case," Livingston said. "When we discovered the ransom money with Jared's prints on it, I pulled the original files. Mr. Thompson, you stated you and your wife were at a charity event at the country club about two miles from this house on the night Jesse disappeared."

"Is it really necessary to drag this up again?" Quentin's sharp tone suggested he thought otherwise.

"In light of your son's confession, I think so," Livingston answered.

"Then yes, we were at the club that night. Ruby had been on the committee to raise funds for a local children's charity." Quentin again reached for Ruby's hands, but she linked hers together instead. "Which charity was it for, my dear?"

Ruby didn't want to revisit that evening, but after a few seconds, the name of the organization came to her. "The Children's Hope."

"How much did the event raise for the charity?" Collier asked.

Ruby looked down at her hands. She could do this. She could relive the worst night of her life yet again. Drawing in a deep breath, she let it out slowly. "I think it was nearly a quarter of a million dollars. In addition to the dinner, we had a silent auction with some remarkable items, including a necklace worn by Princess Grace of Monaco and a signed first edition of *To Kill a Mockingbird* by Harper Lee. That one sold for more than twenty-five thousand dollars."

"I don't think you need to give the detectives a laundry list of the auction items, my darling." Quentin had pitched his voice to sooth, but, instead, Ruby bristled at the implication she was oversharing. It was his son who had taken advantage of their grief and fear and added to it with the bogus ransom note and payment. While Melender had put things into motion, Jared had done something even worse—given them hope Jesse would be returned once the ransom had been paid.

Ruby turned to her husband. "You didn't think the list so

insignificant when the item you wanted was sold right out from underneath you."

"I've never been to a silent auction," Collier interjected before Quentin could respond. "How does it work?"

"For the auction, you submitted sealed bids for the items, which were on display for a week before the dinner and dance. Then on the night of the event, the winners were announced," Ruby explained. "You had to be present to win. Quentin had the winning bid but wasn't in the ballroom when the results were announced. So the winner of the charming little woodcut of a mountain laurel I wanted for my birthday went to someone else."

Beside her, Quentin tensed slightly. "I had a phone call, so I excused myself."

"What time did the announcements take place?" Livingston said.

"It must have been close to ten o'clock because it was after dinner but before the dancing commenced." As if Ruby could forget one single moment of that awful night.

Collier jotted something down in a small notebook. "Mr. Thompson, where did you go?"

"The patio."

"Who called you?" Livingston asked.

Quentin grimaced. "The later events of the evening overshadowed the mundane, so I can't recall exactly. Probably related to my business, or I wouldn't have taken the call. We were negotiating a particularly tricky deal."

"Any idea when you returned to the party?" Collier poised her pen over her notebook.

"Maybe an hour or so later?"

Her husband's uncertainty prompted Ruby to assist with his recollection of the evening. "I think it was about eleven. He found me as the band started playing a fox trot. Quentin dances the fox trot as if he was channeling Fred Astaire."

Even as she kept her tone light, the peevishness she'd felt that night by his prolonged absence came flooding back and another

249

memory assailed her. She eyed her husband. "But you weren't in a good mood. You were scowling and out of sorts and didn't even finish the dance with me. Instead, you practically thrust me into the arms of Harvey Johnson." She flashed the detectives a brilliant smile to hide her remembered discomfort. "Thank goodness, Harvey didn't mind."

"I don't think the detectives want to rehash our entire evening." Quentin took her hand in a firm grip she didn't resist, then shifted his focus back to the detectives. "Exactly where is this going?"

"Jared said he was in the house that night," Livingston stated crisply. "The nanny said you had left him in charge of the younger children because Melender was at a high school graduation party down the street."

"Are you suggesting Jared and Melender were in it together?" Ruby couldn't keep the horror from her voice.

"The investigation didn't find Melender had anything to do with the ransom note or drop," Livingston said. "Just the opposite. She was either being questioned by police or in custody at the crucial times for the ransom. That's why she was never charged with that crime."

Quentin tugged Ruby to her feet as he stood. "This is old news, detective. Unless you have something new to add, we're done here."

Livingston reached into the bag and brought out a clear plastic bag with something blue inside. "Today, this was hand-delivered to Melender Harman's door." Livingston extended the bag to Ruby. "Do you recognize it, Mrs. Thompson?"

Ruby reflexively accepted the bag, her eyes widening. She shook her head. "Oh, no." Raising her head, she glanced at her husband. "It's Jesse's blue bunny."

BROGAN HIT SEND TO FORWARD FALLON THE STORY ON THE RECOVERED ransom money and Jared's confession. Livingston had reluctantly agreed to allow Seth to photograph the bunny, since it pertained to a closed case. Fallon had hinted the story might make the front page of Wednesday's midweek edition.

His desk phone buzzed. Fallon's extension flashed on the display. "Hello?"

"In my office. Now." Fallon clicked off.

Brogan replaced the phone and grabbed his notebook. On his way to Fallon's office, he tried not to worry about the summons. If his editor had a problem with Brogan's work, Fallon wouldn't hesitate to let him know.

Fallon's secretary waved him through to the editor's office.

"Ah, Brogan. Have a seat." Fallon removed his reading glasses and tossed them on top of a pile of papers. "I finished your piece on the ransom money and Jared Thompson's confession. Solid writing."

"Thank you." Brogan settled into one of the chairs in front of the desk.

"And good work getting Seth to photograph the child's stuffed animal. We're going to hold off on that part of the story for now. I think there's more to be said than a rabbit belonging to Jesse Thompson showing up on Melender Harman's doorstep. I want you to get the reaction from the Thompsons and also verify if the stuffed animal actually was Jesse's. What do the police think?"

"About the bunny?"

Fallon nodded.

Brogan shrugged. "Livingston wouldn't speculate on how the bunny got to Melender. He was taking it to the Thompsons' this afternoon to see if it was Jesse's."

"And you'll follow up with the detective?"

"Livingston said he would call me after the visit," Brogan said, adding, "I'll contact him in case he forgets."

"Good." Fallon picked up his glasses but didn't perch them back on his nose. "When we break this story tomorrow morning, it's going to generate a public feeding frenzy. The Thompson case was big news when it happened, and Quentin Thompson has only become more powerful in the intervening years. He has many friends in high places, and this kind of revelation will not be welcomed by his business associates."

Brogan had considered that as well. "Which is why we need to be on top of this story."

"Exactly." Fallon placed his glasses on and reached for a red Sharpie. "I think this story will break, and we have a real opportunity to scoop the big boys. You have the inside track on this one. Don't squander it."

"I won't." Brogan rose as his cell phone buzzed. Out of the office, he answered. "Brogan Gilmore."

"It's Detective Livingston." The other man cleared his throat. "We have confirmation from the Thompsons the bunny was Jesse's, last seen in his crib the night he went missing."

"Go on." Brogan bit back the questions he wanted to ask and let the detective unspool his thoughts in his own time.

"We also discovered Quentin Thompson was absent from the charity event for an hour or so that evening."

Brogan did a fist pump in the air at the news as he settled into his desk chair but kept his tone neutral. "That corroborates the nanny's testimony she saw him on the phone outside during the event."

"True, but it's still not enough to actively reopen a closed case. However, we do have a solid case against Jared for the attempted kidnapping apart from his confession."

Brogan wedged his phone against his ear and opened his notepad. "Can you give me the details?"

Livingston sketched out the facts. Finding Jared's fingerprints—which were on file because of Jesse's disappearance—on some of the ransom money, connecting with an officer on the drug squad who had Snake under surveillance, and getting photographs of Jared and Snake on the night in question. Then Jared confessed he was behind the ransom.

"What's going to happen to him?"

"He will be formally charged with attempted kidnapping."

"Whoa, only attempted kidnapping?" Brogan didn't bother to hide his surprise. Jared's involvement in the kidnapping surely opened up the possibility he had something to do with Jesse's disappearance.

"Since Melender's been convicted of killing Jesse, that means Jared couldn't have actually kidnapped his younger brother. Not in the eyes of the law," Livingston said.

"Which means this ties up one loose end related to the case but does nothing to point to Melender's innocence." Brogan's heart ached for Melender, who would be glad to be cleared of suspicion of kidnapping Jesse but disappointed it hadn't led to overturning her murder conviction.

"That's right." Livingston paused. "Listen, my boss has told us to lay off questioning the Thompsons again. There's nothing in Jared's confession about the ransom that sheds new light on Harman's conviction, since she was never officially charged with kidnapping Jesse."

Brogan rubbed the bridge of his nose. "Yeah, that's what I figured would happen." The Thompsons, with their money and connections, had most likely made a few phone calls to stop what Quentin would undoubtedly have labeled as police harassment.

"So that's it then." At least from the police perspective, Brogan had hoped Livingston would look at the case with fresh eyes.

"From the Fairfax County Police Department's perspective, yes."

"I appreciate your call."

"The brass said I could let you know on the record about it, since your tip was instrumental in cracking that part of the case."

Brogan wanted to slap his forehead. He had been so focused on the Thompson angle, he nearly forgot to follow up on the Williams murder. "Did you find out who killed Williams?"

"Yep, Fernando Jones, a junkie who didn't have enough money for his next fix."

Brogan jotted down the name as he asked a few other questions to wrap up his story on the murder. "Thanks, detective."

"There is one more thing."

Brogan waited, his mind already busy composing the lead to his story about the Williams' death and Jared's confession.

"I'm going to be taking a few hours off, starting tonight. My lieutenant's been after me to whittle down my accrued PTO or lose it," Livingston continued in a casual tone. "But with my missus off visiting her sister, I'm a bit at loose ends. I don't suppose you have any reading material that might make the time pass by a little quicker?"

The import of Livingston's words hit him square in the jaw. He strove to keep his tone as nonchalant as the detective's. "I think I just might, if you care to stop by my uncle's house later today."

"Give me a good time to drop by."

"Come around seven."

Livingston agreed and ended the call. Brogan sent Melender a series of texts to update her on what had happened but didn't mention Livingston coming over. She would be at work when the detective arrived, and Brogan didn't want her hopes raised that Livingston was on their side.

CHAPTER

THIRTY-ONE

L ivingston riffled through a box, reading file labels but not extracting any papers to peruse as Brogan set down two mugs of coffee on the table.

"Thanks. This is regular, right?" The detective didn't wait for Brogan's answer before lifting his mug and taking a sip.

"Yes, as strong as I could make it." Brogan took a tentative sip of his own cup, and the hot liquid nearly scalded his mouth.

Livingston had arrived a few minutes after seven wearing Bermuda shorts, a faded Police Academy t-shirt, and sandals. The transformation from all-business cop to weekender jarred Brogan, but he wisely didn't quip about the clothing option. The detective projected the appearance of someone off the clock, but his manner was serious.

"You've organized this nicely." Livingston tapped one of the boxes. "How far have you and Harman gone through these?"

Brogan brought him up to speed on the slow progress they'd made. "We kind of got sidetracked with Jared's arrest related to the ransom."

"Yeah, that was a bit of a surprise, I'll grant you. I knew something was off about Jared Thompson, but since the FBI handled the kidnapping part, I never got to question him beyond his initial statement."

"We were hoping his confession would open up new avenues to explore in Jesse's disappearance."

"We?" Livingston raised his eyebrows. "Seems to me you're losing your objectivity with this story."

Brogan didn't take the bait to discuss his involvement with Melender, not when he couldn't be honest with himself about his feelings for her. Instead, he switched topics. "What I don't understand is why everyone accepted the Thompsons' version of events without question."

"Early in the investigation, it looked like a case of a missing child. That's treated very differently than if we thought it was a homicide case. So yes, we gave the family the velvet-glove treatment because we had no reason to suspect any of them of foul play in Jesse's disappearance."

"When did Melender's name come up as a potential suspect?" Brogan flipped through the pages on his yellow pad to refresh his memory of the interviews he'd read.

Livingston sipped his coffee, his posture relaxed but his gaze sharp. "When it became obvious the child had been taken, not wandered off."

"How did you determine that?" Brogan strived to sound friendly, not antagonistic. The detective had volunteered his time to read the files, but that didn't mean Livingston thought Melender innocent. Brogan pegged the man as someone who liked to have all his questions answered about a case, and this was one instance where loose ends had dangled for nearly two decades.

"The usual trio of means, motive, and opportunity. Given the testimony of the other household members, Harman appeared to be the only one with all three."

"But you discounted the nanny's testimony about Quentin leaving the charity function for an hour and you never fully interviewed Jared about his whereabouts that night." Brogan tried to mask his frustration with how things had unfolded nineteen years ago.

Livingston didn't change his posture, but a slight tightening of his lips indicated he wasn't pleased with Brogan's statement. "I'm surprised you haven't figured that out yet. You were a big shot investigative reporter. Surely you've discovered life isn't fair, especially to those who haven't the ability to ensure an equal playing field."

Brogan scrambled to interpret the words in light of Melender's case. Then a snippet from an article about Quentin flashed in his mind. "Quentin played golf with the police chief." He met the detective's eyes. "But this wasn't a traffic ticket. It's a woman's life. It's a child's life."

"The results are the same. When your boss tells you to lay off questioning the immediate family, you push back as much as you can because you believe there is more to the story. Then comes the ransom note, and the FBI takes over the case. Finally, the prosecutor swoops in to say there's enough circumstantial evidence to hold a grand jury, and voila. Indictment, trial, conviction, sentencing."

The picture of how easily that had happened to Melender unfolded in Brogan's mind like a silent movie.

"Unfortunately, this isn't the only time where the wheels of justice crushed someone instead of serving the public."

"What would you have done had you been fully free to do your job?"

Livingston blew out a breath. "I would have questioned the family members more thoroughly, followed up on the nanny's testimony, looked into Jared's background. In other words, I would have done some old-fashioned investigative work until I figured out what happened to Jesse Thompson." The detective's phone buzzed. Frowning, he picked it up and checked caller ID. "I better take this. It's the forensics lab. Must be important for them to buzz me while I'm off the clock."

Brogan rose and grabbed the empty coffee cups. "I'll get us a refill." He left the room to give Livingston privacy. After making two fresh cups, he returned to find Livingston tapping his phone on the table, his gaze fixed on the opposite wall.

"Bad news?" Brogan set down the cups and retook his seat.

"No, not at all. Just very surprising." Livingston made no move to pick up his coffee mug. "I've been a detective for twenty-three years, and believe me when I say, I've seen humanity at its worst. You kind of stop believing in miracles." He met Brogan's gaze. "Then you get a phone call like this, and you start to wonder if there is a God after all."

Brogan's investigative antenna went on high alert. "What did the lab say?"

"It was the darndest thing. We'd sent the blue bunny to the lab after the Thompsons positively identified it as belonging to Jesse. Not that we were expecting anything, given someone obviously sent it to Harman to scare her, which surely meant there was nothing of forensic value to be found."

Brogan wanted to shake the other man to get to the point, but he restrained himself. "But that's not what happened."

"No. The technician scanned the bunny and discovered a small recording device where the bunny's heart would be. If stuffed rabbits had hearts, that is."

Brogan's mouth dropped open. "What?"

"That was my reaction too." Livingston shook his head. "I mean, what are the odds of recovering what might turn out to be the equivalent of a smoking gun after nearly two decades?"

"What was on the recording?" Brogan could hardly wrap his mind around what the detective was saying. The blue bunny had a secret recorder installed within its stuffed body. The possibility of Jesse's last moments being captured on audio stirred a mixture of excitement and fear.

"The technician said she hasn't listened to it yet. It's so old, she has to jerry-rig a way to play it." Livingston scrubbed a hand over his face. "I told her this was a top priority, so she's going to get started right away."

"How long do you think it will take?"

The detective shrugged. "Daisy's one of the best, so I imagine she'll have something figured out in a couple of hours. Might take longer because she'll have to move slowly to avoid damaging the device. There's no guarantee there's anything on the recorder."

"But if there is, surely it will be around the time of Jesse's disappearance."

Livingston took a sip of coffee. "While we're waiting, let's make good use of our time. Do you want the housekeeper's folder or the head gardener's?"

Brogan hadn't read either one yet. "I'll take the gardener's."

Livingston handed him the folder, then bent his head over the housekeeper's.

As Brogan read the initial police interview with Dwayne Poteet, who had worked as a gardener for the Thompsons for five years prior to the disappearance, he couldn't tamp down the excitement that the case was about to break wide open.

"HE'S NOT MY ATTORNEY." JARED CROSSED HIS ARMS AND LEANED BACK IN his chair. He glared at Dan Stabe, who sat beside him. The two detectives on the opposite side of the metal table exchanged glances but said nothing.

"Jared, your father sent me to look after you," Stabe said.

"You no longer practice criminal law." Jared didn't want to air his family's dirty laundry in front of the cops, but he also didn't want this bozo representing him. Stabe had defended Melender, then joined the law firm that represented his father's energy company. Even though Jared had been pleased with the outcome of his cousin's trial, he didn't trust Stabe to have his best interests. Not with Quentin paying the bill.

"Granted, I haven't practiced criminal law in several years, but I am capable of representing you in this matter." Stabe smiled, but it didn't reassure Jared.

"I. Want. A. New. Lawyer." Jared enunciated each word as if speaking to a child.

Stabe looked at the detectives. "Would you excuse us for a moment while I confer with my client?"

Collier and a different detective whose name Jared had forgotten stood as one. "Sure. Knock on the door when you have this resolved," Collier said.

Jared waited until the interview room door closed behind the cops before turning to Stabe. "Listen, I don't care what my father told you to do, I don't want you representing me."

"You were fine with my help yesterday." Stabe dropped his solicitous manner, his expression morphing from confident to concerned. "What's going on?"

"I had a change of heart overnight." Jared wasn't about to explain that he wanted to cut a deal by revealing what he knew about the night Jesse disappeared. His father would kill him if he found out, and Jared wasn't sure that the sentiment would only be a figure of speech. Dad had given him a home after the acrimonious divorce from Jared's mother, who had been quick to abandon her son in favor of jetting around the world with various lovers. Jared and his father had gotten along fine until Ruby entered the picture. Then his father's allegiance had been to his new wife followed by his new children. Jared had been relegated to the sidelines, which he hadn't minded too much, since he had been a teenager when they married.

But his father wouldn't hesitate to sacrifice Jared if it meant keeping Ruby and Jillian safe. Jared suspected that Stabe wouldn't let a little thing like attorney-client privilege stop him from sharing what Jared said in confidence.

"A change of heart." Stabe narrowed his eyes. "Listen up. You better not be changing your story at this late game. Your father—"

"You see, that's the problem. This is not about my father. It's about me and my life. You are more concerned with how this will play out for my dad than you are in making sure I get a fair deal. So I repeat. I do not want you as my attorney."

Stabe held his gaze for a long moment, but Jared didn't waver. Finally, the older man shrugged. "Have it your way." He grabbed his briefcase and stalked toward the door, knocking firmly before turning back. "You'd better think long and hard about whatever it is you're planning to do. Your father has many friends in high places."

"I'll take my chances." Jared broke eye contact as the door opened.

"Everything okay in here?" Collier asked, her gaze swinging from Jared to Stabe.

Stabe paused in the doorway as if giving Jared one more chance to change his mind, then shook his head. "I'm no longer representing Mr. Thompson."

CHAPTER
THIRTY-TWO

Melender slid her omelet onto a plate next to two slices of buttered toast. Her breakfast plate in hand, she stepped around the Trents' cat, who had sprawled in a patch of late afternoon sun. She couldn't wait to introduce Goliath to the orange tabby named Bo, but her cat needed some more time to adjust to his new surroundings in the downstairs apartment.

"I wish I could sleep more." It had been hard to fall asleep this morning following her overnight shift. She eyed the cat for a moment, but the feline didn't even bother to open his eyes.

After a quick blessing over the food, Melender dug in, hoping the meal would revive her sluggish brain. Brogan had taped a note to her door alerting her that Livingston was helping them. Surely that meant the detective thought justice had not been served with her conviction, but she couldn't quite banish the small voice that said maybe Livingston simply wanted what everyone else did—for her to reveal the whereabouts of Jesse's body.

Her cell phone rang. As Brogan's name flashed on the screen, a smile blossomed on her face. "Hello?"

"I was hoping you were awake." Brogan's excitement hummed

through the phone. "I'm about ten minutes away. Can you be ready to go when I get there?"

Melender shoved her messy hair back. She always showered when she got home from work in the morning, but she had yet to get dressed. "I think so. What's up?"

"I'll tell you when I see you." Brogan clicked off before Melender could question him.

After quickly finishing her meal, she dumped her plate in the dishwasher, then dashed for the stairs. Nine minutes later, she buckled her seatbelt in Brogan's SUV. "What's going on?"

Brogan grinned at her. "You'll see."

"You're not going to tell me?"

When he shook his head, she playfully slapped his arm. "Brogan, that's not fair."

His expression turned serious. "If I explain it, it won't make as much sense as if you hear it. We'll be there in a few minutes. Can you trust me?"

"I suppose so." His words sent the butterflies in her stomach racing at top speed. She pressed a hand over her midsection, but it didn't help to calm them.

The two rode in silence until Brogan pulled into the parking lot of a nondescript building. "Where are we?"

"One of the labs that processes evidence for the Fairfax County Police Department." Brogan parked in a visitor's slot, then opened his door.

Melender joined him on the sidewalk. "Why are we here?"

"You'll see." Brogan reached back and grabbed her hand. The unexpected gesture warmed her insides but did little to settle the butterflies.

In the lobby, he strode to the receptionist and gave their names. "Detective Livingston's expecting us."

"I'll let him know you're here. If you care to wait over there..." the receptionist gestured toward a grouping of couches and club chairs around a low glass coffee table spread with magazines.

"Thanks." Brogan led the way, then took a seat. He tugged her onto the couch beside him, angling to face her.

"Brogan, what are we doing here?" Melender stared into his blue eyes, which danced with excitement.

"Patience." He rubbed his thumb on the top of her hand.

The physical contact tangled her nerves. Her insides were turning to mush, and she was having trouble holding onto a coherent thought.

"Your face still looks pretty raw."

She fought the desire to lay her head on his shoulder. "The doctor gave me a prescription for ibuprofen, and it helps keep most of the pain at bay."

"I wish I had been there." Brogan squeezed her hand. "With our work schedules, we haven't had much time to talk. How are you doing otherwise?"

"I'm okay." Her eyes transfixed on the shape of his mouth as he formed a gentle smile. She drew in a deep breath to reorient her thoughts away from Brogan's lips. If she moved her head a tad, she could easily bring her mouth into contact with his. But that was madness. Brogan wasn't sure of her innocence. She'd watched enough dramas to know girls like her rarely ended up with guys like him.

He shifted closer to her. "You know the altercation means we must be getting closer to the truth."

Detective Livingston cleared his throat. "Am I interrupting something?"

Melender jerked back, heat flooding her cheeks.

"Not at all." Brogan's voice was as unemotional as if he were discussing the weather.

She got to her feet but averted her eyes, her emotions topsy-turvy.

"Follow me." Livingston led the way to the bank of elevators. "I got called in this morning for an unexpected development in the

Williams case. This isn't for publication yet, but it appears your cousin wants to cut a deal."

Melender brought her gaze from the floor to the cop. "I thought Jared had confessed to sending the ransom note and picking up the money."

"Yep, and he told us where the rest of the cash was stashed." Livingston punched the down button. "In a safe deposit box at his credit union."

Brogan shook his head. "That sounds like something from a crime caper movie."

The elevator dinged, and Livingston held the door back. "You know the old saying that life imitates art." As they stepped inside, the detective selected the B3 button. "Jared said he had information about Jesse's disappearance, but he wanted to talk to his lawyer first."

Melender had reached for Brogan's hand before even realizing she'd made the gesture.

"What does he know?" Brogan interlaced his fingers with hers and squeezed, sending a tingle throughout her body.

The elevator arrived at the third floor of the basement, and the door slid open. "We've yet to find out. He fired the lawyer his father sent and requested a public defender, who arrived at the jail about half an hour ago. My partner will give me a call after Jared and the attorney talk."

"What was the name of the lawyer Jared fired?" Brogan let go of her hand to hold the door open.

"Let me guess. Dan Stabe?" Melender exited the elevator.

Livingston shot her a look as he stepped into the hallway. "That's right. Wasn't he your attorney?"

"Yes." If you could call him that.

The detective led the way to a door close to the elevator. The small, dimly lit room held a bank of computer monitors, keyboards, and sound boards.

A woman sat with her back to the door, large headphones

covering much of her head. She held up one finger at their entrance, and Livingston laid a finger on his lips to signal silence. A few seconds later, the woman removed her headphones and swiveled to face them in what Melender now recognized was a wheelchair. "Detective Livingston, I presume?"

"Ha, I haven't heard that one before." The cop gestured toward Brogan and Melender. "This is Brogan Gilmore, a reporter with the *Northern Virginia Herald*, and Melender Harman. And this is Daisy Sullivan, who I've heard is the best audio technician in the Commonwealth of Virginia."

"I bet you say that to all the technicians." Daisy smirked. "But in my case, it happens to be true."

Livingston nodded toward Daisy. "Rumor has it the FBI has tried to poach her more than once, but for some reason, she likes her little hovel below ground too much to leave us."

"Let's just say my heart belongs to Old Virginny." Daisy tapped the arm of her chair. "But what's with the civilians in the crime lab?"

"I got clearance from my lieutenant," Livingston said. "Since this is officially a closed case, he was willing to give us leeway on protocol."

"All righty then." Daisy repositioned her chair to face the computers. "I have a hot date tonight, so enough with the chitchat."

"Yes, ma'am." Livingston chuckled. "Bob indicated the device was pretty degraded. Were you able to recover any audio?"

Daisy snorted. "Bob's an idiot. The device was just fine for its age and location stuffed inside a rabbit."

"Where was the device in the bunny?" Brogan pulled out his notebook.

"Smack in the middle of the bunny's chest." Daisy held up a small, square black box. "As you can see, it's a pretty basic voice-activated recorder with a twenty-hour recording capacity."

Melender stared at the device, just over an inch square. "That was inside Blue Bunny?"

"You betcha." Daisy clicked some keys. "It's a continual loop mechanism, so it's set to record over itself."

Brogan looked up from his notebook. "So it filled up the twenty hours, then started recording again?"

"That's right. But it always recorded the date and time, so you can tell which part of the recording is from which time period." Daisy fiddled with some of the console controls.

"Melender, any idea where the bunny came from?"

"I gave it to him on his first birthday." An image of Jesse hugging the small stuffed animal tightly to his chest after opening the gift came to her mind. "But I had no idea it contained a recording device."

"The packaging didn't say so?" Livingston asked.

She bit her lip as she dredged up the memory of where she'd purchased the toy. "I bought it second-hand at a thrift store. No packaging, but it did have the original price tag on its ear, so I thought it must have been brand new."

"Can you tell if the recordings were ever listened to?" Brogan leaned around Melender and took a closer look at the device.

She drew in a breath as the scent of soap and cedar teased her nostrils. After this case ended, she would forever associate that smell with Brogan. The knowledge ushered in a wave of sadness. Once they solved this mystery, he would politely say goodbye. After all, he had a career to resurrect, and when he had her story, there would be no need for him to stick around.

"It appears the recordings could be downloaded, but I haven't had time to decipher if any were." Daisy threw Livingston a look over her shoulder. "A certain someone has been pushy about hearing the audio."

Livingston held up his hands in a who-me gesture. "Hey, I'm just trying to solve a crime."

"A crime that's already been solved," Daisy shot back. "I know your reputation. You don't like unanswered questions."

Livingston shrugged. "I prefer hard proof to support circumstantial evidence."

"Then you'll be interested in listening to what I've managed to pull off the recorder." Daisy put her earphones back on and hit a few buttons. "I think this little bunny recorded the murder."

THIRTY-THREE

B rogan nearly dropped the notebook at the lab tech's statement.

"There's about an hour relating to the night of the child's abduction," Daisy said. "I'll play that part."

Brogan snuck a look at Melender, whose gaze remained fixed on the computer screens. Her pale face and rigid shoulders spoke of her tension. He wanted to put his arm around her, but something about her stillness warned him it wouldn't be welcome. Shifting close enough that their arms brushed, he prayed for God's peace to wash over her.

An automated voice announced the date of Jesse's disappearance and the time of nine o'clock. A toddler's cries filled the room.

"That's Jesse," Melender whispered. "That's Jesse," she repeated in a louder voice.

Jesse's cries continued for several seconds, then a muffled child's voice attempted to quiet the toddler. "No cryin', Jesse."

"Jillian," Melender supplied.

Jesse wailed louder. "What's going on?" A male barked.

Brogan didn't need Melender to identify the man as Jared, but she confirmed it anyway.

"He feels hot," Jillian said.

"Seriously? I don't need this hassle right now. Oh, man. Snake's not gonna wait for me." Jared's annoyance came through loud and clear. "Stay here. I'll be right back."

"Twinkle, twinkle, little star, how I wonder what you are," Jillian sang offkey. "Up above the world so high, like a diamond in the sky. Twinkle, twinkle, little star, how I wonder what you are." Jesse's cries lessened into hiccups as Jillian repeated the song twice more before Jared returned.

"I'm going to give your brother some medicine so he will go to sleep," Jared said. "Open your mouth, Jesse."

Sounds of the crib mattress crinkling, coupled with Jesse's sniffles, a wet cough, then silence. Brogan recalled Melender saying Jesse had a runny nose in her police interview. He made a note to follow up to see what medicine Jared had given his little brother.

"Jilly, stay with him until he's asleep."

"I wanna finish the movie," Jillian whined.

"Later." Jared's voice took on a menacing growl. "Right now, play the peek-a-boo game with the bunny."

"Okay," Jillian huffed out. "Peek-a-boo, Jesse."

The recording continued with the sounds of Jillian playing the game with Jesse, who giggled a couple of times. Before long, silence filled the room.

Daisy hit pause. "That's the first bit from that night."

Brogan didn't stop to think. He reached out for Melender and wrapped his arm around her stiff shoulders. It was like hugging a statute, but he didn't let go.

"So Jared was taking care of Jesse that night." Livingston kept his gaze on screen.

"According to this audio," Daisy said, "which hasn't been authenticated."

"Don't worry. This is strictly off the record." Livingston looked at

Brogan. "And remember, you agreed to hold this until I tell you otherwise."

Brogan nodded his head. He squeezed Melender's shoulders, then took her hand in his. The iciness of her fingers chilled him, but he rubbed her hand to infuse some of his warmth to her.

"The next time the recorder comes on is forty-five minutes later." Daisy resumed the audio, which began with a mechanical voice giving the date and time.

"Jesse," Jared said. "Jesse?" His voice grew more panicked. "Oh, no. Jesse!"

The crib springs creaked, and the mattress rustled, then Jared said, "No, no, no, no, no. This can't be happening."

The recorder's mechanical voice gave another time stamp five minutes later, followed by Jared's voice. "Dad, Jesse's not breathing. Something's wrong."

A brief silence, then Jared said, "He was snotty nosed and hot. I gave him some medicine."

Another pause. "Some cough and cold stuff Ruby had in the kids' medicine cabinet plus some baby Tylenol."

"I know how to read a label," Jared's voice rose in agitation. "I only gave him the minimum dose."

A longer pause, then Jared said, "Jilly was playing peek-a-boo to calm him down. Dad." His voice choked. "I found the blue bunny over Jesse's face."

"No!" Melender's body slumped against Brogan. He cradled her in his arms as she buried her face in his chest, her hands bunching his shirt as her tears dampened it.

"Shut it off," Livingston snapped, his voice tight.

Melender's sobs filled the space with an inconsolable ache. Brogan stroked her back, not knowing how to comfort her. Hearing what had actually happened the night Jesse disappeared was heart wrenching. Brogan wasn't sure what to make of the audio, but one thing was crystal clear. Jared had discovered his younger brother in

273

the crib not breathing. Melender shuddered in his arms, and he pulled her closer.

"Brogan." Livingston touched his shoulder. "I think perhaps you should take Melender out for some air."

He nodded and guided Melender out of the room and over to the elevator bank, Livingston at his heels. While they waited for the car, Livingston raked his fingers through his hair. "Daisy said the recording wasn't graphic. That's why I didn't hesitate to ask you two to come along." The detective furrowed his brow. "Is she going to be okay?"

"I hope so." Brogan firmed his arm around her waist. "This recording changes everything."

Livingston blew out a breath as the elevator doors dinged open. "It definitely does." He stepped into the car after Brogan maneuvered Melender and himself inside. "I'll call the Commonwealth's attorney's office as soon as we reach the lobby. She's not gonna be happy about what's been uncovered, especially with her re-election campaign receiving substantial contributions from Thompson Energy."

Brogan had a million other questions but didn't voice any of them in the short elevator ride. Fallon would know how to cover this scoop ahead of their competition once they got permission. While part of him itched to get in front of a computer and start pounding out the story while the recording was fresh in his mind, his concern about Melender overrode his reporter's instincts. In the lobby, Livingston gave them a distracted goodbye, his attention fixated on his own cell phone.

By his side, Melender straightened, pulling away from his embrace. "What's going to happen now?"

"I'm not sure. Livingston's calling the Commonwealth's attorney." Brogan studied her washed-out features. There was a haunted look in her blue eyes that shimmered with tears. "Come on. I'll take you home."

"What time is it?" Her eyes widened. "I have to go to work.

Brogan glanced at his phone. "It's 4:50."

Melender's startled expression relaxed. "I have a little time before my shift starts." She gazed over his shoulder. "It sounded like Jared found Jesse not breathing in his crib with the bunny on his face."

"That's what I heard too." Brogan again placed his arm around her shoulders and gently moved her toward the revolving door. "It appears the Thompsons covered up whatever happened and left you to take the blame." He wedged both of them into one of the door's slots and pushed on the glass to exit the building.

Outside, Melender halted, turning her face up to the afternoon sun. "What do you think happened to Jesse?"

"I think..." Brogan, his arm still around her, glanced at the trickle of people moving past them from the building toward the parking lot. "Let's get in the car first."

Melender opened her mouth, but instead of speaking, nodded. He removed his arm from her shoulders to access his pocket for the car fob, ready to chirp open the doors as they approached the SUV.

He snapped his seat belt into place and tried to organize his thoughts. No matter which scenario that came to mind, all pointed to the Thompsons hiding the truth of what happened to Jesse and deliberately allowing Melender to take the blame. The injustice of it made his blood burn hotter than asphalt pavement under the 90-degree sun.

"You asked what I thought happened to Jesse." He drew in a deep breath. "I think there was a terrible accident and Jesse died. And rather than face what happened, the Thompsons choose to cover up his death and shift the blame to you."

"Brogan, you believe in God."

"Um, yes." He'd fallen away from his faith in his pursuit of journalistic fame, but his very public fall had ripped the scales from his eyes and exposed the sin in his heart. Repentance had started with a return to reading the Scriptures on a daily basis and humbling his heart before his Savior. Now he wouldn't change those lean years when he struggled to find work in his field with a Pulitzer because of how God had worked in his life and heart to draw him ever closer to Jesus.

"Then you know that all things work for the good of those who love God."

His anger rebelled against her words even as his heart agreed. Brogan reached across and wiped a tear from her cheek. "I'm familiar with the verse. Romans 8:28."

She placed her hand over his and brought it back to cradle her cheek, leaning her head into his hand. Her eyes never left his. "Brogan, I believe with all my heart God graciously put me in circumstances designed to strengthen my faith."

Brogan shook his head, his hand falling away from her face. She spoke the truth, but the peace in her eyes sliced into his very soul. She had been through so much more than him, and yet her faith had flourished, while his still struggled at times.

Melender held up her finger, silencing him any protest he might have formed. "It was for my good and His eternal glory that I went to prison for a crime I didn't commit. That didn't mean I gave up trying to find justice in this world. It meant I didn't despair when justice didn't come."

She smiled, and his heart thumped double time in his chest at the determination in her eyes. "No." He couldn't be reading her thoughts correctly. His gut clenched. "You can't, that's not right."

"Yes, I can. I've lived with this my whole adult life, and it hasn't crushed me yet. But the truth will devastate my family." She sat back and clicked her seat belt into place.

"They tried to destroy you." He wouldn't let Melender give up, not when they were so close to exonerating her. "They wanted you to rot in prison and are probably behind the apartment break-in and attacks against you."

"That doesn't matter. My actions aren't predicated on the actions of others."

His frustration spilled over. "Fancy words aren't going to change the fact they deliberately sent you to prison to cover up a crime."

She turned back to face him. "But from the recording, you can tell it was an accident. Jesse died because of a mistake."

He had to make her understand. He couldn't let her throw away the rest of her life because of some noble thought of saving her family by not pressing for her conviction to be overturned. If she did, she would also be throwing away any chance they had of a future, and he very much wanted to explore the possibility with her. "I'll grant you Jesse's death might have been an accident, but what happened after that most certainly was not."

"What if Jillian inadvertently killed him while playing peek-a-boo with the blue bunny?"

The question hit Brogan in the gut, pulverizing his ire into bits.

"She was barely three years old. She had no idea what she was doing." Melender's voice dropped to a whisper, her hands clenched on her lap as she stared straight ahead. "If this comes out, how could Jillian live with the knowledge that she accidentally killed her baby brother?"

"I don't know." He placed his hand over hers. "But it's not up to you. Livingston called the Commonwealth's attorney's office, which will determine if a crime has been committed and if there was a miscarriage of justice in your case."

She moved her hands away from his and bowed her head. "Can we go now?

He wanted to argue with her, make her see the wheels were in motion on the pathway to clearing her name, but things were too raw right now for those arguments to make sense to her. While he didn't agree with her point of view, she wasn't wrong. If Jillian had suffocated Jesse by playing a game with him, carrying that guilt around for the rest of her life would be a terrible burden.

Of all the outcomes for this case, that was one neither one of them had considered. And Brogan was very much afraid it would mean the demise of his budding relationship with Melender as well.

CHAPTER

THIRTY-FOUR

"He did what?" Phone to his ear, Quentin stalked to his office door and slammed it shut.

"He fired me," Dan Stabe said. "Jared said he didn't think I would have his best interests at heart."

Quentin blistered the air with a string of curse words. His plans were crumbling before his eyes. All because of Melender Harman. Nothing had gone right since she'd come out of the mountains and infiltrated his life. He should have listened to Ruby when she'd begged him not to allow Melender to stay in their home, but no, he had to play the magnanimous uncle. It's as if Ruby had known the destruction that would follow in Melender's wake.

He'd missed whatever else Stabe had said but didn't bother asking the attorney to repeat it. Without caring of the consequences, he barked, "You're fired."

"What?" Stabe's indignation mimicked his own. "You can't do that."

"I most certainly can." A grim smile curled the corners of Quentin's lips. "If you recall, your current position is based on my recommendation."

279

"That may be true, but I remind you that I know things about the past."

"Don't threaten me. If you want to go running to the cops or the Commonwealth's attorney, go right ahead. Whatever you say about me, you're the one who faces disbarment for your conduct during the trial."

"You're so sure this won't come back to bite you, but I'm not as incompetent as you think."

The best way to deal with people like Stabe—make sure they know you're not worried about being blackmailed. "So I paid you to make sure you only put up a facsimile of a defense. That's a minor offense compared with taking a bribe to throw a trial. Oh, and don't forget, breaking attorney-client privilege to keep me informed of everything Melender said to you."

"You could let that particular cat out of the bag, but I don't think you will."

The assurance in Stabe's voice alerted him to be wary, but Quentin had other things to think about, like how he was going to keep his son from making a huge mistake.

Stabe resumed. "There's also the matter of conversations we've had since then. I think the FBI will be very interested to listen to what you had to say about a certain senator and a bill that grants you mining rights in Shenandoah National Park."

"What exactly are you saying?"

"That I hold all the cards."

"Do you?" His longtime subordinates would have instantly recognized the menace behind those softly uttered words.

Stabe ploughed forward. "I recorded our conversations, and will turn over the recordings to the FBI, unless..."

Quentin opened a desk drawer and extracted one of his burner phones. Powering it up, he asked the question Stabe was waiting for. "Unless what?"

"I don't see why things can't continue as before."

Stabe's actions read like a script, so predictable. Quentin would have laughed at the sheer pedestrian aura of it all, but he didn't have time for frivolity. "You're right," Quentin finally responded.

A short pause, then the other man ventured, "I am?"

"I was too hasty in my decision to fire you. Consider yourself rehired." Quentin thumbed in a number on the burner phone without hitting the connect button.

"Great." Stabe cleared his throat. "What about Jared?"

"I'll take care of my son. And Stabe?"

"Yes?"

"I expect those recordings to be destroyed immediately." Quentin knew Stabe wouldn't do any such thing, but his tone didn't convey that knowledge.

"Absolutely. I'll take care of them right away."

Quentin ended the call without replying, then touched the connect button on the burner phone.

"Yes?" The other man's voice had a husky timber to it.

"Jared fired Stabe." In his leather executive chair, Quentin leaned back and let his head rest against the upholstered leather.

"And?" By the inflection in the other man's voice, he had picked up on the tension in Quentin.

"The little weasel tried to blackmail me, so I fired him too."

A short bark of laughter on the other end of the phone. "Lawyers can be so smug."

"Stabe said he made recordings of all of our conversations."

"I see. What did you do?"

"I rehired him and told him to destroy the tapes. Immediately." Quentin's personal cell phone sounded with Ruby's ringtone but he swiped to ignore the call. "I don't expect Stabe will be a problem much longer, if you get my meaning."

The other man disconnected without replying. The understanding between the two needed no explanation. He would take care of Stabe and those blasted tapes, if they even existed, and Quentin could focus on saving his family. A picture of Ruby right after she'd given birth to Jesse filled his mind. The radiance of her countenance had been brighter than any star. He had tried so hard to shield her, but he couldn't hold back the landslide any longer. Maybe one day, she would find it in her heart to forgive him. *Oh, my darling wife. I'm so sorry.*

~

JARED TILTED HIS HEAD BACK TO FINISH THE LAST SWALLOW FROM HIS SODA can. The remains of his lunch lay crumpled on the metal table. His new defense attorney, a public defender named John Billings, sat beside him jotting notes on a yellow legal pad. After spilling his story to Billings, the lawyer had arranged for Jared to speak with the two detectives and the Commonwealth's attorney.

"I gotta say, this sounds rather fantastic." Billings removed his glasses to rub the bridge of his nose.

"It's the truth." Jared shrugged. "Isn't there some saying about the truth being stranger than fiction?"

Billings smiled. "They do indeed say that."

For the first time in as long as he could remember, Jared didn't have a tightness in his chest. Guess sharing what had happened the night Jesse disappeared had been good for his body as well as his mind. The door opened, and the two detectives entered, followed by a slim woman with cropped hair.

Billings stood, his hand outstretched toward the detectives. "I'm John Billings, representing Jared Thompson."

The male detective shook Billings's hand. "Detective Livingston. This is my partner, Detective Collier, and Commonwealth's Attorney Nina Valbuena."

Jared didn't rise but nodded his greeting in their direction, second thoughts about this course of action tying his stomach up in knots. No, he needed to look after himself, and this was the only way to mitigate the kidnapping charges.

"Let's get started, shall we?" Billings retook his seat next to Jared as the others sat around the table. "Thank you for agreeing to come down this morning, Ms. Valbuena."

"You're welcome." The lawyer set her briefcase on the floor. "However, the Jesse Thompson murder is a closed case, as far as the Commonwealth of Virginia is concerned."

"And yet you're here." Billings tapped his pen on the legal pad. "I heard there's a recording that will corroborate my client's story."

"What?" Jared couldn't stop the question. "What recording?"

Billings laid a hand on his arm, signaling Jared to not say another word.

Ms. Valbuena shot Detective Livingston a look. The detective shrugged. "What does Mr. Thompson have to say?"

"First, I'd like assurance that my client will not be charged with anything related to what he's about to tell you," Billings countered.

The Commonwealth's representative glanced again at Livingston, who nodded once. "I can guarantee no charges will be filed against Mr. Thompson apart from the attempted kidnapping." She leaned across the table, her finger pointing directly at his chest. "But that guarantee doesn't extend to murder."

Some of the anxiety eased out of Jared at her assurance. Since he wouldn't be confessing to killing Jesse, he should be safe.

"That will do," Billings said. "Jared, the floor is yours."

Jared cleared his throat. "The night Jesse went missing, Ruby asked me to keep an eye on Jillian and Jesse. She and my dad were going to some charity function at the country club, and the nanny would be helping out there after getting Jesse ready for bed." He scrubbed a hand over his face. He'd been so annoyed at being saddled with his half-siblings. All he'd wanted was to score some pills from Snake and get high in his room while listening to his latest heavy metal album.

"Jesse wouldn't settle down. He kept fussing in his crib. Jillian said he wasn't feeling well, so I gave him some medicine. Infant Benadryl and liquid Tylenol." Jared walked them through the rest of the night. Jesse's crying, Jillian playing peek-a-boo with Blue Bunny.

Finding Jesse not breathing with Blue Bunny on his face. Calling his father in a panic.

"What happened after you called your father?" Ms. Valbuena asked.

Jared hung his head. "I checked to make sure Jillian was in her bed, then I left to meet Snake, my dealer."

"You left Jesse lying there in the crib?" Livingston's question cracked like a whip across Jared's back.

Jared flinched at the harshness in the detective's voice. "I couldn't do anything for him." Even as he said the words, he knew how pitiful they sounded. But he'd been only nineteen and jonesing for a fix.

"Why didn't you call 911?" Ms. Valbuena held her pen over her legal pad.

"My dad told me he'd take care of everything." And if the cops came, he could kiss his chance at meeting Snake goodbye. He held his head, and for the first time, the enormity of his actions crashed down on him like a house collapsing in on itself during a fire. The crushing weight of remorse squeezed his chest, making it difficult to answer the questions Ms. Valbuena and the detectives asked.

All Jared could think about was the look of betrayal in Melender's eyes as he lied on the witness stand about his whereabouts that night. At the time, keeping the generous monthly allowance his father settled on him for committing perjury had been his top priority. He'd negotiated the settlement with his father after realizing he could never spend the ransom money. Jared's testimony had been crucial to convincing the jury that Melender had been left in charge of the children. How Melender must hate him for his role in sending her to prison for a crime she didn't commit.

"Mr. Thompson?" Ms. Valbuena's voice held a note of impatience.

Jerking his thoughts away from his cousin, Jared refocused on the attorney. "Sorry."

She didn't acknowledge his apology. "What happened to Jesse's body?"

He shrugged. "I don't know."

"You don't know." Ms. Valbuena tapped the legal pad with her pen, her expression unreadable. "Who would know?"

Jared exchanged a look with Billings, who nodded. Drawing in a deep breath, Jared let it out slowly. He had to take care of himself now. What happened, happened. He couldn't go back and change the actions of his nineteen-year-old self, but he could help his thirty-nine-year-old self. Straightening in his chair, he looked the prosecutor directly in the eye. "My father took care of it."

CHAPTER

THIRTY-FIVE

Melender rolled onto her stomach in bed. Three hours after she'd clocked out at work, she still couldn't fall asleep despite being physically tired. She'd done her shift last night by rote.

The voices on the recording kept playing over and over in her mind. The fear in Jared's voice. Jillian's high-pitched singsong as she entertained Jesse with a game of peek-a-boo. The snuffles and cries of her littlest cousin. She hugged a throw pillow to her chest. She thought the truth would ease the ache in her heart but instead, it had increased it.

During her incarceration, a dozen different scenarios as to what had actually happened to Jesse, mostly involving a kidnapping gone wrong, came to mind. But she'd never considered that Jillian accidentally smothered her younger brother and her father had spirited the body away rather than let his daughter discover what she'd done. Melender figured Quentin had allowed her arrest because of his love for Ruby and his children.

On her back, she stared at the ceiling. If she were being honest, it wasn't only the recording that kept her tossing and turning. Thoughts of Brogan also vied for her attention.

Brogan's disappointment remained baffling. Maybe he'd been upset because her decision to protect Jillian from finding out the truth had hampered his ability to report the entire story. After all, he had been upfront about his interest in the story and the potential it had of catapulting his career back into national prominence.

As she recalled the kiss with Brogan, her body warmed. *Love.* The one word Melender hadn't successfully guarded against when it came to Brogan had allowed Cupid to aim his arrow directly at her heart.

She'd asked Sudie about love once after her grandmother had related one of her stories about star-crossed lovers. Her grandmother smiled as she rocked in a wooden chair, her hands busily knitting a baby blanket for a young family in the hollow. Sudie's words now replayed in her mind.

"Child, sometimes, people do fall in love at the drop of an acorn." Her hands stilled in her lap as a faraway look came into her eyes. "The summer I turned twenty, I met my future husband at a barn raising. Even in patched overalls and scuffed work boots, Trilby Harman caught my eye. My, how that man could swing a hammer." Sudie smiled, her faded blue eyes twinkling with the memory.

"Trilby was too shy to ask me to take a spin during the dance that evening, so I grabbed his hand and pulled him out on the floor. We were married three months later, and I never regretted a moment of our life together. We had fifty years of wedded bliss before the Lord saw fit to call Trilby home."

Sudie resumed knitting and rocking, her eyes on fifteen-year-old Melender. "You're coming of an age to think about young men." Then her grandmother had pointed her knitting needle at her. "Find a young man who loves the Lord more than he loves you, and you won't go wrong."

Oh, Sudie. If only I'd had more time to glean additional wisdom from you before you joined Grandfather Trilby in heaven. Melender blinked back tears as a wave of homesickness crashed over her.

Maybe returning to the little log cabin tucked into the foothills of the Blue Ridge Mountains would banish unrealistic thoughts of a relationship with Brogan. Surely there were still people there who would remember her. She didn't need much and could easily leave behind the trappings of the modern life to forge a living on the mountain. No one there would care about her recent past, only that she had once belonged to the mountains. That was her true heritage, and she would be welcomed back when she chose to reclaim it.

A gentle smile curled the corners of her lips as the words of the nineteenth-century naturalist and preservationist John Muir summed up her desire. *The mountains are calling, and I must go.*

Melender tossed back the covers. She pulled on a pair of denim shorts and a t-shirt, then loosely braided her hair. After slipping on a pair of tennis shoes, she sat on the edge of the bed and brought up Jillian's number on the phone. Maybe Jillian would know what happened to the rest of Melender's things, including the keys to Sudie's cabin. Before she could talk herself out of it, she hit the call button.

"Hello?" Jillian answered after the first ring.

"Jilly, it's Melender." She would be careful not to say anything about knowing what happened the night Jesse disappeared or Jillian's role in his death. She would tell Jillian she wanted to go home but wouldn't offer an explanation.

"Why are you calling?" Jillian's voice held a cautious tone.

"I just have a quick question. Do you know what happened to the rest of my things from the house? I'm specifically looking for the keys to Sudie's cabin."

"Is that all?" Jillian blew out a breath. "This isn't a good time."

"Can I call you later?"

"That might be best." In the background, Melender heard a muffled voice, to which Jillian responded, "Mom, I got this."

Ruby. No wonder Jillian didn't want to talk.

289

"Mom wants to talk to you." Jillian gave Melender only seconds before Ruby came on the line.

"You have some nerve calling my daughter," Ruby hissed.

Melender gathered her wits. "Actually, you probably know the answer to my question."

A short pause, then her aunt said, "What could you possible want to ask me?"

"What happened to the keys to Sudie's cabin?" Melender wasn't holding her breath her aunt would even answer her.

"The prodigal daughter wants to go home?" The sarcasm in her aunt's voice sliced into Melender like a scythe, but she ignored the pain.

"Yes, I do."

"Well, you can't."

Melender sucked in a breath. "You don't have the keys?" She reeled in her impatience. If needed, it would be a small bother to have a locksmith rekey the doors and the benefits far outweighed any inconvenience.

"That's right," Ruby said. "Forget about that place."

Melender's stomach clenched. *No. Please, God, no.* "What did you do?" The words came out in a whisper.

"I sold the cabin." Ruby's malicious satisfaction barely registered as the content hit Melender hard.

"You had no right to sell my inheritance."

"So the kitten does have claws." Ruby clicked her tongue. "I had every right. Sudie didn't leave a will, and as her closest living relative, I was named her heir."

"What?" Melender put a hand to her head. "She told me she was leaving the cabin to me."

"She might have told you that, but she never made the time to write a will." The smugness came through loud and clear. "That means the state had to determine her heirs, and a granddaughter trumps an underage great-granddaughter. I suppose the state thought I would share the proceeds with you, but you killed Jesse, so that was out of the question."

Melender tried not to cry out in pain and frustration.

"One more thing." Ruby spat out the last few words. "Stop calling my daughter. There's nothing here for you anymore." She disconnected the call.

Melender let the phone slide from her hand onto the bed. The thought of returning to that cabin had been a comfort during the long nights in prison. Now she truly had no place to call home. She kicked off her shoes, then fell back onto the mattress. Curled in a fetal position, she stayed dry-eyed as inside, her heart was breaking.

INSTEAD OF HEADING TO THE OFFICE THIS MORNING, BROGAN STOPPED BY HIS aunt and uncle's to read more of the Thompson case file in the hopes of finding more inconsistencies that could help to build a stronger case for Melender's innocence. His phone rang beside him on the dining room table. A glance at the screen revealed the call to be from an unknown party.

"Gilmore." Brogan answered with his standard greeting.

The caller whispered something he couldn't decipher. "I didn't catch that."

"It's Dan." The man cleared his throat. "Dan Stabe."

Brogan straightened in his chair. "Mr. Stabe, what can I do for you?"

"I think someone's following me." The lawyer spoke an undertone.

Brogan depressed the record button, then pressed the device back to his ear. "Where are you?" He tugged his notebook out from underneath a file and picked up a pen.

"I should have known this was a trap."

"Mr. Stabe—"

"Listen carefully. I don't have much time. I left a package for you at the front desk of my law office. You must leave immediately to get it. Do you understand? Time is of the essence. If they figure out I've called you..."

"Mr. Stabe."

Although Stabe's s voice trailed off, fear behind the attorney's words motivated Brogan to get moving.

"I'm heading there now. Tell me, what was a trap?"

"Tell Melender I'm sorry. I'm a weak man."

"Mr. Stabe, I want to know where you are." Brogan halted. He pressed the phone more firmly against his ear. "Hello?" Awareness set in at the sound of silence. The call ended. He stopped the recording while contemplating what to do next.

"Was that Dan Stabe?"

Brogan whipped toward the woman's voice. Melender stood on the landing of the stairs, her phone and earbuds in her hand.

"Yeah, he called me." Given Melender's casual attire of denim shorts, t-shirt, and sneakers, his first thought was to ask why she was awake. "Don't you have to work tonight?"

"My question first. Why is Stabe calling you?" Melender took the last step and stood inches from Brogan. She'd removed the bandage on her face. The stitches now rested in a purplish bruise that covered the right cheek.

"Brogan, will you please answer me?"

The sharpness of her tone yanked him back. "Stabe said he thought someone was following him. He also said he'd left a package for me at his law office. That's where I was headed when the call abruptly ended. My turn. Aren't you working tonight?"

"Yes, but I couldn't sleep, so I'm up earlier. I'm coming with you to pick up the package." Melender's statement startled him given her declaration last night of wanting to let sleeping dogs lie.

He hesitated, then pulled open the front door and held it for her to proceed. "After you."

"Thank you."

Brogan didn't attempt conversation on the drive to the attorney's office. Instead, he vacillated between wanting to convince her that finding the truth about Jesse still mattered and telling her how beautiful she looked, which could make him appear unprofessional under the circumstances.

Melender huddled against the passenger car door. Although her stillness concerned him, he wasn't quite sure how to broach the subject. During the fifteen-minute drive to Stabe's office, she kept her head turned toward the side window but clearly wasn't taking in the scenery. Something had made her skittish, something beyond the recording yesterday.

He pulled into the parking lot of Davis, Ramsey, and Stevens, and slipped into a visitor's spot near the front entrance. "I'm not sure what's going on. You stay put. I'll only be a few minutes."

Melender nodded but didn't turn toward him.

Brogan jogged to the office building. Once inside, he punched the elevator number and took the car to the eleventh floor. The receptionist looked up when he approached her desk. "Good morning."

"Hello."

The receptionist looked past him, then back to him. Maybe checking to see if Seth had accompanied him? Brogan smiled. "Brogan Gilmore. Dan Stabe left a package for me." He refrained from tapping his fingers on the raised glass countertop that encircled the area as she clicked a few keys.

"May I see some identification?" Her smile broadened as she extended her hand toward him. "I need to make sure you're who you say you are."

"Of course." He dug out his wallet and flipped it open to show his driver's license. She studied it before standing to move to a bank of cubby holes. After extracting a bulky, banded accordion file folder, she returned to the desk. "Here you go."

Brogan thanked her and tucked the package under his arm as he hurried to the elevator. During the short ride to the lobby, he resisted the urge to flip through the papers.

293

In the car, he placed the folder on the console between them. Melender rested her hand on the package. "What's this?"

"Something Stabe wanted me to have." Brogan put the car in reverse and backed out of the space

Her fingers lightly tapped the folder. "It looks like his notes from my trial."

He raised his eyebrows. "What makes you think that?"

"I recognize the folder." She pointed to a circular stain on the light brown surface. "He set his coffee mug here and some of it spilled." Melender pointed to another marred area. "This greasy spot is from a sandwich wrapper. And that"—she indicated a smudged shape—"is where I drew a wood anemone blossom. It's kind of our family flower."

Brogan pulled onto the main street. "I'm impressed with your memory. Half the time I can't recall a stain on my shirt from the same day, much less what happened to an accordion file from eighteen years ago."

"Don't envy me." She shrugged. "I had a lot of time in prison to go over the events that led up to my incarceration."

Her solemn declaration gripped his heart. "Are you okay? You seem a little..." He searched for the right word. "Sad."

Hot on the scent of piecing together the truth of what happened to Jesse, he'd overlooked this case was more than a mystery to be solved and a story to be written. To Melender, it was about reclaiming her adult life from its dark past and bringing it into the light of truth.

Melender swiped at her cheek. "Why do you think Stabe gave you the folder?"

He smiled at her diversionary tactic. While accelerating through a yellow light, Brogan glanced over at her. "Melender, something's wrong. Is it the recording?"

She shook her head, not meeting his gaze but staring out of the window. "Please—" Her hand grasped the armrest. "Brogan, watch out!"

He jerked his attention back to the road. A black SUV swerved into his lane, bumping his vehicle into the oncoming traffic. Horns blared as Brogan twisted the wheel hard to the right to regain his lane, but the SUV slammed into them.

"Brace yourself!" He stomped on the brakes and swerved to the right but couldn't completely avoid an oncoming pickup truck. The pressure of his seatbelt held him tight as the high-pitched whine of tearing metal and the loud pop of the deploying airbags filled his ears.

The impact sent his SUV spinning into an unyielding object, whipping Brogan's head against the door frame with a thunk. Light flashed and sparkled as pain exploded across his skull. He fought the enclosing darkness but was no match for the blackness that over-whelmed his senses.

THIRTY-SIX

R uby firmed her lips, not caring that such an expression marred the smooth contours of her face. She didn't want to see the detectives, who showed up yet again unannounced on her doorstep. After their last visit, Consuela had been instructed to leave them standing outside if they returned. She was through offering them hospitality, since they insisted on tormenting her family rather than finding her baby boy.

After yanking open the door, she glared at Livingston and Collier. "If you don't stop harassing my family, I'm going to report you to your superiors."

"Ma'am, I have a warrant to search the premises." Livingston handed her a piece of paper.

Only then did Ruby notice the pair weren't alone. Uniformed officers milled about on the paver-stone driveway. She craned her neck to see behind the two detectives. In the driveway, a woman unloaded two dogs from the back of a van. "What's going on?"

"The warrant explains we will be searching the grounds and the house," Livingston said as his partner waved to a waiting group of men and women, who started toward them. "Who's currently inside?"

Ruby crumpled the warrant in her hand. "My housekeeper and daughter."

"Where's your husband?" Livingston put his hand on Ruby's arm and gently guided her inside as men and women filed in behind them.

"Quentin's at work." As if saying his name broke a spell that had held her immobile, she shook her arm out of Livingston's grip. "I've got to call him." She hurried to the kitchen as she pressed the call button on her phone. A female police officer positioned herself within earshot of Ruby.

Her husband picked up on the first ring. "Ruby, I told you I have meetings all day today. In fact—"

"The police are here with a warrant to search the house and grounds." The words tumbled out in a rush.

Silence.

"Did you hear what I said?" From the corner of her eye, she could see Livingston had joined her in the kitchen.

"I'll be there as soon as I can." Quentin disconnected the call.

Ruby laid the phone on the counter, her husband's decisiveness bolstering her courage to face the police alone. Her daughter stormed into the kitchen, followed by a uniformed female cop.

"Mom? What's happening?" Jillian pointed at the police office behind her. "She kicked me off my computer and told me I had to come to the kitchen."

Livingston answered. "We have a warrant to search the house and grounds. You'll need to either vacate the premises or stay in the kitchen under supervision."

Jillian's mouth fell open in the classic expression of disbelief.

The fear in her daughter's eyes paralyzed Ruby for an instant, then she rushed to gather Jillian in her arms. "It's okay. Everything will be all right."

Jillian shoved back out of Ruby's embrace. "It won't."

Ruby reached for her daughter, but Jillian shook her head. "Your father's on his way. He'll sort this out."

"Not this time." Jillian's mouth tightened. "He can't."

"Of course he can." Quentin always took care of his family first. That was one of the things Ruby admired and loved about her husband.

Jillian snorted. "Don't you see? Don't you get it?"

Ruby shot a quick glance at the detective, whose attention was fixed on mother and daughter. After stepping closer to Jillian, she hissed, "You need to calm down and pull yourself together."

"I need to calm down?" Jillian's voice rose. "Of all the times to not be cool and collected, I think this ranks as one of them. They're going through my stuff!"

Ruby reined in her own emotions, which were steadily rising in correspondence to her daughter's see-sawing outburst. "This is just another incidence of police harassment, and as soon as your father comes—"

"What?" Jillian snapped the question. "What will Dad do? He can't make them stop searching. They have a warrant."

Ruby didn't have an answer to that, but Jillian wasn't waiting for one anyway, as her daughter plowed on. "And you know what? I hope they find whatever it is they're looking for." She lowered her voice. "Then at least we can finally get all of our dirty little secrets out in the open instead of them festering and poisoning all of us."

Jillian dashed tears from her cheeks with the backs of her hands, then turned to face the large kitchen window. Before Ruby could go to her daughter, a suited technician entered the kitchen.

Livingston and the man held a short, murmured conversation before the detective slipped out of the room after the technician. Ruby rubbed her hands on her arms, a chill in the air despite the warm September day. Things had gotten so topsy-turvy, she doubted anything could put them right side up again.

"Ruby?"

She turned to see Quentin pause in the kitchen doorway, another uniformed police officer at his heels. Wordlessly, she held out her hands and her husband hurried across the kitchen to take them in his. At his touch, her composure crumbled.

"My poor darling." Quentin pulled her into his arms.

She laid her cheek against his crisp dress shirt, his heart beating beneath her ear. The tranquil rhythm helped to slow her breathing. Quentin was here. He would make everything better. He always did.

"Mr. Thompson?"

Livingston's voice jerked Ruby out of her comfort zone. She twisted out of Quentin's embrace to face the detective alongside her husband.

"Detective Livingston, isn't it?" Quentin's voice held no hint of distress, and his warm grip on Ruby's hand renewed her confidence in his ability to handle any situation. "What can I do for you?"

"We've discovered a safe hidden in the master bathroom linen closet. Would you please open it?" Livingston gazed directly at Quentin. "We can call a locksmith to drill the lock but thought you might prefer the safe not to be damaged."

Ruby's mind raced. What was he talking about? The only safe in the house was in the study behind her portrait.

But her husband's expression stayed the same, leaving her to believe he didn't seem flummoxed by the discovery. "I can give you the combination." He then rattled off a series of numbers that the detective jotted down. As soon as Livingston left, Quentin dropped her hand and paced to the sink. He grabbed a glass, filled it with water, and drank it down in one long, gulp.

Ruby plucked at his sleeve. "What safe? Quentin, what was he talking about?"

He didn't answer, his shoulders a tense outline in his dress shirt. Ruby aligned herself with him to follow the direction of his gaze. Men and women swarmed over their backyard using long poles to poke into shrubbery, while two women walked behind leashed dogs that sniffed the ground. One dog promptly sat beside her prized rose bushes. The ones her husband had planted in the days after Jesse had disappeared.

~

BROGAN GRITTED HIS TEETH AS THE SURGEON DREW THE NEEDLE THROUGH A laceration in his forearm. Even though the woman had swabbed the area with numbing gel, he still felt the tug of the thread. He'd already been checked over thoroughly and pronounced ready for release once this cut had been stitched. A butterfly bandage closed a cut on his forehead, and other than bruising on his shoulder and hips from the seatbelt, he had come through the accident relatively unscathed.

His questions about Melender had been fruitless beyond the fact that she was somewhere in this hospital. Once the surgeon finished her handiwork, Brogan would roam the hallways until he found her.

"All done." The doctor tied off the suture and stepped away to allow a nurse to bandage the arm. "Keep the dressing on until tomorrow, then change it every day. The nurse will send home instructions with you." She peered closely at Brogan's face. "And some prescription strength ibuprofen for the pain."

"Thanks." Brogan stifled the urge to leap off the bed and find Melender.

With a wave, the surgeon departed the cubicle, swishing the curtain back into place. The fabric hadn't stopped swinging when someone pushed it open again.

"May we come in?" Detective Livingston, followed by a man in a suit Brogan didn't recognize, entered the cubicle. "You don't look so hot."

Brogan grimaced. "Being rammed by a SUV into oncoming traffic can do that to a person."

"I heard about your accident." The other man held up a hand as if to stave off questions Brogan would ask. "Melender's fine. She has some lacerations and bruising, but she's being cleared for release."

"Thank God." Brogan sincerely meant what might sound trite.

"But I didn't come to the hospital just to see how you're doing." The detective remained quiet as the nurse tied off the bandage.

"I'll be right back with the ibuprofen, instructions, and discharge papers," she said.

Once she had gone, Livingston gestured to the man beside him. "This is Detective Tom Billets. He's in charge of investigating the accident."

"It wasn't an accident." Brogan flashed back to the deliberate actions of the other driver and suppressed a shudder. "We could have been killed. The other driver was trying to make us crash."

"We know," Billets said. "The other driver fled the scene, but we recovered his cell phone, which had texts between the driver and someone else directing the driver to make sure you had an accident after leaving Stabe's office."

The folder. "Did you recover an accordion folder from my vehicle?" Brogan had a sinking feeling what the answer would be.

Billets frowned. "No, there was nothing like that in the vehicle, but we might have missed it, as we weren't conducting a thorough search. I'll call the impound lot and have the guys there go through the SUV again. Can you describe the item?"

"It's about yea big"—Brogan demonstrated with his hands, wincing as the gesture pulled at his fresh stitches—"so it's not likely you missed it." Frustration tightened around him like a vice. "Then there was someone else there, someone who followed the driver and managed to get the folder from our car before help arrived."

Billets flipped through a small notebook. "A couple of witnesses said a man had been examining your vehicle immediately after the accident, but they thought he was trying to help you and Ms. Harman."

Livingston's eyebrows rose. "What was in the folder?"

"I'm not sure." His focus slipped as a pounding headache galloped into place. "Stabe called to tell me he had a package at the front desk of his law firm. He wanted me to pick it up right away."

The nurse whisked back the curtain. "Here you go."

Brogan took the paper cup the nurse held out, then took a sip of water from the cup on the bedside tray table.

"These instructions outline how to care for your arm wound and when to seek additional medical help." She handed him the papers.

"Thank you." He signed the discharge papers and returned them, keeping the copy for himself.

"You're all set to go." She gave him a cheery smile, then departed.

The two detectives, who had been carrying on a muted conversation during the nurse's visit, stepped toward the bed. Billets spoke first. "I think that about wraps it up on my end. We'll be in touch, although I don't hold out much hope. The other vehicle was reported stolen this morning."

Brogan wasn't surprised. "Thanks for stopping by." He eased himself off the bed as Billets exited the cubicle while Livingston lingered. "I thought you were on leave."

"Circumstances required my return."

Something else had happened, but Brogan's sluggish mind couldn't form the questions to ask, not when he needed to have eyes on Melender. "I need to check on Melender."

Livingston smiled. "I thought you might. Come on."

Brogan managed to keep up with the other man as he wove his way through the crowded emergency department. Curtained beds fanned out in a ring around a central hub where medical personnel checked computers and snatched papers off a bank of printers.

On the opposite side of the room, Livingston stopped beside a closed curtain. "She's in here."

"Melender?" Brogan eased back the curtain to find an empty bed. Whirling around, he snapped, "Where is she?"

CHAPTER
THIRTY-SEVEN

Melender dried her hands in the single-stall ER bathroom but avoided looking in the mirror. She didn't need it to tell her she resembled something the cat had dragged home, one of Sudie's favorite sayings. Fatigue pulled at her. She hadn't felt this beaten down since the days after her conviction. Every step had been hard, every breath even harder. Only the continual loop of Sudie's voice in her mind, quoting and singing Scripture, had gotten her through those dark days.

Now her quest for the truth threatened to drag her down again. She had never considered Jesse's death might have been an accident and the coverup designed to keep Jillian and Ruby safe. But then Jared had tried to cash in on his little brother's disappearance, and things had snowballed beyond Quentin's control. Melender had no doubt her uncle was behind the coverup. Even as a teenager, she'd known his love for Ruby was like an all-consuming fire, gobbling up everything in its path and leaving only ashes in its wake. Everything that had happened to her and Brogan since Ruby had accosted her at the Kwikie Mart took on new meaning when viewed through the lens of Quentin struggling to keep Ruby from finding out the truth.

Maybe more answers would be forthcoming now that the police had heard the recording. She exited the bathroom, moving slowly as her body responded to new aches and pains, courtesy of the car accident. Wait a minute. Had the truck driver deliberately rammed Brogan's SUV? Her recollections of the accident were fuzzy. Brogan's memory might serve better to answer that question. A nurse had said he was in the ER as well with non-life-threatening injuries. Outside the bathroom to steady herself, Melender nearly lost her balance as someone brushed by.

"Watch—"

Someone put a hand on her shoulder and hissed, "Don't say a word if you want to avoid a shootout in the ER."

Her Don Quixote-quoting assailant was back. Melender stiffened as the man pressed the barrel of a gun into her back, his body pressed close to hers.

"We're going to turn to the left and exit the ER through the stairway door. Do you see it?"

She turned her head in the direction he indicated and spotted the glowing Exit sign, then nodded.

"Good." He slide his arm around her waist from behind and hugged her closer, the gun boring into her side. "Let's go."

Melender kept her body facing forward but tried to look around the busy ER, hoping to spot Brogan or one of the detectives who had briefly talked to her about the accident. No one paid any attention to her or the man at her back. All too soon, she pushed open the stairway door.

The man maneuvered her through it into the deserted stairwell. He pocketed the gun and grabbed her by the elbow. "Keep moving."

With his fingers digging into her arm, Melender went along with him as he tugged her down a short set of stairs and out a door that led to the hospital's parking garage. Another few steps brought them to a black SUV with tinted windows.

The man unlocked the vehicle, twisted her arms behind her. and in one fluid movement, shoved her face down into the back seat. She had no time to protest or fight before plastic zip ties secured her arms, then her feet. The restraints brought memories of her arrest, and helplessness clawed at her like a hungry mountain lion.

"I'll leave a gag off if you stay quiet. Will you be quiet?"

Melender nodded, her heart pounding. The man's identity again tickled her memory. She'd seen him before the warning he'd delivered outside her work but couldn't place him.

"One peep out of you and the gag goes in." Don Quixote slammed the door. Within seconds, he'd settled into the driver's seat and backed the SUV out of the parking space.

As the vehicle exited the parking lot, Melender closed her eyes and concentrated on slowing her heart rate. *Lord, you are my refuge, you are my champion.* Bits of Psalms she'd memorized in prison flitted through her mind, kicking the panic out as the peace of God filled her soul.

If she hoped to get out of this alive, she needed to have all her wits about her. Sudie singing the hymn "Everybody Will Be Happy Over There" echoed in her mind. Melender's body relaxed against the seat as she sang the lyrics into the seat, careful to keep her voice low. "There's a happy land of promise over in the great beyond, where the saved of earth shall soon the glory share. Where the souls of men shall enter and live on forever more. Everybody will be happy over there."

BROGAN RUSHED TO THE NURSES STATION, WHERE AN OLDER WOMAN wearing bright green scrubs with dancing frogs tapped on a keyboard. "Do you know where Melender Harman is? She was in cubicle C."

"And you are?" The nurse met his eyes.

"I'm a..." Brogan wasn't sure what to call his relationship with Melender. "Friend." Livingston came up beside Brogan.

"I'm sorry, I can only give that information to family members."
She turned her attention back to the computer.

"Ma'am, Detective Livingston, Fairfax County Police Department." Livingston flipped open his badge to show the nurse. "Ms.
Harman was in a suspicious car accident along with this gentleman."
The detective indicated Brogan. "I need to question her further about
the incident."

"In that case, let me check." The nurse typed for a few minutes.
"It says she signed her release papers twenty minutes ago." She
glanced up from the screen. "She might have gone into the waiting
room to make a phone call. We don't allow cell usage in the treatment areas."

Brogan took off toward the waiting area, Livingston right behind
him. An initial sweep of the filled room didn't turn up Melender. A
slower perusal had the same results. She wasn't there. Brogan
stepped outside and scanned the sidewalk on either side of the
sliding glass doors. No Melender.

His heart pounding, Brogan slipped back inside. Livingston stood
in conversation with a doctor at the far end of the waiting area. The
doctor left just as Brogan reached the detective.

"She's not outside," Brogan said.

"A doctor saw her go into one of the restrooms in the ER. I'm
going to check the security cameras to see where she might have
gone after that." Livingston started down the hall.

Brogan followed him, relieved the detective was taking her
disappearance seriously. His heart rate accelerated as his thoughts
ping-ponged around to various scenarios, each more dire than the
last. *Please, God, keep her safe. Help us figure out where she went.* He had
no doubt she was in some kind of danger. No way would Melender
simply vanish without telling anyone, not after all that had
happened over the last couple of days.

Ten minutes later, Brogan and Livingston crammed into the
small security office with Tavon Carstairs, head of security. Sasha

Brown, a female technician on the security team, keyed up the ER cameras for the right time frame.

On a surprisingly clear recording, Melender exited cubicle C and went into the single-stall restroom on the far side of the busy ER. A few minutes later, she left the bathroom and paused. Then someone wearing a baseball cap and a hoodie bumped into her and touched her shoulder. A minute later, Melender and the person, who appeared to be a man by height and stature, walked to the stairway exit door and disappeared from view.

"I'd like a copy of that footage, please. Do the stairwells have cameras?" Livingston asked.

Brogan stared at the monitor. The stiffness of Melender's posture attested that she hadn't gone willingly with the man.

"Yep." Carstairs motioned to Sasha to tap into that camera. Minutes later, Melender and the man appeared on the other side of the stairway door. The man kept his head down and his body turned away from the camera as he put something in his pocket, then grabbed Melender's arm to hustle her down the stairs and out another door.

"Was that a gun he put in his pocket?" Brogan figured his guess was spot on, given Melender's acquiescence in the ER.

"That's what I think," Livingston concurred. "Where does that door lead?"

"To the parking lot." Carstairs didn't have to ask the tech to move to the parking lot cameras. "Last year, we had a rash of parking lot thefts, with the thieves disabling our security cameras. So we beefed up our video coverage in all of our garages and installed hidden cameras in addition to the visible ones."

On the bank of screens, multiple images of the area near the exit door Melender and the man used popped up. Sasha reversed the recording to reach the right time frame, and soon Melender and the man appeared again in the far-left screen. Cameras tracked them to a black SUV, where the man opened the back door and shoved Melender into the car face first.

The camera didn't capture what the man did, but Brogan caught sight of a plastic zip tie in the man's back pocket. "He's tying her up." The thought of Melender being trussed like a turkey made his blood pressure rise, but Brogan tamped down his anger. He needed to keep his cool to figure out where this man was taking her. He couldn't ever remember getting this worked up over a story before, but then this wasn't just the injustice over something happening to a source. It was a woman he cared about being manhandled.

"That's what it looks like," Livingston agreed.

The man got into the driver's seat and backed the car out of the space. The license plate was missing from the front of the vehicle, but another camera showed the back plate, slightly smeared with mud but still readable.

"Pause it there, please. Can you zoom in on the plate?" Livingston waited until the tech enlarged the plate area, then he jotted down the number. "Thanks. Would you print that for me?"

"Sure." Carstairs leaned over and moved the mouse to access another camera while the tech printed the blown-up license plate screen shot.

"Any way to tell which exit he took?" Brogan asked while Livingston made a phone call to request a check on the plates.

"There." Carstairs pointed to a screen on the right. "He's exiting onto Blue Road, which will take him straight to Gallows Road."

"Stop it right there," Livingston requested.

Carstairs complied. Through the SUV's windshield, the camera captured a partial view of the driver's face.

"Can you enhance that at all?" Brogan leaned closer. The man looked familiar. He had a good memory for faces, an asset in his line of work.

"Gonna take a while, since he's in the shadows." Sasha isolated the photo and clicked over to another screen. She glanced up at Carstairs. "I'll text you when I have something."

"Sounds good," Carstairs said. "Let's grab a cup of coffee."

Brogan started to protest, but over Sasha's head, Carstairs

nodded toward the door. The trio departed, leaving the tech muttering to herself as she manipulated the photo.

Once outside, Carstairs led the way toward one of the hospital cafes. "Sasha's my best tech. She'll work much faster if we're not looking over her shoulder. Detective, I hear you know Bob Knightman."

"Yes, we go way back," Livingston answered.

As the two talked about Bob, Brogan prayed again for Melender's safety. *Please keep her safe. Help us to find her. And let the truth about Jesse finally come to light.* She'd become so much more than a source, than a story. He had to find her, to tell her how he felt. For the first time in a very long time, he had found someone to share his life with, the good and the bad.

He only hoped he'd have an opportunity to tell her.

THIRTY-EIGHT

"Remember, one peep and I'll gag you." The man roughly shoved Melender onto a stack of bagged fertilizer. They had driven for what seemed like hours before the vehicle stopped. When he'd hustled her from the SUV to the shed tucked behind a stand of tall evergreen shrubs, Melender had caught a glimpse of a large house a hundred yards away.

A single bulb dangled on a cord, but the man didn't turn on the light. Late afternoon sunlight streamed through a window set on the wall opposite the door. The lawn equipment and gardening tools had been neatly stacked on shelves and the floor, which had been recently swept. She fervently hoped no eight-legged or four-legged creatures hid in the recesses.

"I've got her." The man spoke into his phone, his back to Melender. "Be here within the hour." He ended the call, slipping the phone into a pocket and turning to face Melender. He'd ditched the baseball cap upon arriving at their destination.

"Who are you?" The question burst out of her before she'd had time to think.

"John Smith."

Melender snorted at the absurdity.

The man's smile broadened. "You don't believe me."

"No."

"They never do." Smith looked around him, then grabbed a folded camping chair from a shelf. After shaking it out, he sat across from Melender. "I told Quentin you would be trouble, and here you are, stirring up all kinds of trouble."

Melender straightened, the man's words sparking anger. "I don't call trying to clear my name of a crime I didn't commit stirring up trouble."

"I suppose if I were in your shoes, I'd feel the same way." Smith shrugged. "But since I'm not, it's irrelevant what you think."

Smith's words, spoken so causally, warned she was dealing with a man without a conscience. She had encountered her fair share of sociopaths during her imprisonment but never ceased to be amazed at the how they justified their actions. "Are you always this indifferent to truth?"

"Ah, a jailhouse philosopher." His eyes brightened as he leaned forward. "Whose truth? Yours? My truth is that I want to live my life on my terms. Your truth doesn't interest me in the slightest."

"Unless my truth helps you gain yours."

Smith spread his hands out, palms up, in a as-you-see gesture. In that instant, a long-ago image of Smith popped into her head. If her hands had been free, she'd have snapped her fingers together. "You worked for Senator Johnston. I remember seeing you at one of the Thompsons' parties."

Another image clicked into place, and Melender's heart dropped. Oh, no. Snippets of an overheard conversation during a party at the Thompson house the day before Jesse went missing involving the senator, her uncle, and Smith echoed in her mind.

Something in her face must have alerted Smith to her memories. "You've remembered."

"The map." More memories clicked into place.

Her captor leaned back. "I knew you would eventually recall that piece of information."

Melender closed her eyes briefly as the long-ago conversation flooded her mind. "My uncle wanted to get the rights to an old gold mine that straddled the boundaries of Shenandoah National Park. The senator told him a congressional okay to extract anything from the mine on the park's portion would be a no-go, so you were discussing options."

"You overheard more than we thought."

It had been the mention of the Blue Ridge Mountains that had captured her attention. She'd tucked herself into a window seat in the study, the only room closed off to guests during the party, with Catherine Marshall's *Christy* as her companion. The long, heavy curtain had hidden her from view when the trio had entered the room. At first, she hadn't paid much attention to what they were discussing, but when she realized she knew the area in question, she listened more closely.

Now she stared at Smith. "You altered an old map to show the boundaries of the park different so you could tap into a mine purported to still have gold deposits." Rumors of gold had circulated among the residents of Sudie's holler for years, but most of the mountain people hadn't believed the old Shade Mine had anything left. Apparently, Quentin had believed enough to want to steal the rights. "What happened? Did he get access, then discover the gold was a myth?"

"Something like that, but at the time, it seemed very promising." Smith scowled. "That's why I was against trusting the system to incarcerate you."

"What?" A rush of emotion flooded her body. "I never said anything about the map."

"Not then, but you would have, once you heard about the mining permits." He crossed one ankle over the opposite knee. "You wouldn't have allowed anything to harm your beloved mountains."

He was right. Lord have mercy, he was right. She would not have

315

kept quiet once she'd learned about the mining on park land. She knew the park's boundaries as well as the lines in her grandmother's face. She would have known in an instant someone had altered the map. Then the further implication of Smith's words sank in.

"You deliberately set me up to take the fall for Jesse's disappearance so I wouldn't say anything about the map and mining?"

"I..." Before Smith could answer, someone knocked on the door. "Come in." He stood as the door opened.

Melender turned her head to see her uncle step into the shed.

QUENTIN AVOIDED MELENDER, WHO WAS PERCHED ON A PILE OF FERTILIZER bags, her hands wrenched behind her back and her feet tied together with a plastic zip tie. Instead, he focused on John Smith. He'd known John for more than three decades, a man always in the shadows. A man you called to fix your problems. How Quentin wished he'd never called John the night Jesse died. But the thought of Ruby learning what her daughter had done drove him to make a choice that continued to haunt him.

"Quentin." John consulted his phone. "You cut it a little close."

"I'm here now." Quentin didn't move from his position near the shed door. "Why did you take Melender?"

"I'm just following your orders." John's tone held a mocking note.

"I never said—"

"You said she needed to be taken care of."

Quentin couldn't disagree, but that was before police dug up his rose garden. "It's over, John."

"It is not over." John pointed a finger at Quentin. "I will not be left holding the bag on this mess. You are in neck deep too."

"You're right." Quentin's admission sailed right past John, as the other man continued his tirade.

"You're the one who wanted to make it look like Jesse

disappeared."

Memories of that night flooded Quentin's senses. He could almost hear Jillian asking why her daddy was crying.

"You're the one who came up with a plausible tale to spin to throw suspicion off of your other children." Each word John said twisted the knife in Quentin's gut.

The coldness of his plan hadn't seemed that stark to him as he pushed down his grief over Jesse's death. Jared's panic and Jillian's cries had only fueled his calmness. He put out fires constantly in his line of work. Keeping his head in the midst of this family crisis had been second nature. Gazing down at Jesse's lifeless body in his crib, the story of what might have happened unspooled in his mind until it became what actually happened, supplanting the truth with a more palatable lie.

"You're the one who suggested putting the blame on your niece."

He couldn't have Jillian grow up knowing she'd killed her baby brother by accidentally smothering him with his blue bunny. While his older son had his share of problems, Quentin wasn't about to let his own flesh and blood go to prison on a drug charge or child neglect. In the end, the decision to sacrifice a niece he barely knew had been easy—it had seemed like the only way to keep what remained of his family intact.

John stared straight at him. "And you're the one who picked out the burial place for your son."

A burial place now being disturbed by shovels. Quentin bowed his head. Every word John said pierced his heart, but instead of fear or anger, relief was the emotion that rose to the top. He'd kept company with this secret for nineteen years. Letting go brought a relief sweeter than he'd ever imagined. His phone buzzed. Automatically, he pulled it out of his pocket to see a text from Jillian.

Dad, where are you? You've got to come home. Now. They found something in the garden. Won't tell us what it is, but Mom's falling apart.

"Bad news?" John's tone indicated he couldn't care less if it was.

"No." Quentin looked at the man as the last vestiges of self-preservation evaporated like the morning mist on a mountain top. He drew in a deep breath to gather the courage to put the unimaginable into words. "They've found Jesse."

"What?" Melender's voice came out in a whisper. "Where?"

Quentin finally turned to his niece. Strands of her long, blonde hair had escaped her braid and bunched around her face. Sorrow infused his entire body. "They found Jesse's grave in our rose garden."

In the hospital café, Brogan stared at Livingston. He couldn't quite comprehend what the detective had just told him after Carstairs had stepped away to confer with a colleague. "They found human remains in the Thompson's rose garden?"

"Yes, but not an adult's." Livingston's mouth settled into a grim line. "An infant's."

"Jesse." Brogan stated the obvious as more pieces of this intricate puzzle slipped into place.

"It seems highly likely." Livingston's phone buzzed. "I need to get this." The detective walked a few steps away and answered the call.

Melender was missing. Jesse's body had finally been found, just yards from his home. Would everyone believe Melender had buried Jesse's body in her own backyard? Or would the police try to uncover what really happened that night? Part of him itched to phone Fallon with an update, but he resisted. Finding Melender took top priority.

"Brogan!" Seth approached the table. "Fallon wants to know why you're ignoring his texts and calls."

Brogan had texted Seth about the accident while waiting to for the doctor to put in the stitches. Now he motioned for Seth to have a seat, then filled him in on what had happened.

"Melender's missing?" Seth latched on to what concerned Brogan the most.

"Yes, we're hoping the tech can clean up the photo enough that we'll be able to ID her kidnapper and give us a clue as to where he might have taken her." Brogan fidgeted with his empty coffee cup. "I don't understand why he'd take her now. Whoever rammed into us already got the information Stabe left for us."

Livingston returned to the table but didn't sit down. "Stabe's dead."

"What?" Brogan couldn't believe it. "How?"

"Shot in the head," Livingston said. "It's too soon to tell if it's suicide or murder."

Brogan jotted the info down in his reporter's notebook. "Where was he found?

"At his condo a couple of hours ago. The body was still warm, so he hadn't been gone long." Livingston tapped his phone against his leg. "You said he called you this morning?"

"Yeah." Brogan summoned his recall of the conversation. "Stabe was scared, said he thought someone was following him. Also said he didn't think he had much time."

"Time for what?" Livingston asked.

"Wouldn't say." Not for the first time, Brogan wished he'd kept Stabe talking.

"Did he say anything else?" Livingston pressed.

"Just that he'd left something for me at reception at his law office, and I'd better go get it fast." Brogan shoved a hand through his hair and winced as the movement pulled at his stitches. Fatigue pressed down on him as if the news of Stabe's death had released an avalanche and his body couldn't handle the additional news. The car accident. Stabe's death. Infant remains recovered on the Thompson property. Melender missing. The only thing he cared about was finding Melender. *Please, God, keep her safe!*

Carstairs rejoined them. "Sasha's got the photo ready."

Brogan rose, along with Seth, and they followed Carstairs and Livingston to the security suite. Sasha didn't look up when they entered the room with the bank of computer monitors.

"Here you go." She pointed to an enlarged photo of a man, his features a little blurry.

"Recognize him?" Carstairs asked.

Livingston squinted at the screen. "There's something about him that looks familiar, but I can't quite place him."

"Can you run it through facial recognition software or something?" Seth queried.

"You've been watching too many cop TV shows. The Feds have access, but we have to have a pretty high-profile case to ask them for that kind of favor," Livingston said. "Can you print out a half dozen copies and email me the file?"

Carstairs nodded his approval, then Sasha hit the print button. "What's your email address?"

As Livingston rattled it off, Brogan leaned closer to the screen. The man's unremarkable features tickled something in his brain. He'd seen him before. Not recently, but back in his past. He focused his entire attention on the screen and blocked out the conversation around him. An image of a Washington, DC, Christmas party coalesced in his mind. He'd been there to meet his source for the charity story that ended his journalism career. While seeking a quiet place to talk, Brogan and his source had stumbled upon the man who had kidnapped Melender deep in conversation with a senator.

Pulling up the senator's name from memory, Brogan pointed to the screen. "That looks like Senator Johnston's former guy."

Livingston turned to him. "Who?"

"I think he worked for United States Senator Johnston from Virginia. I saw him and the senator talking at a party a decade or so and asked someone who he was." Brogan concentrated on dredging up more information from the long-ago party.

When Brogan didn't immediately continue, Livingston prodded, "And did you find out?"

The name came to Brogan in a flash. "John Smith."

"John Smith." Livingston narrowed his eyes. "You're not joking."

Brogan shrugged. "I know, it sounds like it can't possibly be his real name. And it might not be, but that's the name everyone called him." He once again indicated the photo on the screen. He wasn't sure how Smith figured into all this, but it looked like the man was trying to erase all evidence related to Jesse's death and disappearance.

"Hard to believe there are people actually named John Smith, right?" Seth smiled, but it quickly faded.

"We'll run it through the system, along with the Senator Johnston connection. That might narrow down the search." Livingston accepted the photo printouts, then turned to Brogan. "Don't worry —we'll find her."

As he followed Livingston and Seth out of the room, snippets of other information he'd gleaned about Smith rose in his mind. The man had a hard reputation for handling all manner of dirty work, including bribes and making people disappear. Brogan prayed they would locate Melender before Smith finished tying up loose ends.

CHAPTER

THIRTY-NINE

As twilight cast long shadows over the lawn, Ruby sat dry-eyed on the back patio, watching crime scene technicians uncover her son's bones underneath her roses. Her precious baby boy had been surrounded by the fragrant blossoms of the Virginia rose during his eternal rest. Quentin probably thought his placement there would make Ruby feel better. The look on her husband's face when he realized the warrant covered the grounds was enough for Ruby to know Jesse would be found on the property.

"Mom?" Jillian touched her arm. "Are you okay?"

Ruby glanced up as Jillian dropped into the chaise lounge beside her, eyes red-rimmed and cheeks pale. She should comfort her daughter, but Ruby had nothing left to give. For years, she had fanned her anger at Melender to hold the sorrow over Jesse's disappearance at bay. Discovering she had been tending to Jesse's grave as she tenderly cared for her roses had drained her of all emotion, leaving a hollow shell inside her core.

"Mom? You're scaring me." Jillian whimpered, her voice dropping back into the cadence of a preschooler.

"He was there all this time." Ruby stared at the mound of dirt, so much dirt to extract so little a body.

"Ma'am?" Collier's softly spoken question pulled Ruby's attention away from Jillian and the excavation. "Do you know where your husband is?"

Ruby pressed her fingers into the lounge cushion as her heart rate increased. "He's around here somewhere. He said he had to make some calls. Why do you need him?" Even as she asked the question, she knew. Because Quentin had morphed from the father of a missing-presumed-murdered child into a person of interest in Jesse's disappearance.

"We have some questions for him," the detective replied with professional smoothness.

But Ruby had stopped caring what happened to her husband, not when the evidence of what he had done had been uncovered inch by inch in her garden. Ruby leaned her head back, allowing her eyes to drift close. "I suppose you do."

"Did you know that a child had been buried in your garden?"

Collier's question snapped Ruby out of her apathy. She opened her eyes to meet the other woman's gaze. "No." She swung her legs over the side of the lounge and rose. "And please don't insult me by insisting it can't be confirmed to be my son your crime scene technicians are uncovering. We all know it's..." Her voice broke, but she summoned the will to finish, "...it's Jesse out there."

The detective said something else, but Ruby stopped listening, her gaze focused on the men and women crouched down among her roses. *My little Jesse, who didn't like the dark, had been buried in a black hole for nearly two decades.* How often had she waved off help from the lawn maintenance crew and attended to the rose garden herself over the years? Almost as if she'd instinctively known there was something special about that plot of land. Under her care, the bushes had flourished as if honoring sacred ground.

A sob escaped, followed by another one. Ruby no longer had the strength to hold back the tidal wave of tears breaking over the dam

324

she'd constructed in her heart. With a hand over her mouth, she raced for the house. She'd carried this grief around inside of her for too long to share it with anyone else. Ignoring the people milling about the house, Ruby maneuvered her way up the stairs and into her bedroom.

Two men dressed in white jumpsuits stood near the bathroom, bags of gear at their feet.

"Get out!" Ruby pointed a trembling finger to the door. "Get out of my room now!"

The two exchanged glances, and one reached down to pick up a bag.

On the dresser, Ruby spotted a framed photo of Quentin and herself at some long-forgotten charity event. Rage at her husband supplanted the grief for an instant, and she lobbed the photo in the direction of the technicians. The frame shattered against the wall, sending the pair scurrying with their bags out the bedroom door.

Collier appeared in the doorway. Ruby snatched another heavy crystal frame, not even bothering to look at the photo inside. She hurled it toward the detective, who sidestepped to avoid the missile. The knickknack hit the doorframe with a satisfying thunk, crystal breaking into tiny pieces as it showered the carpet.

"Mrs. Thompson," Collier began, her voice pitched low.

But Ruby wasn't going to be talked out of her anger or grief. She'd held it bottled inside for too long to be soothed by a police officer or anyone else. "Get. Out."

"I know it's been a shock."

"You know nothing about it." Ruby stalked toward her, stopping a foot away. Her entire body trembled with the effort to not scream or hurl more things as her heart cried out for release from the torment. "You haven't clipped blossoms for a bouquet while your child's little body lay buried under your feet."

Collier opened her mouth to reply, but Ruby held up her hand. "You don't get to tell me you understand. Because you can't possibly. My husband allowed me to cling to the tiniest bit of hope that maybe, just maybe, Jesse was still alive somewhere. That he had been taken and given to another family." She laughed but choked on the sound. "You want to know the real irony is?"

"Mrs. Thompson, is there someone we could call to sit with you?" Collier interjected.

"I've spent the last eighteen years hating a woman who had nothing to do with my son's disappearance. A hatred my dear husband fanned with comments over the years. Because as long as I was fixated on Melender, I wasn't asking the questions I should have been asking. If I hadn't been blinded by my grief and despair, I would have seen the inconsistencies years ago. If I had, Jesse might have come home sooner."

"Mom? What are you saying?" Jillian pushed past Collier. "Are you saying Dad had something to do with Jesse's death?"

"Of course he did." Ruby snarled, her sharp tone sending Jillian reeling back a step. "You think someone buried your little brother in our backyard without his knowledge? I doubt he did the dirty work himself because he had people for that sort of thing. I have no doubt Quentin knew exactly where Jesse was all these years for one reason. Your father put him there."

Jillian's eyes widened, and she stumbled back to sit on the bench at the foot of the king-sized bed. "Oh, no." She pressed the heels of her hands to her eyes, bending over at the waist to rock back and forth. "It wasn't a dream, it wasn't a dream."

"What wasn't a dream?" Collier stepped to Jillian, laying a hand on her shoulder.

Her anger spent, Ruby gaped at her daughter. "Oh, dear God." She covered her mouth with her hand. "Jillian, what happened?"

CHAPTER

FORTY

Melender tried to process what her uncle said to Smith, but the words didn't make sense. Even after hearing Jillian and Jared on the recording, she was sure Jesse had been buried where his body would never be recovered, casting suspicion on her forever.

"The little tyke's final resting place was underneath his wife's prized roses," Smith said, the gun still resting comfortably in his hand.

"Cat's got your tongue, Quentin?" Smith glanced at Melender, swung his gun toward Quentin, who tightened his lips into a firm line. "I get it. You don't care to repeat it in front of the niece you threw to the wolves."

Smith paced a few feet toward the only window, moving the faded curtain aside to peer out. "Your uncle wanted Jesse close by, though he was the only one who knew exactly where the body was buried. Well, except for me. After all, he doesn't like to get his hands dirty, figuratively or literally."

Melender hoped her face didn't show revulsion. All these years, Jesse had been buried in the Thompson's backyard. Another thought

327

rolled through on the heels of that revelation. Jillian's nightmare wasn't a dream at all. Was Smith the man Jillian had seen taking Jesse out of the crib?

The truth was much uglier than anticipated. Once the recording came to light, Jillian would come to know she had accidentally killed her baby brother. When Melender set out to clear her name, she hadn't wanted to destroy her cousin in the process.

"Got nothing to say, Harman?"

Smith's question jerked Melender out of her thoughts. "About what?"

"Surely you know by now your uncle orchestrated the events leading to your arrest and conviction." Smith waved his gun as he spoke. "What punishment should Quentin get for his role in putting the blame for Jesse's disappearance on you?"

Melender turned to look at Quentin, but he stood with his body angled away from her. Her pulse quickened at the slump of her uncle's shoulders and the scent of despair permeating the shed. From her prison experience, hopelessness made people do the unexpected, often with disastrous results.

"Quentin paid your attorney to put up a minimal defense and funnel inside trial information to him. Then your uncle prepped the family witnesses to testify in a way designed to put you behind bars." Smith's voice had an admiring tone. "I knew Quentin could be devious in his business dealings, but I had no idea how diabolical his mind worked until I got a firsthand glimpse during your trial. It was a masterful handling of the case. And no one suspected a thing. Especially with Ruby wailing and gnashing her teeth at you for killing her baby boy. Truly a work of art."

Hearing about her uncle's machinations turned her stomach, but Smith's adulation for Quentin's shenanigans poured acid on her churning insides.

"After you served your sentence and came back here," Smith continued, "you started poking around, wanting to find out what happened. I knew it was only a matter of time before you picked apart the flimsy evidence that sent you away."

"Quentin called you to clean things up once and for all," Melender interjected.

"By Jove, she's got it." Smith touched the side of the gun to his forehead in a mock salute. "I told Quentin you had brains as well as beauty. You and your boyfriend nearly figured everything out. If Jared hadn't panicked, the cops would still be in the dark."

"You leave my son out of this," Quentin snapped, turning to face Smith.

Smith snorted, derision tightening the lines of his face. "All you rich people are alike. Covering up for your offspring."

As the two men argued about Jared, Melender shifted, her shoulders aching from her wrists being secured behind her back. She tried to reposition on the plastic sacks, but with her feet bound, she slipped onto the dusty floor, and her hands brushed against something hard. Rotating her shoulders up and down brought her fingers into contact with the object. Tentatively, she explored the outline. Gardening shears. Maybe she could maneuver the shears enough to cut the plastic ties around her wrists. To even attempt it, she would need to distract the men from her movements. Fanning their animosity toward each other ought to work.

She broke into their argument. "It wasn't Jared who brought the cops to the Thompson house with a search warrant."

Both men turned to stare at her.

"What are you talking about?" Smith narrowed his eyes.

Swallowing hard, Melender looked from one to the other. "The recording."

"What recording?" Smith stalked a few steps closer to her.

Melender jutted her chin toward her uncle. "The one in Jesse's blue bunny."

"How did you get the stuffed rabbit?" Smith said.

"I don't know. It was sent to my house anonymously."

Smith whipped the gun in Quentin's direction. "You sent her the kid's stuffed animal?" His threatening tone caused Melender to draw back against the fertilizer bags.

She took advantage of Smith's distraction to wiggle her body down into the crevice in between the stacked bags. Her fingers grazed the closed clippers. Another shimmy, and she managed to grasp the shears by the handle. Straightening, she paused to check on Quentin and Smith.

"I don't owe you any explanation." Quentin's voice lacked its usual bluster.

"Oh, I think you do." Smith aimed the gun straight at Quentin's head. "I repeat. What recording?"

Quentin shook his head. "I don't know anything about a recording." Smith took another step closer to him, and her uncle raised his hands. "Yes, I sent the bunny to Melender to scare her into giving up the search. But I swear, I don't know what she's talking about."

Smith swiveled to face Melender, his gun now pointed at her head. "You'd better start talking. Fast."

Melender gripped the shears as tight as she could to avoid dropping them. When she did so, she discovered the clippers had a release button that kept the blades locked into place. "The bunny had a recording device inside."

"What?" Quentin raised his eyebrows, his face the picture of confusion.

"Keep going," Smith growled.

"It was voice activated and recorded up to twenty hours before recording over itself." She drew in a breath to steady her nerves. She needed to keep talking while she figured out how to cut the plastic tie on her wrists. Pitching her voice low and soothing, she continued. "The police discovered it when they X-rayed the bunny."

"The police." Smith spat out the word like a curse. "What was on the recording?"

Melender found the release button on the shears and flicked it up. The blades separated with a soft click, but both men stayed focused on each other. "The night of Jesse's death."

Quentin staggered backwards as if punched in the gut. He blindly reached behind him and bumped into a stack of rakes, which clattered to the floor. "That's not possible."

"You're lying," Smith snarled, his gun trained on Melender.

"I'm not." She kept her body hunched to portray submission. "The recording is at a Fairfax County Police lab. The detective called the Commonwealth's attorney to let her know what they'd found."

Smith shrugged. "At this point, it really doesn't matter." He refocused his attention on her uncle. "You have made a mess of this whole thing—and now I have to clean it up. I never should have agreed to your plan in the first place. Too many variables."

"But it worked." Quentin had recovered, some of the color returning to his face. "She took the blame, and no one suspected anything."

"Until Harman got out of prison and started poking her nose around." Smith narrowed his eyes. "We wouldn't be in this position had we gone with my plan all those years ago."

Melender didn't like the look in Smith's eyes, which had dropped to an even darker shade of mean. She'd seen that look often enough in the eyes of fellow prisoners right before an attack on another inmate. Trying to keep her upper body as still as possible, she held her wrists as far apart as she could, ignoring the plastic bands that cut into her skin. Then she worked the shear blades into place, hoping she had calculated the proper position between the plastic bands.

"What are you saying?" Quentin's question drew Smith's attention back to him.

"She's a loose end that needs snipping." Smith kept the gun at waist level but no longer pointing directly at Melender. "I should have ignored your instructions and capped her when this whole thing went down originally, but no, you didn't want her dead. You wanted her locked away. But see? If we'd done it my way, we wouldn't be in this mess today."

Melender stretched her fingers around the handles and

331

squeezed. The blades closed, but the plastic tie didn't snap. She'd positioned the blades in the wrong place. Smith and Quentin continued to argue while she maneuvered the shears into position again. *Please God, let this work.* The blades met with resistance as they closed, and she summoned all the strength she could muster in her hands and applied more pressure on the handles. The plastic snapped with a soft ping. *Thank you, Jesus.*

She didn't change her body's position even though her shoulders screamed for her to relax them. Keeping her hands behind her back to give the illusion of being restrained, she locked the shear blades closed. Her hands might be free, but her feet were still bound. Getting her ankle restraints snipped would be impossible to manage without the men noticing.

"We're doing it my way." In one fluid motion, Smith swung the gun toward Melender.

The deadly intent in his eyes registered a split second before she acted. Melender brought her hands around to the front and dove over the back of the fertilizer pile as a shot rang out.

CHAPTER

FORTY-ONE

Brogan tossed his phone onto the cluttered desk. He'd spent the last hour trying to track down the whereabouts of John Smith, but the man was as elusive as his reputation indicated. Even though the police had issued a BOLO for his vehicle, there had been no sightings. Senator Johnston, who'd retired from public life two years ago, had been unable to shed any light on his former employee, who was indeed legally named John Smith. "John's a man who likes to live off the grid," was how the senator had put it. "If he doesn't want to be found, he won't be."

Maybe Seth had more luck on his end. Brogan rose and headed to his colleague's desk.

Seth had the desk phone handset tucked under his ear while he made notations on a stickie pad. "Thank you very much." He replaced the receiver and grinned at Brogan.

"Tell me you have good news." Brogan needed some. Every minute Melender stayed missing was like a stab in his heart. He could tell himself it was all about the story, but the anxiety flooding his veins told a different tale.

"I have very good news." Seth stood and held out the note. "I found an address for Smith."

Brogan bit back a sigh of disappointment. "I've found six addresses for Smith, and none of them panned out."

"Ah, but this one is different." Seth raised his eyebrows. "This one is the property he inherited from a cousin, so it didn't pop up as directly related to Smith."

Brogan straightened, his senses tingling. This could be the break they needed. "Where is it?"

Seth rattled off an address in Fairfax County. "It's in one of those five-acre estate subdivisions, but get this—it's only fifteen minutes from the Thompson house."

"Let's go. We'll call Livingston on the road." As Brogan hustled to the elevator with Seth at his heels, he prayed Smith had taken Melender to the house.

And that they would be in time.

ON THE BENCH AT THE FOOT OF THE BED, RUBY ROCKED HER SOBBING daughter, ignoring the presence of the detective, who hovered just inside the room. Somehow, she'd found the strength to offer comfort, when all Ruby wanted to do was sink into the four-poster bed and sleep away the nightmare unfolding around her. "Shh. It will be okay, Jilly."

Jillian shoved back, her face splotchy and wet. "No, it won't."

"I think you'd better start at the beginning," Collier suggested, her tone gentler than Ruby expected from a cop.

Jillian hiccupped. "I can't."

Ruby's heart constricted even tighter at the pain behind her daughter's words. In her grief over losing Jesse, had she failed to see the hurt Jillian hid from the world? "Yes, you can."

Jillian jumped to her feet, moving several steps away from Ruby and Collier, who had stayed near the door. "No, I can't."

334

"Why not?" Collier interjected.

Jillian whirled to face her mother. The anguish in her eyes sent another stab to Ruby's heart. "Because if I do, you'll hate me like you've hated Melender all these years."

"No, my darling. I won't." But even as she said the words, Ruby latched onto the implication behind them. What had Jillian done? No matter what happened, Jillian was her flesh and blood, her only living link to being a mother. "You're my daughter. Whatever happened couldn't have been your fault. You were only three years old."

"I think I killed Jesse." Sobs overtook Jillian, doubling her over. She dropped to her knees on the plush, white carpet away from the shattered picture frames, her arms wrapped around her middle.

Her words froze Ruby to the bench, unable to move or process what Jillian had said. She could only watch her daughter cry for several long moments. The detective hadn't jumped in with questions, for which Ruby was grateful. Surely Jillian would continue when she could and explain what she meant.

Jillian finally straightened and wiped her eyes with her sleeve, then blew her nose from a tissue she pulled from her pocket. She locked eyes with Ruby, the pleading in them for understanding nearly breaking Ruby's fragile composure. "Jared was watching us while you and Dad were at that charity event," she whispered, her words carrying clearly through the otherwise silent room.

Her daughter drew in a breath. "Melender wasn't at home. She was at a graduation party down the street for the evening."

Ruby listened quietly, not wanting to interrupt the flow of truth from Jillian's lips. Strange how unreal the true events of that night sounded after nearly two decades of clinging to the alternative version they had told themselves—and the police, the FBI, and a jury.

"Jesse was fussy. Isadora had given him a dose of Tylenol before she left to help you at the country club, but I guess it had worn off because he wouldn't stop coughing and crying." Jillian's fingers shredded the tissue into confetti as she continued. "Jared gave Jesse some medicine, then he told me to play peek-a-boo with Blue Bunny to calm him down. So I did. Only I was tired too. It was late, really late. Jared left to meet Snake, so he wasn't there any longer. I stopped playing when Jesse calmed down and left Blue Bunny in the crib."

Ruby drew in a ragged breath as Jillian paused. Pain sliced through her at the thought of her baby boy, lying helpless in his crib, sick. She should have been there. She should have ditched the charity event and stayed home with her precious children. She certainly should not have left them in the care of Jared, who at nineteen, was already a disappointment to Quentin. But the lure of adoration from all their friends as they oohed and ahhed over the event she'd organized had been too strong for her to stay home.

"I didn't realize anything was wrong until voices in Jesse's room woke me up. I tiptoed through the bathroom to see a man picking up Jesse from his crib." Jillian started crying again. "And Dad was there too."

The revelation shocked Ruby. She'd figured Melender had buried Jesse in her rose garden. But hadn't the police searched the freshly planted area after Jesse disappeared and found nothing? That would mean her son's body had been kept elsewhere, then moved to the garden. Her niece had been in custody awaiting trial, then immediately sent to prison.

Collier questioned Jillian, their voices a soft murmur in the background as more questions swirled in Ruby's mind. The mist of grief cleared enough for one thought to come to the forefront. Whatever had happened that night, her niece had had nothing to do with it. And that meant coming to grips with her part in sending an innocent woman to jail for seventeen years.

～

"LET'S GO!" BROGAN SNAPPED HIS SEATBELT INTO PLACE. "TAKE I-66 TO the Beltway."

"Got it." Seth threw the car into gear and squealed out of the *Herald's* parking lot.

Brogan speed-dialed Livingston's number. "Detective, it's Brogan. I think we have a lead on Smith."

"Go on."

Brogan recapped Seth's detective work in locating the McLean property, giving Livingston the address on Jarvis Court. "I know it's a long shot, but since the other leads haven't panned out, Seth and I think it's worth taking a look. Google Earth shows the house and grounds are fairly isolated, one of those large estates with lots of privacy. We're thinking Smith might believe no one would be able to connect him to that property, and it's only fifteen minutes from the Thompson house."

"You could be right. Hang on a second. I've got another call coming in."

"Take I-495 toward Tyson's Corner," Brogan directed Seth while he waited for the detective to come back on the line.

"Brogan?" Livingston didn't wait for a response. "Quentin's no longer at the house."

"I thought you'd assigned someone to keep an eye on him after the discovery in the backyard." Brogan wasn't sure what Quentin's absence meant. He only cared about finding Melender before Smith hurt her.

"We did, but Quentin managed to slip away without anyone noticing. Where are you now?"

"With Seth." Brogan hesitated about telling him they were en route to check out the property.

Livingston sighed. "What's your ETA to Jarvis Court?"

So much for pulling a fast one on the detective. "Let me check GPS." Brogan toggled between screens to view the navigation app. "About seven minutes."

"I'll meet you there. I'll request backup. Wait until an officer arrives before exploring. From what we've gathered about Smith so far, he's not a man who likes to leave loose ends."

Brogan tamped down the fear that rose in his throat. "Melender's a loose end."

"Exactly. Don't try to be a hero. Wait for backup."

"We'll be careful." Brogan ended the call. *Dear God, please keep her safe.* If Melender was on that property being held captive by Smith, no way was he waiting for the police to arrive.

CHAPTER

FORTY-TWO

Melender crouched down behind the pile of fertilizer bags. She had managed to hang onto the shears in her dive to safety and now used the clippers to slice through the plastic ties binding her ankles. Free from her restraints, she duck-walked toward a covered riding lawnmower, its metal bulk appearing safer than the fertilizer bags.

She peeked around a corner. Quentin and Smith continued to wrestle for the gun. A second shot shattered a flowerpot on the opposite wall as the men grappled for the weapon. Quentin must have rushed Smith to prevent him from shooting her. Why he did so was a mystery, given her uncle's role in setting her up. Questions popped into her mind. Had Jillian accidently smothered Jesse? Or had Jared given the toddler too much of the wrong kind of medicine and that killed him?

Shaking her head to clear the questions she couldn't answer, Melender refocused her attention on the fight. She edged around the lawnmower, keeping the shears in her hand. A third shot, then a grunt. Her heart rate accelerated to warp speed. The sound of a body hitting the floor echoed in the sudden quiet.

Dropping to her belly, Melender peered under the tractor to see Quentin lying on the floor, blood spreading rapidly from his upper thigh. Her uncle's face contorted in pain as he clutched the wound.

Smith stood over him, gun firmly in his hand. "You'll bleed out soon enough. After I kill your niece, I'll make the whole thing look like a shootout. An all-too familiar scene among family members these days."

The shed door burst open, and Brogan raced inside. Melender sucked in a breath at the sight of him. She wanted to run into his arms but didn't budge. Best if she stayed hidden for now.

Brogan took a step toward Quentin, whose moans had quieted.

"Stop right there." Smith squeezed off a shot that whizzed past Brogan to the opposite wall, hitting a bag of potting soil sitting on a shelf.

Brogan froze. "Let me help him."

"Stay where you are."

Her uncle's gray pallor revealed he didn't have much more time. No matter his role in her conviction, she couldn't let him die. But to save him, she needed a bigger weapon than gardening shears. Rising to her knees and carefully keeping her head below the top of the lawnmower, she slowly scanned her surroundings.

"The washed-up reporter seeks redemption by proving an ex-con innocent of murder." The derision in Smith's voice chilled Melender as his words pierced her heart. "If that isn't the ultimate cliché."

"The truth is never a cliché." Brogan's reply countered the coldness seeping into Melender's bones.

"Ah, the truth." Smith made a circular motion with the gun. "The truth is whatever the person holding the winning hand says it is."

"You'd like to think so, wouldn't you? That way you don't have to live with the consequences of your actions."

Melender spied a heavy metal garden rake on the floor a few feet away from her position. The short, sharp tines would make a good weapon.

"I've lived my own truth for years, and no one has objected yet."

"Maybe you have 'gotten away with it.'" Melender could hear the air quotes in Brogan's statement. "But that doesn't mean what you've done isn't wrong."

She eased close enough to the rake to touch the handle, then maneuvered herself to the front of the lawnmower. Smith stood a few feet away, his attention focused on Brogan. With a prayer for success, she rose to a half crouch, keeping her upper body level with the lawnmower's height.

"While I find this philosophic discourse interesting," Smith said, "I—"

Melender stood to full height, lifting and swinging the rake toward Smith with all her might. As if sensing movement behind him, Smith turned and raised his gun.

Melender continued the forward motion of the rake, which hit the man square in the shoulder, the metal tines digging into his flesh and sending the gun skittering to the floor. Brogan dove for the gun as Smith careened into shelves holding terracotta planters. The shelving toppled, bringing Smith down with it in a heap of broken pots.

Brogan aimed the gun at Smith. "Don't move."

"Quentin!" Melender dropped the rake and scrambled to her uncle, who was unresponsive. She had to stop the bleeding. A pile of old towels on a shelf a few feet away caught her eye and she sprinted to the shelf and grabbed them. Back at her uncle's side, she held one of the towels over the leg wound, pressing down as hard as she could manage. "Stay with me."

Her uncle's eyes fluttered open. "Melender. You're okay."

"Yes." In the background, Brogan requested an ambulance on his phone. Sirens punctuated the air, their strident call music to her ears. Maybe Brogan had called in backup before coming to rescue her. She leaned over the wounded leg, keeping the pressure steady.

"I'm sorry." Quentin's voice held a weary note. "I shouldn't have..."

"We can talk later. Save your strength. Help is coming." *Please,*

341

God. Don't let him die. She gazed into her uncle's eyes, where regret mingled with the pain.

Quentin placed his blood-stained hand over hers. "Why are you helping me? Why don't you hate me?"

"I did at first for what you and your family did to me." But during her incarceration, she'd seen firsthand how anger fueled many of the prisoners' waking moments. Sudie's calming words had echoed in her mind whenever temptation to give in to despair and fury tried to rule. *Child, when we allow anger over wrongs done to us to take root in our hearts, we're saying to God Almighty that crimes committed against us are worse than crimes committed against Jesus. Our crimes against Jesus were nailed to the cross. How can we hang on to unforgiveness when our Savior does not?*

"Something Sudie said to me made me try not to let hate stay in my heart." Melender shifted her position to keep the pressure steady on the wound. "Because of Jesus, I don't hate you."

"How is he?" Brogan's question startled Melender.

For a moment, she'd forgotten everything but her uncle and the past. "He needs medical attention." She sent a worried look at her uncle's ashen complexion. Quentin had closed his eyes again, giving his countenance a death-like hue. A quick glance at Brogan showed he kept his attention and gun trained on Smith, who now sat amidst the pottery shards with his head in his hands.

"Seth says the cops have arrived," Brogan said.

"And the ambulance?" She repositioned her hands on the bloody towel. The blood flow from the wound appeared to have eased, but she didn't dare remove the towel to check.

"On its way." No sooner had the words left his lips than the shed door burst open. A stream of police officers rushed into the space, guns drawn.

"Drop your weapon! Put your hands in the air!" one of the officers commanded.

Brogan complied. Several officers hurried to Quentin. Melender briefed them on what she knew, and one of them coordinated an exchange of positions, taking over from her.

She rose, but her legs nearly gave out from the adrenaline depletion and kneeling.

"Steady there." Brogan cradled her against his body, taking the weight of hers as she faced him. His arms encased her with strength.

Melender closed her eyes and collapsed against his broad chest. Words failed her, so she simply wrapped her arms around his waist and allowed her mind to relax for the first time in nearly two decades.

CHAPTER

FORTY-THREE

An hour later, Brogan still didn't want to let go of Melender. The visual of Smith with a gun, Quentin bleeding on the floor, and Melender held hostage had faded, but the emotions pulsating throughout his body had not. He'd guided her to an old stone garden bench pushed against one wall and sat, tugging her down beside him. Now she rested against him with her head buried in his shoulder and her arms around his waist. All the tension of the past few hours drained away as he held Melender close. Paramedics had whisked Quentin to the hospital, but cops and crime scene technicians milled about processing the scene while he and Melender nestled in a cocoon of relief. Brogan used the oasis to thank God for her safety and for Quentin to recover.

"Brogan?"

He lifted his head to see Livingston. "Hey."

"How is she?" The detective spoke softly.

Brogan glanced down at Melender, who had closed her eyes. Her breathing had slowed to a steady cadence. "Okay, I think."

"She asleep?"

"Maybe." Brogan didn't want to move to find out, content with the warmth of her body so close to his. He brushed his hand down her back over the long single braid, the gesture more intimate than he'd intended, but he found himself not caring what Livingston thought.

"You two need to give statements, but given everything's that happened, I'm sending you both home for the night."

Brogan nodded his thanks.

"Come by the station in the morning, say ten o'clock, to give your statements. I know you have questions, so we can address those tomorrow too." Livingston pulled out his phone. "Excuse me. I've got to take this call."

As Livingston left, Seth approached. "Hey."

"What did Fallon say?" Brogan had asked his colleague to update their editor on the evening's events.

"He's waiting for your story." Seth bounced lightly on his toes. "I got some amazing shots with my phone, and statements from the police."

"Great." He shifted slightly and accidentally jostled Melender, who lifted her head.

"Brogan?" The breathy tone of her voice sent his pulse racing. As he looked down at her mouth, the desire to kiss her nearly overwhelmed him.

Brogan yanked his gaze from her lips. "Let's go home." Brogan helped her upright even though he longed to pull her closer. Later, Lord willing, there would be a more opportune time for a kiss.

"Don't we need to give statements to the police?" She hid a yawn behind her hand, then stretched her arms. A shadow of pain crossed her face as she put a hand on her shoulder, sharply reminding Brogan of all she had been through these past hours.

"Livingston said we could come to the station in the morning." Brogan rose, extending his hand to her. "Come on. Seth will drive us back to the Trents."

"Okay." She accepted his assistance, tucking her hand in his.

Once standing, Brogan drew her hand through the crook of his arm to pull her closer. "Hi, Seth."

"Hello, Melender. I'm glad you're okay." Seth smiled, then led the way through the throng of police officers and crime scene technicians.

Brogan skirted the blood stain covering the middle of the floor. "Any word on how Quentin's doing?"

"He's at the hospital," Seth said.

Brogan kept Melender close as they walked into the cooler night air. A full moon shone brightly above the treetops. The moonlight picked up the silvery highlights of her hair. Brogan made a mental note to take Melender on a walk during the next full moon when he could take full advantage of the romantic atmosphere.

"Is Smith his real name?" Melender asked as they paused for Seth to chirp open the car.

"Ironically, yes." Brogan opened the back door for Melender, then climbed in beside her.

Seth got behind the wheel and started the car. "Gonna treat me like an Uber driver, eh?"

"Yep." Brogan fastened his seatbelt.

Melender clicked hers into place. "Did you know Smith used to work for a senator?"

Brogan nodded. "Senator Johnston of Virginia."

"A couple of days before Jesse went missing, I overheard the senator, Smith, and my uncle talking at one of the parties Ruby and Quentin threw that summer." Melender sounded sad, and Brogan reached across to hold her hand.

"What were they talking about?" Brogan used his thumb to gently massage her hand.

"Gold mining. Quentin wanted the rights to an old gold mine that straddled the border of the Shenandoah National Park. The senator was helping him get federal permission to explore and potentially open the mine. But with part of it in the park, permission would have been denied outright. An old map Smith found put the park borders a little bit more to the west, which gave them more wiggle room for the permit."

Brogan's stomach clenched. In the back of his mind, he'd known there had to be more to Quentin's putting the blame on Melender than a desire to protect Jared and Jillian. "They must have realized you overheard the exchange."

"That's what Smith said. I think Quentin called Smith after Jared phoned him with the news about Jesse. Smith saw an opportunity to get rid of me as well as have Quentin in his debt. And have a clear way forward for the mining permit. Win-win all around."

"Except for you." Brogan tightened his fingers around hers.

"I was expendable. The orphan niece from the mountains." Her voice hitched, and her hand trembled in his. "I can't even go home."

Brogan frowned. "What do you mean?"

"Ruby sold Sudie's cabin."

The pain behind those words tore at his heart. "I'm so sorry, Melender."

"Me too." She sighed again. "It's probably for the best."

"How's that?" The pain behind those words tore at his heart, but at the same time, he mentally fist-pumped the air. A tinge of guilt crept in at his elation. He considered coming clean about wanting her to remain in the area so they could see one another on a regular basis, but he opted to wait and hear her out.

"When I was inside, I used to long for the quietness of the mountains. But now, I find I don't mind people so much."

Her words made him bold, even with Seth probably eavesdropping from the driver's seat. "Anyone in particular you like to be around?"

Their eyes met. She raised her free hand to cup his cheek. "Yes. A certain journalist with a pair of blue eyes and a talent for helping me out of trouble."

CHAPTER

FORTY-FOUR

Melender bit into her cheeseburger and chewed slowly. Although Brogan's response to her romantic declaration the night before hadn't been negative, it lacked any passion to show her feelings were reciprocal. Seated across from him now, she couldn't help but regret choosing one of the most popular gourmet burger restaurants in town for lunch. The line of customers snaked from the registers out the front door. A sudden outburst of laughter from a group of women in the next booth drew not only Melender's attention but also Brogan's.

"Is this place always so crowded?" Brogan dunked several fries into a ketchup cup on his plate, then leaned across the table. "Don't get me wrong. I'm not complaining. The saying goes, if you want good food, look for long lines."

She blotted her mouth with a paper napkin. "It's pretty much always crowded, but if you like, we could wrap our food up and take it to the park down the street."

"Nah, this fine." He picked up his double cheeseburger with both hands and bit into it. The smile in Brogan's eyes reminded her that the way to a man's heart was sometimes through his stomach, even if the cooking wasn't her own. "You look refreshed."

She swallowed her food. "I slept surprisingly well last night. Maybe because all of this is finally over."

Brogan took a swig of iced tea. "I can't believe as soon as Quentin could speak coherently after his surgery, he insisted on giving a statement. At least he owned up to his part in the whole thing."

He shook his head. "Calling Smith to help bury your one-year-old son to hide his accidental death is cold and calculated."

Melender set the napkin she'd used to blot her mouth beside her plate. Any appetite she'd had waned. "My uncle wanted to protect his living children and get his mining permit. I guess we'll never know exactly how Jesse died."

"Livingston said the ME couldn't immediately determine a cause of death." Brogan took another bite of his burger. "They'll run more tests but those will take a while."

"Do the police have a theory as to what happened to Jesse?" Melender smiled as Brogan pointed to his mouth.

After another longer swig from his iced tea, he spoke. "Livingston said the ME's best guess was the cold inhibited Jesse's breathing, and the medicine made him sleepy When Jillian played peek-a-boo, then left the blue bunny on his face, he simply couldn't breathe and was too drowsy to remove it."

Sadness over how Jilly must be feeling with the knowledge she could have inadvertently killed her baby brother knotted Melender's stomach. Brogan pushed his plate aside. "I know your heart aches for Jillian."

Oh, Jilly. "How will she recover from it?"

"The ME did say Jesse might have died for an entirely different reason that had nothing to do with what Jared or Jillian did that night."

"That's true." Melender took sip of iced tea to clear her throat of emotion. A change of topic was in order, or she'd shed more tears.

"How did your story turn out? I didn't have time to look for it before heading to the station this morning."

His eyes lit up. "Fallon said it was one of the best pieces of investigative journalism he'd read in a long time. It took me half the night to write it, but Fallon had very few edits."

Brogan wiped his hands on his napkin, picked up his phone, then handed her the device. "Read for yourself."

DECADES-OLD CHILD DISAPPEARANCE SOLVED
New evidence points to family coverup; remains discovered on Thompson property.
By Brogan Gilmore, Herald reporter
Infant bones discovered yesterday in the backyard of Quentin and Ruby Thompson are believed to be those of Jesse Thompson, who disappeared nineteen years ago. Quentin Thompson has confessed to burying his son's body in a rose garden on the property with an alleged accomplice, John Smith. Thompson also said he and Smith conspired to frame his niece, Melender Harman, for the disappearance. Harman, convicted of killing the toddler, served her entire seventeen-year sentence while maintaining her innocence.

Melender skimmed the rest of the article, which contained info they'd already discovered together. "Nice job." Brogan's phone jangled, and she handed it back to him.

Checking the caller ID, Brogan said, "It's Fallon. Mind if I take it?"

"Go ahead." She munched on a fry, her appetite returning a little. Brogan's story had gone national, and it was only a matter of time before a bigger news outlet decided to give him another chance. She tried to be happy but couldn't help the melancholy mood that gripped her heart each time she looked into his blue eyes. Would he even want her to come with him when he moved to the big leagues? Or would she be a liability, given her past? Even though exonerated in the press, she still had a conviction on her record. She didn't even know how to start getting that expunged.

Brogan sat back and squared his shoulders "Yes, I see."

Her phone buzzed. An unfamiliar number with a Virginia area code flashed on her screen. The phone buzzed again. It could be a reporter, but something prompted her to answer it. "Hello?"

"May I speak to Melender Harman?" a female voice asked crisply.

"Speaking."

"I'm calling from the governor's office."

"The governor's office?" Melender's voice came out in a squeak as a million thoughts raced through her mind.

"Yes. Please hold while I connect you with Governor Conner." Without waiting for Melender's acquiescence, the woman clicked off, then a male voice boomed on the line.

"Melender Harman? Governor Blake Conner."

Melender couldn't formulate a suitable greeting and stayed silent while the governor continued.

"Quentin Thompson told me the entire story." The governor's tone sobered. "You might not know this, but Quentin and I went to high school together. He's been one of my closest friends for many years."

Melender held her breath, not sure where Conner was going with this. If they were friends for that long, would the governor believe in Quentin's guilt?

"I guess you can never really know someone, can you? What he did, I can only chalk up to a father's grief and fierce protective nature."

That was one way of processing what her uncle had done. She longed to ask if Quentin had confessed to the map alternation as part of his impetus for framing her.

"But I didn't call to speculate about Quentin's motives. I've spoken with the attorney general, and we're drafting an official pardon for you."

"A pardon?" Melender had hoped her conviction would be expunged, but a governor's pardon would amount to the same thing and be a more public proclamation of her innocence.

"Yes, your record will be wiped clean."

"How long will it take?" The question burst out of her before she had time to consider how ungrateful it might sound.

Her query must have amused the governor because he chuckled. "I would be anxious to put all this behind me too. It should be ready for my signature later today. My office will send out an official statement to the press about the pardon this afternoon."

Melender glanced at Brogan, who appeared to be wrapping up his own call. While her heart didn't want to help him solidify his return to journalism on a national scale, her head wanted to help him succeed in his chosen profession. "Maybe you could give a quote to Brogan Gilmore with the *Northern Virginia Herald*? He's with me right now."

"Gilmore? He wrote a fine piece about the case. Quentin said he had a hand in saving his life."

"Yes, he did." She smiled at Brogan as he ended his call.

"Put him on, and my office will be in touch once I have the pardon signed. Miss Harman?"

"Yes, sir?"

"On behalf of the Commonwealth of Virginia, my sincere apologies for your wrongful conviction."

"Thank you." Melender managed to speak around the lump in her throat. "Here's Brogan."

She handed her phone to Brogan. "It's Governor Conner."

He raised his eyebrows as he accepted the device. "Brogan Gilmore with the *Northern Virginia Herald*."

Melender couldn't concentrate on Brogan's side of the conversation because she kept replaying the governor's words "sincere apologies for your wrongful conviction," "your record wiped clean," and "pardon." She closed her eyes as the reality of his words washed over her.

Finally, her life would be her own. Finally, she had closure on what happened to her darling nephew. Finally, she could think about her future—maybe one that would include a certain blond-haired, blue-eyed reporter. A smile tugged at the corners of her mouth. But somehow, she didn't think what she felt for the handsome reporter had much in common with the infatuation of youth. This was the real thing, a love that would last a lifetime.

Her eyes popped open. Love. Yes, she did love Brogan. The way he had protected her, had believed in her when no one else did. The way he'd come to her rescue in the garden shed. The way he'd kissed her. Her lips tingled at the memory. Her gaze drifted to his lips, watching as he formed words she ignored. The longing for his mouth on hers sent another wave of warmth throughout her body. But a niggling doubt crept in. Would Brogan even want her now that the story was complete?

She could have misread the signs he meant for friendship where she saw love. After all, she had zero experience in the romance department. There was that kiss, but since then, he'd never even tried to capture her lips with his. Sure, he had held her hand, and the look in his eyes at times had made her heart skip quite a few beats.

"Melender?"

She jerked her gaze from his mouth to his eyes. By the look of bemusement in their blue depths, she must have zoned out for longer than a few seconds. "Uh, I was woolgathering, as Sudie used to say."

He smiled as he reached across the table for her hand. "You appeared to be miles away."

"How was the governor?" Melender interlaced her fingers with Brogan's, not wanting to discuss exactly where her thoughts had gone during his phone conversation.

"Great. He gave me an exclusive interview with the caveat that I can't hit publish until 4 p.m. today when he makes the announcement about your pardon." Brogan's blue eyes brightened. "You must be so happy."

"I am." Melender didn't add that much of her happiness had to do with the man sitting across from her rather than an official pardon. "It's a lot to take in, after all that's happened."

"I know." He squeezed her hand, then extracted his and cleaned up the remains of their lunch. "But I've got a lot of writing to do between now and 4 p.m."

Melender rose to help toss the wrappers and cups into the trashcan. She tried to focus as he chatted about the story and the news Fallon had given him by text that his story had been picked up by the Associated Press and broadcast across the country. But she couldn't entirely fight off a wave of melancholy that swept over her. As he walked her out to the parking lot, tears suddenly pricked the backs of her eyelids. Blinking rapidly, she willed them away. No way did she want to cry on Brogan's parade. He deserved this moment of journalistic redemption.

At their respective vehicles, she pulled keys from her purse. The evening ahead stretched out in front of her like a blank canvas. Maybe she'd curl up with Goliath and binge-watch an entire season of "The Office."

Brogan touched her arm.

She met his gaze briefly before sliding hers to the ground. "I know you'll write a good story about the pardon."

"Melender." He gently lifted her chin, then cupped her cheek. "There's something I've been meaning to tell you."

"Oh?" Her eyes entangled with his, the seriousness in their depths sending a tingling sensation down to her toes.

"We've had a wild ride, haven't we?" His lips curve into a brief smile. "I can't believe we've only known each other less than a month. And yet..."

Instead of finishing his thought, he encircled her waist with his other hand, drawing her body closer to his. "And yet?" His nearness played havoc with her senses as she breathed in a hint of cedar underlined with a clean soap smell that she identified as all Brogan.

"I've found myself thinking about you all the time, not as a source but as someone with whom I'm falling in love." He brought his lips close to hers. "I have no intention of walking out of your life, Melender Harman. I'm in it for the long game."

With those words, he closed the distance between them and pressed his lips against her mouth. As Brogan deepened the kiss, Melender wrapped her arms around his neck and allowed herself to simply enjoy the moment—feeling at home in his arms.

THE END

About Sarah Hamaker

About Sarah Hamaker

Join Sarah's newsletter and receive one of her romantic suspense novellas for free! She shares about her writing journey and other Christian romantic suspense authors, plus subscribers get a chance to win a romantic suspense book each month! Join here: https://sarahhamakerfiction.ck.page

You can connect with Sarah on her website, sarahhamakerfiction.com, or on these social media platforms:

BookBub: https://www.bookbub.com/profile/sarah-hamaker

Facebook: https://www.facebook.com/authorsarahhamaker

Goodreads: https://www.goodreads.com/author/show/1804799.Sarah_Hamaker

Instagram: sarah.s.hamaker

LinkedIn: https://www.linkedin.com/in/sarah-hamaker-7295a01/

OTHER BOOKS BY SARAH HAMAKER

The Cold War Legacy Triology

Compelling stories about ordinary women uncovering extraordinary secrets of the past that could cost them everything.

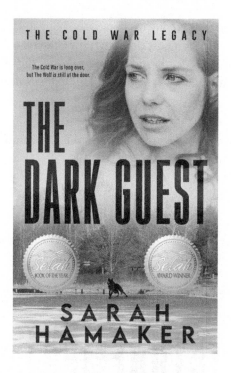

The Cold War Legacy Book One: The Dark Guest

The Cold War is over, but The Wolf is still at the door.

"Once I started reading *The Dark Guest*, I could not put it down. The story captures the reader in the first chapter and doesn't let go until the last.

Sarah Hamaker has created wonderful characters to root for as she takes them on a dangerous, twisty journey to the truth."

—Patricia Bradley, author of The Natchez Trace Park Rangers Series

When Violet Lundy isn't cleaning rooms at Happy Hills Assisted Living Facility, she loves spending her free time with resident Rainer Kopecek. Hearing his stories of the dangerous life he led behind the Iron Curtain in East Berlin makes her own life seem more tolerable. But when Rainer is found dead and his room in disarray, Violet suspects foul play.

Dr. Henry Silverton lives among his books, teaching and writing about the Cold War. A letter about an East German traitor known only as "The Wolf" propels Henry out of academia and into Violet's life. Together, they embark on a perilous quest to uncover the truth about Rainer's death and the traitor's identity.

Can Violet and Henry uncover the secrets of the past before one of them ends up as The Wolf's next victim?

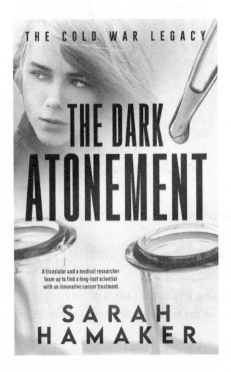

The Cold War Legacy Book Two: The Dark Atonement

A translator and a medical researcher team up to find a long-lost scientist with an innovative cancer treatment.

German translator Lena Hoffman thought her grandfather died years ago. But the unexpected arrival of a cryptic postcard seems to indicate otherwise. As Lena delves into her grandfather's past and uncovers information about him and his cancer research work in East Germany four decades ago, she unwittingly puts her own life in danger.

Dr. Devlin Mills works as a cancer researcher at the National Institutes of Health and lives across the hall from Lena, although they've never formally met. But when Lena is nearly run down by a vehicle, Devlin finds himself thrust into the role of protector. As their lives intersect, the pair find themselves in a race to discover the whereabouts of her grandfather—and whoever wants to silence him—before the past catches up with the present.

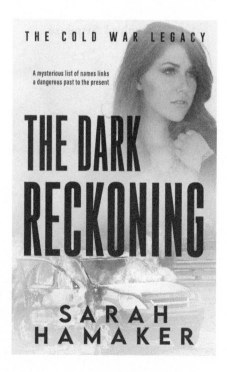

The Cold War Legacy Book Three: The Dark Reckoning

A mysterious list of names links a dangerous past to the present.

When Isana Thomas finds a smartphone among the cherry trees, her life is put in jeopardy. Isana discovers the phone belongs to Lillian Hillam, whose son, Cyrus "Cy" Hillam, works at The Heritage Museum with Isana. But Lillian is missing, and someone doesn't want the pair to find her.

Cy can't believe his mother would disappear without telling him, not after his father's suicide when he was a child. Then kidnappers claiming to have Lillian contact him, asking to exchange her life for a list of names. Cy and Isana must delve deep into his parents' past to find the list and save his mother's life.

But someone doesn't want them to succeed and will do anything to stop their search. Will Cy and Isana uncover the truth about the list before their lives are snuffed out?

Love Inspired Suspense

Dangerous Christmas Memories

A witness in jeopardy...and a killer on the loose.

Hiding in witness protection is the only option for Priscilla Anderson after witnessing a murder. Then Lucas Langsdale shows up claiming to be her husband right when a hit man finds her. With partial amnesia, she has no memory of her marriage or the killer's identity. Yet she will have to put her faith in Luc if they both want to live to see another day.

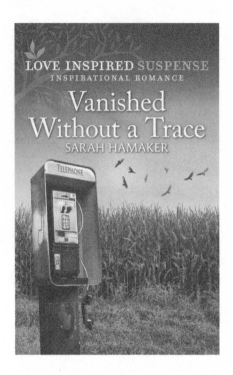

Vanished Without a Trace

A missing person case. A new clue. And a fight for survival.

After nine years searching for his missing sister, attorney Henderson Parker uncovers a clue that leads him to Twin Oaks, Virginia—and podcaster Elle Updike investigating the case. Partnering with the journalist is the last thing Henderson wants, until mysterious thugs make multiple attacks on both their lives. Now they'll have to trust each other...before the suspected kidnappers make them disappear for good.

Standalone Romantic Suspense

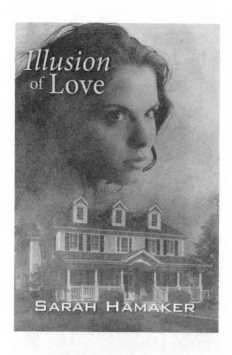

Illusion of Love (Seshva Press)

A suspicious online romance reconnects an agoraphobe and an old friend.

Psychiatrist Jared Quinby's investigation for the FBI leads him to his childhood friend, Mary Divers. Agoraphobic Mary has found love with online beau David. When David reveals his intention of becoming a missionary, Mary takes a leap of faith and accepts David's marriage proposal.

When Jared's case intersects with Mary's online relationship, she refuses to believe anything's amiss with David. When tragedy strikes, Mary pushes Jared away.

Will Jared convince Mary of the truth—and of his love for her—before it's too late?

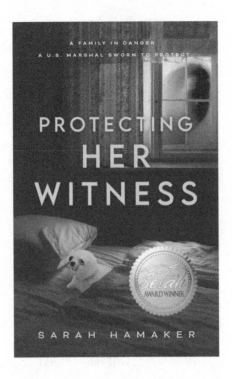

Protecting Her Witness (Seshva Press)

A family in danger...a U.S. Marshal sworn to protect.

U.S. Marshal Chalissa Manning has been running from her past and God for most of her life. When she meets widower Titus Davis and his son, Sam, her well-built defenses begin to crumble. But someone is targeting Titus and Sam, and it's up to Chalissa to both protect them and to find out who is behind the attacks.

As the threats pile up, will Chalissa be able to keep the family she's grown to love safe?

Novellas

Deadly Diamonds (Seshva Press)

The race to find missing diamonds puts a widow in danger.

Three years ago, Dulce Honeycutt's life imploded when her husband died after a robbing a jewelry store and her 18-year-old son, Kieran, landed in prison as an accessory. The uncut diamonds were never recovered, and when rumors fly that she and Kieran know where the gems are hidden, their lives are in danger.

Veteran insurance investigator Miles Sharp believes Dulce knows more about the diamonds than she's revealing. But as the attacks on the beautiful widow's life multiply, he struggles to maintain his professional objectivity. Is Dulce a victim or is her story a sweet web of lies?

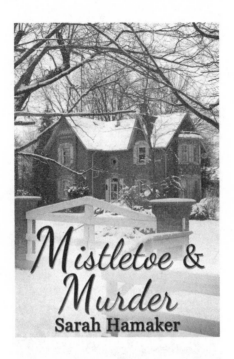

Mistletoe & Murder (Seshva Press)

Alec Stratman comes home to Twin Oaks, Virginia, after his Army retirement to contemplate his reentry into civilian life. Instead he's greeted with the murder of his beloved Great-Aunt Heloise.

For Isabella Montoya, the loss of Heloise Stratman Thatcher goes beyond the end of a job. Heloise had encouraged Isabella to follow her dreams and helped fund her studies. Now, accused of her mentor's murder, Isabella is scrambling to prove her innocence.

Since his great-aunt had written glowing letters about Isabella, Alec is unwilling to believe the police's suspicion of the former housekeeper. Instead, he works to help clear her name.

Will Isabella and Alec be able to navigate the secrets that threaten to derail their budding romance and uncover the truth about Heloise's death before the killer strikes again?

Christmas Cold Case (Seshva Press)

All she wants for Christmas is to solve her parents' murders—and stay alive.

Noelle Chastain has returned to Twin Oaks to discover who killed her parents thirty years ago. When the Shenandoah County Sheriff's Office declines to reopen the cold case, citing lack of new evidence, attorney David Keener steps in to help her search—and keep her safe from someone who doesn't want her digging up the past.

Will they find out who's behind the increasingly personal attacks on Noelle before she suffers the same fate as her parents?

Made in the USA
Middletown, DE
23 May 2024

54506809R00223